WHISPERS
— of —
Deception

Behind every
deception lies
a deadly truth.

RENÉE
GALLANT

For my family
With love

The rule of thumb regarding death—there are no rules.
The unavoidable truth—there are no exemptions.

Chapter One

ELAINA STARED OUT THE CARRIAGE window at the empty expanse of the field, its full view dulled by the continuous curtain of falling rain. If she were to look out the other window, she would see her parents' graves and, beside them, the blurred form of her brother, William, standing regal in his officer's uniform, receiving condolences. For a fleeting moment, guilt pinched her heart. She'd abandoned William and escaped to the waiting carriage after Father Kent had droned on for nearly half an hour and she could take no more of the kirkyard or his voice.

Their father had told them he once cheated death. Three days ago, death had come calling on the Spencer family and collected its debt twice over. The news came in the form of a General standing in the salon with his tricorn hat dutifully tucked under his arm. Rays of light from the late afternoon sun through the window had fallen across the officer's chest, illuminating the bottom third of him and his brilliant red uniform. The shadow laying across his face had done nothing to soften the grimness of his expression. William had been staring into the fire in the hearth and not acknowledged her when she entered the room. She'd stared in confusion at his back while the General spoke. The news of their parents' demise on an empty strip of road between Edinburgh and Newcastle had taken her to her knees. It was only then that her brother had turned from the flames.

The family had arrived in Newcastle Upon Tyne four months earlier, having spent the previous twenty years in the Province of North Carolina in the royal colonies of North America. The untimely death of their father's only living relative, an older brother James the Earl of Strafford, had forced the family's return to England for her father to claim his short-lived title as the 2nd Earl of Strafford.

Their grand adventure had begun one day after Elaina turned one and twenty. It was now a nightmare from which she could not awaken. She wanted nothing more than to return to a land and a culture she knew—to hide in the mountains of the Province of North Carolina, far from the world and all of its cruelty. An impossibility unless she wanted to make the journey alone, and she did not. William's duties lay solely with the king's army, and they wanted him in Scotland.

Their arrival on England's glorious shores had been met with orders for the two officers, her father, a captain, and her brother, a lieutenant, to report for duty in Scotland. Whispered rumors had circulated about a prospective Jacobite uprising, and the British army proved determined to quell it before it gained a sound footing.

Elaina knew little of the Jacobite cause, only that it existed and had since 1688 when the Stuart King, King James II, was deposed during the Glorious Revolution. Several unsuccessful attempts were made over the last fifty years or so to return a Stuart king to the throne. Now, here they were in 1744 and rumors once again flitted about. The continuing conflict had not been a significant cause of concern for the Spencers living in the colonies, especially to a precocious and head-strong lass who cared nothing about politics, nor cooking or knitting for that matter. She spent as much time out of doors as possible.

The carriage swayed as William stepped inside, the latch clicking after him. Elaina did not turn her eyes from the window as he took the seat across from her. To do so would take more countenance than she possessed at the moment. She swallowed the lump in her throat as the carriage started with a soft jerk, out of the kirkyard and toward Whitman Hall.

The siblings rode for several minutes before William broke the silence. "It is perfectly normal to grieve, Elaina."

"I am grieving."

"It is okay to cry. No one will think less of you."

"I do not tell you how to handle your emotions." Her words were sharp, though she wanted nothing more than to throw her arms about her older brother and weep into his chest. The truth of it was that if she started, she might never stop.

The rain slowed as they made the turn up the long drive to their current home. The ghostly shape of fruit trees rose through the remaining mist and into view in the gardens south of the sprawling manor. The house and acreage, their mother's estate in Edinburgh, and the title of 3rd Earl of Strafford were now William's responsibilities. The siblings would make their move to Scotland by the end of the week. Alone. Their parents had traveled ahead to ready Duart Manor for the family's arrival. Their murders had occurred on their return trip to Newcastle. The authorities had no suspects and no motive.

She dragged her eyes away from the rain-washed grounds to the dim interior of the carriage. William stared out of his window. With his black hair and square jaw, he held a strong resemblance to their father. So much so it pained her to look at him. Her gaze traveled down her brother's rigid form and came to rest on the white lilies she'd intended to lay on her mother's grave. In her haste to escape the kirkyard, she had forgotten the flowers now lying crushed at her brother's feet. Water dripped from the sleeve and hem of William's coat, creating a puddle around the petals that were tinged a rusty red from the mud on the carriage floor. They seemed the perfect metaphor for the siblings' newly upended, messy lives.

———— ✦◇✦ ————

The wood of the paneled wall was rough under her hand as she steadied herself. The thought of entertaining friends and acquaintances of her parents made her stomach knot.

"Are ye well, then?" Caitir, her Scottish lady's maid, asked as she came to pass her in the hallway.

"Yes. Attempting to gather my courage is all." Elaina gave her servant a half-smile.

"Well. Deep breath and go. Ye'll not gain any just standin' in the hall quiverin'. If ye need anythin'," she said, bobbing her head and then continuing toward whatever errand she was running.

Two years older than Elaina, Caitir was a true gift. She was attentive without being overbearing. She knew when Elaina needed her space or when she needed a companion.

Taking her maid's advice and a calming breath while smoothing the bodice of her black silk gown, Elaina braced herself and entered the formal dining hall. A few servants fussed over platters of food that adorned the sideboard along one wall. Opposite the food, the heavy drapes on the great windows stood open, filling the room with the afternoon light. She had insisted the servants open them. She could not stand feeling as if she were living in a cave, even if she was supposed to be in mourning. From the descriptions given by the servants, this funeral was a subdued affair. Often, services were held at night while the mourners consumed copious amounts of alcohol and were deemed too dangerous for women to attend. Elaina buried her parents how she wished and had no problem telling anyone who objected where they could go.

Eads, the lanky gray-haired butler, appeared at her elbow. "Good for your constitution." He winked as she took the crystal tumbler from his hand.

The whiskey burned as it slid down her throat, drawing her attention away from the ache in her heart.

William stood engaged in conversation with a short, robust gentleman dressed in a deep plum ensemble. The man had tried to speak to her at the cemetery. She had entertained him for only a moment before she continued her escape to the waiting carriage. William caught her eye and waved her over. With a sigh, she forced her feet into motion and joined the pair.

"You remember His Grace, the Duke of Newcastle Upon Tyne?"

"Of course." Elaina lowered a curtsy before the man who bested her height by only an inch or two. "I'm sorry if I was rude earlier." She cringed over her actions at the cemetery. She hadn't been entirely sure he'd finished giving his condolences, but at the time, hadn't cared. Would her behavior have been different had she remembered he was a duke? The answer, unfortunately, was no.

"Not at all, my dear. Quite understandable. My heart is devastated at losing the friendship of your parents. I am sure not as much as your own."

Hasty introductions had been made to the Duke in a chaotic flurry of activity on the wharf upon their arrival in England. So many new faces and names had been thrown at her and William as the family tried to find their belongings and get their land feet under them, she was surprised she recognized his face at all. Her father had been whisked away to discuss business while the family found lodging and arranged for their belongings to be shipped ahead to Whitman Hall, the Spencer family's estate.

Interrupting her thoughts, the Duke said, "My associates and I hope to continue our business enterprises with your family and to make the transition as effortless as possible." His voice was light and almost feminine, which contrasted shockingly with his portliness and his bulging eyes. His gaze rested on William while he dabbed at his ruddy face with a silk handkerchief.

Elaina took a long draw from her glass and wondered absently if his cravat was too tight, resisting the urge to re-tie it.

"I'm sure it will be painless, although possibly bumpy," William said. "Father had his irons in many fires."

"Some of them dangerous, it seems," Elaina added, continuing to study the Duke.

Her face, as always, must have been easy to read for he answered quickly. "It seems so. I pray you do not suspect me of anything to do with your parents' demise, my lady?" He placed a hand over his velvet-clad chest. "Your father was as a brother to me."

"I would like to think not. Unfortunately, being so new to the country, I am afraid I harbor suspicions of everyone." In a morbidly amusing way, Elaina could picture her mother cringing in her grave at her bluntness. Her mother never had appreciated her candor. *Sorry, Mama.*

William cleared his throat. It seemed he did not appreciate her candor either.

"I take no offense, Lord Spencer." The Duke laid a hand on Elaina's sleeve, not moving his hard-gray eyes from hers. "I admire your truthfulness, Lady Elaina. I will do my damnedest to earn your trust. Your parents helped me at a time when I could not help myself. I will forever be indebted to them. I would have gladly given my life for your father and mother both. I am prepared to do it for their offspring as well."

"I appreciate your honesty as well, Your Grace. Hopefully, it never comes to that," Elaina said, her eyes traveling to something of interest across the room. "If you two will excuse me, I will let you return to your business discussions. It seems I have some business to attend to myself." Elaina nodded to the two gentlemen, keeping her eyes on the flustered butler.

She pasted a fake smile upon her face as she wove in and out of mourners offering their condolences, all the while, watching Eads muttering to himself as he rearranged already tidy platters of food.

"What is it, Eads?" she asked, coming to stand between him and the doorway leading to the stairwell to the kitchen, blocking any quick attempts at escape he might think to have.

"Nothing for you to worry about, my lady. I think it is over now." He spoke with calm assurance, but the tense clenching of his jaw did not diminish.

"What is over?" Elaina arched an eyebrow at him.

Eads's gaze moved to something behind her.

Elaina turned. The cook's assistant, Missie, peered at them through the door she held cracked open. She blanched and retreated as her employer's eyes met hers.

"Let's go." Letting out a sigh that seemed to come from her toes, Elaina caught William's attention before setting her glass on the sideboard and leading the reluctant butler down the stairs.

Their destination was in an uproar. Flour filtered through the air, dusting tabletops and servants alike. Bowls had been upturned and stools knocked over. Arms crossed, Elaina waited in silence on the stairs and chewed the inside of her cheek to keep from screaming like a madwoman. Missie, the timid lass, stood to the side with her eyes trained on the floor. One servant caught sight of Elaina and froze for the space of a heartbeat before his eyes too turned downward. It spread like a plague. Where chaos once ruled, there was silence. Elaina scanned the tops of their heads while squeezing her arms, trying to force her temper into submission so she could speak like the lady she was.

When she thought she held enough self-possession, she turned to the substantially sized cook. "Mrs. Davies."

"Yes, my lady?" The cook raised her head and bobbed a curtsy, her face scarlet under the smudges of flour.

"What's amiss?"

"Well, m-my l-lady," she stuttered, wringing her hands. "We are missing a bottle of brandy I was to use for the poached pears. Missie saw Angus with it—"

"I didna take it!"

Elaina glanced at the small stable lad. His dark eyes glared at the cook from under a mop of shaggy brown hair. His childish features did nothing to diminish his angry expression. She thought him to be all of nine years of age.

"Honest, my lady. I did take a sip, but I put it back." He dropped his head once more.

"If the lad says he didna take it, he didna take it," a curly-headed boy said to Elaina. He stood tall and spindly next to the much shorter Angus, his hand resting on the boy's shoulder.

Elaina took him to be the lad's brother. She knew two brothers worked in the stables. The older of the two, Ainsley, was about fifteen if she remembered correctly.

"Ainsley is nothin' to do with you." The cook turned a stern look on the lad.

"Aye, it is when ye stand there accusin' my brother of thievery."

"We are missin' a bottle of sherry as well," Missie squeaked without lifting her gaze from the floor.

Mrs. Davie's eyes darted to the young Angus.

"I didna take it!" he yelled again.

"That's enough! Mrs. Davies, do you truly think if this lad had disposed of not one but two bottles of drink, he would be standing in this kitchen with you? Do you not think he would be hiding somewhere getting blootered out of his senses?"

Mrs. Davies opened her mouth, then snapped it shut again, her lips set in a thin, hard line.

"Someone took them for they are not here, but I do not believe this boy did it. I cannot believe all of you are fighting and carrying on today of all days. I do not even want to know how the rest of this began." She waved a hand over the tumble of stools and bowls littering the kitchen floor. "Pull yourselves together and act like proper help or every one of you will be released without references. Do you understand?"

"Yes, my lady," they all mumbled, most still staring at their feet.

The back door to the kitchen area opened, and Caitir stepped through with a small basket of herbs. Her gaze traveled over the scene. Her eyes at first full and horrified, narrowed to angry slits. Elaina did not think she wanted to be on the receiving end of whatever the lady's maid thought to render.

"Angus?" Elaina said.

The lad raised his eyes to meet hers.

"If anything else happens, report it to me. Got it?"

"Got it!" He beamed proudly. "I will search for the missing bottles."

"That sounds like a good task for you. Run along."

"I'm sorry I walloped ye with the pot," Mrs. Davies said to the retreating boy.

He turned to stare at the cook, seeming to contemplate his words for a moment. "I'm sorry I thought ye a crabbitbawfacedcow."

His words ran together so fast, Elaina wasn't sure she heard him correctly. The cook, however, did and the lad escaped out of the door only steps ahead of her.

"Mrs. Davies," Elaina called out, trying to stifle the laughter in her voice. "Your turnovers are burning."

"Crivens!" That brought her back around.

"Caitir?"

"Yes, my lady," she answered, her voice holding the throaty sound of laughter being quelled.

Elaina directed her gaze over the girl's head, not trusting herself to make eye contact. Nerves strung to the point of breaking, she fought against losing the tenuous grasp she held on her amusement at the lad's words. It would be more inappropriate for her to lose herself in a fit of hysterical laughter on the day she buried her parents than it was for the help to fight.

Elaina cleared her throat. "Will you see things are put back together here?"

"Aye, my lady."

"A small matter with the servants," she answered William's questioning look as she took her place at his side. "Caitir has it under control."

"Woe to the offender," William said with marked sympathy.

"That would be the entire kitchen staff and whatever wrath she unleashes upon them, they deserve it. Don't let me interrupt." Elaina glanced at the woman William had been chatting with upon her return.

"I'm sorry. How rude of me. Lady Caroline Taylor, this is my sister, Lady Elaina."

The two women nodded a cordial dip of the head at each other.

"Papa has…had…business dealings with her father. They live in Edinburgh but are in Newcastle on holiday."

Lady Caroline leaned towards William and Elaina, smiling. "Papa is on business; the rest of us are on holiday." She stood several inches taller than Elaina—most people did. Her hair, the color of wheat ready for harvest, was pinned in neat coils and swirls atop her head and the well-tailored navy frock she wore fit her lean frame perfectly.

"Thank you for coming," Elaina addressed the posh young woman.

"I am truly sorry for your loss. I cannot imagine. It must be dreadful."

"Dreadful does not come anywhere close in description." Elaina realized the sharpness of her words by the wounded look on Caroline's pretty face. *Why can you not control your tongue?* "I apologize. My mouth and my emotions tend to get the better of me. It's a terrible curse invoked upon me at birth, I'm afraid."

"You need not apologize. The death of both parents at once is a tragedy no one should have to endure. You have every right to feel angry." Caroline's kindness caused Elaina to balk at her actions even more. "Lord Spencer was regaling me with stories of your life in the colonies."

Caroline's lingering touch to William's arm did not escape Elaina and she smiled sideways up at her brother before replying, "It was a wonderful home for many years."

"Maybe we could take tea when you have settled in Edinburgh, and you can tell me all about it?" Caroline asked with a timid smile.

"Perhaps."

Lady Caroline turned her attention to William. "We should have dinner," she gushed. "I mean so you and Papa can get acquainted since you will be conducting business together. He couldn't be here." The last statement she directed to Elaina, her hand still resting on William's arm. "There was trouble with one of the ships or something. You will come, won't you? Both of you?" she asked, her gaze trained on William as she added Elaina's invitation almost as an afterthought.

Elaina discreetly poked William in the back, receiving a penetrating stare in return.

"My lady?" came a timid squeak from behind Elaina.

Elaina turned to the speaker. "Angus." Turning back to her brother and Caroline, she said, "Excuse me, won't you?"

She took the young boy by the hand, led him to a discreet corner, and leaned over with her hands upon her knees so the entire mourning party wouldn't overhear. "What's of it?"

"We found it!" he exclaimed, his dark eyes dancing with pride.

"Stop grinning like the cat that caught a canary. Out with it."

"I went to the stables to search. I didna find anythin', but when I was leavin', I heard this ruckus in the closet where the farrier keeps his tools. Sounded like a wild pig rootin' for 'shrooms. I opened the door, and there was my lord's footman, snorin' like a hog and pissed out o' his head. Beggin' yer pardon, my lady." He grimaced.

"No offense taken."

"I told ye it wasna me!"

"I never doubted you. You are a good investigator." She ruffled his hair. "Now scoot and tell Missie to give you a treat. My orders."

"Thank ye, my lady." He gave her a solemn bow before scampering away.

William appeared at her side. "You do have a way with the men."

She straightened, stretching her back. "I have a soft spot for the lad—don't fault me for it. Meanwhile, you have a way with the lovely Lady Caroline."

"She is only paying respects for her family."

"Mmmm."

"What's with the servants?" William handed Elaina a glass of whiskey.

They stood side by side surveying the room and the strangers within—ghosts of their parents' past, a past they would have to learn about second hand.

"Your footman has stirred up a hornet's nest pilfering alcohol. He's passed out in the farrier's closet," Elaina said.

"Good God." William sounded as exasperated as she felt.

"How much longer do we have to do this? I am over this day and want nothing more than to retire to my room. I'm not sure how much more my nerves can take, whiskey or no. Also," Elaina paused, not believing what she was about to say, "I am sorry for snapping at you earlier." She slid her arm through her brother's.

"Elaina Spencer is apologizing? This day will forever stand in the history books."

"You think you're clever." She bumped him with her shoulder.

William chuckled. "Apology accepted, and I will not make you cry if you do not wish to."

"If only you were that thoughtful when we were children."

William kissed her on the side of her head. "What would have been the fun in that? Lady Caroline is leaving. I must see her out." And he was gone, leaving her standing alone.

The simple act of him leaving her side to bid someone farewell struck her so viscerally she found it hard to breathe. It seemed everyone was abandoning her.

Pull yourself together. He walked across the room, not out of your life.

Tears springing to her eyes, she watched William helping Lady Caroline with her cloak, envious of the easy way he had with everyone. Swallowing the remainder of her whiskey, she turned from the room and once again left her brother to deal with the mourners.

Chapter Two

ONE WEEK FOLLOWING THE SPENCER sibling's arrival in Edinburgh, Scotland, the constable hand delivered a box of their parents' belongings recovered from the crime scene. Elaina sat in William's study with the unopened box on her lap as she fought the urge to throttle the daylights out of the flippant lawman. The imbecile's dismissive attitude toward William's argument that their parents' deaths reeked of something more sinister than a simple highway robbery made her head want to explode. As William started in on the condition of the bodies that he had identified, Elaina could stomach no more and excused herself from the discussion. The siblings knew almost nothing about their parents' youths spent on this side of the ocean and absolutely nothing about their recent trip to Edinburgh. There was no way to know if they had enemies and if so, who they might be.

She placed a note to William on a table in the salon under the box of her parents' items before she fled the house. Saddling her horse against the will of their coachman, Wallace, Elaina disappeared into the glade bordering Duart Manor. Nothing soothed her frazzled nerves better than being on the back of a horse, yet her trick did not work today. The air hung heavy with the threat of coming rain and an unshakable fear that followed her like a shadow.

After exploring the woods for a short while, the sound of running water caught her ear. Dismounting and hobbling her mare to a tree, she pushed her way through a thicket and into a small clearing with a running stream. Stripping off her boots and stockings, she plunged her feet into the freezing water. The shock of it took her breath but, unfortunately, not her thoughts.

Water striders flitted about on the dark surface of the brook, creating tiny ripples in their wakes. She flicked a bare foot at them, splashing the small insects and sending them floundering into the air only to settle once again. Leaving Newcastle and her parents' graves had been difficult. There had been discussions about whether to bury them in Edinburgh, at her mother's family estate, or in Newcastle at their father's. So much suppressed angst existed between their mother, Diana, and her mother, the late Dowager Countess Leicester, that the siblings saw little argument for burying even her mother in Edinburgh. The two women had not spoken in the twenty years the Spencers resided in the colonies. Thus, their parents' bodies remained in Newcastle in the Spencer family cemetery while the siblings continued their life in Scotland.

A horse whinnied in the distance. Sadie, her backstabbing equine, answered in kind, betraying her whereabouts. William had come looking for her. The note she'd left for him should have counted for something, but she knew it wouldn't. Being back in the saddle and not barricaded in a coach or a house was worth whatever ire he unleashed on her for leaving the house alone.

Major nickered at Sadie as horse and rider approached. She would know the sound of that horse anywhere. Branches crunched under William's feet as he made his way through the brush.

Her eyes remained on the stream as she cringed inwardly, awaiting the tongue lashing she was sure to receive.

Without speaking, William removed his boots and stockings, sinking beside her on the grass and testing the water with his feet.

"Plunge them in, William. Your breath will come back eventually." She turned a sideways smile to her brother.

He gasped as he did. "Jesus. It's freezing."

"Yes, isn't it marvelous?" Elaina swished her feet through the dark water. "Maybe it will cool your temper a bit."

"Doubtful."

She hadn't held out any hope.

"You cannot run off alone."

"I couldn't take it any longer, William, and you were busy. I went for a ride is all. I left you a note." Her argument held no merit, but it didn't stop her from speaking it. What could he do? Punish her? She would like to see him try.

"It is dangerous. Until we catch the culprit, you must not leave the house alone."

Silence filled the space between them for a long moment.

"I hate this place," she whispered, tugging at the moss decorating the ground where she sat. "I want to go home."

"I know you do. I would love nothing more myself. Unfortunately, that is impossible. Duart Manor and Scotland is now our home. You must come to terms with the fact."

Elaina swiped the tears she could no longer suppress. "Father told me he would take me hunting once we got to Edinburgh, dammit! It is not supposed to be like this." She buried her face in her hands.

William wrapped an arm around her, pulling her close. That was all it took for the soul-crushing sense of powerlessness to take her breath. She collapsed into him, weeping for the first time since their parents' deaths. She could not survive here in this brash place surrounded by strangers. At her age, she should not need her parents so desperately, and perhaps back in the colonies she would not have, but here in this strange place, she felt small and exposed. She lay in William's arms inconsolable for several moments, her chest squeezed tight as she let go of all she'd worked so hard to keep at bay.

A thought niggled in the recesses of her mind. Appalled at herself, she attempted to brush it aside, but it kept resurfacing until it was all she could think about. It was no thought for a lady, but she was no ordinary lady. She had grown up in a place where it was kill or be killed. It was animals like bears and wild boars they were on the watch for, but these people, whoever they were, they were animals also. They had taken from her those she loved, and with that act, they had also stolen her sense of freedom and security. Whoever killed their parents had thrown her and her brother into a turbulent situation in a foreign country with no other recourse.

She pushed herself out of her brother's arms. "I am going to kill them," she whispered.

"What?" William asked as she took his offered handkerchief and wiped at her nose. "What did you say?"

Their father, though it seemed he had been distant and removed from her most of her childhood, had insisted she learn to hunt and survive in the wilderness, much to her mother's chagrin. Mama wanted her in the house, learning how to be a good wife one day. Elaina preferred the woods to the kitchen. Her knack for hunting and sharpshooting were uncanny. She thought back to the look of shock on William's and her father's faces the first time she took down a buck at one-hundred-fifty yards with a long rifle. She had been ten. The stag did not die immediately, however, and her father had insisted she finish the job. Hesitating but a moment, she slithered through the grass to gain an advantage on the struggling deer. Only a waif of a child, she still managed to pull back the massive deer's head with her thin arms and slit its throat as she had seen her father do. The stern military captain had hoisted her on his shoulders that day—one of the few times in her life when he had shown her affection.

"We are going to hunt down whoever took our parents from us, and we are going to exact justice."

"Like hell we are," William answered, staring at her as if she wore two heads. "We will let the authorities handle the matter. We will follow the letter of the law."

"Just as they did?" Elaina arched a brow at her brother. He indeed was just like their father.

"I will not reduce myself to becoming a common criminal to avenge my parents. There are laws, Elaina. I am a lieutenant. I could be brought up on court-martial."

"Well, I do not belong to the military. I cannot be brought up on court-martial, and I cannot be deterred."

Elaina sat in the sunroom of Duart Manor staring out the window at the mountains to the north, wondering what creatures abided there. Had Papa taken her hunting as promised, what would they have found? Her mother had talked of the great red deer of her homeland with reverence.

The hum of conversation around her did little to distract from her imaginary trek into the hills searching for fox and Scottish wildcats. William's kick to her ankle did bring her back to the here and now, however. Startled, she nearly upended her tea in her lap, then she cast him a withering glare that he returned in kind.

"You were saying?" Elaina asked him stiffly.

William had insisted they invite a few guests for tea to take their minds from the turmoil that was now their lives. Several women Elaina could not remember the names of and some of William's comrades milled about the sunroom in various groups. It felt more like a matchmaking party than a casual tea. Lady Caroline, unfortunately, had seated herself squarely before Elaina and William. She wanted nothing more than to remove herself from the situation and hide in the stables. More than likely, it was for this reason alone that William had penned her in.

Whatever retort William opened his mouth to utter was cut short by a frantic Angus bursting through the door, yelling, "My lord! My lord!" He stumbled across the floor and landed face down at William's feet.

Elaina dropped to her knees, grabbing the lad under his trembling shoulders and then raising him to a seated position. "Calm down, Angus."

The boy opened his mouth but couldn't speak for gasping for air. Drops of sweat glistened on his forehead and upper lip. He swallowed hard, his eyes wide with fear.

William appeared on his knees alongside Elaina. "Catch your breath, son, then tell me what is wrong."

Dread filled Elaina, and she innately knew that she did not want to hear what the boy had to say. She understood fear to be a contagious state and felt it seeping into her hands from the trembling child, working its way up her arms until it seized her heart, causing it to beat wildly.

"Can you speak?" William asked softly.

"Aye," the boy gasped. "Wallace...Wallace is dead."

Elaina studied Angus's face. "What do you mean Wallace is dead? The coachman? He is more than likely drunk." The man had a penchant for his liquor.

"No, my lady. He has been stabbed. There is...there is a paper..."

"Elaina, stay here." William sprang to his feet, motioning to another member of the military who was in attendance.

As the two men ran through the door, most of the other guests followed closely behind them.

Elaina and Lady Caroline helped Angus to a seat between the two of them on the sofa, catching each other's eye over the top of his head.

"Take a drink, Angus. Calm yourself." Caroline pressed a cup of tea into the boy's hands.

He gulped it down, resulting in a coughing fit.

Pushing his mop of hair from his eyes, Elaina wiped the sweat from his face with a damp rag that Eads produced. "Can you tell us what happened?" she asked when she thought he had recovered enough breath to speak.

"I-I cleaned Sadie's stall like he told me, and I went to find him to tell him... to tell him... I dinna ken what I was goin' to tell him." The boy shook until Elaina thought he would rattle her and Caroline both from their seats.

"It's ok." Caroline patted his small knee and took one of his hands in hers and squeezed it. "Don't fret about it. Can you tell us what happened next?"

"I couldna find him. I went out to the corral to see if he was still workin' the filly. He was seated on the ground, leaned up against the post with his back to me. I called his name, but he didna answer. I thought he was drunk like ye said, my lady, but when I rounded the front of him, that's when I saw it…the knife sticking out of his chest." The boy shuddered and wrapped his arms around himself.

"You said there was a paper. Were there words?" Caroline asked.

"Aye, but I couldna read them. I dinna ken how to read."

"You were too unsettled to bring it with you?" Elaina smoothed his hair away from his forehead.

"I didna want to touch it. It-it is stuck to his chest with the knife."

<hr />

William's study was still in a somewhat state of disarray, sparsely furnished with few books upon its shelves. Two leather chairs, an oversized sofa, a desk, and few pictures were all that resided there. The remainder of the books and furnishings were en-route from Newcastle to Edinburgh and Duart Manor, the estate her mother had inherited from the Dowager Countess Leicester. It came as a surprise and a fortuitous coincidence that the matriarch of the Leicester family had left the estate to her estranged daughter, whom she had not spoken to in twenty years. The family had assumed the estate would be auctioned off after the Countess's death. It had been a stipulation in the will that Diana Leicester Spencer was not to be told of the bequeathment and would only receive it upon her return to Scotland. She had to return of her own volition, not because of an inheritance.

None of that mattered now as Elaina sat in the study like a dutiful young lady. William had sent her and Angus there as he rid the house of guests and, once more, greeted the constable. Ainsley joined the pair to help comfort his terrified brother.

Elaina paced the floor, stood by the window, stirred the fire in the hearth, and picked bits of paper from the drawers of the large oak desk while Angus and Ainsley whispered together and watched her. She needed to get a grip on her emotions and help this young boy ease his fears.

"Do you know how to read, Ainsley?" Elaina questioned the older boy.

"A wee bit, my lady, and mostly Gaelic," the lad confessed.

"Well, let us take our minds off our troubles, shall we?" She studied the few books on the shelves until she found one she thought they might enjoy.

Elaina positioned herself between the two boys. "Have you heard of Robin Hood?"

Both boys shook their heads.

"You are in for a treat. Robin and the Merry Men of Sherwood Forest are an adventuresome lot. Would you like to learn more?"

Angus nodded, picking nervously at his fingernails.

"It will be all right," Elaina said, wrapping an arm around the boy and pulling him close. Propping the book on her lap, she kept her arm around a trembling Angus while Ainsley helped her hold the book open and turn the pages.

The boys became fascinated by the story, and it seemed to take their minds off the murder in the stable. Her fingers traced the words, letting the two follow along as she read the words. Three chapters in and William appeared at the study door, two tumblers and a glass bottle of whiskey in hand.

"Boys, I hate to interrupt, but I must have a word with the lady alone. Run on down to the kitchen and have Mrs. Davies feed you."

"Aye." Ainsley stood, reaching for Angus's hand.

"What happens to Robin now?" Angus asked, his eyes full of curiosity.

"You will have to wait to find out. We will read more of it soon, I promise." Elaina ruffled his hair.

"Finally," Elaina admonished a gray-faced William as the brothers exited the room.

Instead of responding, he clunked down the tumblers upon the desktop, filling them both with whiskey. "Sit," he commanded.

Ordinarily, she would have a snide comment for an order like that, but the look on his face warned her against it. She planted herself in the chair across the desk from him.

William drained his glass and refilled it. Elaina left hers untouched. He stared at the desktop, but she knew he was not studying the design of golden diamonds displayed there, produced by the sunlight shining through the cuttings in his whiskey glass. She did, however, trace each line with her eyes until she could stand the silence no longer.

"What is it, William? Do you know who did it?"

"We have our suspicions. Unfortunately, we still have no idea."

"That makes no sense whatsoever. How can you have suspicions and no idea?"

William reached into his pocket, pulling out a piece of paper, and unfolded it on the desktop.

There were bloodstains on the page. Elaina tried to ignore them. Clasping her hands tightly together, she leaned forward to read the words. 'The price for treason' was scrawled across it in blotchy black ink. The writer seemed to have been in a hurry.

She looked up at William and asked, "He was treasonous? What do you think he did and why was he not arrested instead of being killed, in our corral no less?"

"This note was not meant for him."

"What are you talking about?" Elaina chose this time to pick up her glass. Perhaps she needed it after all.

"It was meant for us."

"I am not understanding, William. Just come out and say it." Elaina tried to ignore the trembling in her voice and the hairs rising on the back of her neck.

"The note was pinned to his chest with Father's knife."

Her glass shattered onto the floor. "I-I'm sorry," she mumbled, stumbling out of her chair. She made her way to the fire on shaking legs, ignoring her whiskey-soaked shoes.

William opened the study door and spoke in low tones to someone in the hallway. The earthy sound of a broom across the wooden floor and the tinkle of glass being swept into a pile sounded moments later. The timber, grating to Elaina's ears, bristled her skin as if the broom raked across her flesh instead of the floor.

With the study once more in order, William came to stand by his sister's side.

She held a handkerchief in her hands, her fingertips worrying the design of the lace border from one corner to the next, then back again. She waved off the second glass William offered. "How could it be so?"

"How can you be sure it is Father's? There could be any number of knives resembling his."

"It is his. There is no doubt." William's voice was as soft as the arm he lay about her shoulder.

"The price of treason. What does that even mean? Father was a loyal member of the king's army. He was a devout and honorable man. No one could think that he would commit acts of treason." Her voice sounded hollow to her ears. They had been away from Britain for twenty years. Their father had returned several times throughout the years to conduct business, visit his brother, and check on the family's holdings on this side of the ocean. Any manner of business may have taken place, but Elaina would be willing to bet her soul that her father was no traitor. The Spencer men ate, drank, and breathed all things military. They were rule followers. Her father had lived and died by them. No. Whoever had murdered their parents and now Wallace was wrong. Categorically wrong.

Chapter Three

BLASTED HORSE'S ARSE! ELAINA SHOT daggers into her brother's back as he lectured the household staff on safety and what to do if they saw anything out of the ordinary and that his baby sister must have an escort at all times. Anywhere she went on the grounds, she was not to be alone. All eyes turned to her, and her face warmed under their scrutiny. Eads at least looked sympathetic.

They employed far too many servants as far as Elaina was concerned, especially now that they were all staring at her. Eads, Mrs. Davies, Angus, Ainsley, and Caitir had made the move to Edinburgh with the Spencer siblings. There were over twenty staff in all. Twenty-whatever pair of eyes trained on her as her brother continued his instructions. She arched an angry eyebrow at a particularly interested stable hand. Turning crimson, he lowered his gaze to his feet. The firm hold she'd thought she had on the household help was slipping away. He made her sound inept. How was she to govern with a gaggle of servants babysitting her?

With the help dismissed and William retired to his study, Elaina lingered in the dining hall attempting to contain her anger. She appreciated her brother's concern, but there was nothing she despised more than to be dressed down in public and made to look like a half-wit. She clenched and unclenched her fists, eyes closed, face turned toward the ceiling as if the heavens would open and the loving light of God himself would fill her with forgiveness. Not bloody likely.

Entering his study without knocking, she perched herself on the edge of the writing desk and rolled the feather of the quill between her thumb and forefinger, trying to think of a tactful way to tell him what an arse he was. "A word?"

"Do we have to do this now, Elaina?" He rubbed his face. "I have to read over these reports before my morning meeting with the investors."

"Now is as good a time as any," she replied, earning her a stern blue glare before his gaze returned to the papers littering his desktop. Taking a deep breath, she abandoned the quill and placed her hand on top of the documents. "Was that necessary?"

"Yes, I believe it was," he answered, leaning back in his chair. "We cannot be too careful."

Elaina stared across the room as she nodded and chewed her lip. "I agree," she eventually replied, narrowing her brown eyes at him. "I do not, however, agree to you not discussing with me beforehand the babysitting you would be imposing upon me. I do not appreciate having to stand there while you portray me as some simple-minded, blundering child still suckled at her mother's tit."

"I did not—"

"You did!" She slapped the table for emphasis. "How do you expect them to respect me if they are watching over my every move? You have blurred the lines between the help and the employer just when I think I have gotten somewhere with them."

"It's not like that, Elaina."

"What is it like? You go to extravagant dinners, and I sit in the parlor under lock and key? You hunt with Dukes and Lords, and I sit in the sunroom and gaze demurely out the window? Wait. May I? Do I have your permission, my lord? I must have an escort to go to the garden. May I even go to the privy alone or do I need an escort for that as well?"

"You are being dramatic. This is why I did not want to tell you beforehand. You cannot control your temper."

"Dramatic? If anyone is dramatic, it is you, William."

"I don't want to fight. I am tired. I have work to do. If you don't mind?" He tried to shoo her from his desk.

How dare he! "I am not some insolent child without a brain."

"Never claimed you to be." He turned his focus back to the papers, more or less dismissing her.

She wanted him to fight back, to yell. She needed to scream at him—with him, at anyone. "If I am expected to care for this household, I must have the confidence and respect of the staff. I would also demand some respect from you if I am to manage the estate while you are out gallivanting around, posing as the

Earl of Strafford." She could not keep the disdain from her voice. She knew it was harsh, but at that moment, she didn't care.

William shoved himself away from the desk and to his feet, leaning close enough she almost felt the need to retreat, but the word retreat was not in her vocabulary. "You demand respect? Well, might I remind you, Lady Elaina," he scoffed, "I, in fact, run this household. I will run the half dozen businesses. The servants will answer to me. As far as you are concerned, I am the heir to Duart Manor and Whitman Hall and I. Am. The. Earl of Strafford. And you would do well to remember it!" He stormed from the room, the door slamming hard enough behind him to rattle her teeth.

She had what she wanted—a fight. It did not feel as vindicating as she'd thought it would, mostly because now she knew where she stood. William was now her superior when they had lived their entire lives as equals. She was no more to him than a member of the household staff.

Caitir pulled the pins from Elaina's hair, letting the glossy curls unwind down her back.

"I can brush my hair, you know?" Elaina said locking eyes with the maid in the looking glass. She was an attractive girl, with her strawberry blonde hair pulled back in a chignon at her neck. They were also near opposites, Caitir with her light red hair and sky-blue eyes a stark contrast to Elaina's chestnut hair and dark brown eyes.

"'Tis my job, my lady. Sit there and enjoy it."

Elaina and Caitir had known each other only a short time. Elaina's mother had hired the maid while on their fateful trip to Edinburgh. Lady Diana Spencer had searched for the woman who worked for them previously, before their move to the Colonies. Unfortunately, that woman was no longer alive, but her daughter, Caitir, happened to be available for hire. Caitir had helped Lady Spencer ready the manor and the household staff during the Earl and Countess's brief stay in Edinburgh. She'd arrived at Whitman Hall a week ahead of the lord and lady. The Countess had sent her early to help Elaina make the transition to Duart Manor when the time came, not knowing at the time that they, themselves would not be with them.

Caitir treated Elaina with sympathy but did not coddle her. Having lost her mother several years earlier, Caitir seemed to know the right words to say. Elaina found herself amused at the lass's no-nonsense approach to her job. The fact that the brazen girl was able to give sympathy yet was not afraid to be blunt with her employer truly delighted Elaina. The women did not dwell on the subject of Elaina's dead parents. It was a welcome respite from the turmoil that was now her life.

"I will admit, it does feel good to have someone else brush your hair." Elaina closed her eyes and emitted a small sigh.

"Ye didna have a personal maid in the colonies?" Caitir asked, leaning around her.

Elaina heard the soft *plink* of hairpins dropping into the small glass dish on the dressing table. "No. We employed only a few servants. It was a much simpler life."

"Ye miss it, then?"

"Tremendously," Elaina whispered with a half-smile. Each stroke of the brush seemed to pull tension from her body. Her shoulders had felt scrunched up around her ears all day.

"Did ye have a special man whilst there?"

Elaina opened her eyes at the question and arched an eyebrow at her maid. "Aren't you the forward one?"

Caitir shrugged in answer.

"No. I was to be married two springs past, but it wasn't in the cards, one might say." Elaina stared at the looking glass, not seeing the images reflected in it.

"I'm sorry. I shouldna be so bold. Did he…?"

"Did he what?"

"Die?" Caitir said with a grimace, pulling the brush through Elaina's hair.

Elaina burst out laughing, causing Caitir to drop the brush. "One could only be so fortunate. He left me standing on our wedding day. Oh, don't feel sorry for me," she said in response to her maid's sympathetic look. "I didn't want to marry him in the first place. As business partners, our fathers arranged it. If we were to wed, it would make Spencer and Travis the largest fur trading company in the colonies. It was a blessing Richard lost his shirt at cards the night before and drank himself into oblivion. Papa and Richard's father finally found him the next afternoon, passed out in a whore's bed. I am only glad I learned what kind of man he was before I was bound to him for the rest of my life." The last statement was no lie, but it did little to erase the sting of embarrassment at being jilted. "Our fathers tried to reconcile us, but I would have none of it. I would rather die a spinster."

That was a subject best left in the past. As much as Elaina liked Caitir, she disliked the subject of Richard even more, so she turned the tables. "Do you have a beau?" The weight of the day lay heavy in her bones, and she rose from the chair stretching and groaning. She drew a deep breath as her bustle was removed and stays unlaced. If only her worries and fears could be alleviated as quickly as a dress could be removed.

"Who has time for a man?" Caitir said gathering Elaina's dress and laying it across the bed. "There is so much still to be done to settle ye in and tryin' to get all these eejits to work together is a job within itself." Caitir paused with Elaina's silk sleeping gown in hand, touching a sizeable crimson mark on the back of Elaina's thigh, just under her right buttock. "What is this?"

"You are just now noticing it?" Elaina stood naked in front of her maid, covering her breasts with her arms and craned her neck around to look down at the mark. "It is a birthmark. Isn't it lovely?" she said with sarcasm.

"'Tis vivid. I dinna ken how I missed it before."

"At least it's hidden," Elaina said as her head popped out of the neck of the gown. "Back to the subject of eejits, that nonsense the other day in Newcastle was ridiculous."

"Aye, it was. Mrs. Davies has a temper to rival yer own." Caitir grinned at the glare she earned. "I near died when Angus called her…what was it…a crabbit, baw-faced cow?" She giggled, scrunching up her freckled nose.

"What is the situation with Angus and Ainsley? Angus seems so young to be away from home, working in a stable."

"Their parents are poor farmers with too many bairns."

"So they send them off to work? Alone? That seems a bit callous."

"They have each other. 'Tis just how it is, my lady. It's that or they starve."

"Well, that is just sad to me."

"Sometimes 'tis better to be alone in a bonnie situation than to be with a bevy of folk in a bad."

"Ah, the poetic voice of wisdom," Elaina said, crawling into bed.

"Go to sleep, my lady. Yer cattiness is coming out." Caitir gave Elaina a sideways glance. "Besides, ye need to recover from yer fight with Lord Spencer," she added casually as she straightened things here and there.

"How do you know I had words with Lord Spencer?"

"The entire city of Edinburgh may ken, the way the two of ye were yellin'. I kent it was comin'. I could see it in yer eyes at the meetin'. I only wish I had been there to witness the whole thing. The door slam nearly knocked the portraits off the wall."

"He had it coming," Elaina huffed, laying back on her pillow.

"He only means to protect ye. He doesna ken how to do it otherwise."

"Taking his side, are you? And here I thought you sympathetic to my cause," Elaina said with sarcasm. "I need no protection, Mistress Murray. I am more than capable of taking care of myself."

"Hmph."

"Goodnight, Caitir," Elaina called out to her retreating maid who picked up the last of the lit tapers and headed toward the door.

"Goodnight, my lady."

Elaina could hear the smile in Caitir's voice as she closed the double doors to the room behind her, leaving her staring at the ceiling in the dark.

Her mother had done well. Caitir was going to be a valuable asset to the household. God's hand had been at work the day Lady Spencer found her. He knew what Elaina would need to get her through.

———— ◆◆◆ ————

Even in the heat of July when it was sweltering inside with no breeze, the stables smelled like heaven. It was the only place that felt like home anymore, where she wasn't drowning in grief. Elaina inhaled the scents of fresh hay mixed with the ripe smell of manure and the warm musk of the horses.

Major accepted his carrot with a velvety nibble, the muscles in his jaw working under the palm of her hand. "Major, *bon gentil garçon.*"

"*C'est un cheval très savant.* To speak French, I mean. With a name like Major, I assume he also speaks English?" a male voice said from behind Elaina.

She spun around, dropping her handful of carrots.

"I'm sorry. I didna mean to frighten ye. Here, let me." A tall blonde Scot bent over and retrieved her dropped vegetables.

Elaina took a step back. "He does…speak English, I mean." She moved closer to the pitchfork in case it was needed. She was not alone in the stables, several men lurked about, but she spotted none at the moment. The one time she would appreciate someone watching over her. "Although, I think Latin may be his favorite language," she added.

The gentleman extended the carrots to her. "*Et Latine? Valde infigo.*"

"He is a worldly gelding," Elaina responded, also in Latin. She raised an eyebrow as she looked up at the kilted gentleman.

He stood with his hands clasped behind his back, his green eyes inspecting her with interest. "Italian?"

"*Sì, un po,*" Elaina replied. "Although, I believe four may be our limit."

"Verra impressive. English, French, Latin, and Italian. *Feumaidh sinn a bhith ag obair air teagasg Gàidhlig dhut.*" The stranger gave Major a smile and a wink, running a hand down the gelding's nose and under his jaw, scratching and massaging.

Elaina swore she heard the horse emit a small sigh. "All I caught out of that little tidbit was the word Gaelic," she smiled. "I'm afraid you have one-upped me. Can I be of some assistance to you, Mr....?"

"I said we have to teach him Gaelic," he replied with a brilliant smile. "Rabbie MacLeod, yer servant, madam." He bowed his blonde head low, extending her an elegant leg. "I am in search of Lord Spencer. They told me he might be in the stables. I am to assume that you are not Lord Spencer," he said with a raised brow and a twitch of a smile.

"How astute of such an educated gentleman," Elaina replied. "Lady Elaina Spencer. Lord Spencer's sister." She extended her hand.

"Lady Elaina. A pleasure." He took her hand and brushed it lightly with his lips.

Elaina extracted her hand from his grasp, trying not to notice the fine hairs standing up on her arms. "Pleased to make your acquaintance. I'm afraid I am not sure where William, that is, Lord Spencer is at the moment. Is it a matter I may help you with, perhaps?" she asked.

"Mr. MacLeod! There you are," William exclaimed, appearing out of nowhere and striding across the stable to shake the Scot's hand.

Relief flooded Elaina. Though the man had been nothing but a gentleman, she appreciated her brother's presence, nonetheless.

"Lord Spencer. Your servant, sir," the gentleman replied just as heartily.

"You have met my sister, I see." William turned a smile to Elaina that did not reach his eyes. He, apparently, still harbored hard feelings from their fight yesterday.

"Indeed."

"Excellent. Will you excuse us? We've much to discuss," William addressed his sister.

The two gentlemen nodded absently in her direction as they turned toward the large double doors, exchanging pleasantries as they went.

"Hmm. What is up with that, I wonder?" Elaina mused to Major in Latin.

The gelding snorted and shook his head, nudging her skirt, searching for more carrots.

"One more," she said, rubbing his head as he retrieved his treat. "Rest easy, big fellow. I think I will go be nosy."

She strode out of the stable and across the dark gravel lane, toward the large main house. The blooms from the rose bushes lining the small walk filled the air with their scent while bees flitted in and out of the delicate petals. The beauty of their place here in the outskirts of Edinburgh did much to lift Elaina's spirits. Far enough from the city to feel like country, yet close enough to be convenient for William's work and her snooping. Not that she had learned anything. She'd yet to meet enough people for it to make a difference.

She'd hoped the authorities in Edinburgh would have found something by now, but it was not the case. They were treating their parents' murders as a simple highway robbery. The note found impaled to their coachman had made no difference. They attributed it to Wallace, not her family, no matter how much she and William argued their point. The fact that her mother's jewelry had still been on her person gave them no pause. Their theory being, the thieves might have considered it impossible to sell the lady's jewelry without being caught. Elaina didn't think one needed to be a schooled investigator to know that their theory was a bunch of horse shite.

William would be attending a meeting with a military council this evening in Edinburgh. Perhaps, she would venture into the city and see what information she could dig up on her own.

Chapter Four

"I CANNAE BELIEVE YOU, MY LADY," Caitir hissed through her teeth. "Ye are a daft woman to be sure."

"That's not nice after I let you tag along," Elaina whispered back.

"Let? Ye didna *let* me. I am no here because I want to be."

Elaina shushed her maid, who seemed on the verge of violence. "You have bound me so tight, I can scarcely draw a breath." She squirmed under the muslin wrapping.

They'd pilfered the breeches and a coat from one of the stable boys and Elaina had coaxed, bribed, and cajoled her maid into binding her breasts as flat as possible. A little dirt smeared on her face and her long brown hair shoved underneath a knit cap, and her disguise was complete.

"Serves ye right. 'Twill never work. The first time ye open yer mouth they'll ken ye are a lass."

"I won't speak. You will speak for me."

Caitir huffed at her.

The women left the manor shortly after His Lordship. If William knew what she was up to, he would brain her. After their little servants' meeting, Elaina dragged Caitir along in case she was discovered. Not that it mattered. It was her life, and she wasn't going to be sitting at home twiddling her thumbs. Someone in Edinburgh must have seen her parents while they were here.

"I dinna ken why ye couldna be yerself."

"Because I don't want word getting back to Lord Spencer that his sister was exploring the taverns with her maid, and,"—Elaina lowered her voice to a whisper as they passed a small cluster of men roaring with laughter—"if they recognize me as a lady, they may not be as free speaking."

The Sheep Heid Inn was a disorderly place stuffed with men and women at every stage of drunkenness. The sweet smell of ale and the overwhelming stench of sweat and urine hung heavy in the air. Elaina's shirt clung to her even before they elbowed their way into the heart of the tavern. Her woolen hat made her want to claw her head and raised her body temperature to near unbearable levels.

It didn't take long for Caitir to begin sweating too. Whether it was from the shoulder to shoulder abyss they were in or the gleaming eye and a wink aimed at 'Jasper' from the voluptuous barmaid, Elaina couldn't be sure. For good measure, she gave the wench a wink and an eyebrow wiggle. Caitir rewarded her with a swift kick under the table.

"Och, and what ye ken aboot that?"

A rowdy game of Loo was taking place at the neighboring table. A large, obnoxious man aimed a yellowed, gapped toothed sneer at a shorter man across from him.

The smaller man threw his cards down. "I ken ye're a pile of horse shite's, wha' I ken."

The crowd gathered around the game erupted in laughter.

"I'm oot." The man left the table, bellowing for Morag to bring him another ale.

"Who's the next unlucky laddie then?" The man looked around the group, his eyes lighting on Elaina. "You?"

Elaina looked at him and pointed at herself, glancing at Caitir who glared at her. She shook her head and grinned, hooking a thumb at Caitir with a shrug.

"What? Yer lass has got her tongue as well as yer bollocks?"

A ripple of laughter passed through the crowd of spectators.

"He cannae speak," Caitir piped up. "He's mute and no, he's no bettin'."

"He's dumb? They cut out his tongue?" The man's curiosity seemed piqued.

"No, he has a tongue. He just cannae speak. I dinna ken why. He just cannae." Caitir glared at the man and grabbed Elaina by the arm to pull her away.

Elaina shrugged at the man.

"Eh, Monroe, leave the lad be. I'll be willin' to skelp yer arse for ye." A man plopped himself down at the table, taking the attention from Elaina and Caitir.

Morag, the attentive wench, kept the two women well supplied in drink, conveniently brushing her ample bosom across various parts of 'Jasper's' body each time she came around, so often that Caitir would lean closer to Elaina, blocking the bar maid's way. Elaina nearly choked on her drink at the look on Caitir's face more than once.

After several hours of useless eavesdropping and too many rounds of drink, Elaina felt the need for a privy and a change of scenery. The two women stumbled out into the street, sucking in the fresh night air.

Caitir pulled her bodice away from her chest, sighing. "Christ, what a hullabaloo."

"What a complete waste of time."

The only information the women had gleaned from their spying was that the men at the card table worked at the docks. But that hadn't been hard to deduce by the stench of dead fish and saltwater that infiltrated the air around them.

"I need a tree." Elaina was not about to use the loo at the Sheep Heid for fear of being found out. She glanced around for a private place to relieve herself and then froze, looking at something over Caitir's shoulder.

"What is it?" Caitir asked, in the motion of turning to look.

Elaina grabbed her by the head and planted a kiss on her lips. She turned Caitir's back toward the road, all the while being pummeled by her flailing fists. When the carriage passed, Elaina released a startled and angry lady's maid.

"What the hell do ye think ye're doin'?" she hissed, her face scarlet.

"What? You didn't enjoy it?" Elaina ducked away from her, laughing. "That was Lord Spencer. I was saving your job and my arse."

Caitir's eyes widened, and she took a step backward, looking down the road toward the retreating carriage. She crossed herself, whispering what Elaina took to be a Hail Mary. "I didna hire on for this." She turned a fierce gaze on her employer.

Caitir's anger didn't faze Elaina in the least. It could have been the drink making her so bold. "You know, you would be a better kisser if you didn't fight it so." It most definitely was the drink. Elaina didn't move fast enough and caught Caitir's swing on the side of her head, making her laugh and nearly piss herself. "Wait here," she told her. "I need to relieve myself, then we shall find another tavern."

Caitir gave a frustrated groan.

Elaina ducked down between the Inn and the building next to it. She sidled down the dark corridor, squinting, trying to get her eyes to cut through the shadows. The night may have been a bust so far, but it worked to distract her from the worrisome yet mundane life she was being forced to live.

"Oof." She tripped and fell, almost peeing on herself. "I hope that's mud," she mumbled, stumbling to her feet and wiping at her clothes. Her head was swimming from all the drink, and she stumbled again but caught herself before falling into someone taking a piss of their own.

"Watch it, you," the drunk slurred, swiping an arm toward Elaina.

She growled low at him and kept going. A cluster of trees stood behind the row of buildings, giving Elaina the cover she needed. Squatting behind the trees, she sighed with relief, steadying herself with one hand seconds before falling on her face.

"Watch where yer aiming."

Elaina almost toppled over as another gruff voice responded, *"Haud yer wheesht,* ye old goat."

As quietly as she could, Elaina straightened and pulled up her breeches.

"I heard auld Spencer's boy's been nosin' 'round, askin' a lot of questions. Questions that might cause problems."

Elaina's breath stopped. How many Spencers, she wondered, resided in Edinburgh, and how many of those had sons that would be asking problematic questions? She rested her head on the tree in part to hear better, but mostly to stop the world from spinning.

"Hell, I'm no worrit aboot him. I've been workin' on that matter. We'll ken what he kens before he kens it."

"What? Now ye're talkin' oot yer heid, ye drunk auld bastard. Ye dinna make a lick o' sense."

"I make perfect sense, ye daft loon. Ye're just too drunk to hear it. I'll handle His Lordship. Ye needn't worry aboot that."

His Lordship? How was he going to handle him and why?

"The duke—"

Elaina sneezed. She uttered a foul oath under her breath as the card shark Monroe sprung with surprising agility around the trunk of the large oak. A smaller man appeared around the other side.

"What're ye doin' there, boy?" Monroe asked, eyeing her up and down.

Elaina shrugged, her heart pounding. She glanced between the two men, trying to gauge their levels of drunkenness. Who was more intoxicated, them or her?

"Answer 'im," the smaller of the two said taking a step toward her.

"He's dumb, ya eejit. He cannae talk," Monroe said.

"How tha hell am I 'posed to ken that?"

Taking a chance while the pair continued arguing, Elaina made like she was falling and scrambled out between the two older and, she hoped, slower men. A hand seized the hem of her breeches, and she kicked out with the other foot, contacting something. From the muffled swearing, it could have been a face.

She heard pounding feet behind her as she ran up the close, careening off the walls of the buildings while trying to keep her footing in what she now decided was the discarded contents of the Sheep Heid's chamber pots. The putrid mess saved her as a hand grazed her back followed by a thud as one man struck the ground, spewing a stream of profanity. The other was not far behind. Elaina barreled out of the alleyway and collided with a startled Caitir. The two of them tumbled to the ground in a flurry of arms, legs, skirts, and strangled oaths. Elaina's head hit the ground with a solid thud.

"You! Boy!"

The words sounded muffled amidst the ringing in her ears. She tried to shake the stars from her eyes and extract herself from the enormous number of petticoats smothering her face. Why did women have to wear so damn many clothes? She needn't have put much effort into her escape because a second later, she was snatched up, making her teeth clank painfully together.

"D'ya git 'im?" The smaller man stumbled out of the close, reeking of human waste.

"I should take yer ear for eavesdroppin'." Monroe shook Elaina.

"You leave him be!" Caitir yelled and grabbed Elaina's other arm, starting a horrendous game of tug of war.

Elaina opened her mouth to yell at them to stop, but the grisly giant yanked her from Caitir's grasp, sending the girl stumbling backward to the ground. The woman launched herself up with surprising speed for a girl that seemed half drunk and hampered by all those blasted petticoats. She leaped like a wildcat for the man's face.

A fair amount of laughter and jeers erupted behind them, but Elaina didn't have time to worry about attracting unwelcome attention. Monroe held a death grip on her arm, while black spots danced in her eyes. He tried without success to remove Caitir from his person with one arm. Elaina glanced up in time to see her maid's knee contact a delicate area of Monroe's body, and he released his hold on her, collapsing to the ground in a writhing heap. The smaller, foul-smelling man shoved Caitir out of the way.

"Come here, boy," he said, taking a step toward Elaina, then another.

She did the only thing she could think to do. She tucked her head and launched herself with all her might at the man, knocking him backward.

He grabbed at her, his arms flailing as he went down.

Elaina landed on top of him as he snatched the woolen cap from her head. Her long hair came cascading down around his startled face.

"What tha hell?" he hissed.

It was the break she needed. When the man hesitated, Elaina landed him with an uppercut to the chin with all her might. There was a cracking sound as her fist made contact, and the block spots behind her eyes returned.

Someone grabbed her by her coat and hauled her to her feet.

"Go," Caitir hissed, shoving her down the alleyway Elaina had tumbled from moments ago. "Run!"

"...knocked him out cold!"

Elaina barely heard the exclamations and resulting hilarity as the pair fled. They shot out of the other end of the close and veered down a side street. Caitir clung to her mistress's hand, pulling and pushing her down cobblestone streets and closes, zigzagging between buildings and people.

"Where...are...we...going?" Elaina gasped for air.

"I...ken a...place. Come on." Caitir threw an arm around Elaina, pulling her along.

Stumbling and half-blinded by her mass of flying hair, Elaina's lungs burned and she was developing a stitch in her side. Led by her maid and on the verge of collapse, she tumbled through a doorway into a darkened building. The two women fell in a heap, gasping for air.

"Oh Christ...I can't...breathe...sweet Jesus..."

"Ye're...sure...a bletherin'...for...someone...who...cannae breathe," Caitir gasped.

Elaina raised her head, shoving her hair out of her face. Panting, she stared at the shadow of her maid for a split second before she burst into laughter. They clung to each other, snorting and wheezing until they heard the sharp click of a hammer pulled back. Snapping their heads around, they sobered immediately, though still gasping for air.

"Well, have ye quite got yourselves together then?" a male voice said from the darkened staircase.

Caitir squinted into the dimness. "Calum?"

"Caitir? What in the heavens—"

Caitir scrambled to her feet and up the few stairs, throwing her arms around the shadowy figure.

"What in God's name are ye doin' here, lass? Ye almost met yer maker!"

"What are *you* doin' here?" she accused him in return. "I thought ye were in France?"

Elaina inched her way into a standing position, holding onto the wall for balance, grunting and stumbling as she came upright.

"Christ, are ye all right?" Caitir scurried back down the stairs.

"I think so. No…my head," Elaina said with a moan, grabbing the back of her head.

"Crivens, ye've got a lump the size of a goose's egg."

"I smacked it on the ground when I tackled you." Elaina giggled, then groaned as the sound reverberated inside her pounding head. "Oh God." She slid back down the wall.

"Have ye got any light about this place, cousin, or are ye taken to livin' like a savage?"

The man sighed with what sounded like exasperation. Coming down the last few steps, he bent to peer into Elaina's face in the dim light filtering through the fanlight above the door. "She's lookin' a wee bit peely-wally. Is it a she?" he asked, looking Elaina over. "Why is she dressed like that?"

"What the hell does 'peely-wally' mean, and you are a fine one to judge, standing there looking like a porcupine in a dress. Is there any whiskey?" Elaina growled, her bleary eyes taking in her scrutinizer's muss of wild hair and tunic, coming to rest on his muscular bare legs and eventually his bare feet.

"Peely-wally means yer white as a sheet, and I dare say ye need no more drink. Will ye lend a hand, Calum?" Caitir asked, taking her mistress under the arm.

"Hmph," Elaina grunted as her maid and the cousin hoisted her up from the floor. "A Scot thinking there is such a thing as too much drink? Now I've heard everything."

"Sit. Dinna move." Caitir planted Elaina firmly in a chair in a room just off the main entrance. The only light was from the smoored fire in the hearth.

"A porcupine?" Calum asked as the two cousins left the room together.

"She's from the colonies," Caitir said as if that explained her friend's strangeness.

Elaina might have either dozed off or passed out because the next thing she knew, Calum was once again studying her and Caitir was trying to light a taper from the red-hot coals in the fireplace.

"Why is she covered in shite? What are ye doin' out runnin' around with… this… Does yer da' ken? Where yer at, I mean? Christ, how much has she had to drink?"

"Not near about enough for all your damned questions," Elaina grumbled.

Calum ignored her. "Do ye need a place to stay, cousin? Do ye need me to draw some water so she can wash up?" he asked with unmasked apprehension.

If she weren't so bloody drunk with her head feeling like a smashed pumpkin, she would have kicked him.

"No, we cannae stay. We absolutely must get back to the manor tonight. I hope to God almighty we get there before Lord Spencer," Caitir said, wringing her hands after she inspected Elaina's injured head and hand.

"Ye work for Lord Spencer, then?" Calum sounded relieved. "Where is he this evening?"

"There was a gathering…military…with the Duke of Manchester," Elaina mumbled, eyes closed as she cradled her throbbing hand to her chest.

"I'll get dressed and escort ye two back to the manor. I ken a shortcut. Will ye ready the horses while I get dressed?" Calum said to Caitir.

A few minutes later, Elaina sat mounted behind Caitir, her uninjured hand gripped tightly around her servant's waist and her spinning head resting on her back.

"Ye reek," Caitir told her as they trotted as fast as they dared down the stone streets and back alleyways.

"I know. I'm covered in human waste. I think I may be sick." Elaina leaned over the side of the horse and vomited.

"Oh for Christ's sake!" Caitir exclaimed reaching behind her and grabbing Elaina before she tumbled off the back of the horse.

Elaina emitted a strangled half chuckle-half groan and tightened her grip around Caitir's waist. She wasn't sure she could make it to the manor. Her head thumping against Caitir's back was almost more than she could stand. On the verge of telling the pair to let her walk, she was relieved when they finally made it home.

"Ifrinn!" Calum hissed under his breath. "Is that him?"

Elaina glanced up to see William standing under the torches outside the stables, conversing with what looked to be the tall Scot she'd met earlier in the stables.

"Yes," Caitir said. "Best to leave us here. We will sneak in through the side entrance."

Elaina snorted. "Ifrinn!" she imitated Calum's Scottish accent and giggled as Caitir slid from the horse, dragging her staggering and stinking employer with her.

"Can ye handle her?" Calum asked with considerable doubt in his voice. "Should I come help ye?"

"No. I've got her. Bless ye, cousin."

"Caitir? I may be sick again."

Caitir grabbed Elaina's mass of hair out of the way while she vomited beside a nearby tree trunk.

"Good God," Caitir grumbled.

"Watch her close. I'm thinkin' she took a good conk to the head. It will make yer wame turn inside out," Calum said, turning the horses back into the shadows. "Although the drink and the shite doesna help. Goodnight, cousin," he said with a chuckle and then disappeared into the night.

Chapter Five

"MRS. DAVIES SENT YE SOMETHING for yer head." Caitir set the small tray on the table next to Elaina's bed where she had lain suffering through the night and most of the morning. Caitir had bathed her in the servant's quarters in freezing water the night before, claiming it would help sober her up. Elaina thought it to be revenge for the evening's excitement.

"Yuck! What the bloody hell is it? It stinks—"

"Drink it." Caitir forced the cup towards Elaina's mouth.

Elaina held her breath and gulped it down, glaring at a grinning Caitir over the rim of the cup.

"Don't ye dare throw up again!" Caitir said as Elaina gagged.

"It tastes like ash from the fire mixed with what I was wearing last night. Are you trying to kill me?"

"Maybe torture ye bit." Caitir handed Elaina a cup of tea to wash it down with.

"I said I was sorry."

"I ken. I heard it the twenty times ye said it. I must say, that is the most fun I think I have ever had, besides having to clean ye and take care of ye, I mean."

"I'm glad you enjoyed it," Elaina said with sarcasm as she attempted to swing her legs over the side of the bed and stand up. Caitir caught her as she wobbled. Her head felt like it would split in two. She closed her eyes until the world quit spinning.

"Take it easy, my lady. There is truly no reason for ye to be up and around."

"William will be wondering about me."

"I told him Sadie knocked ye into the wall of the stable and ye hit yer head, and she stepped on yer hand." Caitir took Elaina's injured hand, inspecting the purple bruise that had formed across the top of it during the night.

"You lied for me? You *do* love me."

"Dinna push it, my lady," Caitir said helping Elaina out of one garment and into another. "I swear, ye are like no other lady I have worked for."

Elaina laughed. "I grew up in the wilds of the Carolina's. I'm afraid I'm not much of a lady."

"It is good to see ye laugh." Caitir sobered, studying Elaina's face. "Ye are too serious and too stuck in yer own head. I like seeing ye like this."

Caitir's words gave Elaina pause. How had she been? She thought back to the days after her parents' deaths. She had only felt the move from one side of the Atlantic to the other was a change, but now she didn't recognize the life she was living. She'd been struggling to hold on to what could never be again. She needed to pull herself together.

"I will try to be better."

"Good. Now, answer me this. Where did ye learn to throw a punch like that?"

"William and some Indian boys who would visit taught me a lot. Mama was none too happy about it, either. I told you I was no lady."

Elaina found her brother in his study poring over stacks of papers.

"I didn't expect you up and around." He rose from his place behind the desk, coming around to inspect Elaina's injuries. "She did a number on you, didn't she? How are you feeling?"

"Not the best I have ever felt." Elaina took a seat in front of the desk. "Can we pull the drapes and light some candles? The sunlight is painful." She squeezed her eyes shut against the pain in her head and the guilt she felt in her heart about lying to her brother.

"Absolutely." William set about the tasks. "Well, you have no cause to be in that position any longer. I have hired Mr. MacLeod as our new coachman. You need not be in the stalls fooling with horse hooves."

"I can tend to my horse just fine, William." Elaina stared at him over the cluttered desk he was seated behind. He was not going to keep her from the stables. "It was not Sadie's fault."

"I want you to be safe," he said evenly. "I don't know what I would do if something happened to you."

Elaina felt momentarily guilty, but it quickly turned to indignation. "You cannot protect me from everything, William."

"Unfortunately, I know, but let me protect you from what I can."

Elaina grunted. "You will not keep me from the stables."

"I don't mean to. You may go anytime. Just let the men we have hired to care for the horses do their jobs."

Elaina didn't argue. He knew as well as she did that she would do whatever she pleased. Instead, she tipped her chin to the pile of papers littering his desktop and changed the subject. "What are you working on?"

"A headache, that's what. I have to be in Scotland for military purposes, but shipping from Edinburgh ports is not near as easy as from English or the New World ports. We have to expand if we are to make things work while we are here. The Duke of Newcastle is keeping a hand on our ships that come in and out of Newcastle, but I think we need to ship from here as well. If we are going to live here, we need to support its people. After all, they were Mama's people."

The siblings had grown up in a mixed household, if one would call it that, their mother being Scottish and their father British. Their mother had held onto a few customs of her home country, but their father had also kept a firm hand and was a captain, so he expected their loyalty to lie with England. William was every bit his father. Military, business, and Britain. Elaina felt a tug on her heart toward her mother's heritage, perhaps because her mother would indulge her in stories and folklore during the times her father was gone—a secret they shared, mother and daughter. Her mother had told her William was too much like his father to appreciate the superstitions and tales.

"My lady?" Eads appeared at the doorway to the office. "A parcel for you."

"For me? I am not expecting anything. Who is it from?" she asked, waving him into the room.

"The delivery boy did not know," he said, closing the space between them and depositing the small box into her hands. "Only that it was for you."

"Thank you, Eads." Elaina absently dismissed the butler.

William watched her untie the string and unwrap the brown paper from the small box. She lifted the lid, picked up the note laying inside, and read it. Not comprehending its words, she read it again. Her eyes traveled to the item lying in the bottom of the box, and her hand flew to her mouth where it muffled a sob. Flinging the box to the floor, Elaina scrambled out of her chair and across the room.

Coming around the desk, William picked up the package and the paper. His eyebrows pulled together as he read the note.

Elaina's hands trembled as she wiped the tears from her cheeks. Moments ticked by as her brother stared inside the box at the item responsible for her panicked escape to the other side of the room. Eventually, he reached inside and drew out their father's pocket watch.

"Eads!" William bellowed for the butler, his sober blue eyes on his sister.

He immediately appeared at the door. "Yes, my lord?"

"I need to know who brought this package."

"He was just a young messenger." Eads passed a look of confusion between Elaina and William.

"Stay here," William ordered Elaina.

She merely nodded in return. She didn't think she could will her legs to move if she wanted to.

"Get her a whiskey, Eads. Did you at least see which way the lad left?"

"Aye. Toward the city."

William dropped the box and their father's watch onto the desk before running from the room and out the front door.

"My lady?" Eads said, taking Elaina's trembling elbow.

She nodded and allowed him to help her to a chair.

"You will be all right until I return?" the kindly butler said once he'd settled her in the chair.

She nodded, her eyes on the object on the desk.

The watch ticked away the seconds. Her parents had died several months ago, so someone had set the correct time and wound the watch before mailing it to her.

A shawl appeared around her shivering shoulders, and she looked up to find Caitir tucking it around her. Eads stood on the other side, placing a tumbler of whiskey into her hand. Closing her eyes, she hugged the glass to her chest. Why was the package delivered to her personally? A cold chill slid down her spine as she remembered the conversation she'd overheard in the copse of trees the night before. There had been no talk of Lady Elaina, only William. Could there be more than one group?

She opened her eyes to find Caitir standing in front of her with the note in her hand and Eads gone. "What does it mean?" Elaina whispered. "Tick tock little mouse."

"I dinna ken, my lady, but ye must tell Lord Spencer what ye heard the past eve."

"No." Shame churned in Elaina's gut. "He can never know the danger I put you and me in. Swear it to me."

Caitir stared at her for the space of a minute. "I swear it, even though I think ye are wrong."

Rabbie MacLeod's Scots accent drifted through the room in a soothing lilt while he and Eads discussed something in low tones. Elaina looked up to see the two of them standing in the doorway of the study. Rabbie gave her a somber dip of the head before he turned his attention once more to the butler.

"Mr. MacLeod is going to guard you until Lord Spencer can return," Eads said to Elaina.

She nodded, her eyes traveling to the coachman who had not bothered to remove his apron upon being summoned to the main house.

He must have noticed her gaze for he looked down, then grinning at her, he removed it and handed it to whoever was standing behind him. "Run along, lad. Take it back to the stables for me," he spoke to the shadows.

"Aye." Angus's worried eyes met Elaina's as the boy hurried past the doorway to do his bidding.

"If ye need me, I'll be outside the door, my lady," Rabbie spoke softly.

At Elaina's nod, he disappeared. She didn't know who had sent for him—William as he'd left or Eads. She did not think she was in immediate danger, but it did help her feelings to know there was protection if needed.

Caitir folded the note once again and laid it inside the box on William's desk. "If ye need me..."

There was no need for her to finish her thought, Elaina knew.

The minutes turned into hours, and Elaina took her tea in her brother's study awaiting his return. After a time, her nerves settled a bit and she began straightening his desk for lack of anything else to do, stacking papers together according to which company name they held.

Her father's watch stared at her until she couldn't stand it anymore and slid it into the middle drawer of the desk, catching sight of the invitation as she did. Bloody hell. She'd forgotten they were to have dinner with the Taylors tomorrow eve. A welcoming to Edinburgh in honor of the Spencers, as it were. There was no getting out of it. Many of her father's business partners had been invited to introduce William as the new head of the Spencer legacy. Elaina had inherited one company—her mother's glassworks. The three other shareholders were to be present tomorrow as well. She slammed the drawer closed.

"Easy on the furniture, sister," William said, entering the room.

Elaina ran to him, throwing her arms about him. "Thank God you are safe. Where have you been? Did you find out anything?"

William squeezed her tight before setting her back into the chair. "Nothing." He dropped himself into the chair in front of the desk, exhaustion etching his face. "The lad didn't know who the man was that instructed him to bring it. The man was British and paid him a shilling was about all the lad knew. I took him with me to the constable. He could get nothing from him either. So the authorities have been informed, for all the good it does. There are no clues. No trail to follow."

Elaina thought back to the previous evening and was tempted to tell William of what she'd overheard, but what had she heard? A vague threat by two drunk dock workers. No. She couldn't tell him. Not yet. She liked her head right where it was.

"Look in the top drawer on the left," William instructed. "The first note is in there."

Elaina pulled the stained paper with an elongated hole speared through it and lay it on the newly cleared desktop.

William unfolded the second note and placed them side by side. It seemed to be the same scrawling hand on both.

Elaina didn't want to look at them anymore. She crossed the room to the window and pulled back one side of the drapes. Tightening the shawl around her shoulders, she watched the sun as it sank past the horizon.

"We will take the evening meal in here, Eads," William instructed the butler who had apparently entered the room.

"As you wish."

The scraping of the poker sounded on the stone hearth as someone stirred the fire, then wood thumped hollowly against itself as they added fresh logs. The warmth of the bolstered fire surrounded Elaina while she watched the soft pinks and grays of the day ease their way into the deep indigos of the evening.

"What does this mean, William?"

Silence.

She turned in a panic to find him with his head in his hands, still staring at the pages.

"Give me those." She stormed across the room and gathered the notes, shoving them back into the drawer of the desk with a hefty slam as Rabbie knocked on the open doorway.

"Shall I come back later?" he asked, his green eyes traveling from brother to sister and back again.

"No. Come in. You will have a bite with us while we discuss matters." William stood, offering the man his chair, and took his seat behind the desk.

"I couldn't, my lord—"

"Yes. I have called you away from your meal. Please, sit."

Rabbie took his chair as ordered.

Elaina snuggled into an oversized chair by the hearth, tucking her feet under her and closing her eyes. Her head pounded. She heard a drawer slide open and the rattle of papers.

"Ye need to see these." William's voice came from across the room. "This one was pinned to our former coachman with a knife."

Elaina noticed William didn't tell him it was their dead father's knife.

"This one was delivered today to my sister. I want you to be on the lookout for anyone out of the ordinary wandering around here. Tell the lads in the stables. We need eyes everywhere."

"Aye, my lord."

Their meal was delivered, and the men ate and continued their discussion of security around the house.

Elaina hardly heard their words as she stared into the fire. Someone was stalking them. If someone believed her father to be treasonous, why terrorize his children and why take their mother's life as well? Maybe the party at the Taylors' was coming at an opportune time. They would meet the business partners and some of their most prominent investors and get a feel for the life their parents had led. William knew more of it than she did. Well, she would get a peek tomorrow and would keep her eyes and ears open.

Chapter Six

LISBON HALL SHONE MAGNIFICENTLY IN the late afternoon sun. Elaina peered from the carriage window, admiring the three-story mansion constructed of white stone. A rounded portico with massive columns decorated the front, giving it a Romanesque feel. She smoothed the skirts of her champagne-colored gown. Nervous fingers traced the burgundy silk flowers embroidered upon it.

As if reading her thoughts, William took her hand and squeezed it. "It will be a grand time."

"If you say so."

"The little buds in your hair are a nice touch."

"You like them? Caitir's doing. The dress as well. She said it brought out the gold in my eyes."

"At least she did not dress you in deep brown."

"Why?" Elaina asked as they pulled to a stop at the front steps.

The carriage door opened and Rabbie helped her down to the white gravel drive.

"Because it might make your eyes look the color they are when you are angry." William joined her on the ground.

"And how is that?" She raised an eyebrow at her brother.

"Dark, like the waters at the bottom of a burn." He stared into her eyes, a hint of a smile tugging at the corner of his mouth. "That color right there."

"Are you telling me my eyes look like dirty, moss-filled water? That is no way to talk to your sister."

Rabbie tried to hide a smile as he bowed to the pair and set about moving the carriage out of the way of the next arriving guest.

"Welcome, welcome!" An enthusiastic greeting bubbled out of a short, slightly plump woman flanked by an exquisite Lady Caroline decked out in emerald green.

"Mama, these are our guests of honor, Lady Elaina and Lord William Spencer."

Caroline and her mother held no resemblance except for the color of their hair. Lady Taylor's bore a small amount of silver, that being the only difference.

"I would have recognized you anywhere from the descriptions my daughter has given you," Lady Taylor gushed, causing the tips of Caroline's ears to turn pink.

"Come." Caroline slipped her arm through Elaina's as if they were old friends. "Let's get the two of you inside. I will introduce you to Papa."

Elaina smiled to herself at Caroline's rush to get away from her mother and her confession that Caroline had been bending her ear about William.

The guest list seemed a who's who of Edinburgh society. Elaina tried to keep up with the introductions, but her headache was as distracting as Lord Taylor's attitude. The beautiful Lady Caroline might have gotten her looks from her father, but thank the heavens God had endowed her with her mother's charm. Lord Taylor held the personality of a rock.

He introduced William to some of the men, adding Elaina as an afterthought, it seemed. Elaina didn't appreciate his attitude toward her but remained polite while silently cursing Caroline for running off to greet arriving guests and leaving her standing with William, Lord Taylor, and a few businessmen. She remained dutifully quiet during the men's conversation, listening to them ramble on about nothing in particular.

Talk turned to the business of shipping after compulsory introductions had been made. Elaina's ears perked, listening for any clues she could garner. Monroe worked the docks, and he worked for someone who'd wanted her parents dead. She sipped her glass of sherry while one of the men rambled on about the ignorance of exporting whiskey to the colonies.

"...I don't see the importance of it," he was saying. "Money wasted."

He sounded so incredibly haughty over the matter that Elaina couldn't stop herself. "You don't see the importance of exporting Scottish whiskey to the colonies?"

Silence came from the group of previously opinionated men. All eyes stared at her as if she should not be speaking.

The man she'd posed the question to stood a few inches taller than her but shorter than most of the men in the group, and his blonde hair was pulled into a tight, shiny clubbing. "No, madam, I do not. The colonies grow enough barley to produce their own whiskey. If you are so educated on the aspects of importing and exporting, maybe you can explain why we should go to the trouble and expense of shipping it to them?"

There were soft chuckles from some of the men.

William gave an almost imperceptible shake of his head.

She didn't know if he was trying to quiet her or if he was taking pity on the unsuspecting man. Undaunted, Elaina raised an eyebrow at the young gentleman. "Have you tasted whiskey made in the colonies? I dare say they have yet to come close to mastering the art."

"She is correct on that matter," William murmured raising his glass to his sister with an amused look.

The young man did not look as entertained.

Lord Taylor cleared his throat. "Let me introduce you properly. Lady Elaina Spencer, this is my nephew, Harry Everson."

The two nodded at each other.

If Lord Taylor thought the fact that this man was his relation was going to quiet her tongue, the man was dead wrong.

Apparently, Harry felt the same. "And just what would the benefits be, if I may ask, besides providing a decent glass of spirits to the inhabitants of the Royal Colonies?"

"That depends on what you want in return. Tobacco? Indigo? Rum? Ships? Money to line your pockets and increase your ship counts and thus increase your shipping potential. That depends on what part of the coast you are importing to. As of now, ships run from Boston, carrying rum made in New England, to Africa where it is traded for slaves who are then taken to the Caribbean plantations where molasses are purchased and then in return, shipped to New England to make rum. It is a never-ending triangle. You are English, I presume?"

The man didn't answer, his face red.

"If you ship directly from Edinburgh to New England, you cut out the middle-man, increase your profits, and reduce the number of tariffs you pay to your home country. Scotland is under English rule, is it not? Isn't the point of shipping to make all the money you can while keeping as much of the profits as possible?"

"Seems the lady kens her business." A tall and striking Scot had joined the fold, his hazel eyes focused on Elaina.

"Mr. MacKinnon." Lord Taylor pumped the man's hand, clapping him on the shoulder. "When I heard you had returned early, I could not have been more pleased."

It was the most emotion Lord Taylor had exhibited all evening, and it seemed to be that of relief.

"My dear, my dear," a familiar voice cried out from behind her, and she turned to see the Duke of Newcastle lumbering toward her. He grabbed her face, kissing her on each cheek. "Look at you." He stepped back, doing just that. "The epitome of elegance and charm, wouldn't you say?" He directed his question to the men standing around her.

A snort sounded, and Elaina knew it came from the man she had been giving a business lesson to.

"Well, all of the shareholders are present," Lord Taylor's gaze rested on Elaina.

"Shareholders?"

"Yes, Lady Elaina—to your glass company. The one your mother left to you. The duke, myself, you, and Harry."

Elaina's mouth gaped open. This arrogant, pompous twit was a shareholder in her company?

"Maybe ye should introduce us," the gentleman with the hazel eyes suggested, breaking the glare between Elaina and Harry.

"Of course. Begging your pardon," the Duke said. "My dear, may I introduce Calum MacKinnon, one of our most esteemed associates. Mr. MacKinnon, the lovely Lady Elaina Spencer. The daughter of the late Lord Edward Spencer, the 2nd Earl of Strafford."

At the mention of the name Calum, Elaina was sure her heart stopped.

"Lady Elaina, your servant, madam." Mr. MacKinnon bowed over Elaina's hand but not before giving her a dazzling smile, exposing a dimple in his left cheek.

For a moment, his name had given her pause, but relief flooded her just as quickly that his surname was MacKinnon and not Murray. "Mr. MacKinnon, my pleasure," she said.

"Her brother, Lord William Spencer, the 3rd Earl of Strafford," Lord Taylor offered as if to draw attention, once again, away from Elaina and the awkwardness she'd brought to the discussion at hand.

The two men greeted each other with Mr. MacKinnon turning sober. "The *late* Lord Spencer?"

"Yes, unfortunately," William answered. "Our parents were murdered."

"I am verra sorry to hear that," Calum replied, his broad Scots accent coming across. "I was hopin' to meet yer father. His Grace and Lord Taylor have both spoken highly of him and his ships. I hope the criminals have been brought to justice then?" He directed his question to Elaina.

"No, there seems to be no clue as to who or why." Her answer fell sharp from her tongue, and her eyes traveled over the surrounding gentlemen who squirmed under her gaze.

The Duke cleared his throat. "Let's not dwell on this here, shall we? Tonight is to be a festive occasion." He slipped his arm through the crook of Elaina's, giving it a subtle squeeze.

"Of course," William said. "Lord Taylor said you recently returned? You have been out of the country, Mr. MacKinnon?"

"Aye," the tall Scot answered.

"Your travels? Were they business or pleasure?" Elaina asked.

"A wee bit of both. I was visitin' family in France, but I was also attending business while there."

She was grateful for the Duke's arm still linked with hers. Calum stood about the right height. She couldn't tell by his voice because that part of the evening was little more than a blur and she had not gotten a good look at him, being as she could barely open her eyes at the time. It couldn't be. After all, Calum was a common Scottish name, but the fact that he had recently returned from France…

Lord Taylor drew Mr. MacKinnon's attention away from her, thank heavens. She studied him, looking for signs of familiarity as he conversed with the other men. He stood probably six-foot-tall and was broad through the shoulders. The clubbing at his neck let a few dark errant curls escape the leather binding that fought to control them. Her eyes traveled up his square jaw and across his lips where one corner of his mouth twitched. She met his eyes. He was watching her take him in. Heat rose in her face, and she glanced away, raising her glass to her lips.

"Lady Elaina? I believe my cousin may be in your employment?" the blasted man said, bringing her attention back around to him.

The sherry felt like a boulder traveling down her throat. "Oh?" she attempted to sound nonchalant. There did not seem to be any recognition in Calum's eyes. Well, she did look and smell a trifle different this evening, she hoped.

"Caitir Murray?" he asked.

"Yes. My lady's maid. What a small world," she answered, feeling as transparent as glass. To her ears, she sounded guilty as sin.

"Back to the question of exporting whiskey," Harry barked at Elaina, unable to let it go.

"Aye," Calum said. "Exportin' whiskey. Exactly what I wanted to talk to Lord Spencer about. I've heard ye've fine ships. Yer company is reliable and one of the best at outsmartin' and outrunnin' pirates?"

"Your problem is going to be getting your whiskey from the Highlands to Edinburgh to load on ships." Harry sounded smug. "The Watch, I hear, has been loaded up and shipped to Flanders to fight. With no one to police the Highlands, how do you propose to see your cargo safely to port?"

"The Highlands dinna need The Watch's brand of policing with their thievin' and extortions. We can take care of our own."

It was apparent that Calum held strong opinions about The Watch and Harry Everson, and neither were favorable. The announcement of dinner served saved them from further discussion.

It was an informal event, and guests sat where they chose. The Duke seated himself to Elaina's right. Unfortunately, Calum placed himself across the table from them, next to William, with Lord Taylor at the foot of the table. Lady Caroline seated herself on the other side of the Duke, conveniently across from William. Harry, thankfully, sat next to his aunt at the other end of the table. The talk was small as the servants made their rounds with various platters of stuffed pheasant, broiled fish, and roasted root vegetables. The dishes kept coming, and Elaina realized she was famished.

In between bites, she looked at Calum. "So, what exactly is The Watch?" she asked.

"Well, after the risin' of 1715, the British thought the Highlanders were gettin' out of hand. There were disturbances between some of the clans, but when has there not been? The British put together a band of Highlanders from four different clans, all loyal to the British Crown, to keep order between the clans and hopefully stop a Scottish uprisin', if one should start. But there is lawlessness in anythin'. Some of the men servin' are honest men, but there are always those who want more than their share."

Elaina's heart leaped into her throat as the Duke grabbed her wrist, interrupting Calum.

"Whatever happened to your hand?" He turned her hand to and fro, studying the bruise that had become a vivid shade of purple over the last two days.

"Oh," she said. "It's nothing." Extricating her hand from the Duke's grasp, she placed it discreetly in her lap. "Sadie, my horse, knocked me off balance and stepped on it while I was working on her hoof the other day. It's nothing. Just a little bruise," she babbled and drained her glass of wine, gladly accepting another as her heart pounded against the wall of her chest.

"Your horse? Do you not have a groomsman? A coachman? Why were you tending your horse?" His Grace seemed taken aback.

"Our coachman was murdered during a tea party a few days after our arrival in Edinburgh." Her response was sharper than intended and brought a warning glance from William.

"We have a new coachman, Your Grace," said William, as always, more tactful than Elaina. "He hired on this week. There will be no need for her to put herself in that position any longer."

"I dare hope not." His Grace patted his mouth with his napkin.

"I will tend my horse if I see fit. I am quite capable." Elaina raised an eyebrow at her brother. "Coachman or no coachman." She didn't back down.

The two stared at each other until Lady Caroline cleared her throat. Elaina glanced at Lord Taylor, whose gaze flicked from William to her. His hands didn't move quick enough for him to hide his hint of a smile behind his napkin. It was only the second emotion she had seen from him all night. All the men seemed entertained except William.

Elaina shook her head and turned her attention back to her plate, stabbing a carrot.

"You will never believe what Mr. Adair told everyone at the shop today," Caroline said, hastily changing the subject.

The Taylors owned a jewelry store on High Street. Elaina knew Lady Caroline often kept an eye on Mr. Adair, the overseer who liked to have a little nip in the afternoon more often than not. Elaina breathed a short-lived sigh of relief at having the attention drawn away from her.

"There was a brawl outside of the Sheep's Heid," she stated dramatically.

"That's not news. That is a nightly occurrence," Caroline's father replied.

"This one was different, Papa. Just hush and listen."

Dread crept from Elaina's toes, up her legs.

"He said he was leaving the Inn and when he got outside, a vicious fight was in progress. He didn't know how it started, but he knew how it ended." Caroline paused for effect, and Elaina closed her eyes, her face toward her plate. Unease settled in her wame as she prayed to God but knew the truth. "A lass with a waif of a companion brawled with this oversized ape and a short man who seemed to be covered in... Well, I'm not sure I should say, but, well…he was covered in human waste."

Elaina's dress felt too tight, like she couldn't draw a good breath. She squirmed in her seat, trying to force herself to swallow the bite of food she still held in her mouth.

"What in the world?" the Duke muttered under his breath.

"What in the world, indeed," Caroline continued. "The lass takes the large man to his knees with a quite accurate blow to his stones—"

Her father cleared his throat.

"Well, it's part of the story, Papa," Caroline said, laughing. "Anyway, the large man is on the ground, and the waif of a lad right tackles the short man covered in shite."

"Caroline," her father admonished.

"Father, you are ruining the story. The boy tackles the short man," Caroline started again with the emphasis on the short man. "And knocks him out cold with an uppercut to the chin."

"And," her father said.

"Turns out the lad was a lass. He…well, *she* lost her hat in the melee. Mr. Adair said the most glorious wave of chestnut hair came raining down just before she clocked him a good one!"

Elaina choked on her wine.

"My goodness, lass, are you okay?" the Duke patted her on the back as she coughed madly into her napkin.

"Yes, I'll be fine," she managed to croak out, her eyes watering. "What a tale."

"What a tale indeed," Calum said evenly from across the table.

She could feel his eyes boring into the top of her head.

"Sounds like a tall tale." Lord Taylor took a bite of pheasant, unimpressed with his daughter's account.

"No. I believe it to be true. I heard the same earlier," a gentleman offered, keeping the conversation going.

As everyone debated on the who and the why of things, Elaina excused herself from the table, refusing to make eye contact with Calum or William. She made her way out to the veranda as the dinner party started on dessert and continued the gossip. She sucked in the brisk evening air, trying to slow her wildly beating heart.

"Beautiful evening," a male voice said from behind her

She gripped the railing to keep her knees from buckling and cringed as he approached. "Mr. MacKinnon. You startled me." She turned back toward the night, hoping he wouldn't see the trembling in her hands.

"Did I?" he asked, leaning his back against the rail next to her. He was quiet as he looked through the double doors to the party continuing inside.

"Would you care for another drink," he asked finally. "Maybe a whiskey instead of wine?"

"Wine would be perfect. Thank you for asking," she said, hoping the whiskey reference was unintentional, but knowing it was not. He disappeared, and she stifled the urge to run. She couldn't leave William stranded at the Taylors and was no coward, so she held her ground.

He returned shortly, handing her a glass while he sipped his own, still studying the guests inside while she studied the stars in the heavens, praying.

"Ye made a strong argument for exportin' whiskey."

Elaina stammered, "Did I? I wouldn't think as a man you would take much heed to what a woman has to say."

"Ye dinna ken what kind of man I am." His voice was deep and husky.

Gooseflesh rose on her arms. "No. I don't suppose I do, seeing as how we just met."

"Ye seem to have no interest in the rum trade. Have ye somethin' against the West Indies?"

"Not the West Indies per se. I do, however, have a problem with slavery. I do not think it right. Have you witnessed it, Mr. MacKinnon—the shipping of slaves?"

"No, I havenae."

"The ships that transport the slaves…you can smell them before they reach the shore. Many of the men, women, and children are sick and near dead when they arrive. Not many of them make it to port alive. The conditions are horrendous. I do not wish to partake of any part of it. My father was a fair and just man. I believe it to be one of the reasons he built our home in North Carolina. Slavery was not as common as it was in South Carolina. The land was not conducive to plantations."

"Ye seem to be an educated lass."

"About some things. My father tried to make sure of it."

Moments passed, and Elaina sipped her wine as she stared out at the stars, trying to ignore the warmth emanating off of the man leaning so nonchalantly against the railing, his shoulder quite close to her own.

"That was a wild tale, Lady Caroline was recountin'," he said, not looking at her.

She cleared her throat. "Yes, quite."

"It would be hard to believe if only…"

"If only?"

"If only I hadna had the immense pleasure of bein' awakened two nights ago by two lasses, one of whom was covered in shite and had an injured hand. How is your head by the way?"

She could see him turn toward her out of the corner of her eye. "About to burst at the moment," she answered meekly still staring at the night.

"Horse accident?" he asked.

"Um, yes."

"Happened the same day as this?" He took up her hand. His own was large and warm, engulfing her chilled fingers in a secure nest. He ran his thumb across her knuckles, sending chills down her back.

"Yes, as a matter of fact. Sadie was frisky that day."

"Frisky indeed," he said with a hint of laughter.

Elaina mentally kicked herself for her choice of words.

"Knocked him out cold, did she?"

"That's the story Lady Caroline recounted," Elaina said, meeting his gaze.

"Indeed."

They stood staring at each other in the moonlight, the laughter from the dining hall drifting out on the cool night air.

One corner of Calum's mouth turned up. "Do I even wanna know?"

"Probably not," she said.

"Does your brother ken?"

"He may have an idea now."

"Good. Maybe ye'll get yerself a good thrashin' when ye get home."

She snatched her hand from his. "Not unless he wants a good thrashing in return," she said coldly.

"If you were my sister or my wife—"

"It is a good thing I am neither, isn't it?" she said, turning on her heel and storming back toward the party.

Calum grabbed her wrist, twirling her back toward him and squarely against his solid chest. "I dinna ken what's goin' on, but I think ye are puttin' yerself and my cousin in a fair amount of danger and I dinna like it," he stated, his grip tightening.

The bastard acted as if he were her father. She laid her free hand upon his chest, her fingers fiddling with his cravat. Looking up at him through her lashes, she gave him her most seductive look. "Why. Mr. MacKinnon, you do flatter me so. I had no idea our relationship was at this level. I thought us mere acquaintances."

Calum raised his brow, a smile quirking in the corner of his mouth.

"But I tell you what," Elaina pushed herself away from him, glaring. Then, mocking his accent, she continued. "Caitir is a grown woman, as am I, and we will do what we damn well please. I am not your sister nor your wife, and if you ever touch me without my permission again, you will ken the true meanin' of a thrashin', sir." She yanked her arm from his grasp and strolled back to the dining hall, followed out of the veranda by his quiet laughter.

Chapter Seven

THE FRUSTRATIONS AND PAIN OF the previous few months flew from her body, carried away on the wind rushing past her. Warm upon her face, the sunlight seemed to sink through to her soul, but dark rain clouds loomed just past the granite mountains in the distance. True to his word, Rabbie led Elaina out to where the vast open field lay before her and she could let Sadie go at full gallop. He fell back as she urged her mare faster as if she could outrun her troubles. She kept her eyes on a cluster of trees and heather along the base of a rocky ridge, watching them grow larger until she was forced to pull Sadie to a stop. Turning to face the direction from which they had come, she couldn't tell if Rabbie's tiny figure on the horizon was moving or sitting still.

His offer to take her on this outing had surprised her. William's agreement had been more shocking, though he'd also made the stipulation that the new coachman stay with her at all times. She was not to run off by herself.

Elaina had grown impatient as William lay down his rules. He needn't treat her like a child. At this moment in time, however, none of that mattered. Rabbie had taken her to this spot where he told her she could ride free but remain in his sight as her brother wished. If she closed her eyes, she could almost imagine she was back in North Carolina. Turning her horse east, she set out to follow the dense outline of the forest surrounding the open plain laying behind her. Scotland was a beautiful country once you got away from the stench that constantly bombarded you in the city. Waves of heather blanketed the hills around her with every shade of purple as far as her eye could see, dotted with bits of pink and occasionally white. Her mother had recounted stories of the heather of her home country to Elaina when she was a small child, along with legends and myths of her homeland. Elaina wished she had paid more attention. She could feel her mother's presence around her, in the hills and mountains and in the pines rising majestically toward the heavens.

Reaching into a secret pouch of her skirt, she pulled out the pendant she kept hidden there. She laid the reins across the pommel of the saddle, trusting Sadie not to throw her off. She turned the amulet over in her hands, admiring the smoky stone. It was exquisitely unique, not brown, not quite gray, not opaque, yet not translucent. Fixed to the top of the crystal was a silver bell cap decorated with three silver pinecones. Etched down the sides of the elongated stone were the fine needles of a Scotch pine. It had been a gift from her mother on her twenty-first birthday two days before they'd set sail for England. Cairngorm stones brought strength, her mother had told her, and it would help to keep her safe. If this was the case, her mother should have held onto it for herself, Elaina thought cynically. Lady Spencer had claimed the stone was only powerful if she kept it close to her person. Her mother was Scottish. Scots and superstitions went hand in hand.

The English part of Elaina thought the whole power and protection thing pushed the limits of realism. The Scottish part didn't want to press her luck, so she kept the pendant hidden from everyone, even William. Caitir had seen it, or felt it rather, while helping her undress. Elaina showed it to her with reluctance, explaining why she kept it hidden. She didn't want to reveal the stone to anyone fearing it might lose part of its magic—the magic tying her and her mother together. She may be holding onto a ghost, but so be it.

Sadie leisurely picked her way back toward Rabbie, drawn by the other horse's presence. Elaina let her choose her speed and didn't interrupt when she stopped to feed on shrubbery.

Rabbie sat on a large outcropping about halfway back, whittling on a stick. She returned the amulet to its hiding place after kissing it for luck.

"There is a burn where we can water the horses," he said, rising to his feet and tucking the small knife and the stick away. He tossed an apple core into the bushes as Elaina slid from the saddle. He took her reins, and she followed the lanky Scot and the horses down a steep incline toward the sound of running water.

"The stream is up," Rabbie said, trying to squint through the trees toward the mountains. "Means the cloud is to be a heavy one. I'm no meanin' to rush ye after I said I wadna, but we need to be gettin' on sooner rather than later."

"I am forever indebted to you," Elaina said. "Whether you rush me or not."

Rabbie smiled, leading the horses to drink from the rolling stream. He handed Elaina a wooden canteen from which she drank deeply.

"Forever indebted? Ye act as if I have done ye a great favor."

"Truly, you have. Thank you." Elaina had been more comfortable with the coachman since his guarding of her after the second letter. It helped that William had confidence in him as well. He had an uncanny way of sneaking up behind her and scaring the living daylights out of her when she was in the stables, but she'd gladly accepted his offer of taking her out for a ride.

"Does me just as much good," he replied. "I dinna like the city any more than you."

"Why are you there?" Elaina asked splashing water from the stream onto her hot face.

"It's a long story," Rabbie replied. He stretched out full length on a patch of mossy ground lit by the sun.

Elaina sat beside him, her knees drawn up to her chin, skirts spread around her feet. "So, you are not going to tell me?" she asked, watching the horses.

"My job played out. I needed a new one. Here I am."

"Fascinating."

He only smiled, crossed his arms behind his head, and closed his eyes.

"Where are you from?" she prodded.

"North."

"North is a large place." She tore leaves from a twig and tossed them in the flowing water.

"Not as big as it sounds."

"Well, I can't imagine my brother bringing you on if he knows nothing of who you are or where you are from."

"I've high recommendations."

"I'm sure you do." She studied the long line of him. Ankles crossed and hands under his head, the man was stretched out taught. The muscles in his body banded tight against his bones, much like a cat. She could see and trace every dip and curve.

Thunder sounded faintly in the distance, and Rabbie opened one eye.

"It's gettin' closer. We best be on, then." He rose gracefully from the ground, tying his sandy blonde hair back with his leather thong that had come undone. His piercing green eyes turned to Elaina as he stretched out his hand and helped her to her feet.

Accepting her horse's reins, she waved him off once again when he tried to help her onto Sadie's saddle. He shook his head and emitted an exaggerated sigh before he swung himself up into his own. Turning the horses back toward Duart Manor and the city of Edinburgh, Elaina let out a sigh of regret that their ride would soon end.

"Ye ken that ye are a lady, aye?" Rabbie asked.

"In what manner are you referring? That I am female or a member of British high society?" She cut her eyes at him.

He chuckled, shaking his head. "Both. Ye ken it is my job to help ye mount yer horse, aye?"

"As you can see, I have no problem setting myself upon a horse."

"Aye, I see that fine enough, and I dinna care what ye do if we are in the middle of nowhere, but when we are in public or in the presence of Lord Spencer, I would appreciate ye lettin' me do my job so that I might be able to keep it, ye ken?"

It was Elaina's turn to laugh. "Aye, I ken."

Not in any hurry even as the storm loomed behind them, they loped their horses along in silence.

"So, yer ma was from Edinburgh?" Rabbie asked.

"She was. Leicester was her maiden name."

"And yer father was British?"

"He was."

"Did it pose problems for yer family? The English and the Scottish have had a rough go, no?"

"I suppose it may have. I know my mother had a falling out with her mother not long before we moved to the colonies. They never spoke again, as far as I know. I don't know if her marriage to my father had anything to do with the rift."

"Why did yer family leave for the colonies? Why there?"

"You sure ask a lot of questions for someone who enjoys his secrets." Elaina raised a quizzical eyebrow toward Rabbie.

"What can I say?" he grinned.

"You could tell me about your family. Are your parents living?"

My da is. My mam died while givin' birth to my brother."

"I'm sorry. How old were you?"

"Ten.

"Is your brother still living?" She almost didn't want to ask.

"He is. He is a farmer back home."

"North, right?" Elaina said, cutting her eyes at the coachman.

"Ye catch on fast, my lady." He grinned, looking straight ahead.

"Hmph. Any other siblings?"

A streak of lightning split the sky, startling riders and horses alike.

"Enough with the interrogations!" Rabbie called out over the thunder, and the pair urged their horses into a gallop to outrun the storm.

They arrived at the manor already drenched to their skin but entering the stables a moment ahead of a deluge that made it impossible to hear each other over the roar of the rain pounding the roof. The pair worked without speaking, removing saddles and pads and wiping down the horses. Steam swirled off animals and humans alike. The rain pounded on the roof, and whiskey from the flask warmed Elaina's bones even as her wet clothing chilled her skin. Rabbie settled himself onto a pile of hay, pulling out yet another stick and his small knife. Elaina propped herself on a box and watched, entranced as curls of wood fell to the floor of the stables like waves of blonde hair against the dark stones. She wondered what secrets he hid. He did have excellent references. William told her as much, but the man kept his personal life private.

She pulled her knees to her chest and rested her head on them while watching the rhythmic action of the blade against the wood. She dreaded going back to the real world—the world where her parents no longer existed, where everything was dangerous, and where she didn't know who to trust. She felt almost normal when she was with the horses, like maybe the world wasn't such a dangerous place after all.

Eventually, the rain began to subside, and it eased Elaina out of her trance. Her clothes hung heavy on her slight frame as she pulled herself to her feet. She wasn't sure if it was the weight of her wet garments or her grief trying to drag her back down.

Her face must have betrayed her emotions for Rabbie placed a hand upon her shoulder. "Is it that bad lass, ye dinna want to return home?"

Elaina forced a smile she did not feel. Patting his hand, she replied, "No, I don't suppose it is. Thank you again for the ride." She turned to leave.

"We will go again," he called after her.

She nodded her agreement, then wept on her walk to the main house.

Chapter Eight

"WHERE ARE YOU GOING?" WILLIAM asked, eyeing Elaina as she came waltzing into the study where he spent most of his days poring over charts, billing receipts, orders, and inventories.

"Lady Caroline invited some ladies to tea. I thought I would mingle a bit, get to know some of the locals." Elaina feigned innocence while she pulled on her white gloves.

"Nose around. Spy," William said, the sides of his mouth turning up. He leaned back in the brown leather chair, stretching his arms and groaning. Worry lines were etched deep in his forehead, and his face held the pallid cast of the unwell.

"If I just happen to hear something helpful, that is only a bonus." Elaina sat in the chair across the desk from him. "Why don't you take a break, William? You look terrible."

"I will after I finish this." He waved a hand over the papers scattered on his desk.

"Let me help you," she pleaded. "I don't want to go to teas and socials. You know how I feel about people."

He grinned at her confession. "You can't go to the docks. It's no place for a woman. Besides, the men wouldn't listen to a woman over business matters anyway, no matter how much sense she made or how loud she yelled."

She cut her eyes at him. "I didn't ask to go to the docks." Leaning forward, she placed her arms on the cluttered desk. "Let me do some of this. I want to take part of the burden from you, and it would give me something to do. We've so many servants in this place I can't even sneeze without someone running over to wipe my nose."

William sighed, looking over the massive pile of papers scattered every-where. "I don't know. How are you going to spy if you are stuck in here doing paperwork all day?"

"I bet I can do it twice as fast as you."

"It's not a competition, Elaina."

"Everything is a competition, William. Otherwise, what is the point of liv-ing? I'm going to be late for tea." She jumped up, running around the desk to kiss him on top of his head.

"Never thought you would be so eager to take tea with a bunch of cackling, gossiping women," he said rising to escort her out.

"We are playing Penneech…for money." Elaina waggled her eyebrows at him.

"Oh, ho." William rocked back on his heels, his hands in his pockets. "Watch out, Edinburgh. You're not looking to make a lot of new friends, then?"

"No. I'm looking to win."

⁂

Elaina left Caroline's house on a high note having won a bit of money. Her thoughts, however, were not on the winnings—she would donate those to a local charity. It was the image of the mysterious Monroe that replayed in her mind. She needed to find him but wasn't sure where to start. She couldn't ask William without having to tell him how she had found out the name. She didn't want to ask Rabbie because he might be William's eyes and ears as well as the coachman. Besides, being tied up working in their stables left him little time to be snooping around the seaside. She needed someone with ties to the docks, someone who would possibly know the regulars who worked there. Calum. Did she trust the pompous arse, though? Well, he had not spoken to William about what happened. She smiled, thinking about her adventure-filled evening.

"Lady Elaina! What's the matter? Are ye not well?" Rabbie scrambled from the waiting carriage and hurried to her side.

Her heart leaped into her throat. "I'm fine. What?" she asked, turning her hands and arms inspecting them and looking herself over as best she could. "What is it?"

"Ye're smiling," Rabbie said, the corner of his mouth turning up.

"Horse's arse," she said, smacking him on the arm. "You scared the hell out of me."

"Well, isnae somethin' ye see often. Ye had me worrit."

"I smile." *Don't I?*

"Ye do smile," Rabbie agreed. "Ye smile at horses. Ye smile at Angus, who, might I say, is a wee bit on the young side for ye."

"You are insufferable."

"I know," Rabbie said, opening the door to the carriage for her. "Home?" he asked.

"No, I have a little business I need to attend to while in the city. And then I believe I would like to wander around the shops on High Street," she said. "You can let me out and go do what you like for a while." Hopefully, she sounded innocent enough.

"I dinna ken what yer brother would have to say about that." Rabbie gazed down at her, carriage door in hand. His statement confirmed her suspicions about William's version of spying.

"Well, you are welcome to come along. I need to talk to Mr. Lawrence about new drapes for the study. I told him to pull out a dozen samples for me to go over. Of course, I will have to have a matching sofa in a coordinating pattern, which will involve a visit with Samson and more talk of fabric choices. Then, I planned to have a new ball gown made. That will involve—"

"Aye, fine," he huffed, rolling his eyes.

"It's the middle of town. I don't think anything will become of me in broad daylight, on one of the busiest streets in Edinburgh."

"I didna argue." He took her hand, helping her into the carriage.

"You didn't have to."

Rabbie did reluctantly let her out at the end of High Street. They planned to meet in two hours at a little tavern at the bottom of the hill.

Elaina had planned to perform most of the tasks she'd laid out for Rabbie. She'd set them in motion weeks ago and thus completed them quickly. Afterward, her mission was to find Calum MacKinnon. That drunken night in Edinburgh was a blur, but she believed Calum's building lay somewhere in the vicinity of her errands. However, she didn't know if she was looking for a shop, an office, or a private residence. She stopped a few people and asked about Calum MacKinnon, but none had heard of him.

Elaina sighed, looking around for something to strike a familiar chord. The city bustled on this unusually dry afternoon. The cobblestone streets were still damp from the morning rain, but the sun had decided to show itself about mid-day and the residents of the city took advantage. She squinted against the sun, stepping into the road to get a better view of the buildings farther up the way.

"Madam! Watch out!" Someone jerked her violently backward.

"Mother of God!" she squealed as a pair of short but stout arms kept her from falling over. "What was that?"

"Cows."

"I have never seen cows like that before. Why on earth are they in the middle of the city?" Elaina leaned back out into the street, craning her neck to watch the scurry of people avoiding the enormous, although mild-mannered, shaggy beasts on their leisurely afternoon stroll.

"Cows are about as much as people on these streets. Ye must be new to Edinburgh if ye dinna ken that nor what a Scottish cow looks like." The older gentleman was about Elaina's height with a head full of bright red hair unsuc-cessfully contained under a slouched hat. He produced a friendly smile, making his hazel eyes almost disappear.

"I arrived several months ago," Elaina admitted. "Thank you for saving me."

"Nay trouble 't all." The gentleman touched his hat, turning to leave.

She touched his arm. "Begging your pardon, but I am looking for a friend. Maybe you can help me?"

"Well, I dinna have many friends so I suppose I could use another." He grinned at her, his weathered face crinkling in amusement.

"I would be honored to have you as a friend," she laughed, "but I am look-ing for a Mr. Calum MacKinnon. Have you heard of him, by chance?"

"Aye. I have," the man said, studying her face. "As it happens, I was just on my way to see the wee bugger."

"Were you? What a small world. Would you mind if I tagged along? I can-not seem to remember where his building is, having been there only once."

"I would consider it a privilege to accompany such a bonny lass." The gentleman crooked his elbow, and Elaina inserted her arm through it. "It is the next street over and up a few."

"Good God. I would never have found it." Elaina laughed. "Thank you for your help."

"What brings you to Edinburgh?"

Something in the man's manner put Elaina at ease, so she explained their move from the colonies to Scotland as they turned down a close to cut across to the next street. She considered omitting the part about her parents but decided, in the end, it would not make much difference either way.

"Aye, I heard about the death of the Earl and his wife. My sincere condolences, my lady." He removed his hat and held it to his chest in earnest.

Before she could respond, they were both shoved roughly into the stone wall of the close.

"What have we here?" A drunk with no teeth breathed into Elaina's face.

She turned her head, trying not to gag from the stench of the man.

"Bugger off," her red-headed companion growled. "We've no business with you."

"No? Well, we've business with you." A second man stepped forward. He was a bit larger than his friend, and it seemed not near as inebriated. "Money. Hand it over."

"We've none," Red retorted.

"No? This one looks like she does." The soberer of the two grabbed Elaina by her throat, dragging her tightly into him. One hand remained around her neck while the other began to make its way down her bodice, groping and searching.

Red sprung forward, but the drunken dimwit blocked him with his body.

Her captor's hand began to ruck up her skirts, and damned if she would let him violate her. She stomped on the man's foot with her boot heel and threw her head back. In a series of strangled swears and gurgles, the man released his hold on her. Faster than he looked, his friend punched Elaina before she could react further. She wasn't sure what happened next because she was bent over, her eyes watering.

"Come on," Red said, wrapping an arm around her. "Let's get movin'."

She glanced back to find both men lying unconscious on the ground. She wondered for a moment if they were only unconscious.

The two ran to the end of the close and then slowed to a walk for the next two blocks to Calum's building. Her companion entered without knocking as a small bell chimed over the door. Elaina didn't remember it from her previous visit. Perhaps Calum didn't appreciate surprise visits.

"One moment," a male voice called from the back.

It was a small office of sorts. The red-headed man led Elaina, who held her pounding eye, into a familiar room and planted her in an all too familiar chair. It seemed to be an entirely different room, though it was now broad daylight and this time Elaina was sober. A large table with numerous maps spread across the top stood beside a wall of books. A smaller desk, more neatly arranged, sat in the center of the room with two chairs in front where she assumed Calum and whatever kind of customers he had dispensed with their business tasks.

"Good after—" Calum stopped in his tracks, looking from Elaina to Red and back to Elaina in a state of confusion. A slow, sly smile spread across his face as he took in Elaina holding her eye.

"Here ye are again. I'm no physician. I dinna ken why my kinfolk keep poppin' ye in here for me to patch ye up."

The man looked confused.

"Uncle." Calum nodded to the man.

"Uncle?" Elaina questioned.

"She said she was a friend of yers." Calum's uncle cocked his head in her direction, looking between the two.

"Did she now?" Calum crossed his arms and leaned against the doorframe. "I didna ken I had moved up to the status of friend. I thought I still resided somewhere between horse dung and a midge."

His uncle gave a deep, boisterous laugh. "She kens ye fair well, I'd say."

"You wear me out, Mr. MacKinnon." Elaina sighed, leaning back in the large wingback chair.

Calum pushed himself off the door facing. He chuckled, crossing the room to where she sat. "Let's have a look at yer eye, then."

Elaina moved her hand and closed her eyes.

Calum gently probed the bone around the socket. "Uncle, was she spoutin' off and ye had to throttle her?"

Elaina opened her eye and glared at him.

He grinned down at her, his eyes twinkling. His shirt sleeves had been rolled up to his elbows, revealing a pair of well-muscled forearms. He wore a leather apron over his clothing, and beads of perspiration dotted his forehead.

Elaina didn't know what their arrival had interrupted, but it had been physical. He smelled vaguely of dust and whiskey…and distinctly of man. His dark curly hair pulled back and clubbed at his neck escaped its bindings in small wisps about his face. A particularly long curl tickled her chin. She closed her eye before he caught her ogling him once again.

"We were set upon by muggers. The lass might have held her own had she no been caught unawares," the uncle said with what sounded like pride.

"I heard she is quite the wee scrapper." Calum continued his probe of Elaina's eye.

She tried to ignore his warm breath on her face and the proximity of his body to hers. What the hell was wrong with her? The man was a lout. She told herself her aggravation with him caused the warmth in her face and the tingling feeling where his fingers roamed over her skin.

"She also seems to attract trouble like fleas to a hound."

"That I will not argue with," Elaina said, her eyes still closed.

"Let me grab a poultice and then we can all talk." The sudden loss of his warm fingers on her face gave Elaina a shudder and an uncomfortable sense of… what? Longing? She absolutely, without a doubt, had lost her mind.

Calum left the way he'd come, wiping at his face with a handkerchief as he went. He returned not only with the poultice but also, thankfully, with a decanter of whiskey, which his uncle poured them each a glass from while Calum gently placed the rag-wrapped concoction on Elaina's eye.

"So," Calum said after they settled and softened their edges a bit. "What brings ye out on this fine day, Lady Elaina."

"I have a favor to ask," she replied, looking at him speculatively. She could not believe she was about to ask this man for help. *This tall, handsome—*

"Doctoring yer wounds is not favor enough?" he teased, interrupting her thoughts.

"Are you ever serious?" His sarcasm brought her out of her stupor.

"Not usually," his uncle answered.

"For one moment, try. I came to ask if you know a man named Monroe? I don't know if it is his surname or given name. He is a large, rather hairy man, and is missing a front tooth. His hair is dark, I think, but I'm pretty sure he never bathes so it may be anyone's guess. He works at the dock, but for whom I don't know. I think he has a friend or works with a shorter just as hairy gentleman. I believe they may be involved in my parents' deaths somehow."

"Could ye be any more vague?"

The death glare Elaina gave him would have withered any other man.

Calum merely added, "The two men ye and Caitir had yer encounter with?"

"Encounter? Caitir?" his uncle asked.

Elaina filled the two in on what had taken place at the Inn that night. Calum filled his uncle in on what had taken place here in this room. Red expressed concern at appropriate moments and nearly roared with laughter at others, making Elaina's face turn crimson in memory.

"Dinna be embarrassed, lass." The man wiped his eyes with his sleeve. "I never in all my years... I am so glad I saved ye from the cattle today. This is the most fun I've had with a lassie with my clothes on in a verra long time."

"She's entertaining to be sure," Calum grinned.

"I am so glad my disasters are amusing to the two of you," Elaina said, removing the poultice pack from her eye so she could adequately glare at them.

"What are ye going to tell Lord Spencer about that one?" Calum asked, pointing to her eye.

"William? Dammit! Rabbie!"

"What?" the two men said in unison.

"Rabbie, the coachman! I was supposed to meet him at the pub probably twenty minutes ago." She jumped up from the chair, downing the remainder of her whiskey in one gulp.

"We'll take ye," Calum said motioning to his uncle who was already grabbing his hat. "I will keep a look and an ear out for the men ye asked about," he assured her as the trio hurried toward the pub on High Street. "But may I ask why me and not your brother?"

"I can't tell him about the tavern incident. He would kill me, and Caitir might lose her position. I cannot lose her. She is more of a blessing to me than either of you may ever know." She looked desperately at the two men. "You are the only one I could think of—the only one I thought I could trust not to say anything. Crivens, there he is, and he doesn't look happy," Elaina said spying Rabbie leaning against the carriage with his arms crossed.

"Where the hell have ye been?" he asked, turning a disparaging look at her two companions. "What happened to your eye?" He took a step forward.

"The cows," she blurted out.

"The cows?" he asked.

"Did you not see those giant hairy beasts traipsing right down High Street as if they owned it?" she asked a tad too high pitched. "I have never seen such creatures."

"Ye have never seen a cow?" Rabbie asked, crossing his arms again.

"I have seen cows, just not cows in desperate need of having their hair cut. This gentleman saved me from being trampled, but in the act, I accidentally hit myself in the eye."

"Did ye now?" Rabbie asked, his voice registering the doubt she could see plainly on his face.

"I did. By pure coincidence, this gentleman happened to be Mr. MacKinnon's uncle. I met Mr. MacKinnon at the Taylors' dinner party. He made me a poultice to put on my eye. I am so sorry I kept you waiting," Elaina babbled but couldn't stop herself. She didn't know why she thought she felt the need to answer to the help. Guilt for having lied about her intentions for the day, she supposed. Turning her back to Rabbie, she spoke to Calum and his uncle. "Thank you, gentlemen, truly. For all your help." Elaina met Calum's gaze and held it.

He smiled, bowing to her. "My pleasure, my lady."

"'Twas my pleasure as well, madam. Until we meet again." Calum's uncle took her hand and kissed it.

"In all the excitement, I never did get your name," Elaina said.

"Everyone calls me Auld Ruadh," he said, smiling at her.

"Old Red," Rabbie said behind her, causing her to glance at him. He stared with unmarked hostility at the two gentlemen.

Elaina cleared her throat loudly.

Rabbie blinked, looking down at her. "Your pardon, my lady." He bowed his head and turned his attention to something attached to the carriage.

"Well, Auld Ruadh, I look forward to our next meeting. May it be a longer visit and not quite so full of excitement." She leaned forward and kissed him on the cheek. "Thank you for saving my life." She held up two fingers in front of her chest, out of sight of Rabbie, and mouthed "twice."

Rabbie helped Elaina into the carriage before exchanging wary glances with her two companions.

Auld Ruadh touched the tip of his cap, and Calum gave her a nod and smile as the carriage started with a jerk.

She tilted her head to them in reply before collapsing back against the seat. The trip back to Duart Manor passed too quickly for Elaina's liking. She chewed her lip, wondering exactly how bad her eye looked and whether William would believe her story. Not that it mattered, it was the story he would get. The carriage pulled to a stop in front of the stables.

"Lady Elaina, may I be frank with ye?" Rabbie asked, helping her from the carriage.

"Of course," she said.

"I dinna believe yer story about yer eye. I dinna ken what did happen, but I ken ye need to be careful who ye trust. Ye are new to Edinburgh and Scotland in general. These are dangerous times, my lady. There are many a wolf in sheep's clothing."

"Do you know something about Mr. MacKinnon that I need to know?" Elaina asked, slightly affronted.

"I am just givin' ye a bit of advice to watch with whom ye associate. Not everyone nice to ye is yer friend. Pick the wrong ones, and it may cost ye yer life." With those final words, Rabbie turned and started to unhook the team of horses.

Elaina stood staring at his back, not sure what to think. She headed to the house without further discussion, but with gooseflesh broken out over her body.

Chapter Nine

ELAINA NEEDN'T HAVE WORRIED ABOUT what William would think of her black eye. Upon her return, she learned Lord Spencer had left for Newcastle on urgent business and no one knew when he would return. The fact that he had not told her about his trip left a sour taste in her mouth. She should have concerned herself more with what Caitir would have to say.

"Oh for Christ's sake, my lady. Can ye no stay out of trouble? Just stay home."

"I'm pretty sure I can get in plenty of trouble here, as well." Elaina examined her eye in the looking glass. It wasn't bad. Calum's poultice had worked wonders. By the time William returned, he would never know anything had happened. She recounted her tale to Caitir, who had been delighted to know Auld Ruadh was in the area. Elaina gave her leave to visit with her kinsman.

With William and Caitir gone and her with nothing to do, Elaina moped about the house for a bit before she set out for the stables. It was time she got to know the two young boys better.

"Angus?" Elaina called into the stables, searching for the young lad.

"Yes, my lady?" He came scampering out, grinning from ear to ear.

"Will you fetch me a big apron and tell Ainsley to grab the axes?"

"Aye, my lady." He looked at her quizzically before running back into the stables.

"Angus? Fetch us some bows and arrows also. We are going to make a day of it."

Several minutes later, Angus, armed with the bows and arrows, and Ainsley, sporting a pair of axes, emerged from the stables.

Elaina, decked out in one of the grooms' leather aprons and toting a basket of food Mrs. Davies threw together for the trio, followed the boys to the woodpile in a little clearing behind the garden and down a hill away from the main house.

"What are we goin' to do, my lady?" Angus practically jumped up and down with excitement at the attention from the lady of the house.

Ainsley remained silent while fidgeting with the handle of the ax he still held.

Elaina tried to hide her amusement at the lad's wary gaze. "First off, we are going to set up a target and the two of you are going to practice your shooting skills while I split some wood." She placed the basket on the ground and stood surveying the small clearing. "I think over there."

The two boys erected the target out of a piece of muslin Elaina had snatched up on her way out of the house. Angus scampered off to find some berries and returned, making a small red circle in the center.

Elaina inspected their work. "Brilliant! Now, have you two shot a bow before?"

"Aye," the pair said in unison.

"Well, get to it then."

"I be Robin Hood, and ye be Little John," Angus instructed Ainsley.

Elaina smiled to herself. She had created a monster with her readings to the boys. She rolled up her sleeves while watching the enthusiastic pair. They had escaped the drudgery of scooping horse shite in favor of shooting arrows. Their excitement was palpable.

She turned to her task at hand. It had been some time since she had split wood and it took her a bit to get into the rhythm of it. She would be sore in the morning. The muscles in her back and arms tightened with each swing of the heavy ax. She could feel it in her thighs and buttocks. To move again—breathing the fresh air, not cooped up in a house making nice with people she didn't know—lifted her spirits. Her thoughts turned to her family as she lost herself in her task. The smell of fresh split wood brought back images of her father in his study in North Carolina. She closed her eyes, picturing his large frame sitting hunched over papers for hours until his eyes were red and his nerves on edge. The office smelled of pine from newly hued boards. Once William was old enough, her father brought him in to help with the business end of things. He would talk with William for hours about different ventures and ideas. Captain Spencer, for he was a captain in the army but not yet an Earl, made sure Elaina was well educated, but as far as discussions about business or such, she seemed to be more of a nuisance than a confidant. Perhaps he'd thought her interests should lie elsewhere, her being a female. She'd managed to absorb much of what he'd taught William, however, by eavesdropping on their conversations and picking William's brain later.

If she were honest, she and her father hadn't talked much at all. He had involved her in other things most young girls were unlikely to do. They had hunted together, but it required silence. Elaina was a natural, and her father, an avid hunter himself, had seemed pleased with this aspect of his daughter's personality. With her mother always harping for her to act more like a lady and her father avoiding conversation, there had been times when Elaina felt like she didn't quite belong in the mix. So, she'd attempted to spend as much time out of doors as she could.

Her body staked out a rhythm all its own while her mind found its way back in time to her childhood in North Carolina. The lush forest grass under her bare feet. The rough branch of the massive oak tree scraping the backs of her thighs while she tried not to giggle as William and the two small Indian boys who visited the Spencer family with their father for weeks at a time practiced their tracking skills, trying to find her. She became excellent at hiding and even better at tracking, much to her mother's dismay. Diana Spencer thought the wilds of the wood no place for a young girl. She'd tried desperately to keep Elaina at the house, attempting to teach her knitting and needlework, cooking and other womanly things she thought any self-respecting prospect for a wife should know. Elaina held no interest. She would rather butcher a hog or split wood. Splitting wood was something she'd truly missed. William detested the chore, so Elaina had often offered to do it for him if they could hide it from their mother.

Sweat dripped down her nose, and she paused, wiping her face with her sleeve while watching the two boys. Ainsley was a fair shot. Angus needed some work. Who knew how often he got to shoot, being removed from his parents' home so young and put to work. Her heart went out to the boys. She knew how lonely she was without her parents, even if they didn't always see eye to eye. She wondered if the pain was the same, though their parents were still alive. Who knew when or if they would ever see them again.

She watched them for a few minutes, catching her breath and observing their technique. "Here, Angus. Let me show you." She leaned the ax against the tree stump, wiping her sweaty hands on her apron. "Feet square while facing the target. Grip your bow," she instructed, coming to stand behind the young boy.

"Now, you want to rest the bow on this fatty part of your hand, just under your thumb. See?" She adjusted the boy's grip. "But relax the rest of your fingers. You are not trying to squeeze the life out of it. Do not pretend it is Mrs. Davies's neck."

The two boys giggled.

"Okay, nock your arrow and draw it back."

The boy did as told.

"Relax. Get your shoulder out of your ear." She tugged at his ear, causing him to giggle again. "Now, let's straighten this arm parallel to the ground. There you go. Raise your draw hand just a smidge until your finger is just at the corner of your mouth. You are going to use all your muscles, not just your arm. You should feel it here and here." Elaina touched the boy's back and shoulder. "Perfect. Now sight in your target and gently release."

The arrow flew, nearly hitting the center of the target.

"Woohoo!" Angus exclaimed.

"Fantastic!" Ainsley clasped his brother on the shoulder, giving it a tight squeeze. "That's the best ye've ever done!"

"You shoot, madam! You do it!" Angus pushed the bow toward her.

"Very well, but I will need a slightly larger bow than that one." Elaina tested a couple of the extra bows they had brought with them before settling on one that fit her the best. "Pass me an arrow, please." She sighted it in and let it fly. Bullseye. She reached out for another arrow.

"Is there anythin' ye cannae do, my lady?" Angus asked in earnest.

"Well, let's see." Elaina pondered while sighting in her arrow. "I cannot sing. I sound like a dying goose." She laughed as she let her arrow loose, causing it to go slightly off course.

Angus handed her another one.

"I cannot play the pianoforte." She cast a sideways glance at the two boys smiling at her. "My knitting is atrocious, so do not beg me to knit you a hat." She let her arrow fly. "And," she added, arching a dramatic eyebrow at the pair while nocking another arrow. "I cannot seem to stay out of trouble." In one swift movement, she turned her head, lifted her bow, and released the arrow without pausing to aim. Bullseye.

Both boys broke out in enthusiastic applause.

She gave them a bow, a hand to her chest and the other arm outstretched.

"Now ye are just showin' off," a voice sounded behind them.

All three whirled around to find Rabbie sitting on the splitting stump. "I wondered where the two of ye ran off to."

The boys backed up a step as if afraid, and Elaina put her hands on their shoulders.

"I bid them come with me. I needed the company and someone to carry all this wood back." She smiled down at the two boys.

"Well, 'tis about time they get back to it in the stables. The horses are needin' their mash."

The boys began to gather the wood and axes together.

"Just a moment." Elaina stopped them. She reached into the basket and stuffed the boys' pockets with an apple each and cheese and bannocks before ruffling both their hair. "Grab what you can of the wood and go tend the horses. You can come back and fetch the remainder later. Mr. MacLeod and I will bring the axes and the other things. You boys did well today. We will do it again sometime, only next time you may chop wood while I shoot the bow." She winked at them.

"Thank you, my lady," Angus beamed proudly at her.

"Yes, madam, thank you." Ainsley bowed his head to her.

The boys gathered the wood and set off back to their work giggling and talking under their breath as they went.

She watched the retreating boys with her hands on her hips.

"Aren't you just the mother hen?" Rabbie said.

"If that's what you call it. They need some fun and happiness in their lives, I would think. Would you care for a drink, Mr. MacLeod?" she asked, spreading her skirts and plopping herself on the ground by the basket. She pulled out a stone bottle and drank from it before passing it to Rabbie.

He took the bottle from her hand, studying her. "Do ye no think the boys are happy havin' a roof over their head and a bed on which to sleep? Food in their belly?" He slid down onto the ground in front of her, leaning back against the stump and stretching out his long legs.

"I think maybe it takes more than the bare necessities to make a person truly content. Anyone can have shelter and food and still feel alone and unhappy. One also needs a sense of belonging, a feeling of being wanted and appreciated."

"And do you feel that way, my lady? Do you have a sense of belonging?"

Elaina stopped chewing the piece of cheese she had been nibbling on. *Why skirt the question?* "Not always, no. Do you, Mr. MacLeod?"

"Not always, no. Especially when ye call me Mr. MacLeod." He imitated her with a haughty shake of his head.

She half-heartedly threw an apple at him. "Fine. Rabbie. Do you feel wanted and appreciated?"

He picked up the fruit and studied it before taking a large bite and chewing it while watching her. His green eyes pierced her own until she looked away. "At times," he said after swallowing. "Do you feel wanted and appreciated?"

"This is getting redundant." She laughed and then grabbed the bottle, taking another drink of the ale.

"I answered you." He raised his brow at her.

"Not always." She looked pointedly at him.

"Ye cannae just repeat my answers," he teased. "All of this and ye are not happy?" He waved an all-encompassing hand at the house, stables, and land.

"You didn't ask if I was happy. You asked if I felt wanted and appreciated. Those are three different emotions."

"Are you happy, then?"

"You ask too many questions."

"Are you happy?" he repeated slower, stretching his leg over and tapping the bottom of her shoe with his leather boot.

She looked up at him. "Mostly."

He only nodded in response.

It was quiet while each of them got lost in their thoughts for a few moments. Rabbie said, "Even with all of this, you're no happy?"

"What is your obsession with 'all this'? Things do not equal happiness," Elaina said. "Happiness comes from a sense of being loved."

"If ye did not have a fancy house, a fancy horse, fancy clothes, fancy friends, do ye think ye wadna be any more unhappy than ye already are?"

Elaina sighed with exasperation. "That is a question I cannot answer. Do I live comfortably? Yes. Do I think I could live without all this? Yes. Could I be happy doing it? Depends. If I have the love of special people in my life, yes. I do not think I could be happy alone."

"Ye are not alone here, and yet ye are not completely happy," Rabbie said. "Ye dinna think Lord Spencer loves ye and appreciates ye?" he asked. "If he didna, he wadna leave me in charge of lookin' after ye while he's away."

"I know William loves me. And what do you mean in charge of looking after me? You knew he was leaving?"

"Aye," Rabbie answered. "He told me before ye left to go to Caroline's. He asked me to watch over ye."

"Why didn't he tell me? I'm his bloody sister, and I don't know why he thinks I need someone to watch over me. I can watch over myself just fine."

"Of course ye can," Rabbie said sarcastically. "That's why I leave ye to go shoppin' and ye show up with two strange men and a black eye?"

"Those men are not strangers," Elaina said. "Calum is Caitir's cousin."

"How do ye ken ye can trust him?"

"Why are we on this subject again?" Elaina's voice rose along with her temper. Where in the hell did William get off telling the coachman of all people he would be gone but not his sister? And why the hell was Rabbie questioning Calum's trustworthiness again?

"Because he is someone's cousin doesna mean he is honorable."

"Well, who are you that I'm to trust you? I don't know you either, Rabbie MacLeod, and my brother leaves me in your care without even discussing it with me."

"And would ye have felt any different on the matter if he had told ye about it first or would ye still be sittin' there with yer knickers in a knot?"

"You bloody horse's arse." Elaina stood and snatched the basket, the bows, and the quiver of arrows off the ground.

"Seems to be yer pet name for me." Rabbie rose as well, grabbing the two axes and grinning at her.

Blood boiling, she didn't speak on the way back to the stables. With her hands full, she couldn't hold up the front of her skirts and stumbled over them, nearly falling on her face. Rabbie grabbed her elbow to catch her, and she wrenched it from his grasp. She could hear him chuckling behind her and had half a mind to grab one of those damned axes and put it through his skull.

The boys came running out to greet her but pulled up short when they saw her face. "Here, my lady, I'll take that from ye," Ainsley said glancing from Rabbie to Elaina as he reached for the bows and the quiver.

"Thank you, boys. I had a wonderful time today. We will do it again soon," Elaina said, nodding to them. She turned and stared hard at Rabbie, thinking of all manner of things she wanted to say to him. And none of them lady-like.

"Yer hair is the wrong color for that temper of yers," he said with a big toothy grin as he leaned against a post with his arms crossed.

Elaina glared at the man with his cocky smile and his cocky attitude.

Looking back at the boys, she spied the bucket of water sitting by her feet. She snatched it up and doused Rabbie with it, the cold water taking his breath and sending him stumbling off the post.

Ainsley and Angus covered their mouths, trying to suppress their astonished laughter.

"If these young men were not standing here, I would've knocked the bloody hell out of you with the bucket instead," Elaina said with a raised brow. "My temper suits the color of my hair just fine."

The boys snickered, and Rabbie gave her a sly grin and a nod as she headed toward the main house.

Elaina stormed up the stairs and into her bedroom, slamming the door behind her. Fuming, she paced the floor. How dare William leave that man in charge of her. *That arrogant son of a...* Her chamber held a perfect view of the stables, and she stared at him through the window. *The bastard.*

She turned from the window, her eyes lighting on a small box upon her pillow meticulously wrapped in gold paper with a bow to match. She stared at it for a long moment before venturing over to pick it up. Sitting on the edge of the bed, she unwrapped the box and opened it, her breath hitching in her throat as she caught sight of her mother's necklace inside. Hesitantly, she reached out a finger to touch it. Her mother had never taken this necklace from her person. As long as Elaina could remember, she had worn it around her neck.

The box could be a peace offering from William. If so, he could have skipped it and simply told her of his trip. The alternative was someone had been in her house—in her chamber, someone who had access to her mother's necklace and possibly her father's watch and knife. With a churning in her stomach, she set off in search of Eads.

"Have you received a package for me, as of late?" she asked after tracking him down in the pantry where he stood inspecting the collection of bottles of whiskey and other various spirits.

"No, my lady. Are you expecting one?"

"No. I just...never mind. It's not important." Elaina left him staring after her as she returned to her room to double-check the pistol she always kept in the drawer by her bed—a habit her father had instilled in her several years ago. She refused to rile up the help over something that may be purely innocent, but she felt better after inspecting her weapon.

Chapter Ten

HER FIGHT WITH RABBIE AND finding the necklace shook her more than she wanted to admit—not to mention the fact that Eads knew nothing of the package. To help settle her nerves a bit, she sent Missie to the stables to fetch the boys. Their reading sessions had become a Thursday afternoon tradition, but Elaina moved it up a day after her argument with Rabbie the day before. Nothing would settle her nerves better than time with the two boys. She had grown quite fond of them and didn't have to wait long before they appeared in the doorway to the study.

She motioned them to sit, and they took their usual positions, one on either end of the long sofa with a sizeable gap between them.

Ainsley leaned across it to swat at his brother's swinging legs. "Stop with the fidgets," he hissed

Elaina hid a smile as she plucked *Robin Hood* from the bookshelf once more. "Excited, are you?" She patted Angus on the knee as she took her place between them.

"Verra." Angus wiggled closer to Elaina.

"Come." She waved Ainsley closer as well.

Ainsley could read better than he let on, and she enjoyed teaching him some of the words and taking turns when he felt comfortable with a sentence. Ainsley was as quiet and humble as Angus was spirited and precocious.

Angus lay his head against Elaina's arm as she read. Tears pricked her eyes, and she struggled to keep the swelling emotion out of her voice. Her heart ached for the two lads on their own in this vast and dangerous world. Knowing she could not replace their mother, she still vowed to herself to give the boys a good start in this world. She would teach them all she knew and what she didn't know

William could teach them. Laying her cheek against the top of Angus's head, she gave his mass of wild hair a kiss. The smile she received in return nearly melted her into a puddle on the floor.

"I ken that word," Angus piped up, poking his finger at the book.

"What word do you know?" Elaina prodded him.

"This one is wood. That one is John."

"Impressive." Elaina beamed at her little prodigy. Both of the boys were clever beyond measure.

They continued, taking turns between Elaina and Ainsley reading and Angus belting out words he recognized. Eads arrived with tea things, prompting a break in the adventures.

"Do ye think Robin Hood be real?" Angus asked Elaina around a mouthful of scone.

"Dinna talk with yer mouth full," Ainsley scolded his brother.

Elaina stifled a laugh. "I'm not sure. Some think he was real."

"I hope he is, and when I meet him, I will join his band of Merry Men and together we will hunt down the evil Sheriff of Nottingham and give him what he deserves!"

"How 'bout I give ye what ye deserve, huh? A good knock on the head for thinkin' such things. Ye cannae go around shootin' folks with arrows because ye think they are a fictional character. Robin Hood no be a real person."

"You do no ken. He could be." Angus shot a glare at his brother.

Ainsley ignored him, taking a drink of his tea.

"Ainsley?" Elaina said.

"Yes, my lady."

"Would you like to take this book with you and practice reading? It will give the two of you something to do in the evenings when you are through with work."

"Could we? I might no ken all of the words, but I would love to try to figure them out."

"I can help!" Angus bounced in his chair. "Then I can hear the adventures every night, no just once a week."

Ainsley rolled his eyes and looked like he might have second thoughts on the idea.

"Very well, ye may take *Robin Hood*, and when we meet again next week, we can begin on Gulliver's Travels. He may not be as exciting as the Merry Men, but he has marvelous adventures of his own."

———————— ✦◆◆✦ ————————

She avoided the stables and Rabbie for the next few days. Instead, she roamed restlessly through the house, her bare feet padding through the hallways and stairwells in a never-ending circle as she thought of all the terrible things she would say to William when he returned—present or no present. It was on her third trip around the house one morning when Eads stopped her in the front hall.

"Madam, if I may? You will wear out the rugs with all your pacing, and whatever is bothering you is giving you frown lines."

"I just have so much on my mind. It won't stop raining, and I feel as if I am going to crawl right out of my skin."

"I have a nice bottle of brandy with your name on it, if you would like?" he asked. "Settle your nerves a bit?"

"That may be just what I need. Will you bring it to me in the green room, though? I think I shall like to go through some of the things we have never unpacked." Truthfully, she needed a good dose of her mother.

Settled in with not only a good bottle of brandy but also a tray of fruits and cheeses, Elaina poured herself a glass of courage and opened the brocade curtains to what everyone referred to as the green room. Her late grandmother had an eclectic taste in decorating. Each bedroom in the large manor was a different color and a different theme. Pale green wallpaper graced with delicate cherry blossoms adorned these walls. William found it stunningly hideous. Elaina found it soothing, especially after a glass of brandy.

She sat upon the pale pink settee in front of the window and stared out at the pouring rain while she fingered the long plait of hair hanging over her shoulder. She'd refused to let Caitir pile her hair upon her head this morning. There was no need for it. She was not leaving the house.

It rained in North Carolina almost as much as it rained in Scotland, but the rain was different here. It could have been her attitude was different. She certainly had a bad one at the moment. Everything annoyed her—even things she usually enjoyed, like the soft pattering of rain upon a window. The green room lay three rooms down the hall from her bedchamber, so from her current perch, she could see the stables. She hated having words with Rabbie but did not hate throwing water on the arrogant lout. He'd deserved it, but it was not his fault William had put him in charge of watching her.

She turned from the window, her eyes trailing over the stack of trunks and crates full of some of her family's most cherished belongings. She'd refused to let the help unpack them. She had not been ready. Now, a deep part of her needed the connection she would have with the memories contained within. She poured herself another snifter of brandy and moved to the floor in front of a large crate, prying it open. Inside lay her mother's china, the face of it adorned with hand-painted thistles commemorative of her mother's beloved home country. As much as her father was a devoted British Officer, her mother had been a devoted Scot. Over the years, Elaina had often wondered what her parents' private conversations entailed. They'd always been civil and seemed quite fond of each other, but there were times when small comments were made or shared looks revealed there might have been words during the night. Her parents had been careful not to quarrel in front of their children. Elaina and William never saw the argument, but sometimes they would see the aftermath when their parents weren't speaking to each other.

She opened a few more crates, finding nothing of great interest—some of her father's books and different odds and ends that had been throughout their old home.

She stood, stretching her back, and surveyed her surroundings. In the corner of the room sat a small writing desk. It had been her late grandmother's, one of the few things of hers still in the home. Curious, she grabbed her glass and lamp and settled herself at the desk. She felt almost guilty as she slid her hand across the smooth mahogany cylinder top before rolling it open, careful not to disturb the lamp and goblet she'd perched on the white marble gallery. The interior stood disappointingly empty. The soft leather writing surface showed signs of wear, however, indicating the small desk had been used and not just ornamental decoration. Elaina wondered who her grandmother had written letters to, because it sure as hell wasn't her daughter. She tried to picture her sitting at this desk, quill in hand. Was her grandmother shorter, like her? Did she have brown hair in her younger days and at the end of her life had it been silver? Elaina's mother had had dark blonde hair. Elaina supposed she was a mix of her mother's and her father's, but what if she was the image of her grandmother? There were no portraits of her hanging in the house. Her mother had removed them.

Pulling open drawers and brass hinged cubbyholes, she found them all empty. Disappointed, she reached down to open the last drawer and came close to tumbling out of the chair, her dress slipping on its smooth surface. She stopped her plummet by catching her knee on the underside of the desk. There was a soft clicking sound, and a drawer popped out of the center where none had been before. Elaina gave her deceased grandmother a wry grin. *A secret compartment? How ostentatious.* She peeked into the drawer. Inside was a stack of letters tied with a piece of blue silk ribbon. She glanced over her shoulder before she pulled the items from the drawer. An uncomfortable feeling overcame her, almost as if she were spying into a world where she was not welcome, and she tried to shake it off. Retreating to the sanctity of her private bedchamber, she perched herself in the middle of the bed, the open drapes of her oversized windows casting enough light with which to read.

Several minutes passed as she tried to build up her courage. Taking a deep breath, she dove in, the silk ribbon sliding undone with ease and she opened the first letter, nearly falling over at seeing her mother's handwriting on the page before her. The date read 1742. Two years ago. The year the Dowager Countess Leicester died. Elaina quickly scanned the letter. Diana Spencer wrote that she'd heard from a friend her mother had been ill and prayed for a swift recovery. Elaina was confused and moved at the same time. She went through the letters, not taking the time to read them, only scanning the handwriting. They were all in her mother's hand, the documents dating back to the year they'd first moved to the colonies. All these years her mother had continued to write even though there was never a response from her own mother. Her grandmother had obviously read the letters and thought enough of them to keep them. Lady Leicester had also bequeathed her estate to her estranged daughter. What had happened between the two women to have such a profound effect on their relationship? Whatever it was, it was clear Elaina's mother had not held a grudge.

Elaina put the letters in order from the earliest to the most recent. Maybe the secret would lie within them. With trembling hands, she picked up the first letter dated 1724, Royal Colony of North Carolina. Diana Spencer wrote of their trip over the ocean to the colonies. When she had written the correspondence, the small family resided with a friend and business acquaintance of Captain Spencer's while awaiting the completion of their house. It was nice to hear her mother's voice again, even if it was only through words on a page. The next few letters were much the same, giving details of the burgeoning life in Carolina. By the fifth letter, though, something had changed.

Dearest Mama,

Praying this letter finds you well. Edward and the children are all in good health. I also am in good health except for a nagging issue that seems to grow more significant as the months pass. I first thought your letters were being lost as the post here in North Carolina tends to be nothing if not unreliable, but I have received several correspondences from our mutual friend, Lady Donovan. So, I proposed to ask of you and your health. Gavie happily reports you in excellent health. Unfortunately, she also indicates you have not brought yourself to write correspondence to the family. I fear the grave matter still weighs heavy upon your heart. Edward has adjusted quite well. I pray with time you may be accepting and welcome us back into your good graces .

The letter went on, but Elaina was intrigued by "the grave matter." She scanned some of the letters of later dates, but there was no mention of it again. Jumping off her bed, headed for the green room determined to dig through the remainder of the things sent from overseas, she collided with Caitir as she flung open the bedroom door.

"Where are you off to in such a tizzy?" Caitir asked, extricating herself from Elaina's grasp.

"You scared the hell out of me." Elaina clasped her chest, sidestepping the question.

"Good. Maybe with less hell, there will be room for a wee bit of good sense in there." Caitir knocked on Elaina's head.

"Extra clever today, I see."

"I came to tell ye Calum is downstairs needin' a word with ye, if ye please?"

"Is he?" Elaina's heart leaped, and she forgot her current mission, heading for the stairs. Her excitement was only in hopes of news of Monroe. That's what she told herself anyway.

"So, the two of ye have made amends?" Caitir called out after her mistress.

"Not in so many words," Elaina answered over her shoulder.

Bursting into the salon in a whirlwind of skirts, bare feet, and flying hair, she found Calum leaning casually on the carved stone surrounding the hearth, a glass of amber liquid already in his hands. He straightened when she stumbled into the room and cast her an amused once-over. "Ye ken how to make an entrance, my lady." He took in her appearance from head to toe, causing her face to warm.

She looked down at her bare feet and brushed the hanging tendrils out of her eyes, smoothing her plait over her shoulder.

"You do not have to tend my wounds this time at least."

"The day isnae over yet," he said. "I didna interrupt yer nap, I hope?"

"Nap? No, I was...reading."

"And ye were so pleased to see me ye didna care to take time to dress properly?"

"Are my bare feet too much for your countenance, Mr. MacKinnon?" Elaina devilishly edged closer to him. "Shall I cover them? I wouldn't want to upset your delicate virtues."

Calum leaned in close to Elaina, whispering in her ear, "'Tis not my virtues I am concerned with."

Shivers ran down her spine, whether from his breath tickling her ear or his words she couldn't be sure. The man affected her in more ways than any other man ever had.

Luckily for her, Eads decided to make his presence known with a loud clearing of his throat. "Whiskey, madam?" he asked, looking Calum over with a wary eye.

"I believe I'll have tea," Elaina replied.

Eads left the door to the salon open upon his exit, and Elaina secretly thanked him even though she might prefer to hear what Calum had to say without the possibility of an eavesdropper. On the other hand, she was not sure she wanted to be in a room alone with the lout. She motioned him to a chair as she took another, tucking her bare feet under her. She sat staring into the fire, watching the flames dance and lick the stones around it while awaiting their refreshment to appear.

"Beautiful," Calum whispered.

Startled, Elaina glanced at him, finding his gaze fixed on the fire. "Yes," she answered. "It is. I could sit and watch the flames all day."

Calum raised his glass to his lips and turned his eyes from the fire to her. "I quite agree," he said.

Elaina squirmed, uncomfortable under his scrutiny. She cleared her throat, trying to break what she deemed an awkward silence while refusing to meet his eye. Not many men made her uncomfortable, but it seemed to be a specialty for him. "It was kind of you to brave the rain to bring me what I hope is good news."

"If I waited for the rain to let up, ye would be an old maid before ye heard a thing."

"True. I am ready for some sunshine. I need to get out of this house. I need to ride," Elaina sighed.

"Ye truly enjoy horses, then?" Calum asked.

"Yes. It's been days since I have been to the stables."

"Ye afraid ye will melt?"

"No, I am not afraid I will melt." Elaina turned an amused eye on him. "I had words with Rabbie. I'm avoiding him."

"Did he harm ye in any way?" Calum asked, leaning forward.

"No," she answered. Was it her imagination or did Mr. MacKinnon seem concerned? "He was a horse's arse, so I threw a bucket of water on him. I wanted to smash him over the head with it, but I restrained myself."

Calum laughed, the sound of it deep and rich, warming her to her soul. "That would have been a sight."

Caitir swirled into the room with a tray of tea things. "Eads sent me," she grinned at the pair. "He thought ye needed some supervisin'. I wasna sure if it was because ye were already at each other's throats or...?" Caitir raised an eyebrow.

Elaina blushed, making a move toward her tea to try to hide the fact.

Calum cleared his throat and caught Elaina's eye, making a small hitch with his head in Caitir's direction.

Caitir narrowed her eyes, looking between the two of them. "If ye think ye are keepin' secrets from me, I'm here to inform ye ye're not," she said indignantly crossing her arms. "I'm no leavin'."

"It's all the better," Elaina said. "This way, we can close the door." She checked the hallway before doing just that.

"Where are yer shoes...and what happened to yer hair?" Caitir looked her mistress over critically as she returned to her seat by the fire.

"What is it with your family and shoes? What is wrong with going barefoot? Do you never want to feel the cool grass between your toes?"

"Ye are hardly on grass, my lady, standing here in the salon with an unfamiliar man present. 'Tis no wonder Eads sent me."

"Unfamiliar? Calum? He has seen me worse off, I dare say, and I am tired of talking about my feet. I do not like shoes, and I will not wear them if I don't want to. And what is wrong with my hair? You did it." Elaina felt a surge of self-consciousness wash over her. Did she genuinely look dreadful?

"I did not do that." Caitir swirled a finger at Elaina's head.

"Well, I've unpacked a few things. It might be a bit of a mess. Can we move on from my hideous un-lady like appearance and get to the heart of the matter? What have you learned?" she turned to Calum, finding him looking rather amused at the exchange between the two ladies. With an exaggerated sigh, she took her chair, leaving her bare feet dangling and uncovered in rebellion.

"I have learned some, but not a lot. He is known about the wharf by more than a few souls. He regulates crews to load and unload ships, occasionally taking on as a hand and traveling with the cargo. He moves from job to job, ship to ship. I believe he has even worked on some of yer family's ships, my lady," Calum said.

"Interesting. I will look through the books and see if I can find a record of it."

"I believe he is currently aboard the *Gurney O'Rourke*, set to make port in about a week or so. Perhaps Lord Spencer and I can find him, question him and see what we can learn."

"Will Lord Spencer be home by then?" Caitir asked.

"Who knows? He didn't see fit to tell me about his trip," Elaina said. "If not, I will do it myself."

"Maybe no by yerself," Calum interjected. "If yer brother hasnae returned, I could question him. We dinna want to scare him off before we have garnered any information."

"Scare him off? What do you mean?" Elaina turned a menacing eye toward Calum.

He pointed his finger at her. "That is precisely what I mean."

Elaina raised an eyebrow in defiance.

"Ye always look like ye want to rip someone's head off."

"Maybe only yours." Just when she had started to like the blasted man.

Calum left, promising to send word when the *Gurney O'Rourke* was to arrive in the shipping channel. Elaina still wasn't sure how to tell William of what she had learned. She supposed honesty would be the best policy. After all, what could he do about it this far after the fact? Scold her?

Her skin prickled with anticipation as she climbed the stairs. Answers might be right around the corner to one of the mysteries contained within this house. That left two still to be dealt with, the menacing notes and the "grave matter." Pausing on the landing, she wasn't sure which avenue to pursue first. Should she go to the shipping logs and look to see if there was a record of a Monroe working for them? There would be a week or two for that mundane chore. The project seeming to occupy every corner of her conscience at present was "the grave matter." Would the answer lie in her mother's belongings?

Entering the green room, she found the mounds of unopened crates and trunks a mocking and overwhelming task. The air in the room had taken on a stale fragrance of things tucked away for far too long. The rain had lightened to a slow drizzle, and she crossed the room to the windows and cranked them partly open, inhaling the damp fresh breeze that ruffled the curtains and the loose fringes of hair about her face. Across the way, the men in the stables flung the doors and shutters open wide. She assumed they also appreciated the let-up of the deluge and the clean air accompanying it.

"My lady?" Caitir's soft voice questioned from behind her.

"Yes?" Elaina turned, lifting her great braid and letting the fresh air playfully tickle her neck, causing her to shiver.

"Is there something I may help ye with?" Caitir glanced around the room, taking in its mounds of hapless contents.

"As a matter of fact." Elaina motioned for Caitir to join her on the pink settee. "Your mother worked for my mother for a short while, did she not? Before my parents immigrated to the colonies?"

"Aye, for a short while. It may have been for less than a year."

"Did your mother ever talk about the time she spent here? Do you remember?"

"Not really. What is bothering ye, my lady?"

Elaina chewed her lip and played absently with the ends of her hair. What did she want to ask the girl, and did she truly want an answer? She glanced sideways at Caitir with her perfectly polished strawberry hair and those dancing blue eyes that were trained patiently on her mistress. The girl's hair never seemed to be out of place, unlike Elaina's mad coif, which had a mind of its own.

"Ye're not goin' to have a lip left if ye dinna speak up."

"Have you ever heard your mother mention a 'grave matter' regarding her time spent with my parents?"

Caitir stared at Elaina. She sat so still and unblinking, Elaina almost repeated the question.

"Why do ye ask?" Caitir asked softly.

"So, you have heard of something?" Elaina leaned forward with anticipation.

"Why do ye ask?" Caitir repeated.

Elaina thought about questioning the girl more, but instead, dove right in and explained the rift between her mother and grandmother and told her maid about the letters she'd found in the hidden drawer in the desk. "I hoped to find an answer as to why my grandmother would not speak to my mother. So, I told you. Now, you tell me. What do you know?"

Caitir stood and crossed the room to the old desk, running her hand along its edge. She looked over her shoulder at her friend. "My Mam and Da only spoke of it a few times. Those were the words they used, though, 'the grave matter.' I dinna think they kent I listened in. I was verra good at pretendin' to sleep, and I was but a wee lass. We all shared a room for a while until I was older. Whatever it was made my mother sad, and my father sad and angry the like. I havenae heard those words uttered together in a long while, and never by anyone but my parents. I had quite forgotten about it. I thought it was my own family's secret. Now you have spoken them, and yer own mother's hand has written them. Maybe 'tis yer family secret and no mine." She turned and leaned against the desk, looking Elaina over.

"What if one of these"—Elaina swept her hand over the expanse of the Spencers' belongings—"holds the answer to our question?"

"What if it is somethin' best left unknown? There is a reason why they kept it from ye. Perhaps ye should let it lie."

Elaina sat quietly for a moment. "I don't think I can do that. Not now," she said. She experienced a fleeting moment of apprehension when she almost changed her mind. She blurted out her next question before her nerves could win the battle against her stubbornness. "Will you help me?"

Caitir looked uneasy. "I dinna ken if it is somethin' I want to get involved in. What if 'the grave matter' is a reason your parents were murdered? It may be a dangerous secret."

"All the more reason to know," Elaina said. "How can I protect myself against an unknown enemy. Mama knew about the matter but was still unable to protect herself, if that's what it was all about."

It was Caitir's turn to chew her lip. She stared out the window beyond Elaina for several moments, pondering. "Aye," she sighed. "Let's do it, then."

"Here," Elaina offered Caitir the bottle of brandy she had left in the room. "A shot of courage." Both women drank from the bottle before setting to their task.

Even with the windows open, the air in the room was damp and still. Elaina's bodice clung to her and sweat dripped from her forehead, making a dark circle on the crate in front of her. She sat back on her haunches and wiped her face with the hem of her dress. The pair had been at their task for nearly an hour with no luck, whatsoever. She had half a mind to call it a day when Caitir made a noise under her breath.

"What is it?' Elaina asked. "What have you found? Letters?"

"Nooo," Caitir said slowly. She rose to her feet, crossed to the door, and peeked out into the hallway. Satisfied at what she saw there, she closed the door behind her and leaned against it.

"Why are you acting like that?" Elaina asked, flopping down on her bottom. She slid her skirts up to her hips and tucked the folds between her knees, trying to get a breeze to her damp legs.

"I cannae believe I am about to ask this of ye, my lady. I am trusting ye with who I believe ye to be, and the Blessed Virgin Mother protect me if I am wrong." Caitir crossed herself, still leaning against the door. "What I am about to ask ye stays in this room—between the two of us. Not as employer and employee, but as two women brought together by fate and friendship."

"Quit being so damned dramatic," Elaina moaned. "Out with it!"

"Where do yer loyalties lie?"

Elaina looked at Caitir with unfettered confusion. "I do not get your meaning."

Caitir crossed the room to the open crate. She lifted out Elaina's mother's crystal serving bowl, placing it gingerly on the ground. Alongside the bowl, she stood four crystal goblets. Caitir met Elaina's questioning gaze.

Elaina shook her head with incomprehension.

"Tell me what ye see," Caitir asked.

"Seriously—"

"Tell me," Caitir interrupted firmly.

Elaina sighed. "I see my mother's serving bowl and her glasses. Glassware made by her own company."

"Yer mother was Scottish and yer father British?"

"Yes. You know this already," Elaina said with impatience.

"Did yer father ever see these things? Did yer mother display them in the home, I am asking?"

"Just tell me—" Elaina started.

"Just answer me!"

"I…I don't know. I don't remember. The bowl? Yes. At times when company came, Mother would use the bowl. The glasses? She only had them out a few times that I remember. She kept them in a chest. That chest." Elaina pointed to an oak chest partially hidden in the corner with a small padlock on it.

"Do ye ken where the key is?" Caitir asked, standing and crossing over to the chest, inspecting the lock.

"No, I don't, and I'm not looking for it until you tell me what is going on."

Caitir looked over at her friend, studying her face for answers to unasked questions before crossing back over to the bowl and glasses and planting herself on the floor.

"Who is our king?"

"Are you serious?"

The look on Caitir's face told her she was.

"George II," Elaina sighed, reluctantly playing along.

"Who did your mother believe to be the true king?"

Elaina once again looked blankly at Caitir.

"Ye have led a sheltered life," Caitir sighed, shaking her head. "I ken ye spent yer life in the colonies, but certainly ye must have heard of the Catholic king whom some believe to be the true heir to the throne of Scotland? The Stuart King?"

"Of course," Elaina said, looking at her mother's items sitting on the rug in front of Caitir. "The old pretender to the throne, my father would call him."

Caitir stared at her.

Elaina sat forward, her interest growing. "My mother would sometimes get angry with him when he would say that."

"And his son, the young pretender—this bowl," she held it up for Elaina to examine, "to look at it by itself is just a beautiful bowl with its oak leaf details and delicate acorns, but this bowl with these goblets…this group tells a tale."

Elaina looked at the hand-etched items sitting on the floor. She'd always thought them a hodgepodge mix of glasses and bowl—the bowl with oak leaves and acorns, the crystal glasses with six-sided roses. Her mother rarely used them at all except when some of her Scottish friends would happen by on their way out of the hills, toward the larger cities for supplies. She had wondered why her mother would present her friends with such an odd mix of stemware when they owned a lovely set of matching crystal.

Elaina leaned forward as a realization dawned on her. "Do you think my mother to be a Jacobite?"

"I am no makin' accusations." Caitir threw her hands up.

"No, no," Elaina said, waving a hand without looking at her friend. She stared in wonderment at the items in front of her. How could she be so blind? In bits and pieces, random moments of her childhood appeared to be just that—random. Looking at them now, with these things laid out in front of her and Caitir's leading questions, she began to see the broader picture.

"During times when Papa would be gone, and Mama's Scottish friends would stop by," Elaina said, sliding to her knees and crawling closer to the crystal gracing the floor. "Mama would pour them a claret in these glasses, and they would toast. *Slainte Mhath*," Elaina whispered, reaching out a shaky finger to touch the rim of one of the glasses.

"Good health—the *Gàidhlig*," Caitir whispered in reply.

"I always stayed so busy hunting and acting a boy that I seldom had time for my mother and her friends. Every chance I had, I would escape out of doors. Mama, however, would make me toast with the others before she would let me loose. William was never present. Only myself. It never once crossed my mind why she would not do this when Papa was around. I thought it chance that Papa would be gone when her Scottish friends happened through for supplies." Elaina sat hard on her bottom, shaking her head. She met her friend's gaze—brown eyes staring into blue—calculating.

"I assume' yer father was a loyal British officer?" Caitir asked.

"I assume so as well," Elaina answered.

"Maybe that is why ye know so little of this," Caitir said. "A mairiet couple on opposing sides of a religious and political war. Maybe neither wanted to ask you or William to choose sides."

"But why return to Scotland if things were so… Why would they bring us here if they thought it might be dangerous?"

"Maybe, they didna ken how dangerous it might be. Yer father had to return to accept his title as Earl. Perhaps he did not wish to leave his family behind."

The women turned toward the chest.

"We need in the chest," Elaina said. "But first. Where do you stand? Are you a Jacobite or a loyalist?"

Caitir sat frozen, looking at her mistress. They were at a dangerous crossroads for both of them. "Where do ye stand, my lady?" she whispered.

Elaina was just as frozen. "I-I'm not sure. Let's open the chest. I trust you. Hopefully, you trust me as well and whatever we find, may we both find peace."

Caitir reached down and produced a knife from the vicinity of her ankle.

"Are you going to slit my throat?" Elaina asked with a raised brow.

"I wadna dare attempt it. I've seen ye fight." Caitir smiled. "Hold out your hand." Elaina did as bid, and with a quick flick of the blade, Caitir sliced the palm of Elaina's hand and then her own. She grasped her mistress's bloody hand in hers. "Whatever happens and whatever paths we each choose, we will forever be bound by sisterhood. May we ne'er do harm to the other," Caitir whispered, increasing the force of her grasp. "I swear it to you."

"I swear it to you." Elaina squeezed her friend's hand tight. The closest thing she would ever have to a sister.

"Now let's find the keys." Caitir scurried to put the crystal away and hid its crate amongst the others.

Elaina flew down the stairs to search through William's office. She pulled open drawers and rifled through the contents, careful to not leave a bloody trail, even sliding her hand under the desk to look for secret compartments. Defeated, she sat back in William's leather chair and critically surveyed the office. The key more than likely hung on William's large ring of keys in his pocket in Newcastle. She slumped down in the chair, thinking and drumming her fingers on the desk.

Bolting from the chair, she took the stairs two at a time. "Where are Mother's things," she gasped, falling into the room and startling Caitir. "Mother's things…she wore when…when…"

Caitir perked up. "I put them in yer wardrobe. In the jeweled box."

The two girls sprinted down the hall to Elaina's room, closing the heavy door behind them. Caitir went to the wardrobe and pulled the tiny jeweled box from the back. She handed it to Elaina, who dumped the contents on the bed. Two rings and a small silk purse with a drawstring tumbled onto the bed. Elaina thought her heart would stop as she opened the neck of the purse and dumped the contents into her hand. A handful of coins and nothing more. She sat on the bed looking into the empty bag again and then at her friend. The two of them turned their disappointed gaze to the items, trying in vain to will one of them to be a small key.

"I just knew—" Caitir began.

Elaina held up her hand, then strode across the room and retrieved her mother's necklace, laying it gently on the table under the light of the candle. The delicate brushstrokes of yellows, golds, and browns seemed to move in the wavering light. A sunflower swayed in the breeze of a candle's flame as it danced under Elaina's ragged breath.

The locket, her mother had said, contained a lock of Elaina and William's hair. If you didn't know it was a locket, it would be hard to determine. There was one spot on the delicate, gold lace filigree edge that was the clasp to open it. She flicked it with her thumbnail, and an iron key fell out onto the tabletop. She stared at it, her vision swimming as a cold sweat formed on her lip. Caitir's voice came from far away. Elaina knew at that moment whatever they found in the chest would change the way she looked at her mother forever.

Back in the green room, kneeling in front of the chest, Elaina stared at the lock, her hands shaking. "I don't think I can do it." She gave Caitir a sideways glance.

Caitir took the key and inserted it into the iron lock on the chest, her hands only slightly more steady than Elaina's. With her eyes on her friend, she turned the key and the lock released its hold.

Elaina held her breath as Caitir slowly pushed back the lid. The two women leaned forward and peered into the chest. Laid across the contents was a black and red tartan. Elaina lifted it from its resting place. Bringing it to her face, she inhaled through her nose, hoping to catch the scent of her mother, but the plaid only held an earthy odor like the inside of its recently vacated home.

Caitir reached into the chest, pulling out a sheet of paper.

Elaina inspected the document written in a strange hand in a language she had never seen.

"'Tis *Gàidhlig*," Caitir whispered.

"Gaelic?" Elaina took the sheet from her. "Can you read it? Do you speak it?"

"Aye, I can speak it. Unfortunately, I cannae read it."

Elaina retrieved a handful of papers from their resting place. They were of different sizes and varying hues ranging from the palest blue to the faint yellowing parchment acquires over many years. She shuffled through them. "Most of these are written in Gaelic. This one is written in my mother's hand. How could I have never seen her write in Gaelic all these years? I have never heard her speak it, except for the toast she would make with her friends. She is a Lowlander, born and raised in Edinburgh…was," Elaina corrected herself quietly. "She was."

Caitir pulled another sheet out. "This looks to be a ledger of some sort."

"Who would Mother correspond to in Gaelic?" Elaina shuffled through the remaining papers.

"Perhaps hidin' it from someone…someone like your father," Caitir said matter-of-factly.

"Rabbie speaks Gaelic. Maybe he could translate for us?"

Caitir pulled Elaina back to the floor before she could rise to full standing. "No! Ye must be careful to whom ye show these papers. Treason is punishable by hanging, if not worse."

Elaina's hand went immediately to her throat. "What makes you think these are treasonous?"

"I dinna ken for certain, my lady. 'Tis only the late Lady Spencer kept them hidden for a reason. I want to ken what the reason is before we show them to just anyone."

"Who then?"

"Calum. I was practically raised with him, and I trust him. He will not betray us."

Replacing the items they had removed from the trunk, Elaina closed the lid and locked it. She had more questions than ever and still no answers.

"Let us move the chest to yer room until Calum can look the pages over. There will be no reason for anyone but you or I to be in there."

Elaina mulled over the situation as the two women checked the hallway for privacy and then lugged the chest to her bedroom. Caitir trusted Calum. Rabbie most certainly did not. Did Elaina trust Caitir enough to put her life in the girl's hands? Shoving the chest into a far corner of the room, she looked down at the small cut on her palm. She had little choice. Caitir seemed loyal. There were only two people Elaina knew who spoke Gaelic. Only one of whom Caitir trusted.

"Hide the key." Her maid's voice came from behind her.

Elaina slipped the key back into the locket, adding the necklace to the small drawstring bag and placing the contents into the jeweled box. She hid the item in the back of the wardrobe.

Chapter Eleven

MUD SQUELCHED UNDER HER BOOTS. She had starved her love for riding long enough.

Angus came bounding out of the stable doors at the sight of her. "My lady."

"What is it, Angus? Missed me, have you?" Elaina ruffled the young boy's mop of brown hair, releasing tiny bits of hay and some dust.

"Aye, my lady." He grinned broadly. "Are we going to shoot arrows today?"

"Not today, sadly. Today I have come to ride. Saddle up Sadie, will you?"

"Aye." He trotted off, disappearing into the darkness of the stables.

"Look who decided to show their bright and shinin' face." Rabbie stepped out of the shadows, wiping his hands on a rag. "I started to think ye were scairt."

"Me? Scared?" She narrowed her eyes at his wide grin and turned her face into the cool breeze, ignoring his ribbing. She refused to blow her top today, no matter how much he teased her. She needed to ride, and she needed him to make it happen.

"I want to go out," she said, turning her gaze back in his direction.

"Yes?"

"Will you please take me riding?"

"I'm sorry? What? The horses..." He motioned over his shoulder as if the horses whinnying had made him stone deaf.

"Will. You. Please. Take. Me. Riding?" Elaina yelled, making Angus giggle as he came out trailing Sadie behind him.

"D'ye hear this?" Rabbie hooked a thumb at Elaina.

"She did say please, sir."

"That she did."

Elaina stared impassively at Rabbie.

"Aye, saddle my horse," Rabbie said, untying his apron. "Ye cannae be expectin' me to drop everythin' whenever ye feel an urge."

"Wouldn't dream it." Elaina batted her eyes in feigned innocence, but she narrowed them at him when he offered to help her into the saddle. He huffed at her and rolled his eyes before swinging himself onto his own steed, and they set out across the open field. The horses picked their way around the boggiest areas. It would be a short ride since Elaina had spent most of the day looking for answers to a mystery. It was this mystery that continued to occupy the corners of her mind. The sun touched her skin with a warm embrace, but there was a coolness to the breeze. Fall was near. There was a change in the air, and Elaina didn't think it only the seasons.

The political climate between Scotland and England had not been at the forefront of Elaina's education while the Spencers were in the colonies. Why would it have been? The family had never talked about moving back to Europe. William, being a military man, had to have known how precarious things were on this side of the Atlantic. Apparently, no one thought it important enough a matter that she should know. Elaina felt exposed and unnerved by this intentional oversight. She stifled the urge to look over her shoulder. Caitir had laid forth how dangerous things were between the British and the Scottish. To have to rely on her maid to inform her of such things infuriated her. Damn all of them! How could they bring her across the ocean during such upheaval and not tell her anything? She would see what her mother's documents said and then decide what to do about them.

"Halloo?" Rabbie rode up beside her.

Startled, Elaina turned to face him. "What?"

"I asked ye if ye wanted to water the horses and ourselves?" He waved a flask at her.

"I'm sorry. I was thinking. Yes, let's stop a minute."

"If ye think any harder, yer head may burst into flames," Rabbie said taking Sadie's reins as Elaina slid out of the saddle.

She smiled wryly at him.

"Ye need to talk?"

Elaina studied the back of him as they made their way down to the creek bed. Did she trust him? She didn't know. "No, it's nothing."

"Didna seem like nothin'."

Elaina eased herself down onto the cool grass and leaned against the massive oak shading their resting spot. She accepted Rabbie's flask, letting the whiskey slide down her throat. "I wish to take these bloody riding boots off and plant my bare feet on this grass. Is it going to bother you if I do? I promise to cover them with my skirts." She glanced sideways at him.

"If it doesna bother you, it doesna bother me," he said.

Elaina turned her back to Rabbie while she unlaced her boots and pulled them off. She reached up and untied her stockings from her thighs and pulled them off. She spread her skirts around her as she turned back around. "Oh." She closed her eyes, leaning back against the tree. "Marvelous. Do you know how long it has been since I have felt cool grass upon my bare feet?"

"My guess is some time," Rabbie laughed.

"Too long."

They sat quietly for a bit, occasionally sharing the flask, each in their thoughts.

"May I ask you a question?" Elaina broke the silence.

"Aye."

"Why do you not like Mr. MacKinnon?"

"Isnae anything I can put my finger on. Scots ken who they trust and who they cannae. We feel it."

"Well, I'm part Scot, and I do not have one inkling who I can trust beyond Caitir."

"Maybe ye've too much of yer father in ye?"

"I sure don't feel it. My father was a man who always knew what he wanted and how to make it happen. He didn't seem to question anything."

"And what is it ye are questionin', my lady? What are ye wantin' to do?" Rabbie asked.

After a moment's thought, Elaina answered, "At this point in my life, I have no thoughts other than avenging my parents' deaths."

"That is a lofty goal. And if ye never find the killer?"

"Well, that is not an option. I will not stop until I do. I may have a clue."

"Aye?" Rabbie asked with interest.

"Nothing I can talk about at present. It may not pan out."

"Well, I hope it is a reliable clue, and somethin' comes of it."

"Rabbie?"

"Mm?" he grunted at her over a swallow of whiskey.

"What do you know of the Jacobite uprisings?"

Rabbie choked, coughing and sputtering, "Why do ye ask? Good Lord. Is that where yer mind has been?"

"Partly," Elaina admitted.

"I dinna think the Jacobites are anythin' to worry about, my lady. They havenae had a serious footin' since 1715. The British have them firmly under control."

"So, you believe there is no truth to the rumors? William and my father were sent here to Scotland because of talks that Prince Charles was to make an effort to overthrow the king."

"Nay, my lady. I dinna think much will come of it. The Watch has a tight hold on the Highlands. That is the only place an uprisin' is truly spoken of. Most of the Lowlanders are loyal to George."

"But they said the Watch has been gathered and sent to Flanders to fight the French."

"Aye. They were, but there is still a handful that have enlisted since—nay to worry yer pretty head about. Now, I have some traps in the area I would like to check. Will ye be okay here by yerself for a wee bit?" he asked while rising to his feet.

"Yes, of course. It will give me time to clear my head and maybe figure some things out."

"Dinna wander off. There may be some poachers in the area. I wadna want anythin' to happen to ye on my watch."

"I will stay right here. I promise."

Rabbie headed off into a thicket and Elaina stretched her legs out, letting the cool breeze swirl over her bare feet. She lengthened herself out onto her back, closed her eyes, and lost herself in the sounds of the forest surrounding her. This is what she craved most—to be free. God, she hated staying cooped up in that big stuffy house. She wanted to sleep under the stars as she had back in the colonies when she hunted with her father. An opportunity like that might never happen. Everyone considered everything too dangerous here. She hated to inform them that bears were dangerous, and she'd managed not to get eaten by one.

A rustling sounded in the brush across the burn, and she sat straight up.

A young man stepped out clad in a dark green tartan with bits of red and black throughout, and a slouched hat upon his head.

"Madam? Are ye lost?" he asked, looking across the small stream at the two hobbled horses.

"No." She rose to her feet. "My friend is with me. He is checking some traps."

"What is it?" a deep voice growled from the dense bushes behind the young man and two more men, much older, stepped out behind him.

The foursome stood staring at each other for a moment. One of the older men muttered something under his breath and crossed himself.

Elaina recognized the language as Gaelic. They were Highlanders.

He asked the young man a question in the foreign tongue. The man answered with a shrug.

"What is yer name, lass?" the older gentleman asked in a thick Scottish accent, eyeing her with suspicion. He took a step toward the edge of the stream.

Elaina stepped back and answered, raising her chin a notch. "Lady Elaina Spencer. Sister to the 3rd Earl of Strafford." She wasn't sure why she added the second part except he made her uncomfortable. Dammit, where was Rabbie? She was completely defenseless. She didn't have a weapon of any kind. She glanced around the clearing, looking for a large rock, or anything.

As if reading her thoughts, the gentleman removed his slouched bonnet and bowed to her. "We mean ye nay harm, my lady. Ye caught me unawares. Ye… ye look like someone I once knew." He sounded sad and crossed himself again. He spoke to the men in his native tongue without looking at them. They both nodded to whatever he had said. "May we bring our horses down to the water?" he said to Elaina.

"Yes, of course," she answered, still wary but easing slightly.

The young one ducked back into the rough and shortly returned, leading three horses.

"May I ask your acquaintance?" Elaina asked as their horses quenched their thirsts and her horses nickered across the stream at them.

"Beggin' yer pardon, madam, Grier. Mackenzie, Brian, and Robert Grier." He pointed to each of them in turn. The young man being Robert and the one speaking Mackenzie.

"A pleasure, Mr. Grier."

"The pleasure is ours." Mackenzie appeared to be the leader. The other two remained silent yet watched her warily as they tended the horses.

Elaina opened her mouth to ask what brought them this far south when there was a great commotion behind her, and she was grabbed around the waist and jerked off her feet. The three across the water all pulled their broadswords, and Elaina held her breathe, knowing her life was about to end, but it was Rabbie's voice that sounded loud in her ear, speaking rapid Gaelic. Brandishing his dirk, he shoved her behind him.

The trio across the stream stood steady, crouched and ready to pounce at the slightest movement. Mackenzie called something out across the water, and Rabbie growled an answer low in his throat in return.

"Speak the King's English!" Elaina yelled, startling the men. She stepped around Rabbie, but he caught her by her wrist, holding her back. "What is going on?"

"We need to be goin'" Rabbie pulled her back toward the horses.

"Aye. Ye do," Mackenzie answered. He stared holes through Rabbie, and Rabbie tightened his grip on his dirk. "This, is yer friend?" Mackenzie turned his dark gaze toward Elaina.

"Yes," she answered.

"I may have misjudged ye then," the old man said with a sneer and spat on the ground.

Elaina, stunned, stood unable to speak.

Rabbie did not suffer the same effect, his guttural voice menacing even though she understood no Gaelic.

"Let's go, Rabbie." She grabbed his arm, attempting to pull him.

Snatching her boots from their resting place, she swung herself onto Sadie. She looked at the gentlemen. They glowered at Rabbie, swords in hand. Mackenzie turned his gaze to her, and she saw a slight softening in his glare as he studied her face intently. He whispered something sounding like, "Ye move like her too."

"Gentlemen." She bowed her head to them. "I am sorry to leave you on bad terms." They had been cordial, though wary until Rabbie arrived.

"No offense to ye, madam." Mackenzie had his eye on Rabbie who had mounted his horse, dirk still in hand.

Elaina pulled Sadie's head away from the Griers, leaving the men standing by the burn. Rabbie ran the horses as fast as he dared through the boggy grasses. They had traveled a sizable distance when she pulled her horse to a stop and slid to the ground.

"What are ye doing?" Rabbie snapped, reining in his steed and rounding back to look down at her. He cast his eyes at the way they had come.

"You will explain to me what in the hell is going on." Elaina snatched her stockings and boots from across the saddle.

"I will explain it when we get to the stables." He glared down at her while his horse danced impatiently in circles.

"You will explain it now." Elaina spoke with a calmness she did not feel. She tried to hide the shaking of her hands as she fumbled with her boots. Whether it was from fear, anger, or embarrassment, she had yet to determine.

Rabbie slid from his mount and took her by the arm. "Get back on yer horse," he growled at her. "We need to get home."

"There is no one following us. Look." Elaina waved a hand. "Open land. Not a horse in sight. I do not want to have this discussion at the stables in front of the boys and the other staff." She sat on a nearby rock and stuck her foot in one of her stockings. She raised an eyebrow at Rabbie who angrily turned his back. "Speak." She hoisted her skirt up around her thigh so she could tie her stocking.

"They are MacGregors. Worthless horse shite." He spat on the ground.

"What is it with the spitting? They are Griers, not MacGregors. They told me their names before you came bursting out like a wild man with your dirk in your hand."

"Anyone with half a-a…" Rabbie whirled around as Elaina tied her other stocking to her thigh.

She slowly and assertively lowered her skirts, waited for his eyes to meet hers, and slid one stockinged foot forcefully into a boot. "You were saying?" She fought desperately to keep from screaming at him.

"I said, anyone with half a brain kens Grier is an assumed name, as the name MacGregor is abolished by law."

"For one." Elaina stood speaking calmly into Rabbie's face. "I have a brain. Do not insinuate that I am simple. Two, I am not from Scotland—how am I supposed to know Grier stands for MacGregor. Three, how does it happen a name is 'abolished by law'? It's a name."

"MacGregors have a long history of being murderers, thieves, and altogether a loathsome people. Their name has been abolished several times throughout Scottish history. No one may use the name under penalty of death. A Mac-Gregor may not own land nor take any of the holy sacraments."

"Not take the sacraments? These are human beings." Elaina looked back the way they had come, unsure of what to think. An entire family name abolished? The faces of the three gentlemen danced across her mind. It made no sense, but then neither did thievery and murder. "To judge an entire people by a few? Not every one of them is a murderer. How terrible."

"Terrible? Terrible?" Rabbie raised his voice. "Ye ken what is terrible? Coming down out of the hills and stealing cattle from the farmers, murdering and plundering their way through the countryside. Ye ken what is terrible? The battle at Glen Fruin, that was terrible. In my opinion, every damned one of them should be hanged. Dinna stand there and have pity about matters of which ye dinna ken anythin' about. Ye're liable to get yerself killed."

"Are you threatening me?" Elaina took a step toward him, narrowing her eyes.

"No, my lady." Rabbie took a deep breath, closed his eyes, and forcibly unclenched his fists. "Ignorance in this country is deadly. I am no calling ye daft by any means, but ye need to educate yerself on some things, and I'm thinkin' ye need to do it quick. But, for now, we need to be gettin' on."

The pair remained silent for the remainder of their journey. Elaina dwelled on Rabbie's words, "all of them should be hanged." She began to think she did not know her groomsman at all. Those were the same thoughts she'd had about her mother earlier in the day.

When they reached the stables, Elaina slid from her horse and handed the reins to Angus who said nothing but looked between Elaina and Rabbie and returned to the stables with both horses.

"We need to stay close to the house for a time," Rabbie said. "No long rides and ye need to be verra careful, my lady. They know who ye are now."

Elaina stood silent for a moment staring at Rabbie's green eyes. "They know who I am? Who am I? I do not even know who I am. I am nothing but a girl in a big house in a foreign country. I have no political ties, and no knowledge of the country or its ways. I am just a girl, existing." She looked back at the fields beyond the house that they had silently ridden across. That was where she felt the most peaceful—out in the heather riding free, and now that was gone. Her gaze traveled over the vast expanse of the manor, the gardens, and the stables, coming to rest once again on Rabbie.

"The sorrow in yer eyes, my lady." Rabbie took a step towards her. "I am truly sorry if my words are the cause."

A tear rolled down Elaina's cheek.

Rabbie tentatively reached out and wiped it away with his thumb, his touch lingering for a moment on her cheek.

"I have only come to realize just how small I am in this world." She reached up, taking his hand in hers, and swallowed hard to keep the flood from coming that she could feel rising in her throat, threatening to choke her. "I am nothing," she whispered. "This is all William's. I have nothing he does not give me. I have no knowledge to help me. All the Latin and French in the world will do nothing for me now. I cannot hunt. I cannot ride. I have no one to trust." She was crying now, unable to hold her grief at bay any longer. "I have no protection." She motioned to his dirk. "I only exist. Alone, in this place, with nothing."

"Ye dinna have nothin'," a small voice said from behind her.

She turned, her gaze falling on wee Angus, his eyes welled with tears.

His lip quivered as he spoke. "Ye have me. I do love ye, my lady. Ye have been nicer to me than anyone here. When ye're around, I…I dinna miss my mam near as much."

"Come to me," Elaina managed to choke out.

She gathered the boy up in her arms, and they stood there outside the stables, her holding him and the two of them weeping together with his small arms about her neck. After a moment, a handkerchief appeared over her shoulder.

"Look at us." Elaina pulled away from Angus. "We are both dripping like fountains." She wiped his nose and his eyes and gently placed his feet upon the ground. "There," she said. "Our pity party is over." She smiled at the young boy and his brother standing meekly in the shadows. "Do you feel better?" she asked Angus.

"Aye, my lady." He nodded his head, sniffling.

"I do as well. Run along with Ainsley and tend the horses. They need some love also."

Angus wiped his nose on his sleeve. "Aye, my lady."

Ainsley wrapped an arm around his brother as they made their way back to the stables.

An arm appeared around her own body, a small knife in hand. The blade was about three inches long and the hilt roughly carved from a stag's horn.

"For protection." Rabbie's voice was close to her ear. "A *sgian-dubh*. Wear it here." His hand touched her thigh where she had earlier tied her stocking. "Or here." His hand slid down her leg to her calf.

Chills and heat ran through her body simultaneously. She turned to face him, taking a step back.

"Yer pardon, my lady," he said, his green eyes locked on hers. He slid the knife into its sheath and held it out to her.

She didn't immediately take it. "But don't you need it?" she asked.

"I have another."

"Well…then." She took the knife tentatively from his hand, pulling it out of its casing and studying it.

"D'ye ken how to use it?"

"Yes." She looked at him. "I do."

"Good," he answered. "Now ye have Angus, and ye have protection." The side of his mouth turned up.

She gave him a half-smile in return, his touch still burning her leg. She looked up over his shoulder at a sudden clatter in the drive. "William!" She shoved the knife in her pocket and ran to meet her brother's carriage, pausing briefly to look back at Rabbie and say, "Thank you."

He nodded once to her and turned back to the stables.

Chapter Twelve

ARRIVING AT THE STABLES, THE siblings abandoned the carriage and strolled arm in arm to the house. Elaina left William to freshen himself while she arranged for a light supper to be served out of doors so they could enjoy the sunset together. Settled in the surroundings of the late summer gardens, supplied with sustenance and wine, the brother and sister duo ate in silence while enjoying the fleeting warmth of summer. There was a definite nip to the air as the sun sank low on the horizon casting its orange glow onto the gathering clouds, painting them rose-colored with streaks of violet throughout.

"How was your trip?" Elaina asked as they moved to the iron bench facing what remained of the sunset.

"Difficult," William answered.

The evening breeze grew colder, and Elaina snuggled down into her cloak as she watched the servants remove the remnants of their meal. The beauty and sadness of the failing flowers with their petals fluttering to the ground struck her… their edges tinged brown while the centers remained soft and brightly colored. A breeze gathered several in its swirling grip, and they fluttered, scattered down the garden path much like Elaina's thoughts and now her life, it seemed. She was at the mercy of the world just as the petals had no control over their destination.

"It was such short notice. I was not pleased to hear you left without telling me."

"I didn't think you would be," William answered with a sideways grin at his strong-willed sister. "I am sorry I couldn't tell you in person, though."

"What was it that was so urgent you had to run off straight away?" Elaina took another sip of her wine.

William studied the glass in his hand. "It had to do with donations to a charitable cause. There was some mix-up that needed discussing with the Duke of Newcastle."

"Oh? Did you get it straightened out?"

"You might say that."

Elaina, subdued by the exorbitant amount of wine she had drunk, stared off into the distance.

"What is going on in that brain of yours?" William asked while refilling his glass.

"I'm just wondering…where do I fit in this world?"

"What do you mean?" William's voice held an anxious tone.

Or could she have imagined it? She had consumed several glasses of wine.

"Have you suddenly become a student of philosophy while I was away," he teased.

No, he is definitely himself. Letting the thought go, she replied, "I mean, I need to learn about this country. I need to study the politics of our current homeland. I feel so out of the loop."

"It's nothing to worry your pretty head about." William patted her on the knee.

"That's just it, William. I think I do need to worry about it. I think the more ignorant I am, the more dangerous it is. I am worried. I will not say I am scared, but I am concerned."

"Where is this coming from?" William turned toward her and studied her face.

Elaina relayed the encounter with the men at the stream, including Rabbie's strange behavior. She left out the *sgian-dubh* exchange and Rabbie's forward touch.

William was silent for a long while. "I think Rabbie is right. I think you need to stay close to home for a while, until the political climate settles a bit."

"Maybe," Elaina conceded, the wine having a marked effect on her countenance. She thought of the chest upstairs and its contents, debating on telling her brother. She decided against it for the moment. He had enough on his mind. She rested her head on his shoulder, watching the last of the sunlight fade from view. "I don't know what I would do without you," she whispered.

"Nor I, you." He wrapped his arm around her and pulled her close.

"Do you think there is anything to the Jacobite rumors circulating?"

"I can't say one way or the other. That is something else for you to worry about." He chuckled as she elbowed him in the ribs. "If there is truth to the matter, it should be no problem to quell. There have been a few attempts since they dethroned the Old Pretender." William used their father's term. "They have not managed it yet. I am not concerned, and neither should you be."

Elaina nodded against his shoulder.

"Is there any particular reason you are asking?"

"No. It only came up in a discussion is all."

"Not thinking to run off and join the rebellion are you," William teased.

Elaina elbowed him again. "And risk being haunted by Father's ghost? Not a chance of it."

But what if their mother had been sympathetic to the cause? Would the information gleaned from the papers in the chest have any effect on Elaina's decision? Would her findings hold consequences for her friends or her brother?

Squirming to clear her head, she sat up straight, arching an accusing eyebrow at her brother.

"What?"

How is it you found the time to tell the coachman about your trip and not your sister?"

"I knew you would want to go with me, and it was a delicate matter that needn't have involved you. I am truly sorry."

Elaina studied his face for a moment, and the deep lines etched upon it. "Was that the reason for your gift? To buy my forgiveness?"

"What gift?"

"Mama's necklace. Didn't you leave it on my pillow? The one with the sunflower."

His face paled in the failing daylight as he stared at her.

Chills crept down her spine. "What is it?"

"I did not leave you a present, Elaina. I have not seen Mama's necklace since…"

Servants searched every nook and cranny of the great house even though Elaina told William the gift had appeared the day he left. The constable arrived to question the servants. The only thing anyone could recall out of the ordinary was the back door being found ajar one morning, but a tearful Missie could not remember which day she had found it so.

After a restless night of no sleep, Elaina sat William down after breakfast to tell him what she had learned about Monroe, but only because Calum had shown up with the news that the *Gurney O'Rourke* was set to make port by week's end.

"And just how did you know to look for a man named Monroe in the first place?" William raised a quizzical brow at his sister. "Why didn't you say anything before?"

Elaina cleared her throat as she lowered her eyes, fingering a loose string on the sleeve of her dress. "Well...you see—"

Calum snorted earning him a glare from Elaina.

"I'm waiting," William said.

Elaina grimaced as she turned her attention back to her brother. "Well, I thought you might lock me away in the attic if you knew how I found out about him."

William studied her for a moment, then cast his eyes to Calum.

"Dinna look at me!" Calum threw his hands in the air. "I had nothin' to do with it. I thought she a servant at the time. Who in their right mind would have ever considered what landed on my doorstep that eve to be a member of high society?"

"You think you are so clever." Elaina narrowed her eyes at Calum who only grinned broader, exposing that blasted dimple. She raised her chin a notch and sat up straighter in her chair. "If you must know, brother, the story your little friend Lady Caroline recounted at the dinner party was entirely true. I knocked him unconscious with one punch," She continued to glare at Calum.

"You? You got drunk in a tavern dressed as a man—"

"Dinna forget the part where she was also covered in shite." Calum chuckled.

Elaina closed her eyes against the whole nightmare of it. She would never live this down.

"I do have half a mind to lock you in the attic," William said. "I swear you have a death wish."

She looked up at him, arching an eyebrow. "I do not. I have a desire to find whoever killed Mama and Papa and now to discover who is tormenting me and why it is me that draws their attention."

William stared at her for a moment before rising to his feet. "If Monroe has worked for us, it should be in one of these ledgers." He pulled down several books from one of the many shelves of never-ending books. "Not that I see where it matters if he worked for us or not. In the end, the only thing that matters is if he had a hand in our parents' deaths."

"Maybe it would explain something in the reasoning for their murders?" Elaina took the worn, brown leather-bound book from her brother's hand. "There has to be a motive somewhere." The morning having turned off chilly, she curled up in a wing-backed chair by the fire, like a cat with her feet underneath her.

Calum took another leather-bound book and positioned himself by the large floor to ceiling diamond-paned windows across from her, and William took his place behind the large oak desk looking rather stately.

She opened her book and began to read over the names. It was the most mundane task she had ever performed in her life, and concentrating was damn near impossible. Two-thirds of the way through the large book, her eyes began to water. She closed them, squeezing the bridge of her nose. Resting her head on the back of the chair, she opened her eyes and blinked to clear her vision. William's head was bent intently over his book, his eyes following his finger down the list on the page. She felt a pang of sadness at how much he had changed over the last year. The boyish playfulness he'd once held was gone and in its place sat a severe business and military man with the weight of a family legacy to uphold. Part of her envied him for his purpose, but another part of her was somewhat relieved that it was not expected of her to carry the family. She was not sure she could live up to the challenge.

Against her will, her eyes traveled to Calum bathed in the mid-morning light. His brown hair was bound at his neck, the tail of it falling in soft curls down the back of his dark green waistcoat. She followed the line of his ivory sleeves to the rough hands holding the ledger open in the sunlight. He was not just a businessman. Physical labor created hands like his, not dipping a quill. She wondered what it was about him that made her feel like a clumsy adolescent whenever he was around? Rabbie was an attractive man, but he did not have that effect on her. No one had ever had that effect on her.

She studied his strong jawline, wondering what made the man tick. Maybe that was the difference. She knew where she stood with Rabbie. She didn't have a clue about this mystery sitting in front of her. Did he see her as a child, impulsive and reckless? She would probably see herself the same way if she was on the outside looking in. He had never seen another part of her. He didn't know the part of her that could hunt and shoot with the best of them. Would he be impressed that she had taken down a boar with one arrow from the back of her horse or would those things be off-putting? Maybe he would be impressed if she were a sophisticated lady, hosting dinner parties and impressive soirees like Lady Caroline.

What made her think he thought of her at all? She looked up and found Calum's gaze on her over the top of his book. She tried to hide her smile as she looked back down at the words in front of her, not seeing any of them. Maybe he did think of her after all. She felt her face warm at the thought and internally rolled her eyes at herself. She was certainly acting like a schoolgirl now. She needed to concentrate, not wonder if men thought of her.

"I found something!" William said startling Elaina and Calum both.

"What is it?" Elaina unfolded out of the chair and positioned herself over her brother's shoulder.

Calum took the other side.

William pointed to a passage in the middle of the page. "It is dated 12 March 1742."

"That was the last trip Papa made before Uncle James passed," Elaina said.

"Monroe Abernathy and Rufus Wilkes were relieved of their duties immediately upon making port," William read. "They were part of the crew."

"Does Papa say why?"

"Attempted theft."

"Theft of what?" Elaina asked.

"It doesn't say."

"'Tis a serious offense." Calum looked up at Elaina. "I wonder if they were arrested upon landing?"

"If they were, they are free men now. It makes you wonder." William leaned back in his chair. "But we do have a connection now between Papa and this Monroe. We shall find out more in a few days. What does he look like?"

Elaina gave as much detail about the large man and his companion as she could remember.

"We will see what we can find out, but for now, I have a meeting I must attend. If you two will excuse me?" William rose from his chair and left the study.

Caitir stuck her head through the door and asked, "Anythin'?"

Elaina answered, "Monroe worked for Papa about a year ago, and Papa terminated his employment. That's about it."

"As soon as Lord Spencer is gone, we can take Calum upstairs," Caitir whispered.

"Why the whispering, and why are you taking me upstairs?" Calum asked with a raised brow?

"You'll see," Caitir answered.

⸺ ⊹⊱⊰⊹ ⸺

Elaina groped into the back of the wardrobe, her heart falling to her feet as her hand met empty space. "Oh god," she finally breathed, clamping her other hand to her chest. "There it is. I thought it was gone. Sweet Jesus." Opening the jeweled box, she pulled out the drawstring bag. "Did you look in the chest again?" she asked Caitir.

"No," her maid answered, sounding puzzled.

Elaina could have sworn she had drawn the string closed but who knew. She needed to gather her wits. "It's nothing. I just thought… Never mind." Elaina glanced at Calum, who looked uncomfortable. Amused, she wondered if it was because he was in her private chamber. Kneeling before the trunk, she unlocked it, opened the lid, and pulled out one of the folded papers. She hesitated before extending it up to Caitir's waiting hand.

Caitir smiled with a look of encouragement and took the paper, passing it to Calum who hadn't moved away from the door. "Can you read these?" Caitir asked him.

Looking from the paper to Elaina and back he took the page and unfolded it. "Aye," he said after studying the words a moment. "I can. Whose are these?"

Elaina and Caitir glanced at each other, and Elaina realized she was holding her breath, exhaling it with a great whoosh. "My mother's," she managed to squeak.

Calum leaned back against the closed door and studied the paper for a minute. "'Tis a love letter." He raised his brow and crooked a grin at Elaina.

She felt her face warm under his gaze. "Who is it—" she croaked and cleared her throat—"from whom?" Elaina wished she hadn't sounded so startled by his announcement.

"There is no name, but he was from the Highlands." Calum went on to translate the letter as best he could.

Elaina plopped to her bottom in disbelief. It had been dated a good five years before her birth. Three years before her parents' marriage. It may have been her mother's first love. Perhaps that was why her mother had held on to these letters all these years. Her mother, in love with a Highlander? What a bizarre thought, especially with her marrying a British officer. Talk about two different worlds. She'd learned so much more about her mother after her death than she'd ever known while she was alive and she turned out to be entirely different than what Elaina had ever thought. She believed her to be an overprotective, nagging woman who ran the household while Papa was away. But there had been a hidden rebel inside of her.

"I wonder if this was his?" Elaina pulled a tartan from the chest. "There is no other explanation for why she would have it."

Calum finally left his post by the door and came to stand beside her and the chest. Taking the woolen fabric from her, he rubbed it between his fingers. "Could have been."

Leaning over the chest, Elaina shifted through some of the papers and brought out another sheet, handing it to Calum.

Once again, he studied it for a moment before speaking. When he looked up, his gaze darted from Caitir to Elaina. "This"—he waved the paper—"is considered treason. These are dangerous items to have. "May I?" He motioned to the chest.

Elaina nodded in answer, and he dropped to the floor in front of it, his knee brushing her leg and making her uncomfortably warm.

He seemed not to notice while he picked up paper after paper, studying them and then laying them aside. After several pages, he turned to look at Elaina. "Yer mother sent funds to support the Jacobite cause," he stated bluntly. "She exchanged correspondence with several people on this side of the water. This one is unnamed but seems to be in verra high standin'." He studied a few more pages.

"Do any of them use the words 'a grave matter'?" Elaina leaned forward and peered into the chest.

"Not that I have seen, no," he replied without looking up.

Elaina and Caitir exchanged glances.

After looking over a few more, Calum held a handful of papers up in the air. "It is apparent yer father didna ken of yer mother's dealings. Someone within your father's business helped channel funds from your mother's business holdings. Most likely, she thought yer father would never find out because it came from her glass company. This could have cost yer parents their lives."

"Papa wouldn't have known that their lives could be in danger. Mama may have been so excited to finally return to her homeland that it never crossed her mind the price of the move could be her life." Elaina buried her head in her hands. "This could be why they are targeting me. I am the owner of the glass company now. William has no stake in it. But what do they want from me?" She turned a questioning look to the two cousins sitting beside her.

Calum laid a soft hand on her shoulder. "I dinna ken, my lady. Without knowing who, we will have hell determining why. We need to burn these."

"But…Mama had to have a reason to want to support the cause, to go behind Papa's back. Is there any mention of why?" Things grew more confusing and worrisome by the day. What other secrets had her mother kept?

Calum shuffled through the papers. "Not that I have seen, but it would take several days for me to read all of them straight through."

"Well, they've sat in the chest for I don't know how many years. Surely they could be safe a few more days?"

Caitir snorted. "What will we tell Lord Spencer about Calum coming every day and sitting in your bedchamber?"

Calum interjected, "I will stay today and skim as many as I can, but after that, I dinna ken how we can do it without him findin' out. Do ye ken where your brother stands on the issue?"

"The issue being the conflict between the Jacobites and the British?" Elaina sighed. "I'm sure with the British. He is an officer."

Caitir took a deep breath and squatted beside Elaina and Calum, laying a hand on each of them. "Then that answers it. Today it is, and then we burn them."

Chapter Thirteen

"WE ARE GOING ON A hunt!" William burst through the door to the study.

"I know. I was present for the conversation," Elaina mumbled, still bent over a stack of record books from her mother's and now her own glass company, combing for more clues.

He leaned on his hands upon the large wooden desk, his blue eyes dancing with excitement. "Not that kind of hunt, Miss Know-It-All. We will hunt fowl at the invitation of Lord Taylor. It will be a day-long affair with a grand party that evening. So"—he punched a fist upon the table, causing Elaina and her books to jump—"be prepared to scramble through the brush and dine with the Edinburgh elite!"

"You seem to be quite exuberant about this little excursion." Elaina leaned back in the chair, eyeing her brother suspiciously. It was good to see him genuinely smiling for the first time in a long time.

"It has just been so long. Are you not excited as well?"

"Absolutely." Elaina rose and rounded the desk to face her brother. "This wouldn't have anything to do with seeing the lovely Miss Taylor again, would it?"

"Not in the least," William huffed, then he turned to leave the room but not before Elaina caught the slightest glimpse of a smile. "We will leave long before daybreak on Thursday and meet the others near the moors. Be ready. I will not wait for you," he called over his shoulder.

As if that were a possibility—him having to wait for her.

Elaina hardly slept the few nights before the event. It had been forever since she'd hunted, and the thought of holding a gun in her hand again made her almost giddy. The afternoon before the big day, she and Caitir combed through her clothing, searching for the perfect ensemble. Elaina focused mainly on the practicality of the garments and Caitir on the elegance of the evening attire.

Elaina stood leaning against a post beside the stables when William came trotting out of the house the next morning, both of their breaths frosty on the pre-dawn air.

"It's about time," she grinned up at her big brother. "I almost left without you."

"You wouldn't know where to go," he goaded her, waving to his footman to load his and Elaina's personal items into the coach. "Rabbie will take my footman and Caitir to Lord Taylor's residence while we participate in the morning's activities."

"I would have had Rabbie take me." Elaina cocked an eyebrow at her brother.

"Over my dead body," Rabbie retorted as he led Major and Sadie out of the stables.

"That's right. It would be his dead body," William answered. "He knows where his bread is buttered."

"Don't be an arrogant arse, William. Let's go." Elaina let Rabbie help her onto her horse.

She carried her fowling gun through a loop on her hunting saddle and tied her powder horn and shot around her waist. Her long hair hung in a tight plait down her back, much to Caitir's dismay. She had refused to spend time having it all pinned up on her head, in a hurry to make sure she beat William to the stables. Elaina had informed Caitir she could perform that drudgery later, before dinner. Caitir had won the argument over her wearing a hat. "Any self-respecting lady would be wearing one," the maid had stated firmly.

There was just enough light from the sun inching its way to the horizon for them to pick their way towards the moors lying north-east of Edinburgh where the Taylor family held an enormous country estate. The horses danced and flung their heads, feeling extra frisky in the briskness of the morning. As the siblings got closer to the moors, the road and surroundings were easily more visible.

"I'll race you," William challenged his sister.

"What are we betting?"

"Why does there have to be a bet? Why not only a winner?"

"Fine," Elaina sighed and smacked Sadie on the neck without further notice.

"Cheater," William called out after her.

Elaina leaned low in her saddle, trying to reduce the draw of wind across her body as she could hear her brother and his stallion gaining on her. Her felt hat flew from the top of her head, but luckily the ties did not come undone and the hat merely flopped against her back as she urged Sadie faster. When their hunting group came into view, standing together in the distance, Elaina glanced over her shoulder to see how close her competition was. He was much closer than she had anticipated. She let out a little squeal as she encouraged Sadie faster. William gained ground quickly and overtook her as they came to a skidding halt in front of the group.

"Well done, Major," Elaina panted, patting the large black stallion as he snorted and danced while trying to catch his breath.

"Major? No credit for the exceptional rider?" William feigned offense.

"You too, then, brother. Good job." She reached over and patted him on the head as she had done to his horse.

"Bravo." Caroline applauded stepping forward, her gloved hands muffling the sound. She looked exquisite in her navy-blue riding attire, complete with a large felt hat displaying an extravagant peacock plume.

The siblings both dismounted and greeted their hostess. Elaina felt slightly underdressed for the occasion in her gray, yet well-tailored, woolen frock. Tugging at the hem of her form-fitting riding jacket and smoothing the escaped hairs away from her face, she replaced her modest hat to its rightful place while trying not to notice all the eyes resting on the trio. She busied herself with Sadie's bridle and loosening her girth while Caroline gushed over William's racing prowess.

"Let me help." A large pair of hands appeared from over her shoulder.

"I have it," she snapped. Glancing up, she added, "Oh. It's you."

"I ken ye have it, and ye dinna have to say it like that." Calum gave her a dimpled grin.

"Sorry." She looked over her shoulder at Caroline giggling and fawning over William. Her gaze traveled over the group milling about and found several judgmental glances directed her way mostly by the other women accompanying their companions and dressed in more exceptional attire than Elaina sported. She should have listened to Caitir.

Calum unfastened her gun and cast a sideways grin as she smoothed the sides of her hair again. "Dinna fash yerself about them, lassie." He dipped his chin in the group's direction. "Most of the women are only here to carry their man's shot, no to be shootin'," Calum said as if reading her mind. "You, on the other hand..." handed Sadie's reins to a nearby groomsman for him to walk her and cool her off.

"You only have the one gun, Madam?" a grating voice said from behind Elaina.

She turned to find a finely dressed gentleman referring to her with a look of condescending disdain on his face. His sandy hair was neatly clubbed under his tall black hat—Harry Everson, the cheeky bastard.

Calum merely handed Elaina's gun to her, eyeballing Everson with suspicion.

"I only need the one," Elaina slung the gun over her shoulder and adjusted her pouch and horn.

"Well, you don't plan on doing much shooting, do you? Or are you here to carry Mr. MacKinnon's weaponry?" The man turned another equally disdainful gaze to Calum. "I have brought three guns myself, if you feel the need to borrow one so you can keep up. I'm sure I could find someone to load it for you."

"I am quite sure Mr. MacKinnon is capable of carrying his own weaponry," Elaina replied. "As for loading and shooting, I shan't think I will have a problem, Mr. Everson."

"Harry, you aren't being a rascal, are you?" Caroline came rushing over, laying a hand on Elaina's shoulder.

"Of course not." Harry removed his hat and bowed before Elaina. "My lady," he said, cutting his eyes at his cousin as if to ask why she had invited these people.

"I would say it is has been a pleasure, Mr. Everson, but my mother taught me it impolite to lie." Elaina turned on her heel and stalked away to follow William toward the edge of the marshland that stretched out as far as she could see.

She could hear Caroline stifle a giggle as her cousin muttered under his breath.

"Dinna be shy about speakin' yer mind," Calum chuckled catching up with her.

"Don't start with me."

"Hey, I am on yer side, my lady," Calum said.

"I'm sorry. I didn't mean to snap at you. I feel so out of place already, and Mr. Everson didn't help. 'Three guns,'" Elaina mocked Harry. "These are not my kind of people. I feel like a thistle in the middle of a rose garden."

"Well, thistles are beautiful, my lady, although some consider them weeds because they grow wild and free…and, well, roses have sharper thorns."

Elaina looked at Calum speculatively but didn't have time to reply before Caroline clapped them all to attention. After splitting up into small groups or pairs, they headed out into the boggy moors. Elaina noticed Caroline had conveniently taken up with William. She also noticed that nearly everyone had a boy or man with them to help reload the first gun while they fired the second. She decided to focus on enjoying herself despite the nonsense around her.

As the group inched closer to the area of open water, the sound of honking increased in volume. How many geese were there? They sounded like hundreds upon hundreds. She couldn't help but smile. Feeling a light tap on her shoulder, she looked up to find Calum pointing off in the distance. She stood on tiptoe to see over the brush and saw what he saw—a smaller pond off to the right. The main body of their group headed left, in the direction of the massive honking. She followed Calum as quietly as possible through the underbrush of the marshland, the mud pulling at her boots. If they did it right, they could get several Golden Plover while the others stirred up the geese.

They had nearly reached the edge of the pond when she caught movement from the corner of her eye and turned to find the oily grin of Harry Everson pointed at her. The bloody bastard had followed them with his manservant and three guns in tow. Oh well, no matter. Elaina wasn't worried from the looks of the poor man clumsily carrying the small armament. A mutual look of disgust passed between her and Calum.

She pushed Everson from her mind as she crouched down, pulling her skirts up between her legs and out of her way. Slinging her gun farther around her back, she crept through the brush to a fallen log next to a large tree near the water's edge, downwind of the waterfowl. She and Calum took their place.

"Ready?" she asked him with just a look. He gave her a slight nod, and she deftly swung her gun from over her shoulder, pulled the cork out of her powder horn with her teeth, and poured the powder into her measure. She poured it down the barrel of her gun as she replaced the cork with her teeth. She finished loading and set the hammer, firing her first shot with Calum only seconds behind her. Repeating the process in record speed, she had another shot off before Everson fired his first, her first shot having startled his handler into dropping the ramrod the first time around.

She could hear the shots coming from the larger pond, and a dark shadow formed over their own as a large flock of geese took the air. Elaina and Calum both quickly reloaded and aimed upwards. Elaina got off two shots to every one of Everson's, and she took great joy and satisfaction in that fact. She and Calum kept a perfect rhythm to where when one reloaded while the other fired. A continuous rain of shot dotted the sky until the geese made their escape, then the dogs were released to fetch back their kills. Elaina and Calum leaned their guns against the tree and trudged through the mud, retrieving several that had fallen close to their vicinity.

Picking her loot up and dropping it in the grain sack she carried, Elaina felt elated. She straightened, stretching her back, and gazed out over the moor at the brilliant purple and orange hues spread across the vast expanse of sky with the gray mountains rising faintly in the distance.

"Exquisite, is it not?" Calum said softly from beside her.

"That it is," she whispered. "My mother always called it God's Country. I believe she was correct."

They stood side by side for several moments taking in the beauty of Scotland before a large black retriever dropped another duck at their feet.

Calum rubbed the dog between his ears. "Good boy."

"Is he yours?" Elaina asked, reaching down to pet the pup.

"Nay. He belongs to Lady Caroline's father. He has a whole legion he sends out on these hunts."

"The Taylors are an extremely wealthy family, I take it." Elaina looked about the moor at the significant number of pups retrieving dead fowl.

"Aye, and powerful."

Elaina wondered what powerful meant in Scotland in this day and time, but she didn't ask.

"If ye'll carry my gun, my lady, I will carry yer bag."

"You have a deal, Mr. MacKinnon." Elaina slung his gun over her shoulder.

"I cannae believe ye didn't get puffed up or argue."

"I know a sound proposition when I hear one," Elaina grinned at Calum as he slung the weight of both sacks over his shoulder.

"Hold still." Calum whipped out a handkerchief. "Ye've a bit o' mud." He wiped at her cheek.

"I can get it," Elaina reached for the handkerchief.

"Be still. Ye cannae see it. Ye dinna wish to strut about with mud all over yer face, now do ye?"

"I do not strut," Elaina protested but held still. "I am not a hen."

"No?" Calum asked softly, their eyes locking as his hand stilled against her cheek.

Elaina held her breath. For a fleeting moment, she thought he might kiss her. Then for a longer moment, she almost wished he would. But she blinked, breaking the spell.

Calum's dimple appeared. "No, ye dinna strut. Ye flit about much like a mad bumblebee."

Elaina swatted his arm, scolding herself over her disappointment that the moment had not ended differently. "Watch yourself, or I'll show you a mad bumblebee."

He chuckled behind her as she led the way back to the group. Meeting up with the insufferable Harry who was laden with a much smaller bag than either Calum or Elaina, the pair exchanged a triumphant smile and then grimaced as the man reamed his attendant for shoddy work.

Chapter Fourteen

THEIR ARRIVAL AT THE TAYLORS' magnificent country estate was a rambunctious scene. A multitude of servants greeted the guests and took their kills to be cleaned and dressed for the evening's celebration. There were even more people at the house than there had been in the field, and they came down to greet the raucous younger crowd. Elaina felt particularly out of place once again as many of the hunters' parents were the ones chatting and laughing and garnering the details of the hunt.

"Whose is this?" a high-ranking British officer laid his hand upon Elaina's bag before it was carried off. He was an imposing figure in his white powdered wig and military uniform. His face looked dour and sad, much like a hound's. He appeared to be of about the same age as most of the young people gathered by the stables, but with the way he held himself and his formal mannerisms, the gentleman seemed more mature.

"Lady Elaina Spencer, Your Grace," Calum piped up from behind her, and she very much wanted to stomp on his foot. "With one gun."

Elaina reached back and kicked his ankle that time.

"Quite a haul for a young lady, is it not?" the man replied with a raised eyebrow while seeming to take in her ragtag appearance.

"We were all at the same pond," a sarcastic voice replied. "Could be several people's kills in the bag."

Elaina didn't have to turn around to know who spoke. "True," she agreed without argument.

"But the lady is a fair shot, your grace," Calum spoke again. "Faster than many men I've seen."

"I have an idea." Caroline clapped her hands once again. "Let's have a shooting contest. It is only noon. We have a while to go before this evening. Let's make a day of it!" Her exuberance had started to wear on Elaina's countenance.

"We don't—" Everson started to say.

"Let's do," William placed a hand on his sister's shoulder. "It'll be grand." He grinned down at Elaina, and she discreetly pinched him, causing him to jump and his smile to widen.

Several minutes later, the rules had been constructed and a space determined for the shooting contest. Fastest hand won.

Elaina lingered around the back of the group, hoping to be forgotten.

Calum nudged her with his arm. "Chin up. Ye've got this in the bag, so to say." One corner of his mouth turned up.

Elaina bit her tongue on all the things she wanted to say and instead asked, "Who is the officer?"

"Why that's the Duke of Cumberland," Calum said, staring at the man.

"The Duke of Cumberland? The king's son?" Elaina felt her stomach drop into her shoes. "What is he doing here? I thought he was in Germany?"

"He was. They had a good victory. I heard he was injured in the leg with a musket ball, though."

"He seems to have recovered fine." Elaina did notice a slight limp to the man; however, it did not seem to hinder him much at all as he strode around visiting with the young men.

"Let us begin!" Caroline announced loudly.

They had drawn numbers from a hat to determine the shooting order. It began oddly enough with a set of twins. They were of medium build with bright blonde hair and identical twins, so Elaina could not tell them apart at all. Winston and Watson's shots were near exact in timing too. Watson beat his brother by mere seconds...or was he Winston? Elaina found a fence rail with a vantage point to perch herself upon away from the crowd until it was her turn.

"Nervous, are you?" William asked, leaning against the rail next to her.

"Annoyed would be more like it." Elaina cut her eyes at her big brother.

"It's all in fun, Elaina."

"I know. I just...you know how I feel about attention, especially about large groups of attention." She chewed her lip as she watched the people milling about.

"I know, but it is something you will have to get over. You are now Lady Elaina Spencer, and you are expected at these sorts of affairs, and you will have to be polite and pretend you like it. We will even be expected to throw a few of these as well."

"Where is Papa when you need him?" Elaina muttered with a sigh.

"Six feet under. Chin up. My turn." William patted his sister on the knee before he strode off to take his turn.

God. Why did he have to be so callous? That was quite the remark, though it was the truth. All the whining and feeling sorry for herself could not change the fact that she was now the lady of the house. She eyed Caroline, who seemed fascinated by whatever conversation she held with one of the partygoers. Maybe she could try to be more ladylike and civil. She didn't always have to wear a chip on her shoulder. Then her eyes traveled to Harry Everson, and she at once changed her mind. It wasn't a chip—he was just an arse.

William won his shot with no problem. The Duke of Cumberland stood on the veranda with Lord Taylor, taking in the competition with interest. Elaina gleaned the young men who were military by their salute to the Duke after their turn. The Duke returned in kind.

"Your turn," a voice at her elbow said, startling her.

"Crivens? Already?"

Calum gave Elaina's hand an encouraging squeeze as he helped her down from her perch. He handed over her gun, and she nodded to him in thanks and strode to her place.

"Are you sure this is fair? Shouldn't it be women against women and men against men?" the young lad piped up as Elaina took her place next to him.

"The odds should be in your favor. What are you scared of?" someone said from behind the duo.

"I'm not scared of a woman. I would feel bad beating her is all. I would hate to make her cry." He eyed Elaina.

She ignored him. They were shooting balls instead of shot so it would speed things up a tiny bit. She wasn't concerned. She took a deep calming breath, centered herself, and, at the signal, went through her motions calmly and efficiently. She had her shot off before her competitor had loaded his ball.

"I am truly sorry. Do you need this?" Elaina asked him, pulling out her handkerchief.

His face turned crimson at the roars of laughter behind them. Embarrassed, he turned his back to Elaina and saluted the duke.

Seeming to try to hide a smile himself, the Duke gave a rather unenthusiastic one in return. He turned his eye to Elaina and applauded her softly. She gave him a deep curtsy in return.

"Well done, sister." William patted her on the back when she had safely navigated her way to her hiding place.

Blushing, she had nodded at the words of praise extended to her as she made her way through the crowd.

"Thank you, Lord Spencer." She bowed her head to him.

"I see your friend Mr. Everson has made it to the next round as well." William nodded to the unconscionable lad chatting with a group of giggling women but eyeing Elaina with disdain. "What did you do to him?"

"I think I'm breathing is all."

William chuckled. "Well, no worries. He is just a spoiled little boy."

"That's the nice way to put it. Unfortunately, he is also a shareholder in the glass company. I find it hard to believe Mama would have found cause to like the little twit enough for him to be a shareholder."

"I believe Lord Taylor encouraged Papa to let the boy invest. Trying to make a man out of him, I gander. What's the word with MacKinnon?" William asked, catching Elaina off guard.

"What do you mean?" Elaina eyed the large dark Scot taking his turn at the competition. His once neatly clubbed hair had started to lose its battle with some of his curls. His hands deftly went through their moves without the slightest stumble, and he easily beat his opponent. He bowed smartly to the Duke before turning to speak with some of the other men gathered.

"He seems soft on you is all." William grinned.

"He does not," Elaina protested. "We hardly know each other."

"He just seems awful willing to jump to your aid, is all I'm saying."

"Well, don't say it. He is Caitir's cousin. He is helping out of duty."

"Whatever you say." William applauded with the rest of the group as the first round came to its conclusion.

Elaina absently added applause of her own while watching a charismatic Scot interact with those around him.

There was a short break in between the two parts of the competition. Caroline gathered the women together and took them inside so they could freshen up, warm themselves, and relieve themselves.

Elaina eyed herself regretfully in the mirror, trying to tame the stray wisps escaping her plait. She sighed in defeat, took the braid down, and raked her fingers through it. Once again, her judgment stood in question. She supposed Caitir did know best. She should have worn it up. She quickly washed her face and went in search of her lady's maid, finding her with the other maids down in the servants' room.

"My lady." Caitir scrambled from her stool, where she sat talking and laughing with some of the women, and curtsied. "At yer service, my lady."

Elaina had to stifle a giggle. She kept her face as straight as possible. "May I have a word?"

"Aye, my lady." Caitir followed Elaina into the hallway.

Elaina laughed when they were out of earshot of the other servants. "You are so formal."

"It's my job." Caitir eyed her with indignation.

"I know, but it's so funny."

"Do ye need anythin'?" Caitir took in Elaina's appearance from the muddy hem of her gown to her flyaway hair. "Besides a change of clothes, I mean. Christ, ye're filthy. What happened to yer hair? Did I no tell ye to wear it up?"

"Well, we are still shooting. I didn't want to ruin something else with powder or a spark or anything. I did wash my face." Elaina stuck her face out, preening. "But would you re-plait my hair for me? You can get it tighter than I can."

"What? Ye want a pat on the back for havin' enough class to wash yer face even though ye are traipsin' around here in a dirty frock and yer hair all about ye like—"

"Don't say it."

Caitir sighed. "What are ye shootin'?" She twirled her mistress around so she could try to tame the madness on her head.

"Mistress Caroline thought it would be great fun to have a shooting contest."

"And is it?"

"I suppose, if there were not a hundred pairs of eyes on me the whole time."

"And ye in yer filthy dress? Mary, Mother, and Joseph. I will never hear the end of this one."

"Oh hush. I came for some moral support, and all I get is a tongue lashing."

"What else did ye expect?"

"Nothing." Elaina grabbed Caitir's face and kissed her on the cheek. "Thank you for cheering me up."

"Ye are strange, my lady." Caitir shook her head. "Now go show them who's boss before someone catches ye down here and there is more scandal. Shoo!"

Elaina dutifully traipsed back up the stairs with a smile on her face. She would much rather be down in the servants' room with the regular people than hobnobbing with the nobility, but that was her life. Best to perform her duty for William's sake.

Making her way outside, she noticed the shooting had begun without her. Small groups of men and women loitered about, some watching the competition, others lost in conversation from which the sharp staccato of laughter occasionally broke forth. A servant clad in crisp black with stark white gloves presented her a silver tray filled with mugs of steaming cider. Accepting gratefully, she sipped hers with caution as she traversed the curve of stone stairs leading into the throng of partygoers. The brandy infused cider slid down her throat, the warmth of it settling in her chilled toes.

"Careful. You don't want to inhibit your shooting," Harry cast her a disdainful look as he passed her on his way from the stable area to the firing range.

"You better hope it does," she replied, raising her mug to him. She continued through the crowd smiling and nodding as she edged her way toward her hiding spot.

A hand gently grabbed her elbow. "Dinna wander off too far. I believe ye are up next," Calum spoke low into her ear.

"Already? Have you?"

"Nay, not yet."

Elaina sighed, sipping her drink and watching the round at hand. Why did her name have to be drawn so early? She focused on trying to calm herself, watching the man and the only other woman in the competition go through their motions. The woman was a fair shot, beating the man by a couple of seconds. True to Calum's word, Elaina's name rang out over the din of the crowd. Raising her chin, she strode confidently to the front, setting her mug on the table. She took her gun from the servant and gave her competitor a smile for which she received a raised brow in return. The stocky girl rose several inches over Elaina's slight frame even without her severe nose pointed in the air.

Elaina adjusted her powder, shot, and cushions around her waist while noticing the woman had her things spread out on the table in front of her. Several of the men had done the same. She preferred to keep things precisely in the place they were when out hunting. She believed in repetition, memory in your muscles, and routine—where no thinking is involved, everything is automatic. Closing her eyes, she took a couple of deep breaths, then opening them, she focused on the trees ahead just as the signal was given. Quickly and smoothly she performed the machinations, but when she fired several seconds before her opponent, there was a roar in her ear and a shower of molten gun powder. She could feel the burn of it on her neck and the side of her face. She swiped madly at her cheek, brushing at the blistering bits. It took several moments for her ears to stop ringing enough that she could hear a buzzing like bees around a hive. She kept her eyes closed as someone dabbed a cold, wet cloth to her neck and face.

Her brain slowly came back to life, and her immediate thought was why did her gun misfire? She'd cleaned it herself before going to freshen up. There should be no reason. She had handed it to one of the many servants before going indoors. He had left in the direction of the stables. Had someone purposefully sabotaged her? It was a friendly competition. If so, who would do such a thing?

Only one name came to mind.

She waved the hands still dabbing at her away and cautiously opened her eyes. She blinked several times to clear her vision. Thank god she could see. She had witnessed a man lose an eye with a misfire. She had also seen fingers blown off and in a panic, drew her hands up to her face. Spreading her fingers out in front of her, she flexed them, relieved to find all ten digits remaining. A coat of black powder covered them, but they were there. The hand dabbing at her face moved to her hands and patted at the blisters beginning to form. She blinked up to find it was Calum tending her wounds. The dour-faced woman knelt beside her, a horrified look upon her face, and William perched behind her head. The fear in his eyes shook her insides, and she couldn't look at him.

"Are ye all right?"

Elaina could barely hear Calum's question over the din in her ears. The buzzing sound was the hum of spectators gathered around her fallen form. She nodded, realizing she lay on the ground and the spaces between the three kneeling around her were filled with more concerned faces. She waved them away and started rising to her feet, several pairs of hands helping her.

"Where is my gun?" she croaked.

Someone handed it to her, and she began to inspect it. There it was—a pebble. Someone had placed a stone in her gun, causing it to backfire. She was damned lucky not to be injured more than she was. She looked around the group, searching for the little weasel. When she had come down the steps earlier, he was coming from the direction in which the guns were kept.

Harry stared at her wide-eyed and not blinking, his expression owl-like.

She would have laughed had she not been so furious. She didn't know if it was fear or the shock of her knowing it was he who was behind such an act that placed the look upon his face.

"My lady," a voice to her right said, muffled. "My lady," it spoke louder, drawing her attention. "Let us get you inside and tended to." Lord Taylor's concerned face looked down at her.

"I would like to continue," she said, causing his expression to resemble Mr. Everson's. "If someone would be kind enough to loan me a gun."

"Ye can use mine, Lady Elaina," Calum said, helping her to her feet. "I forfeit my position, and ye can use my gun for the remainder of the competition. Ye would beat me anyhow," he said, the side of his mouth turning up.

She nodded in thanks to him, watching his worried eyes take in her appearance, and she wondered just how bad she looked.

"I have inspected it myself." He grinned at her.

She gave him a shaky smile and then turned to her opponent. "Ready?"

The woman shook her head with a nervous glance to Lord Taylor. "You have already beaten me," she said. "You fired before I."

"Well, who is next then?" Elaina said without facing the crowd, her voice echoing in her head. She was afraid she might not be able to continue if she looked at the group behind her.

"Harry Everson."

"Bloody hell," she mumbled under her breath. She glanced at Lord Taylor beside her to see if he had heard her.

The amused look on his face said he had. He waved a hand in the direction of the table. "Carry on, I suppose." He stepped back out of the way.

There was a loud round of applause as Elaina stepped up to the table and attempted to block everything out. Harry would not have the upper hand. She waved to the waiter for another mug of cider. She needed it.

Harry refused to make eye contact or acknowledge Elaina as he awkwardly laid his things out on the table. She took pleasure in the fact that his hands shook as he did so.

Elaina checked to see how much powder she had left. She had enough for Harry, but she would need more before the next contestant—and there would be a next one. She familiarized herself quickly with Calum's gun, trying to get a feel for it. Closing her eyes, she waited for the signal, hoping she could hear it. The caller thankfully yelled quite loudly, that or her hearing had started to return. She swiftly moved through her drill and put Harry out of the competition. He turned without a glance or a word at his competitor. She kept her back turned to the crowd and grinned as the insufferable man stalked away.

There was a slight break for her to refill her supplies. She was not used to servants doing absolutely everything, so she felt quite out of place when one attendant called to the other to get her a refill of powder and cushions. She stood with her back to the crowd, cleaning the burnt remains out of Calum's gun and trying to tune everyone out.

"What the hell happened? Are ye fair?" Rabbie was at her elbow with her needed supplies.

"I'll do. How bad did it get me?"

"Nay all that bad." He studied her face and neck. "Ye have all yer fingers."

"I do." She wiggled them, studying the burns on her palm. "Did you see someone tampering with my gun? Namely that little shite, Everson."

"If I did, do ye think I would be lettin' ye shoot it?"

"Fair enough," Elaina acknowledged.

Rabbie laughed, taking her powder horn from her. "The groomsmen are takin' bets. Several of them were right upset about the last one."

"Good," Elaina replied. "That man is a horse's arse."

"I thought that was my name?" Rabbie retorted, causing Elaina to burst out in laughter. "Aye, he can be right full of himself. Ye need to watch yerself tonight," he added before striding away toward the stables.

Elaina stared after her groomsman, who always seemed to have a dire warning, then caught sight of Harry eyeing her with caution.

Turning her back on him, she wondered if he had the ballocks to do such a thing. He was the only one who seemed put out with her, and why, she didn't know unless it still had to do with their discussion on the shipping of whiskey, and if so, the boy needed to grow up.

Without further incident, she went through several more shooters. One shooter left, thank the Lord. She had grown tired of the pressure of standing in front of everyone. She had begun to feel the burns and desperately needed a drink stiffer than cider and to lie down. The last shooter was William.

Her brother strode up to the table. "You look like hell."

"I feel it," she answered.

"I just wish Papa was here to see this."

"I am glad Mama is not—me in my dirty dress, shooting with the men. She would be appalled, and she would be hovering all around, trying to doctor me."

"That she would," William agreed. "I expect you not to take it easy on me."

"I expect the same." She smiled at her brother and then tried to center her thoughts. She should have centered them a tiny bit more because William beat her by a hair. She turned to him, giving him a deep curtsy, bowing her head. "Well done, Lord Spencer." She stood on the tips of her toes and kissed him on the cheek.

"Well, done to you, my lady. I believe you could have beat me if you were not worn out from all of your other victories and frazzled by your injuries."

"You flatter me."

The pair turned toward the veranda where The Duke of Cumberland stood with a group of onlookers. William saluted smartly, and Elaina curtsied. The Duke gave a salute, looking impressed at the pair.

Elaina made her way through the crowd, nodding at the congratulations and words of admiration from the men and women. She came face to face with Harry Everson, who turned ashen as she approached him.

"And that, sir," she said, "is how you lose graciously. Take note."

She left him standing with his mouth hanging open, and his friends stifling their laughter around him.

Chapter Fifteen

"**M**ARY, MOTHER, AND JOSEPH." CAITIR grabbed Elaina's face, turning it side to side, inspecting her war wounds. "Does it hurt?"

"Yes. It is starting to. Is there anything we can do?"

"Aye, I'll get some salve from the help. Let's get ye out of these clothes. I'll get ye some cold water to wash with." Caitir helped Elaina strip down to her shift, then hurried away to fetch supplies.

Caroline had been kind enough to put Elaina up in a private room. Several of the other women shared chambers, but Caroline thought she could use some privacy after the morning's excitement.

Padding softly to the mirror, she took a deep breath before taking in her reflection. Her hair was wild, falling in strings from her braid. Lifting her chin, she let her fingers glide gently over the angry red marks standing out harsh against the paleness of her skin. Her cheek had taken most of the damage. Several small raised blisters scattered into smaller red dots dusting her forehead, chin, and neck. A soft knock at the door interrupted her inspection, and she turned as Caroline poked her dainty head through the door.

"May I come in?" she asked.

"Yes, of course." Elaina felt absurd standing there in her shift.

Concern etched on her face, Caroline crossed the room and inspected Elaina's face. "I am so sorry. I cannot believe that happened."

"Nor can I." Elaina picked up a light blanket laying on the end of the large bed and wrapped it around her shoulders, hugging it to her.

Caroline sat on the vacated space. "I know you probably think it was Harry, but I am pretty certain it was not."

"How can you be sure?" Elaina sat in a chair beside the reading desk.

"Father spoke to him. Father can get anything out of anyone."

Elaina was not so sure on the matter, but she nodded as if she agreed. "If not him, then who?"

"Excellent question," Caroline sighed. In the next breath, she said, "William told me about the second note and the necklace."

Elaina sat silent for several seconds. Why would he tell her? They didn't know her well enough to be sharing such matters. It was no business of the Taylors'. They didn't know who their enemies were. Hell, it could be Caroline herself, for all William knew. This was her house, after all. She had been in New-castle at the funeral and present when the groomsman was killed. What if her family had arranged the whole thing?

Elaina rose and walked to the window where she stood gazing down at the elaborate gardens, tracing the spiraling curl of the chiseled hedges. The brilliant reds and golds of the Duke of Cumberland's coat glowed in elegant contrast to the green of the surrounding shrubbery as he and Lord Taylor strolled their way through the maze, their heads bowed close together deep in conversation. She thought of her mother's papers. Lord Taylor was a business partner of her father's and a shareholder in her company. He was also an acquaintance of the king's youngest son, a close enough acquaintance for the Duke to pay a visit to his home. What if Lord Taylor had gained knowledge of her mother's treasonous actions? She should have told William about the papers. She had possibly placed them dead center of the lion's den by withholding the information from him.

"I'm sorry if I have upset you," Caroline's voice came from behind her. "Those were not my intentions." There was a moment of silence. "You can trust me," she whispered.

"Oh, can I?" Elaina whirled on her hostess with fire in her eyes and her voice dripping with sarcasm. "How can I be sure? It was at your home, after all, that someone tried to maim me. You, yourself attended the funeral of my parents in Newcastle and were present when we received the first note. What am I to think?"

"I had nothing to do with it." Caroline stood, taking a step toward Elaina.

Elaina took a step back.

"My hand to God, Lady Elaina. How could I have killed your coachman when I was standing in the parlor with you." Elaina's expression must have told what utter nonsense she thought that whole statement was, for Caroline quickly added, "Nor do I have knowledge of who it was."

The door to the room thumped open, and the two women's eyes swiveled toward it as a handful of servants led by Caitir bustled into the room. The servants acknowledged the two ladies and busily set about readying the things they had brought in. Caitir seemed to be the only one who noticed the tension weighing heavy in the air.

"Well, I will leave you to it." Caroline nodded to Elaina and Caitir. "Get your rest, and I will see you tonight at the ball?" she asked as if she thought Elaina might pack up her things and run for the hills.

Elaina was going nowhere. She would stand her ground, but she would also watch her back.

"If there is anything you need…"

Elaina and Caitir both nodded to her before she closed the door behind her.

"What on earth was that about?" Caitir said after the Taylors' servants vacated the room.

Elaina sat down on the chair and let Caitir begin to clean the gunpowder from her wounds. "She claims Mr. Everson had nothing to do with this."

"Humph."

"William told her about the second note and the necklace." Elaina winced at one particularly sensitive spot.

Caitir paused from her efforts, the wet rag in her hand. "Why on earth would he do such a thing?" She glanced back toward the closed door.

"Who knows. I wonder if he told her before we arrived or after the incident? Wait until I see him."

"I dinna want to be present for that one."

With her war wounds tended and having freshly washed, exhaustion overtook Elaina and she collapsed into the bed grateful to Caroline for the gift of privacy. Caitir insisted she rest before the evening's festivities. She didn't think she would be able to sleep but did drift off into a dreamless slumber, waking sometime later to the clanking of china. She sleepily raised her head without opening her eyes.

"Do I smell tea and shortbread?" she mumbled through her veil of wild hair.

"Aye, ye do. Time to be wakin'." Caitir threw open the drapes, bathing the room in the soft golden glow of sunset.

"How long have I been asleep?" Elaina wrapped the blanket around herself as she sat down at the small table next to the hearth. She inhaled the scent of her tea, letting the pungent aroma awaken her senses.

"Long enough. I hated to wake ye, but if ye want to be ready for a fine night of dinin' and dancin', we need to get on with it. We have our work cut out for us." Caitir eyed her critically.

"I have every faith in your abilities," Elaina laughed.

"I'm glad you do," Caitir said, sounding not so sure of herself.

Elaina stood in the small foyer to the winding spiral staircase as William came strolling up. "You look magnificent." He took her hand, taking a step back to admire her properly.

"You are rather dashing yourself," she said, forgetting for a moment about her hard feelings. She picked a piece of lint from his officer's uniform. Every aspect of his dress was perfection—as well it better be with the Duke of Cumberland in attendance.

"I brought you something, a peace offering of sorts, from Caroline."

"You and Caroline have quite the secret relationship going, do you not?" Elaina raised a brow at him.

"It's no secret."

"Oh. So you admit there is a relationship. Who is it not a secret from because it is a damn surprise to me?"

"Language, Elaina, and can we not fight about this here?" William lowered his voice as several other couples approached them, each waiting their turn for introductions. "Do you want the gift or not?"

"Fine. Let us have it then, but when we get home..."

"I have been dutifully warned. Turn around," William instructed.

Elaina obliged, and William slid a circle of sapphires around her neck. Each sapphire was encircled with a small ridge of diamonds.

"Oh," Elaina breathed. "It is beautiful."

"Matches your gown perfectly," William beamed.

Elaina turned to the gilded edged mirror hanging in the hallway to admire the necklace better. The numerous cabochon-shaped Burmese sapphires stood stark against her pale neck, drawing one's eye to her bosom crushed tight under the velvet bodice of her gown. Unlike Caitir's binding on their adventurous outing, her breasts were not being squashed flat—they were being crushed up and out on full display. Not for the first time, she wished she had brought the peridot gown with the higher neckline and the full sleeves, but Caitir had insisted on this little off the shoulder number. Elaina felt like the 'ladies' were on full display with a sapphire sign screaming "look at me!" She smoothed the crushed velvet bodice of her gown, noticing the stones did almost match the color to perfection. Her eyes rose to her face and her neck, and she pulled a few ringlets of hair over her shoulder, trying to disguise some of the red marks adorning her skin.

"Do not be embarrassed, sister. Wear your wounds with pride." His finger lightly touched one of the small blisters. "You are a legend here tonight."

"Nonsense. A legend because someone tried to maim me?" Elaina blushed, turning from the mirror. "I cannot believe Caroline would entrust me to something so exquisite and expensive." Her hand lay on the stones as if to protect the necklace from harm.

"A legend because of your shooting prowess and your refusal to quit under duress, and it is not a loan, Elaina. It is a gift."

"Is she out of her mind?" Elaina's voice was louder than she intended, and she tried to ignore the eyes that had shifted in their direction.

William grabbed her hands as she reached to remove the necklace. "She feels wretched about what happened and that it happened at her home. Before she came to talk to you, she had a peek at your dress and sent a person to her store in Edinburgh to fetch back a peace offering."

"This is unacceptable." Elaina tried to free her hands from her brother's grasp.

"It is rude not to accept. Besides, you would do me a favor by keeping it."

"How do you know she is not the enemy, William? We do not know her or her family."

"There is not a mean bone in her body," William said, holding firm to his sister's hands.

"How do you know? Have you examined all of her bones?" Elaina replied, resulting in a massive sigh from her brother. "Are you in love with her? William, look at me," Elaina demanded, drawing her brother's wandering eyes back to her own.

"Love is a strong term, Elaina. I am fond of her, yes."

"I hope you…*we* do not regret this," Elaina mumbled as an attendant motioned them to the top of the staircase to await their announcement.

Chapter Sixteen

"LIEUTENANT WILLIAM EDWARD TALBOT SPENCER the 3rd Earl of Strafford and his sister Lady Elaina Beatrice Spencer." The booming voice echoed off the ceiling of the room as William and Elaina made their way down the winding staircase to boisterous applause.

Elaina's eyes roved over the sea of faces filling the grand foyer at the base of the staircase. Her stomach began to churn, and she tried desperately to keep her satin skirts from tripping her down the stairs with one hand while holding her brother's arm for support with the other.

"Smile," William hissed out of the corner of his mouth.

Elaina dutifully pasted what she hoped looked like a cheery smile upon her face. She nodded as they made their way down the line of dignitaries, trying to commit to memory all of their names and faces.

"Your Grace." She curtsied deeply in front of the Duke of Cumberland, and William saluted smartly.

"My dear. Let me look at you." He reached out a hand, lifting her chin. "A tad bit worse for the wear, but divine nonetheless," the Duke offered. "You would put any number of my men to shame with your skill and bravery, my dear."

"Thank you, Your Grace. I am not sure I would call it bravery. More to the effect of stubborn pride, I am afraid."

"Stubborn pride is what makes a king a king and keeps him on the throne. Do not underestimate yourself." The Duke turned his attention to William. "Lieutenant Spencer, incredible shooting demonstration this afternoon. I must have a word with you after this"—the Duke waved his hand in the direction of guests still making their way down the staircase—"after this ghastly part of the night has ended."

"Absolutely, Your Grace." William beamed proudly.

The siblings scooted out of the way of the next in line, adding themselves to the ocean of people. Elaina applauded absently at the remaining introductions while she studied the Duke of Cumberland. She was not as impressed with him as William was, but neither was she a member of the military. He was an imposing figure, however, and his little comment about keeping a king on the throne made her stomach knot.

As the introductions ended, they were ushered into a ballroom that glowed with the flames of hundreds of candles glistening off the crystal of numerous chandeliers. An entire wall of the ballroom held at least ten sets of French doors that were thrown open, revealing balconies looking out over Lord Taylor's massive gardens. At the far end of the room on a large rising, the musicians warmed up their instruments before launching into a lively quadrille. Elaina found herself surrounded by a throng of admirers. The men lavished her with praise over her firing abilities and her courage to continue the contest. The women each feigned a swoon at the sight of her wounds, declaring they could never be as strong and brave as she. Elaina found it difficult to keep from rolling her eyes at the whole group. She gladly accepted a drink from a nervous young man who she took to be of about the same age. She drained the glass swiftly, ignoring his startled look, and practically dragged him to the ballroom floor.

The white marble floor, polished to a high shine, made dancing effortless. Nabbing the young man held a second purpose besides escaping that nonsense—it was also the easiest way to see all who were in attendance. Everyone of importance in Edinburgh or Scotland, in general, must be at the party. It was strange to see British military mingling with men dressed in kilts. There were not as many kilts as there were redcoats, but there was a fair sprinkling. She caught a glimpse of a dark head rising shoulders above most as she twirled her way around the dance floor.

Casting an absent smile and nod at her partner, who nervously rambled on about the art of dressing fowl after the kill, Elaina pretended to be interested. She had dressed many a bird after killing one, so it was not the subject that bothered her but rather his spitting and sputtering over his words. Relieved at the ending of the song, she thanked him and made her escape, heading to the nearest waiter carrying drinks.

She was intercepted by a large sweaty man who looked to be her father's age. Without a way of declining his offer for the next dance, she reluctantly took his hand and let him twirl her around the floor. Trying to dodge his massive feet before he stepped on them yet again and trying to ignore the fact that his eyes were trained downward into her cleavage, she told herself she was not searching for Calum although she caught herself looking for his dark curly locks more than once. With the second dance ended, Elaina did manage to find a drink and a tea cake. What she failed to find, however, was a quiet corner in which to collect herself.

She took in the room while half listening to the ramblings and posturing of those vying for her attention. She spied William deep in conversation with Cumberland and another severe-looking gentleman of high rank. William looked quite stern with his hands clasped behind his back, nodding in agreement to whatever the gentleman said. She spotted Caroline across the room with a small group of ladies. She would have to thank her for the too expensive gift at some point. To the left stood another gaggle of girls with none other than one Calum MacKinnon at the center who startled her by standing in full Highland dress. Of course he was a Highlander. How could she be so ignorant? He could speak and read Gaelic, but Caitir made no mention of it, and why would he be in the Lowlands? *You fool.* Her thoughts had rambled on until she finally took hold of herself. *There are a lot of men here in kilts and how the hell would you know a Highlander from a Lowlander in a country you are a stranger to? And have you ever bothered to ask either one of them where they are from?*

She watched him conversing with the ladies and was surprised to feel the twinge of jealousy that rose up in her wame. She tried to shake it off, turning her attention partly to the tall blonde gentleman who now held the floor of conversation around her. She found herself laughing a little too hard at his joke as she watched Calum turn his dazzling smile to one of the women. He extended his hand in an invitation to dance, and the jealousy grew.

Who was she to be jealous? Calum had shown her no form of affection other than lending a helping hand with her search for Monroe and loaning her his gun and forfeiting his round this morning...and carrying a bag of damn ducks. Okay, *and* standing over her with a look of utter concern on his handsome face after the misfire. But, still. She had no claim on him. She didn't even like the man. That is the lie she fed herself, anyway, and in enormous portions.

Elaina grew angry with herself. Downing her glass of wine, she accepted the tall blonde's offer to dance. The gentleman—Elbert, she thought was his name—was a lovely dancer. They reeled and twirled around the floor until the next song turned into a beautiful Quadrille and she found herself face to face with Calum. She prayed to God that he would think the warmth she felt rising in her face was because of the previous dance. Good heavens, he took her breath.

He bowed, and she took his hands, not making eye contact.

"Ye look radiant this evening," he said as they made their way in a circle.

"Thank you," she replied with a hint of aggravation in her voice.

"Did I do something to upset ye?" he asked.

The switching of partners saved her from having to answer. Why *was* she annoyed with him? Then she caught sight of the pretty dark-haired girl in the bright purple satin dress giving Calum her best eye-batting smile and watched him return in kind with his leg numbing grin, and it made her want to stomp his foot the next time he came near. Her feelings had her so disconcerted that when the song ended, she grabbed the nearest glass of whiskey and headed through a pair of doors out to a veranda to collect herself.

Harry Everson leaned his arrogant arse against the railing, and Elaina did an immediate about-face.

"Lady Elaina, a word if I may." His pleading stopped her in her tracks. She stood, trying to decide if she should oblige or not.

"Please." His voice held a desperate tone.

Sighing, she turned to face him.

Harry stared at her with his owl-like expression. He opened his mouth to speak, but then closed it again.

Elaina walked to his side and leaned against the railing. "Well, speak," she barked at him, making him jump.

"I swear upon my honor and my grandmother's grave, I had nothing to do with what happened earlier in the day." The words rushed out of him, tumbling one over the other in a cascading mess and making him sound like a small boy.

Elaina stared into his large, unblinking eyes and sighed again. She looked out over the dimly lit grounds. Lanterns hung from large hooks on poles here and there, and couples walked arm in arm through the swirling aisles of hedges.

"Well, I suppose I can try to believe you. Swearing on your grandmother's grave and all." She gave him a sideways glance.

Relief flooded his face. "I would also like to apologize for my behavior this morning. If I was rude in any way—"

"Well, of course you were rude, or you would not be apologizing," Elaina scoffed.

Harry laughed. An odd sound, coming from the annoying young man. "You are the bluntest woman I have ever spoken to. It is rather amusing."

"Amusing? I find it rather annoying that I am forced to be so." Elaina glared at him.

"I do beg your pardon," Harry stuttered, choking on his laugh.

"Did your uncle tell you to apologize?"

"Lord Taylor? Um, no, although I did receive quite the lecture. No, it was Lady Caroline. She was rather insistent."

"Hmph," Elaina grunted. "Apology accepted. Now if you will excuse me—" Elaina turned to go and ran into Calum making his way onto the veranda.

The look between Calum and Harry was one of mutual distaste.

"Is Mr. Everson bothering you, my lady?" Calum stared Harry down, an easy feat for a man looming at least four inches over the other.

"No. He is apologizing for his rude behavior this morning and swearing an oath he had nothing to do with the accident."

"Was he now." Calum's tone of voice spoke volumes about his thoughts on the matter.

"Indeed." Harry stood up straighter even though he still only came to Calum's chin. He looked the Scot up and down, scowling at his Highland attire. "Returning to your roots where you belong, Mr. MacKinnon?"

"Nay," Calum took a step toward Everson, causing him to back into the railing. "I never left my roots. I've just been slummin' around in the gutters with the British for a time."

It was the first derogatory word about the British that Elaina had heard come from Calum, and it puzzled her. It caused her to think she honestly had no idea who this man was or what he was about. It was possible he had a history with Everson though, and not a nice one.

"I think I'll grab another drink." Harry sidestepped Calum. "Lady Elaina, a pleasure. Take caution with whom you socialize. Enemies can be anywhere." He stalked back into the ballroom, leaving Elaina staring speechlessly after him.

"Daft bastard," Calum muttered under his breath.

Elaina turned on Calum. "What the bloody hell was that all about?"

"I never ken if ye are going to sound like a Brit or like a Scot when ye open yer mouth," Calum laughed.

"Answer the question. What is going on between the two of you? I thought all this time his angst with me was over my comments about shipping at the Taylors' dinner. Now I suspect the two of you have some issues of your own." Elaina crossed her arms, waiting.

"It goes back a few years to school. My da sent me to Edinburgh for formal education. He felt I couldna stay out of trouble while at home. My older brother Aaron and I bumped heads a bit, ye ken? My da thought we might kill each other one day. So, me being the youngest, I was sent to my da's uncle, who has since passed. He kept me through my schooling and taught me the exporting business along the way."

"Interesting," Elaina said with sarcasm. Although it was interesting to learn something about this mystery standing before her, it still didn't answer her question. "What happened?"

"There was a fight. I bloodied his nose."

Elaina shoved a fist on her hip and arched a brow at him. "That's it?" she said incredulously.

"Nay, I may or may not have broken his leg." Calum grimaced at his last remark.

"Broken his leg? What in the world, Calum?"

"He wadna let it go. Claimed I had kissed Jeanette MacCreary behind the shed. He was soft on her. He tried to hit me, but I already stood a good head taller than him. He missed, but he wadna quit. Then the others were laughing at him and made things worse. He kept at me, so I punched him in the nose a wee bit harder than I intended." Calum used his thumb and index finger to express how much harder he had hit the lad than he'd intended.

"And where does the broken leg come into play?"

"A couple of years later. Wee Everson can carry a bit of a grudge, ya ken?"

"Aye, I ken."

Calum laughed at Elaina's Scottish answer. "'Twas over the sale of a horse. Everson is like a little Banti rooster when he gets going. Jumping all around, fists waving. It is a sight to behold." Calum chuckled, shaking his head. "I kicked his legs out from under him—"

"Let me guess," Elaina said. "A wee bit harder than ye meant to," she mocked with a grin.

"Nay, I meant to break his leg, the damned fool. He was speaking his rubbish about worthless Scots and them needing to be taught a lesson. He said my mother was a whore. He had that one coming. It also started a wee stramash between a group of Brits and a group of Scots."

Elaina eyed Calum for a moment. "What do you do for a living, Mr. MacKinnon? If I may be so bold."

"Aye, ye may. I ship whiskey. To France, Italy, the New World."

"Is that all?

"Is that all, she asks? My family has a still in the Highlands. We make the best whiskey in all of Scotland." He turned his attention toward the door. "There may be other matters, but those are better left for another time, my lady." Calum nodded to several figures making their way onto the veranda.

Elaina wondered what else the man could be involved with and just how secretive it was.

Chapter Seventeen

"WHAT ABOUT THE GIRL," ELAINA asked as the pair walked back into the ballroom. "What was her name? Jeanette?"

"Aye, she is here. Just there." Calum's head bobbed in the direction of the pretty dark-haired girl in the purple satin.

Elaina stood stunned for a moment, not quite knowing what to say. "Hmm...pretty girl," she finally managed to get out. "There is William. I must speak with him. If you will excuse me, Mr. MacKinnon." She didn't wait for a reply, needing to remove herself from the situation for some unknown reason.

She sidled up to her brother, slipping her arm through the crook of his. "Well, hello, brother. You have been a busy man this evening. Did His Grace have anything of interest to say?"

"He did." William waved down a glass of whiskey for his sister. "There have been rumors of Jacobites gathering funds for Prince Charles himself."

Elaina choked on her drink.

"Are you all right?" William pulled his handkerchief out and handed it to her, then patted her on the back as she struggled to regain her breath.

"Good," she croaked, wiping at the tears running from her eyes. "Swallowed wrong. You were saying?"

"His Grace wants to put a special unit together, and he wants me to head it. He was impressed with my shooting skills this morning, and my captain gave me rave reviews."

Ah, his captain had been the severe-looking gentleman also embroiled in the conversation. Elaina wondered what precisely the Duke told William, and what the Duke knew. There had to be many sources of funds going here and there. Who was to say their discussion included her mother's acts? Now Elaina felt awkward and exposed. She tried to shake off the feeling that at any moment British soldiers would come running in and arrest her on the spot.

"So, what does he want you to do?" she asked, careful of her tone.

"I'm not sure just yet. His Grace doesn't think much will come of it, but they may send me to either Fort Augustus or Fort William. There is more intelligence to be gathered first. We will see what becomes of it…possibly nothing. It is not even certain if the rumors are true."

"Sounds like a fine mess," Elaina said, sipping her whiskey more carefully.

"That it does. It looks like you have a gentleman caller," William whispered out of the corner of his mouth.

Elaina glanced up and nearly choked again as Harry Everson made his way across the room with a determined look in his eye.

"My lady." Harry bowed low before her. "Would you care to dance."

Elaina was tempted to decline the offer when she caught Harry's furtive sideways glance and followed his eyes to find Calum and Jeanette hand in hand, making their way around the dance floor. "I would be honored," she said instead.

William's jaw dropped as she handed him her glass.

"Close your mouth, William. You are going to catch flies." She strode off with Harry, her chin held high.

The room was like an oven with all the candles burning and bodies whirling, not to mention the amount of alcohol she had consumed. Elaina refused to blame any of the heat on her jealousy. She and Everson danced silently for a bit, neither one being able to think of anything to say, but the pair kept glancing at the other couple who seemed to have plenty to say to each other.

"Mr. Everson, you are such a card," Elaina laughed as they passed Calum and Jeanette.

Calum did a double take, and Elaina gave Harry her most dazzling smile.

Harry caught on after a moment and laughed as well before they moved away from the bothersome couple.

"I truly do feel terrible about your poor face. Does it hurt much?" Harry eyed her injuries.

"Not too much," Elaina replied, trying not to look at Calum or his partner. She instead studied Harry. He was not a bad-looking young man. But his face held no remarkable features either. He had the kind of face you saw and forgot. His eyes traveled over her shoulder, and she knew by the change in his expression what, or rather who, he'd spotted. "So," she said, trying to distract him. "What is your grudge with Mr. MacKinnon?"

Startled, he turned his eyes back to her. "Well…he's a Highlander for one. He doesn't belong down here."

"That is rude," Elaina scolded.

"They are like animals! They are savage people with no respect for authority."

"Mr. MacKinnon seems to hide his savagery well, as are the other Highlanders present. No pillaging or plundering that I can tell."

"You wouldn't understand. You are not from here."

Elaina rolled her eyes. "I'm not a silly little girl with no knowledge of how the world works, Mr. Everson. I do know bigotry when I see it." She raised a brow at him as she subdued the urge to either stomp on his foot or blacken his eye.

"It's not bigotry, my lady. It is the laws of the country that are at stake, and Highlanders are hell-bent on changing the head of them." Harry stared into her eyes. There was a fury there that burned fiercely.

"That is your only beef with Mr. MacKinnon?" She steered the conversation away from politics before things got genuinely heated.

"No." Everson's jaw hardened as he glanced over her shoulder. "He is dancing with her to get to me. He knows I love her. I always have."

The sorrow in his voice almost made Elaina pity him. "Have you ever expressed your feelings to Miss Jeanette?" She had caught sight of the infamous woman looking their way when they made their last turn.

"No. She wouldn't want me. Why would she when she has Calum wrapped around her finger."

"Do you not think maybe she is using Calum to make you jealous?"

"What? No. I do not think so." The song ended, and Elaina looped her arm through Harry's and led him off into a quiet corner to talk. "Women have strange ways of doing things, Mr. Everson. I caught her looking at you a few times during the last song."

"What does that mean? It means nothing. They could have relived old times. Talked about the time the bastard broke my leg."

"He said you had it coming." Elaina honestly didn't know why she even tried to talk sense into this man—into this boy, for that's precisely how he acted.

"I'll kill him!" Harry started to take off, though Calum was nowhere in sight.

"Listen to me." Elaina latched onto him, nearly jerking him off his feet. She grabbed his chin, forcing him to look at her. "You have some growing up to do, Mr. Everson."

"Let go of me, madam." Harry tried to jerk his arm away.

Elaina held tight. "No. You will stand here, and you will listen. How long ago was it that Mr. MacKinnon broke your leg?"

"Four years ago."

"Four years. You have kept this nonsense bottled up inside you for four years? You have not expressed your feelings for Miss Jeanette-whatever-her-name-is. How can you be angry about something you haven't even attempted? And why take your anger out on innocent people. I assume your attitude toward me this morning was because I stood with Mr. MacKinnon. Am I correct?"

"Well, maybe. Partly. Your words at the dinner party still stung, also" Harry looked away from Elaina's piercing stare.

"Look at me," she said. "You have to let things go. Everything that happened today could have been avoided. You could have had a nice, peaceful day instead of being angry the entire time and then being suspected of sabotage. I could have had a nice, peaceful day... Well, except for this." She waved a hand at her face. "Get over it. If you are not willing to stand up like a man and declare your feelings for her, then you have no grounds to be angry when she dances with another man." Elaina felt the irony in her little speech but shoved it down.

"I suppose you're right," Everson conceded.

"I suppose I am."

"Has anyone ever told you that you are brilliant as well as beautiful and strong-willed?" He smiled at her.

"Oh, all the time." She waved a flippant hand.

"Thank you, Lady Elaina, for not holding my ill-manners against me and for your advice. Now, if you will?" He glanced down at her hand still grasping his arm.

"Oh, of course." Elaina smoothed the arm of his jacket where she had held it in a death grip.

Everson took her hand and brushed it lightly with his lips. "My lady, I am off on a mission."

Elaina laughed, watching him cross the dance floor while searching the crowd. She sincerely hoped for her sake and Calum's that everything she had said to him held true.

She grabbed her cloak and escaped out of the side doors and down into the garden area. She didn't want to be present if things headed south between Harry and Calum, and she was overheated from drink and dance. She stopped at the beginning of the twisting maze of shrubbery and closed her eyes for several seconds, letting the crisp fall air caress her skin. Sighing, she opened her eyes and looked around. She could see the heads of a few couples here and there above the well-manicured shrubbery. Sipping her glass of whiskey, she strolled through Lord Taylor's well-kept gardens, her cloak draped over her arm. Making her way farther along the path, she encountered a few souls strolling their way back toward the festivities. Elaina found a stone bench nestled in amongst the shrubbery and sank on it, grateful for its seclusion. She needed a quiet moment to herself. Her blasted shoes were killing her feet after all the dancing, so she took them off. Groaning, she massaged the aching sole of her foot with her thumb, closing her eyes.

"That bad is it?"

The sound of his voice nearly startled her into dropping her glass.

"For God's sake, Calum!"

Calum chuckled and plopped down next to Elaina on the bench, stretching his long legs out in front of him. He leaned his head back and groaned as he closed his eyes.

"That bad is it?" Elaina laughed.

"Aye. It is. I'm just glad Harry Everson came to his blasted senses before that gowk of a woman drove me insane."

"Gowk?" Elaina asked.

"Nitwit," Calum replied.

"So, I was right? Jeanette what's-her-name was trying to make him jealous?" Elaina didn't know why she felt so enormously relieved at the revelation.

"Aye. It was you who talked him into his senses? And here I thought ye truly enjoyed the company of Mr. Everson. Thought ye had a change of heart the way ye laughed at his every word. 'Mr. Everson, you are such a card,'" Calum mocked.

She smacked him on the arm. "You are insufferable."

"Aye, I know," Calum chuckled.

Elaina returned to massaging her foot, and the pair sat in silence for several minutes, enjoying the peace of the secluded little bench. She switched feet, and a small groan escaped her throat.

Calum turned his gaze toward her, his head still resting on his arms on the back of the bench.

She tried not to notice his eyes on her. Closing her own, she took a sip from her glass so she wouldn't have to look at him.

"When I said ye look radiant this evening, I meant it," he murmured in a low voice.

"Thank you," Elaina replied. She knew the color was rising in her face but was powerless to stop it.

Draining her glass and wishing she had another, she squirmed uncomfortably under his scrutiny. She didn't know why his close proximity unnerved her so. He turned his face back to the night sky, and she ventured a look at him. His ankles were crossed and sticking halfway out in the path. Following the line of him, her eyes came to rest on the part of his legs that extended up from his long black boots. How could a knee cause her heart to skip a beat? She didn't know, but it did. Maybe it was not his knees but the thick muscular thighs they were attached to. She dragged her eyes away from the small showing of his leg, feeling almost obscene in her scrutiny. His eyes were closed, and she noticed for the first time how long his eyelashes were, nearly resting on his cheeks. There was a shadow of a beard already coming in from his morning shave. A slow smile began to stretch his mouth, and she knew he knew she was looking at him. She rolled her eyes and went back to rubbing her foot.

"If we were mairiet, I would do that for ye." He stretched his arms up above his head.

"If we were married, I would expect it," Elaina retorted.

"Would ye now?" Calum turned his dimpled grin on her. "One of those, are ye? Demanding and needy?"

"It would be the least you could do for me if I had to put up with all your wise-cracks."

"Aye. If a little foot rub is all it would take for ye to forgive me my wrongs, that's nay so bad."

Elaina squirmed, uncomfortable with the conversation. She bent over and slid her feet back in her shoes. "So," she said. "You and Jeanette what's-her-name—"

"MacCreary. Mistress MacCreary."

"Mistress MacCreary." Elaina could not hide her annoyance at his correction. "You and *Mistress MacCreary* were only trying to make Mr. Everson jealous?"

"Aye. She is a nice enough lassie, but a little too high-strung and—how should I say—simple for my nature."

"Oh. Good," Elaina said, then mentally grimaced at herself.

"Ye're relieved then?" Calum sat up. "Jealous too, were ye?"

God, why did she have to open her mouth? "No." She stood up, trying to wrap her cloak around her and hold her empty glass at the same time.

"Here. The servants will find it." Calum sat her empty glass on the bench and took her cloak from her. His fingers grazed her shoulders as he draped the garment about them, sending a line of fire in their wake.

"Thank you," she said, not looking up at him.

"Aye."

Elaina started walking but not back toward the house. She wanted to get deeper into the garden and farther from earshot of nosy bystanders before she broached the next subject.

Hawkmoths danced among the night flowers, diving and twisting in a nocturnal ballet, while their smaller cousins committed suicide in the large lanterns along the path. The pair walked in silence for a time, both lost in their ruminations and enjoying the chilly night air.

Finally, Elaina cleared her throat.

"What is it, hen?" Calum asked, picking a long white drooping flower, twirling it between his thumb and forefinger and releasing an intense smell, almost like vanilla.

Elaina wondered for a moment if he had said then or hen? It didn't matter, except that hen was a term of affection. *Oh damn, get out of your head,* Elaina chastised herself. "Well, about the misfire this afternoon. I believe it to have been intentional sabotage." Elaina detected the slightest tensing in Calum's fingers.

"And why would that be?"

"We have received two threatening letters since the deaths of my parents—one pinned to the chest of our dead groomsman with my father's knife. The second was sent to me personally. I received it the day after our...um...first meeting, should I say?"

"Oh, aye?" Calum grinned as if remembering the fateful evening. Then she detected the realization come over him as he crushed the delicate flower between his large fingers and tossed it onto the path. "Threatening how?" he asked quietly.

"Well, the first read 'The price of dishonor.' The second came addressed to me in a box with my father's pocket watch, and 'Tick tock little mouse' was written upon it in the same hand as the first."

"Tick tock little mouse?" Calum asked.

"I don't know what any of it means unless it is to do with the money Mama redirected, as it were. There was another incident, as well."

"Aye?"

"The day William left on his trip to Newcastle, a beautifully wrapped box appeared upon my pillow in my chamber. I thought it a possible peace offering for him leaving without telling me."

"And it was not?"

"No. It contained my mother's necklace, the locket that held the key to the chest. He had not seen it since my parents' deaths, and my mother always wore it. We now know why."

Calum stood silent for several seconds. "And now someone has purposefully tampered with your firearm?"

"Yes. I cleaned the gun before our break. A servant took it to the stables with the other guns. There was a pebble shoved down into the barrel."

"Do ye have any suspicions of the culprit?"

"No. I thought it Harry at first. Now I have no idea, and it could be any number of persons. William has spoken to Lady Caroline on the subject. He told her about the notes, even though she was in Newcastle at our home the day of the service and was present the day the groomsman was killed, and it is in her home that I stand here with burns on my face and hands."

Calum stopped in the middle of the path and turned to face Elaina. He took her chin in his warm fingertips and turned her cheek toward the lantern, examining the spots on her face as if it were the first time he had seen them. His gaze traveled slowly across her mouth and up to her eyes. They stood as if in a trance, their eyes searching one another's. Calum cleared his throat and dropped his hand. Elaina's fingers found the button holding her cloak about her neck and unhooked it. Calum's eyes never left hers, yet his expression shifted as she slid the wrap from her shoulders, the cold night air causing gooseflesh to rise on her bare skin.

"Lady Caroline gave me this necklace as a peace offering," she whispered.

His gaze came to rest on the ring of sapphires circling her throat. "That is an expensive peace offering." His voice was thick as his eyes traveled from the necklace to the spattering of dots along her neck, over the prickled skin of her shoulders, and back up to her eyes. He took her by the arm, the swiftness and strength of his movement startling her. Yanking her to him, he whispered, "How do ye ken it wasna me?"

"What?" Elaina stared up at him.

He blinked several times before asking it again, not near as deep and thick as the last but still as menacing. "How do ye ken it wasna me who sabotaged yer gun, my lady?"

Elaina stood stunned for a moment. "Well, was it?"

His hard glare softened, and the side of his mouth turned up into his impish grin. "No, but how can you be certain?"

"Well, I don't suppose I can. I have chosen to trust you because of Caitir, I suppose."

"Ye must trust no one."

"Even you?"

"No one. In fact, if this is the case, why in the hell are ye out here in a dark garden by yerself?"

"I'm not." Elaina threw her cloak back over her shoulders and buttoned it angrily.

"Aye, ye were. Do ye no ken how dangerous it could be? Ye could have disappeared right under our noses, and no one would have been the wiser for hours." His voice had risen through his little tirade, but now he dropped it back down to a discreet hiss as a couple wandered by, eyeing the pair suspiciously. "Ye need someone with ye at all times, my lady. No more wandering around alone."

Elaina glared up at him. "I can take care of myself."

"Ye keep sayin' that and things keep happenin', so I'm beginning to think ye cannae."

Elaina turned on her heel and stalked back toward the party.

"Where are ye goin'?"

She walked in silence.

"Where are ye goin'?" he repeated firmly.

"Inside. You said yourself not to trust anyone, even you."

Calum fell in step beside her.

"Go away." She kept up her quick pace even though she took two or three steps to his one.

He loped easily alongside her, making her angrier. "I willnae. I will see ye safely indoors and then if ye want me to go, I will."

"I can't trust you. You said so yourself."

"That's no what I said." Calum glanced down at her sideways.

"You said to trust no one. How do I know you will not drag me off into the bushes and have your way with me?"

Calum grabbed her arm, whipping her around to face him. "I could have. Several times, Lady Elaina." His dark eyes traveled over her, making their way from her hair to her eyes.

They burned a trail to her mouth where they lingered, and Elaina suddenly had the intense desire to stand on her tiptoes and… They moved down her cloaked body as if they could see every inch of what lay beneath, and she felt heady and unsteady on her feet, making her furious, not only with Calum but with herself. She tried to wrench her arm from his hand.

He held strong. "Go ahead. Pull yourself away from my grasp," he whispered.

She tried. Desperate. When she couldn't wrench free, she stomped on his foot. He still held her tight. She went to slap his face, and he caught her other arm and held it firm.

"You brute," she hissed at him. "Let me go."

"Fight me. Get away from me."

"That's what you would like. Me struggling in your arms. Is that how you get your satisfaction, Mr. MacKinnon? Making women beg for mercy?"

The strength of his grip increased, and she tried to hide the fact that it hurt. If she could get her hand to her *sgian-dubh*, she would cut his throat, but she couldn't, and the realization of his little game sank in. She stopped struggling and stood placidly staring up at him with an eyebrow raised.

"I will not give you the satisfaction." Her voice dripped with disdain.

"Nay. Ye willnae, because ye are a lady and I a gentleman, but if ye did"—he leaned close, his breath warm on her ear—"ye would beg for mercy."

"Why you insufferable, arrogant, son-of-a—"

"Hey. Ye're a lady, remember?" Calum grinned at her.

A couple rounded a curve in the path. "Are ye all right, my lady?" the woman asked.

Elaina recognized her as the dour-faced girl who had stood over her at the shooting match that morning.

Calum dropped his hands to his sides, taking a step back.

"Why, yes," Elaina said glaring at Calum. "Mr. MacKinnon and I were just headed back to the party." She could have made it hard on Calum, but she was ready to get back inside and out of his presence.

"Shall we join you?" the girl asked.

The couple passed a look between themselves, and at Calum, speaking volumes about how much they truly believed her.

"Absolutely." Elaina turned her back on Calum.

The girl slid her elbow through Elaina's and the young man she was with stepped between Elaina and Calum. They strolled back to the ball, making small talk about the cooling weather and the hunt that morning. When they entered the brightly lit ballroom, Elaina turned to look behind her, but Calum was gone.

Elaina laid in bed the next morning, staring at the ceiling. She had been awake for most of the night thinking about Calum and his words. Rabbie had made his thoughts clear that he did not trust Mr. MacKinnon, and she wondered if he was right. But, he'd had ample opportunity to hurt her, and he hadn't. Well, she could still feel the stranglehold grip he'd held on her arms the night before, but never once had she felt in actual danger. He had rattled her in other ways, however, and she mentally berated herself for them. Never in all her one and twenty years had a man ever spoken to her that way, nor had a man ever garnered such a visceral reaction from her. She could not drive the thought of him from her mind and that, in itself, drove her insane.

She could tell by the color of the room that the sun had just begun to make its way over the horizon. Sitting up on the edge of the bed, she shivered at the coolness of the room and hurried to the smoored fire, stirring it, sending dark smoke alight with sparks rushing up the chimney. Tossing a few logs onto the now red-hot embers, she drew her robe over her dressing gown and belted it about her, then rubbed her arms to generate warmth. She wandered to the window and looked down at the gardens and toward the stables. What she saw nearly stopped her heart. A stallion reared on its hind legs, trying to escape the brutal crack of the whip of a stable hand. Even from her perch on the second floor, she could make out the whites of the beast's eyes as it kicked and pawed in fury.

Without hesitation, Elaina flew from her room and down the stairs. She bolted down a hallway and threw open the door. A blasted pantry. How do you get out of this god-forsaken place? She turned, running in the other direction and into a servant.

"The stables," she panted. "How do I get to the stables?"

The confused servant pointed the way, and Elaina fled toward the door the man showed her.

"Stop it at once! You bloody bastard! Give me that!" Elaina ran at the startled stable hand who stared gape-mouthed at her. Ripping the whip from his hand, she threw it to the ground. "Get back!" she barked at him.

She turned her attention to the stallion, keeping her arms at her sides but turning her palms out. She didn't dare approach. His eyes were still wild with fear as he stomped and pawed the ground. Elaina whispered to the beautiful roan steed. He eyed her frightfully. She heard a man's voice behind her and snapped her fingers and pointed at him without turning around, non-verbally telling him to hold his ground and his tongue.

"Do not be afraid," Elaina whispered in French as she edged slightly nearer. "All is well, my beautiful friend. No one will hurt you."

His animations wore down. Shaking his head and snorting, his heavy pawing of the ground eased.

She got within range of reaching his bridle and took it gently in one hand, placing her other firmly upon his neck. "That's it, my friend. All is well." She stood whispering until the stallion's eyes and trembling flesh returned to normal. Without raising her voice or turning from the horse, she asked, "What set him off? And you better speak softly."

"I mounted him and brought him out for His Grace. The horse went crazy and threw me."

"So you chose to beat him instead of checking him over?" Elaina said, then whispered to the horse in French, "Stupid man." In English she said, "Slowly, let us get the saddle and the pad off. Something is not right. I am to assume the Duke of Cumberland's horse would be a well-trained horse unless he is of the mind to ride them green and have to battle for control?"

"No, madam. They are well trained," a second voice said.

"Very well. Lad, approach slowly. If ye spook him, I will let him stomp you to death."

"Aye, mistress." The young lad of about seventeen or so sidled his way up next to her and uncinched the saddle, gently removing it and the blanket underneath.

"Now then," Elaina rubbed the massive horse's jaw and whispered sweet nothings to him. "What do we find?"

"Burrs, madam. Several."

"Who is responsible for the preparations of the Duke's steed?"

"I am, madam. I swear to you they were not there. I checked before I saddled him. I swear to it." The lad sounded truly afraid.

"Did you leave the horse at any time after?"

"Aye," the lad whispered. "I went to relieve myself before—"

"Then they were intentionally placed there. God help the person responsible."

"God help them indeed," the second voice said.

Elaina chanced a look over her shoulder at the Duke of Cumberland staring at her. "Your Grace, forgive me if I do not offer you a proper curtsy at present. My hands are full. I would rather not be trampled this fine morning."

"Forgiven. What seems to be amiss?"

"I witnessed the lad whipping your horse from my chamber window. The horse was crazed, I will not lie, but the beating did not help in the least." Elaina cast a withering glance at the pale stable lad. "Appears someone placed thorns under the steed's saddle while the young man relieved himself. Seems to be quite the weekend for sabotage."

"It does at that, madam. Do you think he has calmed enough to approach?" the Duke asked.

"Yes, your grace," Elaina replied, then she whispered once again to the horse in French as the Duke approached.

The Duke followed Elaina's lead with his choice of language and tone. "Ah, good lad." Taking the reins from her, he lay a large hand upon his horse. "I owe you a debt, Lady Elaina. You do have a way with horses."

"You owe me nothing, Your Grace." Elaina patted the now calm horse that had taken to munching on a patch of grass growing at the base of the post.

With her hands now empty, she offered the Duke a deep curtsy and backed slowly away from the horse. When she had retreated far enough away that she thought no excitement would occur, she turned toward the house. They had drawn a crowd.

"Lord Taylor." Elaina curtsied to the man who stood staring mutely at her.

"My lady," he returned, a smile twitching at his mouth.

She glanced past him at several guests who had gathered to watch the show. Unfortunately, one of them was Calum. He stared at her, his expression unreadable.

It was then Elaina realized her feet were freezing. She stood barefoot on the cold stone walk leading to the house as Caitir rushed from the doorway and skidded to a halt, gaping at her in her gown and robe. Elaina's long hair hung loose and, more than likely, wild. She raked a hand through her hair and strode toward the house with her chin up.

"Mr. MacKinnon," she acknowledged as she passed by him.

"My lady," he replied, looking her over. "Ye look radiant this morning."

"Do not be patronizing, Mr. MacKinnon. It does not suit you." She marched on toward her eye-rolling handmaiden, dreading the tongue lashing awaiting her.

Chapter Eighteen

DAYS LATER, ELAINA, WILLIAM, AND Calum set out for the seaport in search of Monroe.

Rabbie did not hide his unhappiness about her presence on this trip while he grudgingly helped her up into the carriage and glared at her two escorts. Neither of the men had hidden their unhappiness about it either, but she had insisted, and they'd conceded because she was, in fact, the only one who had ever seen the man. Elaina was not pleased to have to share a coach with Mr. MacKinnon, but there was little she could do.

The port bustled in a maddening dance with sailors running about and passengers departing the ships, wobbling on their unsteady sea legs. A great deal of yelling and jostling took place as workers tried to unload the ships' cargos around streaming hordes of people.

"Now, remember," William said as they pulled to a stop and exited the carriage. "You stay with one of us at all times. When we spot this Monroe, Calum and I will talk to him. You need to stay in a safe place."

"I don't know how we will ever find him in this nightmare," Elaina replied, overwhelmed by the throng of people.

"At least we know what ship to look for," Calum said.

William nodded to Rabbie and said, "We shall return."

Rabbie lowered his head in return, then looked at Elaina and discreetly touched his thigh in the area he had told her to wear her *sgian-dubh*.

She patted her leg in answer.

The trio set off on a hunt for the *Gurney O'Rourke* and one mysterious Monroe. William pushed and shoved his way through the crowds, Elaina following behind, one hand holding the hem of his suit coat so as not to get swept away in the flow of bodies. Calum brought up the rear. He and William questioned several persons along the way about the direction of the ship and for any information on the man they hunted. A few of the men pointed down the boardwalk. The heavy smell of saltwater and fish intermixed with the odors of so many bodies crammed together was almost overwhelming. Elaina felt bile rising in the back of her throat. She should have eaten before they came. Now, nerves mixed with obnoxious odors did a number on her stomach.

A more pleasant smell wafted through the air, and she looked around for its source. A small hunched woman sold Scottish pastries her mother had called bridies from a rough wooden cart.

"William." Elaina grabbed her brother's sleeve and when he looked back at her, hitched her head in the direction of the cart. "I have to get something on my stomach."

William conceded, and the trio shoved their way through the crowd, a few choice words given by each of the passing parties.

"Good mornin' to ye," the tiny woman said.

Elaina was not tall herself, but this woman's head struggled to reach her shoulders. Her silver hair lay in a thin plait down her back. She wore a woolen tartan of blues and greens draped and belted over her simple brown dress, something her mother had called an *arisaid*. The two sides, meeting just at her small bosom, were held together by a brooch bearing the head of a wild boar with the words *Ne Obliviscaris* engraved above it.

"Forget Not," Elaina said to the woman while admiring her brooch.

The woman smiled a toothless smile, her weathered face crinkling. She turned, her expression changing as she leered at Calum. "No, we do not."

Elaina was taken aback by the woman's words and attitude. Calum didn't seem phased, only smiling at the tiny woman. William had his eyes on the crowd and missed the exchange. She made her purchase, and the trio quickly moved on.

"What in the world?" Elaina said when they got out of earshot of the woman's cart.

"She belongs to Clan Campbell...rivals of Clan MacKinnon." Calum pointed to the brooch pinning his plaid across his chest. It was also a wild boar but with a large bone in its mouth. "*Audentes fortuna juvat*," he said. "Fortune favors the brave."

"This clan business is so confusing. How is an immigrant supposed to know anything? First the MacGregors, now the Campbells…the MacKinnons. It's too much."

"What about the MacGregors?" Calum asked with unmasked curiosity.

Elaina relayed the tale of her and Rabbie's meeting with the three clansmen. "He said we needed to stay close to the house and not ride for a while because they are murderers and thieves."

"Interesting," Calum said.

William interjected a few words about Elaina's exposure to certain dangers, none of them pleasant, but he cut them short when the *Gurney O'Rourke* rose in front of them. "Here it is."

Before them stood a massive, weather-beaten ship, its crew already unloading the cargo. The trio stood back in the shadow of a row of buildings, watching. Elaina didn't know how the thing stayed afloat because it looked as if it would fall apart on the smallest wave, yet sailors rolled barrels down the gangplank at an astonishing rate. The sailors knew the system well.

"Do ye see him?" Calum leaned close to Elaina so she could hear him over the melee.

"No, but I can't see much of the ship." She strained on the tips of her toes to see over the swarm of people. Frustrated, she glanced around, spying a small stack of boxes, and took Calum's hand as she climbed up to a much better view. Scanning the action aboard the boat, she searched for the large man. There were several who looked to be of the same caliber as Monroe, but none of them were him. Her eyes followed the gangplank lowered to the dock below.

"There!" She grabbed William's shoulder. "Just to the left of the barrels. The big guy with the crate of chickens!" She pointed to the man who was deep in conversation with a shorter, smaller man.

At that moment he looked up and his eyes met hers, her finger still pointing at him. His brow furrowed, and he started to lower the crate.

"Bloody hell!" She jumped down from her perch. "He saw me pointing at him. We have to hurry." She started into the crowd.

"Oh no you don't." William just managed to snag her by the collar and haul her back. "You stay here."

He and Calum took off before she could protest.

"Damn you!" she yelled after them, stomping her foot.

She stood in the shade of the building pouting and watching the workers continue their delicate ballet of rolling barrels and sliding large chests down the plank. Calum and William were gone a fair amount of time, and she soon felt the need to visit a privy. Making her way down the boardwalk, she studied the ship to see if she could catch her escorts questioning the man. There was no sign of any of them.

As she emerged from the outbuilding after taking care of her urgent business, a hand covered her mouth and she could feel the tip of a knife in her side.

"Scream, and I'll gut ye," the man's voice hummed in her ear as he dragged her around to the back of the building and shoved her onto a stack of barley sacks.

She turned around to find Monroe's gapped teeth grinning at her.

"Ye seem ta have a fair amount of interest in ole Monroe. Cannae say I'm no flattered, but what's it aboot?"

Elaina stood tall and squared her shoulders. "I want to know what you know about the murders of Lord and Lady Spencer, the Earl and his wife."

"I dinna ken a thing." Monroe eyed her up and down.

"You do know, and you will tell me all about it."

Monroe let out a hearty laugh, showing Elaina a lot of empty spaces in his mouth. "What makes ye so sure I ken anythin'?"

"I heard you talking by the trees behind the Sheep's Heid Inn."

He looked at her for a moment, uncomprehending, and then she could see it work its way into his brain. "You? It couldna be?"

"It is. Halloo again. Now, let's talk."

Monroe grinned. "Ye are at a disadvantage." He waved his knife. "Why would I tell ye anythin'?"

"I will scream and tell everyone you tried to rape me."

Monroe lunged at her faster than she thought he could move. He clamped a large dirty hand over her mouth and shoved her backward onto the sacks of barley. "Maybe I shall and save ye the trouble of lyin'?" He pressed his body against hers, and she felt the seriousness of his words beginning to take shape.

She reached down, moving just a fraction of an inch, and slid her *sgian-dubh* from the pocket she had hidden it in. She placed the tip of it forcefully on the throbbing vein in his neck while wrapping her fingers in a death hold in the hair on the back of his head.

His eyes locked on hers. "Oh, ho. The lady came prepared," he said.

Elaina tried to grin under his hand that reeked of salt and fish. She raised a questioning eyebrow at him, then gently increased the pressure to the now rapidly pulsing vein. She could read in his eyes that he knew he could not get the knife he'd laid down on the barley sack to her throat quicker than she could pierce his. She felt the slight shift of his weight as he thought to pull away and quickly wrapped her legs around his, locking her ankles and squeezing him to her. She mentally thanked her Indian friends in the colonies for the knowledge and practice as she increased the pressure of the knife once again. He pulled against her legs, but she squeezed them harder and the tip of her knife pierced his skin. His eyes bulged, and he stopped struggling.

"What do ye want to know?" He removed his hand from Elaina's mouth.

"Did you kill my parents?"

"You? You are the Earl's daughter?" His eyes darted down at her while his mouth gaped open as much as the knife at his throat would allow.

"'Tis me," she replied with a grin. "Now answer my question. Did you kill them?"

"No."

"Who did?"

"I…I cannae say. He'll kill me."

Elaina raised a brow at him again. "*I'm* going to kill you if you don't say." She pressed a tad harder.

It was a precarious situation now. She only had so much flesh before she penetrated the artery. She didn't want him to die before she got answers. Blood dripped onto the sack next to her, and if it was possible, Monroe's eyes grew larger.

"Tell me." Her breathing slowed as her body tensed and she pulled Monroe's head back, exposing his neck.

His face took on a petrified expression.

Elaina sneered at him. "I am growing tired of this game and of having to smell you. Maybe I should kill you and find your friend. He may be more cooperative."

The acrid scent of fear began to seep from him, and his eyes darted around.

She supposed he could feel the change in her—the moment she'd made up her mind that he had to die.

"I…I…" He closed his eyes. "Robert Campbell," he sputtered.

"Robert Campbell? Where can I find him?"

A jarring spasm shook his body as it lifted from her with a sudden arch of his back. The deadweight of him collapsed on top of her and crushed the air from her lungs as she struggled to push him away. Then, as fast as he'd fallen, he was gone.

"Are ye all right, my lady?" Rabbie grabbed her face in his hands, searching her eyes.

"Yes…I'm… What are you doing here?"

"Saving yer life. He didn't hurt you?" he asked, his eyes traveling the length of Elaina's body.

"No, he didn't. Why did you kill him?" She pushed his hands angrily from her face.

"He was tryin' to defile ye, my lady." Rabbie looked at her as if she were the most ignorant woman in Edinburgh.

"I had him at a disadvantage." Elaina waved the knife Rabbie himself had given her, now with a light coating of Monroe's blood that she then wiped off on the sacks.

"That was not what it looked like from the back," Rabbie argued.

"Dammit." She slammed her hand down on the sacks of barley. A few more minutes and she might have known the killer's location. She felt the adrenalin ebb from her body, and her hand started to shake as it lay upon the sacks. What frightened her most was that she had been prepared to take the man's life herself. At one time in her life, she would have never thought it possible for her to kill someone in cold blood, but there it stood. She had thought no more of him than an animal.

"We need to be gettin' on." Rabbie looked at Monroe's dead body.

He wiped his knife off, and the two of them sheathed their weapons. He grabbed Elaina by her trembling arm and drug her down the walkway behind the buildings before he turned, stepping casually out into the crowd, well away from where Monroe's dead body lay.

"My Lord!" Rabbie yelled, catching William and Calum's attention. They shoved their way through the throng of people and William snatched Elaina by the arm. "Where have you been? We searched everywhere for you! Did I not tell you to stay put!"

"What happened? What is the matter?" Calum lifted her chin, studying her face.

William looked at him and then at her, realization washing over his face that he had missed something in his frustration.

Elaina's legs quivered so that Rabbie practically held her up.

"She was near raped. I thought one of ye was to stay with her at all times?" Rabbie looked accusingly at the pair of men.

"We saw Monroe and went after him, but he disappeared. Raped?" William exclaimed. "Who?" He looked around the crowd.

"He's dead," she said, her voice shaking. *God, why can I not quit trembling?* "Rabbie killed him. He killed Monroe."

"Monroe? It was Monroe?"

"I needed to use the loo. He grabbed me when I came out and then dragged me behind the buildings. I had him at a disadvantage, but Rabbie couldn't tell. He couldn't see from behind."

"It looked rather like she was being brutalized, not holding a man at knife-point." Rabbie pointed to the artery in his neck.

"Oh!" Elaina remembered. "I have a name."

"A name?" the trio of men asked at the same time.

"Robert Campbell. I was about to learn his whereabouts when Rabbie inconveniently silenced my informant."

"Robert Campbell," Calum said, mulling it over in his mind.

"Do you know him?" Elaina asked.

"No, I dinna think so, but the name is familiar. I've some knowledge of a few Campbells. Some of them are members of the Watch. I will make inquiries and see what I can find out."

"If he's with the Watch, he could be in Flanders." *Dammit. That will put a kink in things,* Elaina thought.

"I dinna mean to interrupt yer sleuthing, but we need to go," Rabbie said. "Surely ye can move yer mouths and yer feet at the same time."

Chapter Nineteen

THE TRIO DISCUSSED ELAINA'S FINDINGS on the way home while the men also scolded her for being reckless.

"I don't know how relieving one's self is reckless," Elaina defended herself, clenching her hands in her lap in an attempt to quell their quivering.

"Ye ken," Calum said. "This is the second time takin' a piss has got ye into trouble. I see a pattern forming here."

William grinned at his sister.

"Laugh all you want, you two, but taking a piss has served me better than either one of you, and I handled myself just fine."

The two men snorted at her.

"I can see that by the way you are about to bounce me off this seat with your quivering." William laid a hand on her fists clenched in her lap.

"I am fine. Can we get back to the matter at hand?" She jerked her hands away from him.

"What I want to know is how you got a knife, and where is it?" William looked his sister over.

She reached into her skirt and slid out her *sgian-dubh*. "Rabbie gave it to me after our run-in with the MacGregors."

"Rabbie, huh?" William took the knife from Elaina's hand and turned it over, studying it before handing it back to her.

"I guess I should thank him for saving your life. Twice."

"Once," Elaina corrected. "I had Monroe under control. The *sgian-dubh* saved my life, not Rabbie."

"Mere technicalities," William answered.

Elaina playfully kicked him.

"Well," Calum began as the carriage pulled up at the house. "I suppose William and I have some work to do finding this Robert Campbell."

"Yes, you do. I only wish Rabbie had killed him five seconds later. Our work would be easier." Elaina gave Rabbie the eye as he helped her from the carriage.

He shrugged in return.

"I need to speak to Caitir for a moment, if I may?" Calum asked Elaina upon his carriage exit.

Elaina nodded. Caitir had been put in charge of burning some of the papers while they were gone and was to hold a few back so Calum could look over them once more before they were destroyed. She turned her attention back to William and Rabbie as Calum headed toward the house.

"Have you ever heard of a Robert Campbell?" Elaina asked Rabbie as he unbridled the horses.

"Nay, I havenae, but I will ask around as well and see what I can learn."

"We would appreciate it," William said. "I also appreciate you taking care of my sister's well-being."

Elaina made a noise in the back of her throat.

"He saved your life," William said.

"The knife he gave me saved my life."

"I dinna see the difference," Rabbie said.

Elaina crossed her arms. "Humph! I will leave you two to flex your muscles and revel in the masculinity of saving damsels in distress. I've things to see about in the house."

It was the men's turn to snort.

⋅—◦⋈◦—⋅

"How is it?"

Calum and Caitir both jumped at the sound of her voice.

"Almost done," Caitir said, holding her chest. "Ye scairt the life out of me. Calum was informin' me of your findin's at the pier. Trouble finds ye like no other, my lady."

"I know. It's a curse." Elaina sank on the floor in front of the fire. "It is only paper, but it tears at my heart to have burned something of such importance to Mama. I wish I could ask her why this cause was so dear to her as to risk certain death, as well it may have."

"Maybe it was the previous relationship with the mysterious Highlander?"

Caitir said softly. "I washed this for ye, my lady." She laid a plaid they had removed from the chest upon Elaina's lap.

Elaina ran her hand across it, wondering what the significance was in the cloth.

"'Tis MacGregor colors," Calum said softly.

"MacGregor?" Elaina pulled her hand away from the plaid.

He eased himself down next to her on the floor, studying her face. "Why does that bother ye so?" he asked.

"Rabbie told me what a terrible clan the MacGregors are. I cannot imagine my mother having anything to do with them, let alone being in love with one."

"Rabbie gave ye one side of a story, my lady." Caitir plopped herself on the other side of Elaina. "Yes, Clan Gregor, or Macgregor as it is now known, is a savage fightin' clan, but circumstance has forced them to be. They have been driven into the most rugged parts of the Highlands where there is little to sustain their families. So many times in the history of our country, Clan Macgregor has been betrayed—their lands taken from them and handed to clans like the Campbells. To say there is bad blood between the two clans is an understatement. Frankly, the MacGregors have a problem with many clans. 'Twas only a hundred years ago or so that MacGregors were hunted with dogs; their women stripped, branded, and beaten naked through the streets, and their children sold into slavery. MacGregor heads were used to gain pardons for thievery and murder. Clan MacGregor had no choice but to hide and steal to survive. The ban on the name was lifted for a while, but unfortunately, it is once again abolished and to be renounced under penalty of death."

"I don't understand. How can a government treat an entire people with such unabashed hatred? It is disturbing." Elaina thought back to the three gentlemen she had encountered at the stream. It was apparent where Rabbie stood on the subject of Clan Macgregor, but where did he stand with Clan Campbell? Could he be trusted to help search for Robert Campbell or would he send out a warning? Surely not. Although he despised the MacGregors, he seemed to be loyal to William and herself—after all, he had saved her life, or so he believed.

"May I ask? Where do your clans stand—MacKinnon and Murray? Are they with Clan Campbell or Clan Macgregor?" Elaina looked from one face to the other.

The two cousins met each other's gaze.

Caitir reached out her healing hand, taking Elaina's in hers. "As a blood sister, I tell ye that our clans stand in alliance with Macgregor. For that fact alone, we are also rivals of Clan Campbell."

Elaina stared down at the red and black tartan on her lap. "Even though I am not a member of a clan, I also stand in defiance of Clan Campbell, for one of their own has claimed the lives of those I held dear."

The room stood quiet for a moment.

"Did you learn anything from the papers?" Elaina asked Calum, breaking the trance.

"Aye. Part of yer mother's money was goin' to a high-rankin' official with Jacobite sympathies. Someone with access to the English parliament and a close affinity with the king's hierarchy, therefore with first-hand knowledge of any sudden movements of the British military against an uprisin'."

Elaina held her breath. So, there was an uprising in the making, and her mother had been a significant player even with an ocean between them. How could Diana Spencer have hidden this from her husband? She thought back to William's unplanned trip to Newcastle over discrepancies in the books of their mother's glass company.

"Was there a name? Did the papers name, in your words, 'the high-ranking official'?" Elaina croaked out the question.

"No. There was no name," Calum answered.

Elaina had two men in mind. One seemed highly unlikely and was already dead. She did not want to believe her father would have ever done such a thing. But the Duke of Newcastle, that was another matter altogether. He was such a good friend of her father's that it seemed hard to imagine. But what was the old saying? Keep your friends close and your enemies…

Robert Campbell was a ghost, or so it seemed. No trace of him could be found in all of Edinburgh. Calum, William, and Rabbie had searched everywhere and questioned everyone they could think of. A few of their contacts had heard of him, but no one knew what he looked like nor much about him. All they knew for certain was that he was Highlander. It was October, and the trail had run cold.

William came to Elaina on a snowy morning as she dug through the study in search of something elusive.

"Good morning, William," she offered, not looking up from her diggings.

"Have you seen the ledger for the glass company? I swear I put it back on this shelf the other day." Elaina pointed to the shelf behind her with one hand and dug through a pile of papers and books with the other.

"No." William looked around the room, his brow furrowed.

"Found it!" Elaina exclaimed, holding the red leather-bound ledger in the air. "I don't know why I would have put it there."

William observed her glass sitting on the edge of the desk. "Maybe too much whiskey?"

"Are you implying I am a lush?"

"I would never."

Elaina sat behind the desk, opening the ledger to the page she was searching for and compared it to another laid out in front of her.

"What are you looking for?" William asked, his gaze taking in her and the two books.

"Clues." Elaina looked at him, wondering how much she should reveal. The numbers in the two books did not add up. They had not in some time—over twenty years to be exact—but the discrepancies ended a few months ago. Right about the same time as his unexpected trip. She studied her brother carefully.

He sighed and turned a troubled look to his sister. "I've something to tell you, Elaina, and I only do so now that you may guard yourself." He closed the study door and approached her again, placing his hands on the desk and leaning down close.

Her stomach started to churn. "What is it?"

"Mother was a Jacobite supporter." His bluntness nearly made her drop her glass, but she caught it and drained it instead.

"I know," she coughed out over the burn in her throat. She pulled out her handkerchief and dabbed at the tears the whiskey had brought forth.

"You know?" It was his turn to be shocked, so he drained his glass as well.

Elaina laughed as he refilled her glass. "If we keep this up, we will both be too drunk to continue this enlightening conversation."

"How do you know? How *long* have you known?" he asked, taking a seat by the fire.

"I found some papers in Mama's things several months ago. I burned them, thinking them treasonous." Elaina decided to leave out the part about them being in Gaelic and Calum and Caitir's involvement. There was no reason to drag them into this. "How do *you* know and for how long?"

"My trip to Newcastle several months ago was about the discrepancies I found in those logs." William waved his glass toward the desk. "I met with our illustrious partner, the Duke of Newcastle. He confirmed the discrepancies, and when pressured with certain arrest and ruin, he filled me in on Mother's little project."

"What is his involvement?" Elaina demanded. *So, the Duke of Newcastle was involved.*

"He claimed innocence. He said Mama arranged the whole thing. It had been set up before we ever immigrated to the colonies."

Elaina frowned, "But he and Father were such good friends. Why would he help Mama support the Jacobites? Father was loyal to the crown, was he not?"

"Yes, he was. The Duke was adamant about that. He said he owed the favor to Mama because her father had saved him from ruin when he was a young man. He was only the middleman. He felt because it was Mama's money and he was only making the transfers that he was not actually at fault. He never thought anything would come of an uprising anyway."

"And do you believe him?"

William hesitated, "Yes, I think I do."

"Why would you tell me this now?" she leaned back in the chair, crossing her arms.

"I've orders to report to Fort William. I am to leave in one week. If I do not return, I need you to know."

"Why would you not return?"

"These are dangerous times, Elaina."

"Unfortunately, I am coming to realize this more and more. Why did no one inform me of such, until this moment? I have learned more from Rabbie and Caitir than from my own family."

"Father and I wanted to protect you."

"So, you did know."

"Of course. I am an officer."

"You of all people, William. I would think *you* would have warned me. You and Papa letting me arrive in Scotland completely unaware of the political climate. And Mama...how on earth could the three of you do that? Do you not think it more dangerous for me to know nothing? Let me tell you, *it is*. Not only are the British at odds with the Scots, but the clans are at war amongst one another."

"I know this also," William said, quietly looking into the fire. "It is the same as back home in the colonies. The different Indian tribes are warring with one another and with settlers, and the British trying to protect its citizens."

"I suppose you are right," Elaina said thoughtfully. "It would have been nice to be warned though, to at least have been part of the conversation. I feel as if the three of you conspired behind my back."

"In a way we did." William turned his gaze back to his sister, his brow furrowed and his blue eyes heavy with worry. "It was Mama's doing. I am sorry, Elaina."

"Even in her death, her overprotective ways continue. Is there something more? Why do you look at me that way?"

"I…that is…I hate to leave you."

"Well, I hate to be left." Elaina crossed the room and sat on her brother's lap the way she had when they were small and Mother made him tell her stories against his will.

"You still have your knife? What did you call it?"

"Yes. It is called a *sgian-dubh*. Caitir said it means something like a hidden knife. You wear it on your thigh or your calf."

"Well, whatever it is, keep it on you at all times. Mama and Papa may have been killed for Mother's Jacobite sympathies, but it could be because of another matter." William lay his head against his sister's shoulder and sighed a sigh seeming to come from somewhere in his soul.

"What matter?" Elaina asked.

"Nothing I can discuss at present because I don't know if it is even true."

"More secrets." Elaina pulled a tuft of his hair.

"I will tell you when I return."

"And when will that be?"

"I'm not sure." William finished his glass of whiskey and wrapped his arms around her, squeezing her.

"The Duke of Newcastle will handle the business end of things, but I am extremely concerned about you staying here alone." William laid his head on Elaina's shoulder.

"I will be fine here. I am surrounded by servants, and I have my bodyguard."

"So you know that too?" William squeezed her hard.

"It was not hard to figure out when I couldn't even breathe without him jumping."

"It's for your own good."

"I know." Elaina laid her head on her brother's and wondered if she would indeed be safe here. She had a feeling she would not be safe anywhere.

Chapter Twenty

A WEEK AFTER WILLIAM'S DEPARTURE, CALUM came to call unexpectedly. Eads escorted him into the now-defunct garden area where Caitir and Elaina sat on one of the iron benches, wrapped in their woolen cloaks and enjoying hot cocoa and sunshine. The brutal Scottish wind had finally dissipated some time during the evening, and the girls had rushed outside the first chance they got.

"How are my ladies faring?" Calum asked them.

"Ye are a sight for sore eyes!" Caitir bounced up and ran to embrace her cousin. "It's been weeks since you've visited."

Elaina rose as well, although she did not bounce into his arms. She did offer him a warm smile and a nod of her head as he addressed her, "Lady Elaina."

Eads asked their guest, "Mr. MacKinnon? Refreshment?"

"Yes, what they're having will be fine." Turning back to the ladies, he said, "I thought I would see how you faired with William gone. It does worry me, two women being alone on the outskirts of Edinburgh."

"Alone?" Elaina scoffed. "We cannot have five minutes alone without some servant chasing me around, trying to cater to my every whim. We are far from alone."

Eads appeared from nowhere with Calum's beverage.

"Do you see?" Elaina laughed, leaving the butler looking thoroughly confused.

"Thank you, Eads." Calum took the proffered mug from his hand. "So this is your secret for surviving out here." He took a cautious drink. "Cocoa laced with brandy."

"'Tis the only way." Caitir raised her brow and her cup to him.

"Truly, what brings you out?" Elaina asked after they settled back in, she and Caitir facing Calum on the opposite bench. "Is there word? Have you found him?"

"Unfortunately, no," Calum said with a sigh. "We ken well enough the man exists, but he is the devil to find. He may have returned to the Campbell lands, or he could be in Flanders. Who is to say?"

"He has to have people here he knows. There has to be a connection to Mama and Papa somewhere. Unless someone hired him to kill them?" Now a sense of unease overtook Elaina as the realization came over her. If he was a hired assassin, who would have hired him and why—and could she or William be next?

"This Robert Campbell is either a man of means and has paid off the people who ken him in Edinburgh, or he is a man to be greatly feared. My money is on the latter. Which brings me to the matter at hand for which I have truly come."

"Which would be?" Caitir asked with what sounded like trepidation.

"I must leave."

"You too?" Elaina moaned. "You just told us how worried you were about us and now you are leaving as well?"

"Believe me, I dinna want to, but I have urgent clan business I must attend to."

"What clan business?" Caitir asked.

"That, I must speak to ye about alone. I beg yer pardon, my lady." Calum bowed his head to Elaina.

"No need. I will leave you to it, and I will check the stables—see how the boys are faring this morning." Elaina patted Caitir on the knee and gave a slight nod in Calum's direction.

She was curious to know what clan business they had to discuss. Entering the stables, she found Rabbie reclining against a stack of hay, carving on one of the many little sticks he always carried. He jumped to his feet at the sight of her.

"My lady." He inclined his head.

"Don't let me interrupt." She glanced at the knife in his hand. "I came to check on things. Where are the boys?" she asked, looking around.

"Down the way, trainin'." Rabbie nodded over her shoulder toward the area where they cut wood.

"Training?"

"With their broadswords, madam. Ye are never too young."

"I believe I shall have a look." She took leave and headed down the hill. She heard the clunking of wood and excessive swearing by Angus before she made the clearing. She stood for a moment, watching until Ainsley noticed her.

"My lady." He bowed his head.

Looking startled, Angus bowed as well.

"Carry on. Let me see what this training is all about."

"It is mostly about Ainsley taking out my legs, my lady," Angus said wryly, making her laugh.

The boys held wooden swords in their hands. Their actual swords were leaned against the stump still in their sheaths, thankfully. Picking one up, she pulled it out and turned it over, admiring it.

"Our father gave them to us before we left, my lady." Ainsley came to stand beside her. "They belonged to his brother and himself when they were boys, God rest Uncle Remy's soul." He crossed himself, as did Angus and Elaina.

"That one is mine," Angus piped up proudly.

"It is an incredible weapon," Elaina responded. The double-edged blade lay somewhat heavy in her hands. The pommel held a stone similar to the stone she carried in her pocket. The grip was simple, as was the blade with the cross hilt sloping down into quatrefoils. It was a sturdy weapon made for battle, not for play.

"Would ye like to try it out, madam?" he asked eagerly. "It might fit ye just right, being a lighter sword and all. It is still a bit long for me."

"He still has growing to do yet." Ainsley ruffled his brother's hair, earning him a hard glare.

"I wouldn't know the first thing about fighting with a broadsword," Elaina said, re-sheathing it. It was a decent size sword and did feel good in her hand.

"Ye would be a natural!" Angus said excitedly. "Ye are bonny at everything. Here. Try." He handed his wooden sword to Elaina and waved her into the middle of the clearing with Ainsley.

Never one to give up a good challenge, Elaina shed her cloak and approached her opponent.

"My lady, if I may?" Angus asked before he touched her.

Elaina nodded, the side of her mouth turning up.

"Stand with yer feet like this." He moved her legs into position. "Now in the heat of battle, ye may not have a chance to think about where yer feet are. Ye need to make it a habit." He spoke with authority as if he'd preached this sermon many times...or had it preached at him.

Ainsley stifled a laugh as Angus continued his instructions.

"All right, then," Elaina said to Ainsley. "I expect you not to hold back just because I am a girl." She raised an eyebrow at him.

He only grinned in return, and the sparring began. Elaina was clumsy at first, and Ainsley most definitely took it easy on her.

"Ye must protect yer legs, my lady," Angus called out as Ainsley tapped her leg with his wooden sword.

She stamped her foot in frustration, causing the boys to break out in laughter.

"A broadsword in the right hands can take yer legs off in one swipe, as well as yer head," he added.

Elaina closed her eyes for a moment, centering her thoughts. She had been playing around before, but no more. Judging the weight of the sword in her hands and the location of all her vital organs, including her head, she took a deep breath. Upon opening her eyes, she took a semi-crouched position and felt the calmness in her muscles. She turned her piercing gaze on Ainsley, who at first seemed taken aback but then gave her a grim nod of the head and bent his knees, taking a defensive stance, both hands on his sword.

The two battled much longer this time, Elaina blocking his sword just in the nick of time on several occasions. The pair twisted and turned, ducking and dodging each other's weapons. Elaina, unencumbered by her swirling skirts, moved in perfect rhythm with Ainsley. The duo began to sweat despite the frigid temperatures. Elaina side-stepped a particularly vicious swipe by Ainsley, who became increasingly frustrated. She grinned at him, increasing his angst. He began to fight with more emotion. Several moves later, he took a massive swing at her head, which she ducked as she swirled around and ended with her wooden sword against the side of his neck.

"You, Ainsley, are a much better fighter than I, but you let your emotions get the better of you. You broke your concentration. For that, you have lost your life."

"The lady is right." Calum stepped into the clearing. "Ye are a braw swordsman, lad, but ye cannae let an opponent get in yer head just because she is a lady, for even a lady will cut ye down. Ye must be wary at all times."

"How long have you been standing there?" Elaina asked, handing her sword back to Angus and wiping her brow with her sleeve.

"Long enough to know I dinna want to tangle with ye on the battlefield. Carry on, lads. I've to have a word with the lady." Calum picked up Elaina's cloak, throwing it over one arm and extending the other to her.

"We will spar again, my lady?" Ainsley asked as the couple turned to leave.

"Absolutely. I have much more to learn from the master." Elaina smiled warmly at the two boys.

She let Calum lead her back toward the garden area while replaying the duel in her mind, thinking of all the different moves she should have made. Nearing the garden, she returned to her senses and the present moment, realizing that her arm remained wrapped around Calum's. He held it close to his side, and she realized she rather enjoyed the protectiveness the act exuded. As much as she hated to admit it, she had missed him.

"Come back, have ye?" Calum asked, a smile tugging at his lips.

"What do you mean?" Her heart skipped a beat as his warm hazel eyes studied her.

He chuckled. "I thought ye would chew yer lip off before ye got out of yer thoughts."

"I was…calculating." A flush crept up her face.

She started to remove her arm from his, but he laid his free hand upon it and pulled her to a stop. She rested her gaze on the safest place she could think of—his hand, but she could feel the heat of his eyes upon her. She studied his long fingers and the back of his hand where fine hairs shimmered in the early afternoon sun.

"Why can ye no look at me?" he whispered. "I've never known ye to be afraid of anythin' let alone a pair of eyes."

She could hear the laughter in his voice. "I'm not afraid—"

His lips, soft and warm, pressed against her own, his nose a cold contrast upon her heated cheek. Her breath hitched, and she was sure her heart stopped as her mouth softened to him, and she raised to her toes. As quick as it came, his touch disappeared, leaving her disoriented.

"I'm sorry," he said, pulling back and now the one avoiding eye contact. "I shouldn't have."

"No," Elaina said, not knowing if she meant 'no, he shouldn't have' or 'no, he should not apologize.'

"That was forward of me."

Elaina slid her arm from his and took her cloak from him, wrapping it around herself even as heat still seared through her body from the recent battle and his kiss.

"I came to tell ye goodbye. I dinna know what came over me, and I truly beg your pardon. It is only watchin' ye move so with the sword, so agile and strong, and then yer touch is so soft and ye are graceful and every bit a woman…" After a moment, he cleared his throat and continued. "I dinna want to leave ye. You or Caitir."

For a moment, Elaina watched his jaw work as he stared off into the distance. Then she reached out a hand and laid it upon his arm, saying, "I don't want you to leave either."

He turned his gaze to hers, and they stood for a moment in silence.

She wished he would kiss her again.

"I must go," he said, laying his hand upon hers and squeezing it tightly. "Ye and Caitir must be careful and on guard at all times. With yer mother's actions and William away, ye are vulnerable. I will see ye again. God willing."

Then he was gone, leaving her standing in the garden confused, her lips burning, and feeling like a part of her had been torn away.

She shivered as sweat dried on her skin, hugging her cloak tighter about her shoulders while she watched him walk away and disappear around the side of the house. A movement from the corner of her eye caught her attention. She turned, expecting to see the boys returning from their sparring practice, but instead, saw Rabbie's blonde head retreating toward the stables. She wondered how much he'd heard or seen.

Chapter Twenty-One

ELAINA INSISTED ON TAKING THE horses instead of the carriage on to-day's venture. She wanted to feel the cold breeze on her face and revel in the snowfall. Caitir agreed readily enough, though Rabbie thought she was crazy. Rabbie, of course, would not let the two women ride into Edinburgh alone. He was currently in the stables, tending to their three horses.

"I am so pleased with your visit," the Duke of Newcastle exclaimed as Elaina shed her snow-dusted cloak.

Caitir took it from her and went after the Duke's maid to dry it for their ride home.

The Duke grabbed her, kissing each cheek in greeting. "Your face is practically frozen, my dear," he exclaimed. "Martin, bring us some tea and some whiskey."

"Right away, sir." The butler bowed and disappeared.

"Come." The Duke led Elaina to the elegant sitting room in the large apartment he used when in the city.

Elaina perched herself on the edge of the pale blue sofa, taking in the Duke's rather garish taste in decor. The over-efficient servants bustled around, one of them stirring the fire in the white stone fireplace. Martin delivered tea, a feat in and of itself on such short notice. Elaina had arrived unannounced, on a whim, when she'd heard the Duke was in town. She accepted the delicate, bone china teacup with gratitude. The ride, although exhilarating, had left her chilled after removing her heavy woolen cloak. Closing her eyes, she sipped her tea, letting the warmth of it slide down her throat.

"I am so pleased with your visit. What a pleasure to gaze upon your lovely face so early in the day," His Grace gushed a little too exuberantly. "What brings you to see me?"

Elaina thought she detected a few nerves behind his words. She took another sip from her cup, trying to pick her words carefully. She glanced at the maid, still puttering over the tea and scones.

His Grace, reading her thoughts, waved the girl away. "Speak it," he said as the girl left the room.

"Aren't you the blunt one?" Elaina laughed, trying to will the butterflies in her stomach to settle.

"No sense dragging things out. I've always found it best to get right down to the heart of the matter." He smiled, sipping his tea.

"I know about Mama's Jacobite connections, and I believe that is why she and Papa were murdered."

"Goodness," he coughed, then he dabbed at his mouth with a lace-edged napkin.

"You said to get to it."

"I wasn't thinking anything along those lines."

"I also need to know if you have any knowledge about Mother, where she sent the money, and something she called a 'grave matter'?"

"I'm not sure what you mean?"

"I am pretty certain you do."

There was a silence between the two as they seemed to be calculating the other's thoughts.

"William said Grandpapa saved you from ruin. Is that why you felt you owed Mama the favor? If you were that close to my parents as to risk your life by committing treason, then you must certainly be close enough to know what went on between my mother and her parents."

"Lower your voice," the Duke hissed at her. "Are you trying to get me hung? William told you about your mother?"

"Yes and no. I knew about the money and my mother. I did not know your involvement until he told me. I found some of Mama's papers written in Gaelic. I know a high-ranking official is involved. After mine and William's conversation, I assumed the official was you, seeing as you know the matter."

His eyes widened. "Do you read Gaelic?"

"No."

"Who do you know that does? Who read them?"

"'Tis no matter. I trust them, and we have burned the papers. I have told no one of my suspicions. I need to know, however, why and where the money goes."

His Grace rose from his chair. Crossing the room, he stood staring out the window at the freshly dusted world. "Why? That is a hard question to answer. I suppose nothing in her papers suggested why?"

"If you mean her former relationship with a Highlander, yes."

The Duke looked over his shoulder. "Yes, your mother was once in love with another man, but the relationship ended several years before she married Edward." He studied Elaina's face.

"Is that why? Is that why she would betray my father and his beliefs and turn against her country? Was she still in love with this other man?"

"Turn against her country? Scotland was her country. She believed in the Stuart King, not this protestant windbag who has brought nothing but the separation of families and friends and destruction of justice, marching his troops into Scotland to subdue the restless natives. Why do the Scottish people not have the right to run their country the way they see fit? It is their country! The British have an army of brutes with absolutely no sense of justice or knowledge of the system in which the Scottish live. If one is Scottish, you are damned lucky to stand a trial before being hanged or cut down in the name of the king." The Duke stared at Elaina for a moment and then grabbed a decanter of whiskey and filled his teacup. He took a deep swallow.

Elaina noticed the smallest of tremors in his hand. He flopped down on the sofa beside her and, without asking, filled her cup with whiskey. The pair unceremoniously raised their glasses in salute and gulped it down, Elaina needing it as much as he.

"I am sorry," he said after a moment. "I am British, and I should not talk of such, but I have many friends who are Scottish. I spent my youth in Edinburgh, and obviously, I do not agree with the treatment of the Scots. I knew your mother before I knew your father, and your grandfather did save me from ruin. I will never be able to repay his debt. I met your father not long after, and he helped me rebuild myself and my reputation. I owe both of your parents."

"If you knew my mother that long, what do you know of the trouble between Mama and my grandmother? What happened between them?"

The Duke slumped against the sofa back. "Well, that is a complicated matter. It started with your mother's relationship with Thamas MacGregor. Your grandmother put an end to it once she caught wind of it. Your mother saw him secretly for months before that happened. There were other things—some big, some small—but when your grandmother felt your mother's personal beliefs caused your family to flee to the colonies, that was the final straw. Whether it was true or not, that was what Lady Leicester believed."

"Grandmother kept all of Mama's letters," Elaina whispered, her finger tracing the delicate edge of her cup. "I found them in a hidden drawer in her writing desk. Why would she keep them if she never responded to them? How bad would a thing have to be to never speak to your daughter again?"

"Your grandmother had her convictions. She felt your mother was dishonoring your father and both families' names. I cannot speak for your grandmother. She was a hard-headed, strong-willed woman."

"William would say that of me. I suppose I took after Grandmama."

There was a pause before the Duke sighed deeply. "Yes, I suppose some might say that."

"Why would Mama risk everything to keep sending money? Was she still in love with this MacGregor?"

"Your mother loved her home country. It was not an easy decision for her to support the Jacobites, but once she made her decision, she never looked back. I suppose she never stopped loving Thamas, even after they both married other people. He died only a few years after they were forced to stop seeing each other. I suppose your mother loved him up until the day she died."

"How sad for Papa."

"Oh, Diana loved Lord Spencer—never doubt that, my dear. She did, however, always hold a special place in her heart for the MacGregor Clan."

"Was that why Grandmother was so against their relationship? Because he was a MacGregor? I've heard they are a dangerous clan, arguably with reason but still dangerous nonetheless."

"Every clan is a dangerous clan if you cross them." He looked at her evenly.

"Was that the grave matter? This relationship with a MacGregor?"

The Duke finished off his teacup of whiskey while studying Elaina's face. "Yes, I suppose it was. Is there any time frame for William's return?"

"No, unfortunately. Mr. MacKinnon is gone as well. 'Clan business' was how he put it. Do you know where the money was going?"

"I do not. I only transferred the funds into a private account. I have no name."

"Did Grandmother know about Mother's involvement with the Jacobites?

Did the money put the family in danger? Was there already talk of a rebellion back then?" Elaina asked.

The Duke stared at her. "Yes, I believe it was." He studied her for a long moment before speaking again. "Would you like to stay in town at my apartment until the men return? I must leave tomorrow, and you may have it to yourself. It may be safer than being out in the county alone."

"Pshaw, I will be fine. I have a house full of servants, and besides, Rabbie is there."

"Be careful, Elaina. Whoever killed your parents is still out there. It does scare me for your safety." His brow furrowed in concern.

Elaina figured she had garnered all the information she could for the day. "It will be fine, I promise. Unfortunately, I really must go if we are to make it back to the manor before dark."

"Yes, I suppose you should if you are sure you won't stay?"

"I appreciate your offer, truly I do, but I must get home. The servants would be worried if we didn't return."

"These are dangerous times, Elaina. Trust no one."

Once again, the dire warning.

⤖⟡⟵

Rabbie helped the two women into their saddles and climbed on his mount, turning it toward home. Elaina mulled over her conversation with the Duke, his parting words haunting her. She purposefully held Sadie back to let Rabbie get out of earshot before she told Caitir what she had learned from her visit.

Caitir replied, "Well, at least ye ken now why yer ma supported The Cause—love of her country and love of a man."

"How strange to think Mama in love with someone besides Papa, and to have that love still consume you to the point of treason. What is the most extreme thing you would do for love?" Elaina asked Caitir.

"I dinna ken. What a question. Who knows what anyone would do for love until put in a position to have to do anythin'?"

"I suppose that's true." Elaina mused over the subject for several moments. "Calum kissed me in the garden." She was not sure why she told Caitir.

The women had lessened the distance between them and Rabbie, and Elaina thought she saw his back stiffen slightly but could have imagined it.

"I knew there was somethin' between the two of ye." Caitir gave a devilish grin.

"There is nothing between us. He kissed me out of the blue and then apologized for it."

"And how do ye feel about it?"

"I don't know." Elaina absently touched her mouth, remembering the feel of his lips on hers. A warmth spread through her, and she coughed, trying to hide the blush she felt rising in her cheeks.

Caitir's smile broadened, but she didn't say anything.

Elaina clicked her tongue at Sadie, urging her forward until she rode even with Rabbie. "What is the most extreme thing you would ever do for love?" she asked him, raising an eyebrow.

They continued to ride in silence, Elaina wondering if he had heard her question. Then he turned his piercing green gaze upon her. "Kill," was his answer.

Silence consumed the remainder of the ride home. Rabbie's look and the tone of his voice had chilled Elaina to the core. She did not doubt that Rabbie would kill, whether it was for love or not was questionable. They arrived at Duart Manor as the sun was setting. Caitir dismounted and headed inside to announce their presence to Mrs. Davies and the rest of the staff. Elaina began to help Rabbie and the boys unsaddle the horses and get them settled. The boys had carried the saddles into the tack room when Rabbie turned on her.

"What are ye doin'?" he demanded.

"I'm helping with the horses?"

"No. What are ye doin' with MacKinnon? I told ye to watch who ye befriend."

"There is nothing wrong with Calum. He is a good man. What is wrong with you?"

"Ye are goin' to get hurt and hurt badly if ye continue on this path with him."

The pair were in Sadie's stall. Elaina's skin had begun to crawl with Rabbie's words. What did he know that she did not? Truth be told, she knew nothing about Calum other than he was Caitir's cousin. She thought back to the night in Lady Caroline's garden, to the moment when Calum had asked what if it was him who had sent the letters and sabotaged her gun. She'd brushed it off when he told her no, it wasn't him. Could it have been him after all?

Rabbie ducked under Sadie's head to stand beside Elaina. She didn't look at him, but continued to brush her horse, her mind spinning in circles.

"Look at me." He took her by the arm. "You will get hurt. Watch yer steps. The punishment for treason is death. I would hate to see your pretty neck hangin' from the end of a rope."

Elaina tried to back up, but Rabbie held on tight. What was he talking about? Her mother's treason or was Calum involved in the Jacobite movement? Her heartbeat pounded under Rabbie's iron grip on her arm, and she tried to wrench it loose.

"Let me go," she whispered, trying to keep her voice from shaking. "What are you talking about? Treason. Where did that come from?"

"I think ye ken good and well where it came from, my lady. I'd advise ye to watch yer step."

"I don't know what you are talking about. Let me go this instant!"

Instead, Rabbie pushed Elaina against the horse stall, his body crushing the breath from her own. His mouth found hers in a bruising intensity that nearly took her to her knees.

"How dare you," she hissed when she broke free. She tried to slap him, but he caught her arm.

"That is how a man should kiss a woman, and I will not apologize." He left her stunned and alone inside Sadie's stall.

The wooden brush felt heavy in her hand. She turned it over and looked at it without truly seeing it. She hadn't told Caitir about her encounter with Rabbie in the stables. It took a lot to rattle her, and Rabbie had succeeded in scaring her. She pulled the brush absently through her hair while pacing the floor. The wood planks chilled her feet, but it helped her feel grounded. Caitir had smoored the fire before she left, believing Elaina would go to bed for the night, but sleep was evasive. She shivered in her thin shift and should have grabbed her robe, but she wanted to feel the cold. She wanted the cold to dampen the fire within her—the heat of fear and the intensity of Rabbie's kiss that lingered on her lips.

She stood at her window, staring down at the stables and ruminating over the events of the last few months. What was she missing? Was Calum a dangerous man? She didn't feel him to be so. Rabbie? Possibly, or was he just a passionate British subject? His statement in the stables had made it clear where he stood on the matter. Where did she stand? Torn between two worlds, she had never been more unsure of anything in her life. Her hand self-consciously went to her throat. Her mother had been sure enough to lay her life on the line. Her brother and father stood stoically on the other side of the issue, and there was Elaina stuck in the middle—lost.

Pulling the long strands of her hair over her shoulder, she brushed through the tangled ends and smoothed them until they turned to silk in her hands. If only untangling the jumbled strands of her life were as easy as brushing knots from her hair.

She sighed, picking up the candle and blowing it out with one last glance at the stables. She crawled into bed, trembling not only from the cold but also from the memory of two very different men and two entirely different encounters.

Chapter Twenty-Two

THE WOODED AREA BEHIND THE manor was dense enough to block most of the overnight snowfall.

"Is that the trail?" Angus whispered to his brother, pointing to something on the ground.

"I'm not sure." Ainsley squatted to inspect what Angus had brought to his attention. "It looks like she went this way but look over there, she might have gone that way. Ainsley studied the area for a few moments. "This way," he said, leading his brother to the east.

When they were out of sight, Elaina scrambled down from her perch in the tall pine. She had made two trails and circled back on herself to hide her tracks. The ruse had worked. As quickly and quietly as possible, she scurried to the edge of the woods, formed two snowballs, and hurried back into the woods to the same tree. She wrapped the snowballs in the hem of her skirts and shimmied up the trunk, scraping the insides of her knees on the rough bark. She settled herself on a large branch and waited.

Angus shouted directions as the boys circled back around. "Look here."

"Yes, I believe you're right. That twig, there. She did come this way." The boys walked closer to Elaina's ambush.

They came into view a few yards away.

"Well, here it runs into another trail." Angus stared at the ground. "Is that right? This is the same place we were a minute ago." He looked up at his brother and spied Elaina grinning in the tree. "Watch out!" He ducked, and Elaina pelted the two boys with her snowballs.

"Trickery!" Ainsley accused her as she scurried down out of her hiding spot.

"Yes, it was, and you two did well. You have good tracking skills."

"Our da taught us before we left," Angus said proudly with a hint of sadness in his voice.

"Och, dinna fret, Angus. Willnae be long. We will go visit, and ye can hunt with Da again." Ainsley thumped his little brother on the back. "Until then…" He pelted his brother with a snowball.

The fight was on. The two made snowballs as fast as they could, flinging them at each other. Then Angus turned his attention to Elaina.

"Oh, ho. Think you are brave enough lad?" Elaina backed away.

"Aye, I do." He launched it, pelting her in the shoulder as she ducked.

She worked as fast as she could but failed miserably at two against one. She finally gave up and launched herself at Ainsley, tackling him and rolling him in the snow. The next thing she knew, Angus was on her back, dumping snow on her head. She reached around and grabbed him by his coat and threw him over her shoulder, sending a puff of white powder into the air. The trio wrestled and laughed, trying to get the better of each other.

"In all my days…" a voice boomed.

They all froze and looked up at Mrs. Davies, looming large over them with her hands on her hips. "In all my days," she said again. "I have never—"

"Been speechless?" Angus piped up, causing peals of laughter to break out behind him.

"I beg your pardon, Mrs. Davies," Elaina snickered behind her hand. She rose, trying to dust the snow from her clothing and hair.

"Get in the kitchen, the three of ye. Ye're goin' ta catch a bloody ague." She turned sharply, her skirts making swirls in the snow.

Elaina and the boys shrugged at each other and followed the mother hen. Once in the kitchen, the heat of the battle began to wear off and the chill of wet hair and wet feet set in. The ever-efficient Mrs. Davies set the kitchen help about fetching blankets and warming pots of water. "Get the good brandy," she called out to Missie.

Caitir appeared, looking her mistress over with a disapproving eye. "My lady, ye are a mess. Come on. We will fix ye upstairs."

"No, I would like to stay in the kitchen. I am tired of being cooped up in this over-sized dungeon by myself."

Caitir shrugged. She was used to her mistress's unorthodox ways. "Well, ye at least need a hairbrush and some dry clothing." She left to fetch the necessities.

The boys and Elaina took turns ducking into the large pantry to change into their dry clothes. Mrs. Davies, however, insisted they each sit with their feet in steaming water. She wrapped a blanket around each of them and placed a mug of brandy in their hands. Shaking her head at Elaina, she lamented, "Yer mother would turn over in her grave if she kent ye were in the kitchen with the help in yer bare feet, after rolling around in the snow with the children, no less."

Elaina gave the distressed woman a shrug of her shoulders and a wry smile that did nothing to improve the annoyed cook's countenance.

"I'm no child," Ainsley piped up. "I'll be sixteen my next birthday."

"Yer birthday is not for another six months," Missie said.

"So!" Ainsley gave her the eye.

"I'm not a child either. I'm ten. I'm practically a man." Angus proudly sipped his brandy.

That sent rounds of laughter throughout the kitchen.

"Well, children or no children, we are doing something with yer hair before ye catch the ague." Caitir swung Elaina around, putting her back to the fire. She pulled the pins out, letting Elaina's wet hair fall down her back. "My word. Ye have pine needles in yer hair…and a stick. More than one!" She pulled the forestry out of Elaina's hair and tossed them into the fire where they hissed and sizzled on the hot embers.

"She was in the tree," Angus said.

"Oh my." Mrs. Davies crossed herself.

"Is it a sin to climb a tree?" Elaina asked, laughing.

"If ye had fallen outta the tree, Lord Spencer would hang us all," Mrs. Davies said. "So, pardon me while I say a prayer of thanks that the good Lord saw fit to save my neck today."

Ainsley snickered behind his mug.

"May I brush yer hair, my lady?" Angus asked Elaina shyly.

Appalled, Mrs. Davies replied, "No, ye may not!"

"Yes, you may." Elaina cast a stern look at Mrs. Davies, who turned in a huff and started barking orders at the other help.

Angus stepped out of his pot of water, placing his mug on the floor by his chair, and padded in his bare feet to Elaina. He stepped up on the hearth and took the brush from Caitir.

"It's glorious," he whispered, running the brush through it.

"I don't know about that," Elaina said. "There is a lot of it though."

"More than my ma. Her hair is long like yer own, but not so much of it. She used to let me brush her hair in the evening. She always wore hers in a long plait though, not piled up on her head like my lady."

In her best thick British accent, like her father's, Elaina replied, "Well, proper English society demands that a lady of stature wear her hair coiffed high upon her head to hide the fact that she has any hair at all."

Angus giggled as he smoothed the back of her hair.

She closed her eyes and sighed. For the first time since the death of her parents, she felt true happiness while sitting in the kitchen with the help, her bare feet in a pot of water and a ten-year-old boy brushing her hair.

Two cups of brandy and a bowl of the cook's infamous fish stew later, Elaina sat drying her feet as Rabbie came through the kitchen door.

"I thought I smelled—" He stopped at the sight of her.

Elaina looked up at the sound of his voice, her loose hair falling around her, nearly dusting the floor as she patted her feet. She straightened immediately, pulling her hair back out of her face and over her shoulders.

"My lady." He nodded his head, looking her over from head to toe.

After their encounter in the stables several days before, the once over made Elaina more than a little uncomfortable. If Rabbie thought anything out of the ordinary, he hid his feelings well.

He turned back to Mrs. Davies. "I thought I smelled something hot to warm my bones by?"

"Aye, I'll fetch ye bowl," Mrs. Davies said, casting Elaina a stern eye.

Elaina took that as an opportunity to escape the kitchen.

Chapter Twenty-Three

"**D**O YOU THINK THIS PLAID was his? The Highlander?" Elaina spread the tartan atop her bed and studied it while Caitir straightened the dressing table and gathered Elain's cloak and her gloves.

"I dinna ken, but it is too small for a man's plaid. Cannae say for sure, but it's cut more like a woman's arisaid, though smaller."

"Maybe he gave it to Mama when they were forced to stop seeing each other, as a 'something-to-remember-me-by'?"

"Possibly. That may be why it was tucked away in the chest. A tartan is usually only worn or given to a member of that clan."

"Really? Tell me more." Elaina perched on the edge of her bed, her curiosity piqued.

Caitir gave her mistress a sideways look and shook her head as she folded the lady's shift. "What do ye want to know?"

"Anything. What is clan life like? What are your customs?"

"Ye talk as if we are a foreign people."

"To me, you are. I'm from across the ocean, remember?"

Caitir sighed and plopped down on the hassock. "Well, ye already ken there are allied clans and rival clans."

"Is there quite a bit of fighting among the clans?"

"At times, yes. I can tell ye if ye ever hear the war cry of a clan, ye better be prepared to run or to fight."

"War cry?"

"Each clan has a clan motto and a call to battle."

"I have seen the Campbell's motto, *Ne Obliviscaris*, on a brooch a woman wore at the seaside."

"Yes, well the Campbell's war cry is *Cruachan*. They are a large, powerful clan. They have a strong political presence. They were one of the first clans in The Watch when the British formed it years ago."

"What is the MacGregors' cry?" Elaina ran her hand along the edge of the tartan.

Caitir gave her mistress a wicked grin. "That, my lady, is a feat to behold— the MacGregors going into battle. No clan, even the Campbells, can strike as much fear in their opponent as the MacGregors. My father has fought alongside them many times. I witnessed it first-hand once when I was a wee lass. It terrified me, and we were on their side. I remember it began with the drums, soft, then steadily louder and louder. They seemed to come from every direction, their rhythm thumping ye in yer chest." Caitir tapped her chest with her fist. "Then the pipes started a wailin' like the screams of women echoing off the hills. *Ard-Choille!* The men roared their cry and then seemed to come from everywhere and nowhere at the same time as if they sprang straight from the bowels of hell itself, their faces and bodies painted. It was one of the most blistering cold days there ever was, and there they were, bare feet, some half-naked, the rest completely naked, screaming as if possessed, with their broadswords in one hand and their dirks in the other."

"Naked?"

"Let me tell ye, it will strike fear right down to the heart of ye to see that coming at ye for more than one reason."

Elaina snickered at the expression on her friend's face.

"Ye will never forget it." Caitir shivered at the memory. "Enough with the tales. We need to be getting on if ye are going to make Lady Caroline's in time."

It had been two weeks since Elaina's visit with the Duke and her encounter with Rabbie. Angus and Ainsley had begged to go hunting for a couple of days, and that had left her with little to occupy her time. And she'd once again avoided the stables. It happened too often for her liking. She might talk with William when he returned. She liked Rabbie and had enjoyed his company on many occasions, but he had unsettled her with his words and his actions. He was supposed to be her protection when William could not be with her. She shouldn't have to worry about him too.

When she received Lady Caroline's invitation to join her for a day at the theater, Elaina delighted at finally having something to do.

"Be still, so I can fasten your cloak proper," Caitir chastised her mistress.

Elaina continued to pull on her gloves but tried not to move as much in the process.

"Are ye meetin' Lady Caroline at the theater or her home?" Caitir asked as she drew on her own cloak and gloves.

"Theater." Donned in a soft woolen gown the color of purple heather in spring, with her matching cloak fastened around her neck, Elaina had been tempted to string her secret pendant on a silver chain about her neck but changed her mind, remembering her mother's words. Instead, she patted the pouch she carried it in and touched the hilt of her *sgian-dubh*. She felt funny wearing such a thing to the theater, but Robert Campbell was out there somewhere and one never knew where he might show up. "What if you finish your running around before the play is over? What will you do with your time?" Elaina asked Caitir as Rabbie pulled the carriage around the front of the house and helped the two women into its waiting form. The horses stomped and tossed their heads, anxious to be on their way. They had been cooped up too long as well. Rabbie acted as if nothing had happened. There were no covert looks or strange actions. He merely helped the ladies into the carriage and took his place behind the reins.

"Dinna fash about me I can find plenty to busy myself with."

The women traveled in silence for a moment. Elaina marveling at the sight of everything covered in white. She watched the road and the trail the wheels of the carriage left and the muss in between where the horses trod. The sight of blankets of unmarred snow seemed magical, and she hated to sully such beauty.

"What are ye goin' to see, again? *Les* what?" Caitir broke the silence.

"*Les Sinceres*," Elaina said as the carriage plowed ahead. "Caroline says it is a comedy written by a Pierre Marivaux. It is about a couple and absolute sincerity in their relationship gone amiss. They say it is quite clever."

"Sounds marvelous," Caitir said absently while peering at something out of the carriage window, her hand tight on the sill.

"What is it?" Elaina asked, switching seats to get a view of whatever had captured her maid's attention.

"British soldiers. They have someone."

Elaina leaned her head out the window. The soldiers' red coats contrasted blood red against the gray November sky. Four of them. They appeared to be in an altercation with a short man. The women watched with mounting curiosity as one of the soldiers struck the man, knocking him into the snow. At that moment a smaller person came into view, held by one of the other soldiers.

"Angus?" Elaina whispered in abject horror, her heart in her throat. "Is that Angus?" She slapped the side of the carriage, yelling at Rabbie. "Hurry, I think it's the boys!"

"Ainsley! Angus!" Caitir yelled out the window.

Elaina tried to will the horses to go faster. The snow bogged the carriage down as a burly soldier drug Ainsley up by his unruly hair and pointed what looked like a knife to his throat. She could hear Angus yell something at the soldiers. The big one turned on him and struck him, knocking him to the ground. "Stop it at once!" Caitir cried out. The soldiers turned their attention to the approaching carriage.

With the soldiers' attention diverted, Angus made a move to raise himself.

"No!" Elaina screamed as the arrow launched from Angus's bow impaled the forearm of the soldier holding his brother. She flung the door of the carriage open as the sharp crack of a pistol echoed through the air, then threw herself from the slowing contraption, rolling head-over-heels in the snow.

"My lady!" Caitir yelled from the open carriage door.

Elaina was on her feet and running.

Rabbie tried to rein in the horses as Elaina rounded the back of the carriage.

"Oh God, the cross of Christ be with me. The Cross of Christ overcomes all weapons," she prayed as she ran, tripping and clawing her way through the dirt and snow. "...everywhere and before all mine enemies..."

She could not move fast enough. Her breath hitched in her throat, struggling against the weight of a boulder lodged firmly on her chest. She slipped and slid through the snow, her heart pounding and a cold sweat breaking out on her brow.

She fell to her knees upon reaching the boy. "Oh Jesus..."

The snow, dirty and trampled by the soldiers' feet, was stained crimson.

"Angus! Angus, my love, can you hear me?" She pushed his dark hair from his eyes and cupped his pallid face in her hands. "Look at me," she urged.

His brown eyes slowly came to focus on her own. "Mam?" he whispered.

A choked sound came from Ainsley as he gripped his brother's hand in a stranglehold. "Brother."

"Did I do good?" the boy whispered, his eyes on his brother. "Did I get him? The evil sheriff of Nottingham?"

"Aye," Ainsley managed to choke out. "Ye did good, Robin."

Elaina ripped open the boy's shirt and froze, her stomach in her throat. She closed it back again. The look of fear in his eyes before his body convulsed into wracking bloody coughs chilled her soul. She wiped his mouth with her cloak.

"I don't want to die," he sputtered, droplets of blood landing on Elaina's face. "The hero never dies, right?"

"Ssssh, my sweet boy," she managed to croak out.

"Momma? Tell me I willnae die."

It took Elaina a moment to realize the dying child thought that she was his mother. "My son." She stroked his hair. "Rest now. You are safe. I have you. You are home. Just rest." She choked on her words, using her thumb to wipe the tears from Angus's ashen face. She gathered the dying boy to her bosom, laying her cheek against his dark hair, and wrapped an arm around Ainsley as he wept upon his brother. Rocking the two boys, she sang in choked whispers a Scottish lullaby her mother had sung to her on nights when she was scared.

"My lady," Caitir whispered, laying a tentative hand on Elaina's shoulder. "My lady, he is gone."

"I know." Elaina continued to rock the boy, her tears freezing in his hair.

"My lady. Elaina, let me take him." Rabbie reached for the dead boy.

"No."

Ainsley raised his head and looked at his mistress, his eyes dark with grief. "I think we do need to go." He glanced over her shoulder at the soldiers tending to their wounded man.

Elaina stared at him a moment before giving a slight nod. She struggled to rise to her feet, hampered by the weight of the dead boy she refused to give up and her stiff legs half frozen from kneeling in the blood-soaked snow.

Rabbie grabbed her under her arms and helped her to her feet. "Please let me take him, only for a moment, until ye can get in the carriage, then ye may hold him again."

Elaina reluctantly acquiesced to Rabbie, and he lifted the boy from her arms. She stared at her blood-soaked gloves and the dark stain on the front of her gown—Angus's blood, the life substance of a boy who had held her heart. Caitir touched her arm, urging her forward, but her gaze fell upon the four soldiers as she turned toward the carriage.

"Why? Why would you murder an innocent boy?" Her voice quivered through her tears as she yelled at them. "How dare you! He was just a child!" She took a step toward one of the men only a few feet away.

Caitir's grip increased on Elaina's arm.

"He assaulted a member of the king's army," one of the soldiers stepped forward as his two other comrades continued their ministrations on the third. "By law, we can dispose of him."

"*Dispose* of him? Is that what you call murder these days? *Disposing* of him? You bloody…you *bastard*." Elaina's gaze flew to the injured soldier who continued spewing obscenities at Ainsley. "Shut him up before I relieve him of his tongue." Elaina lunged at the soldier with her hand on her *sgian-dubh*.

Caitir whirled Elaina around to face her. "Do ye want to die today as well?" she hissed, preventing Elaina from pulling her knife. "I can guarantee yer punishment will not be as swift nor as merciful."

Elaina met Rabbie's eyes, and he slowly shook his head. She looked at the lifeless form in his arms and her knees buckled under the weight of her grief. Merciful? There was nothing merciful about this killing of a young boy.

"Let us go." Caitir and Ainsley wrapped their arms around Elaina's waist, helping her to the carriage.

True to his word, Rabbie lay the dead boy in Elaina's arms for the ride back to the manor. Ainsley sat silent and white as the fallen snow on the seat beside Caitir, his eyes on Elaina cradling his brother and whispering to him between moments of uncontrolled sobbing. "My boy. I am so sorry. My sweet boy." She trembled violently as she cradled him in her arms, her wet cheek pressed against his forehead.

⁂

Mrs. Davies and Caitir washed the boy's body to prepare him for burial. Ainsley helped them wrap his brother's body in a white shroud.

"How far is it to your home?" Elaina asked Ainsley, her voice a hoarse whisper. Her tears had stopped when she exited the carriage at the manor, and not another had fallen.

"About four days ride, my lady."

Elaina looked at Rabbie. "Ready my horse and the sled tomorrow morning by dawn. I am going to take him home."

"Lady Elaina, ye cannae be meanin' to carry him all the way to hi—"

"I will hear no argument," Elaina interrupted. "It will be done. The least I can do is take him to his mother. He was under my care, and I failed him." Her voice broke. Clearing her throat, she added, "The weather is cold enough. Prepare a horse for Ainsley also."

"Ready a horse for me as well," Caitir told Rabbie. "I am going, and I will hear no argument." She looked pointedly at Elaina.

Elaina gave her a slight nod.

"What about the soldiers, madam?" Ainsley asked.

"What about them?" Elaina replied.

"What if they are still out there?"

"What happened? What started the altercation?" It never dawned on Elaina to ask before.

"They wanted our ducks."

"Your ducks?" She stared at Ainsley, uncomprehending.

"Yes, my lady. We killed four ducks, Angus and me. We came upon the soldiers, and they wanted to take our ducks. We didna want to give them up. Angus wanted to show you how much yer lessons had improved his shootin'."

Elaina didn't know if she wanted to cry again or scream. "All this was over ducks?" She stared at the white form that had once been her friend.

"It is the law that the army may confiscate food, weapons...whatever they want," Rabbie said.

Elaina turned on him. "I don't give a damn what the law is! To kill a boy over dead fowl is unconscionable."

"He wasn't killed over the ducks. They killed him for raising a weapon against a member of His Majesty's Army."

"To hell with His Majesty's Army," Elaina spit out. "Those brutish bastards. If I come across them on our path to your home, Ainsley, I promise you I will slaughter every one of them."

"You would hang," Rabbie said flatly. "Ye cannae do it."

"I can, and I will."

"It is the law, my lady. These boys should have handed over their goods and went on their way. It is their fault."

"Their fault? What the hell is wrong with you, Rabbie MacLeod? Look at this boy's face." She grabbed Ainsley by the chin, turning his face toward Rabbie's. Ainsley's bruises showed dark purple in the failing light of the day, his left eye near swollen shut. "Look at Angus' body, and you tell me it is a ten-year-old boy's fault they murdered him while he tried to protect his brother!"

"They could have prevented it."

Elaina could not believe her ears. Rabbie still defended the British bastards.

"No," Ainsley piped up. "We gave them the ducks in the end, but they were not happy with just havin' the ducks. They called us sons of a Scottish whore. They were beatin' us and sayin' all manner of foul things I willnae repeat in front of the lady, and," his voice dropped low, and Elaina strained to hear him. "He said he was goin' to bugger me."

"Sodomy? Rape?" Elaina sat down hard on an upturned bucket, burying her head in her hands. "I can't take this. I cannot do this. Rabbie, have the horses ready at dawn. Ainsley, I will do my best to avenge your brother's death if I go straight to hell for it." Elaina stood up and kicked the bucket as hard as she could, sending it tumbling into the dark.

"I will accompany you," Rabbie said.

"The hell you will," she spit out and turned toward the house, making it to the back door before she collapsed in the snow.

———— ❦ ————

The wet rag was cold upon her face, and she tried to wave away the hand that kept rubbing her with it. Struggling to sit up, she opened her eyes to find herself wrapped tight in Mrs. Davies's embrace.

"There darlin'," she whispered to her. "There ye are."

Concerned faces of the servants peered down at her, and she pushed herself up, the stones of the floor hard and cold underneath her wet gloves. Her head swam, and she closed her eyes against the wave of dizziness and the eyes staring at her.

"Slowly, lass," Mrs. Davies said.

"Ye want I should help ye up?" Ainsley said.

"What happened?" Elaina whispered, her eyes closed.

"Ye fainted. We brought ye inside."

Elaina opened her eyes, bits and pieces of the kitchen coming into view through the legs of those surrounding her. There, still by the hearth, stood the stool she had sat upon a week earlier with her beloved Angus brushing her hair. She pushed herself to her hands and knees. How did they get to this place? Days before they wrestled in the snow. Today he was gone. It was her fault. If she had never introduced him to the legends of Robin Hood, he might still be with her.

Ainsley knelt beside her, his anguished face showing pale in the dancing firelight from the hearth.

"I am so sorry, Ainsley," she whispered. "Please forgive me."

"Forgive? Ye did nothin' There is nothin' to forgive, my lady." He studied her, confusion etched upon his face.

"I killed him."

"Nay. The British killed him. No ye."

"It may as well have been my hand holding that pistol. If I had not read him those stories—"

"If ye'd no read him those stories, his last days would no have been near as happy as they were. No, my lady. Ye mustn't say such. Ye gave him such love—"

"I gave him *death*, Ainsley."

"Stop it," he hissed. "Ye must stop."

"I will not stop. I killed him! I killed your brother."

"I willnae listen to such nonsense." Ainsley stood, but Elaina grabbed the leg of his trews.

The kitchen lay in silence, only the breaths of the bodies hovered around their mistress could be heard.

"He loved ye, my lady," Ainsley's voice came strangled. "And ye loved him. We all ken it. Ye brought him happiness he had no felt since we left home. Ye gave us a home—a true home. Angus made his choice to die when he raised arms against the soldiers. He died for me, no because of you." Ainsley's voice had become a whisper.

He lay his hand upon her head, and she collapsed from that simple act by a fifteen-year-old boy. Her forehead rested on the stones of the floor. The boy had lost his brother mere hours ago. He had no call to be kind to her. If not for her, Angus would still be living. He should hate her. He should run her through with his sword.

Breathing seemed to become something her body no longer knew how to do. Her cries, silent in their fury, wracked her body with the strength of them, though no sound would escape her frozen throat. When finally they erupted, tearing from her in a rage, she slapped the floor with her hands.

"Damn the British!" she screamed. Then her voice fell to a strangled whisper. "Damn them to hell."

Ainsley wrapped her in his arms, burying his face in her hair, muffling his sobs. They huddled together and wept on the cold gray stones.

⟡

"Let me get ye out of these," Caitir whispered to Elaina. She reached out a tentative hand as if afraid Elaina might snap one off if she moved too suddenly.

Elaina didn't respond. She didn't look up or acknowledge that her maid had spoken.

"Get us a dram," Caitir said to Missie who could do nothing but stare gape-mouth at her mistress's blood-stained clothing. "Now!" Caitir hissed. "Bring the whole bottle. Tell the men to bring in the tub and prepare a hot bath. Be quick about it."

The men had gotten Elaina off the kitchen floor and upstairs to her room, where she now sat upon a chair. She could not stop shaking.

"I am going to remove yer gloves?" her maid tentatively said.

Elaina bobbed her head slightly. She could not speak through the chattering of her teeth as Caitir peeled the gloves one by one from her frozen hands.

The servants all moved with great haste, hauling in the giant copper tub and filling it with steaming water. Caitir held the glass of whiskey to Elaina's lips, urging her to drink. Caitir motioned to Missie to take Elaina's hair down. She, herself, moved to untie her lady's stays.

Rabbie stood at the doorway. "Is she—"

"Get out." Elaina's voice was eerie in the quiet room, hollow and frightening to her own ears. She lifted her gaze to where Rabbie stood immobile. "Get out!" she screamed at his startled face.

He looked from Elaina to Missie's wide-eyed expression and Caitir's firm nod, then turned on his heel, closing the double doors behind him.

Elaina grabbed the stool and heaved it at the door where it bounced off and rolled across the floor. Missie and Caitir stood frozen in place until Elaina slumped over, holding her head in her hands, her entire body shaking in great spasms though no tears fell. She allowed the girls to finish undressing her. Her shift clung to her, cold and stiff with blood. Chill bumps rose all over her body. The thin fabric made a horrible sucking sound as the women pulled it away from her tiny frame. Elaina bolted to the chamber pot, hanging her head over it as she retched. Sweat rolled from her forehead while she trembled violently as if ice water pumped through her veins. Caitir wiped her face with a warm damp rag and helped her to her feet. Her servant and friend deposited her into the steaming tub.

"Honey water. We need some water with honey," Caitir whispered to Missie, who ran from the room. Her footsteps could be heard thumping down the stairs. "Ye are all right now, my lady," Caitir said to Elaina while pouring warm water over her shivering frame. "Ye are all right." Caitir crossed to the fireplace and built up the fire into a roaring blaze. Taking up a pot of water she had heated over the fire, she added it to the already steaming bath.

Elaina's eyes stared unblinking at the discolored water in which she sat—his blood slowly leaching from her skin.

Caitir picked up the rose-infused soap and began to scrub Elaina's hands gently.

"I don't understand why," Elaina whispered into the water. Her hand hung limp in Caitir's. Her shivering seemed to be easing somewhat.

Missie returned with the honey water, and Caitir instructed her to feed it to Elaina spoonful by spoonful. Elaina turned her grief-stricken eyes to Caitir, searching her blue eyes for answers no one could give.

"There is no good answer, my lady," Caitir said. "There is just none."

Elaina merely nodded and turned her eyes back to the water, letting Caitir bathe her.

Moving slow and unseeing, Elaina let the two women dress her and put her to bed. Caitir gave Missie orders about what to pack and what to leave behind for the next day's travels.

"Do ye think she should travel in that state?" Missie whispered as she gathered the items Caitir deemed necessary.

Elaina's voice came muffled from the bedclothes. "You will not leave me behind."

"Ye heard her. Get her things ready."

Caitir stayed with Elaina through the night. The two women lay in the same bed, curled together like frightened kittens, neither one sleeping much if at all. Daybreak came as a welcome relief.

Chapter Twenty-Four

THE ENTIRE HOUSEHOLD STAFF MET the trio at the stables as the sun began to show itself on the horizon. Mrs. Davies, dabbing her tears and wiping her nose, loaded the saddlebags with food that would, hopefully, be enough to sustain them on the road. Rabbie tightened straps and adjusted the sled that would take Angus to his family and his final resting place. He did not look happy about the group's intended departure, or the fact that he had been ordered to stay behind.

Elaina handed Eads a letter to dispatch to William at his current post, explaining the situation.

"Please be careful, Lady Elaina, and God speed," the butler said with a slight bow to her.

Elaina stood on the tips of her toes and kissed him on his solemn cheek. "Watch over the house and the help, Rupert. I leave it all in your capable hands."

His prominent Adam's apple bobbed as he swallowed hard. She had called him by his given Christian name, stirring his already high emotional state even further.

A small part of her wondered if she would ever return to this house. Life seemed more fragile than it ever had before. A slight stirring of fear tried to rise inside of her, but she tamped it down. They would deliver Angus to his parents, and she would return to her home and her life—whatever form it chose to take.

There were hugs and tears all around and then the trio mounted their rides to begin their journey. Ainsley sat tall in his saddle, leading the procession down the lane. He attempted to remain stoic, but Elaina heard him sniffle. She and Sadie followed him with their precious cargo behind them on the sled. Each of the household staff laid a hand on the shrouded body of their beloved Angus as it passed them. Caitir rode beside Elaina, dabbing her eyes and blowing her nose. Elaina had no tears left to give. She had no emotion except hate, and no thought but revenge.

The morning ride was a cold one. Elaina pulled her hood over her head and hugged her woolen cloak tighter around her body. The cold was good. They needed it to stay cold at least until they reached the boys' home. Elaina had smelled a decaying body before—it was not a pleasant odor and had the propensity to attract unwanted animal attention. She spent a silent morning mulling over the four soldiers, trying to remember what they looked like. The one who had pulled the trigger had a pock-marked face, she remembered, but as for the other three, she wasn't as sure. She had promised Ainsley revenge if she ever saw them, but now, doubt filled her about her ability to follow through on her promise. Planning it and thinking of it did give her mind something to busy itself with, however, and kept the visions of Angus's terrified eyes at bay.

They stopped at midday after a long morning of lugging through mounds of powdery snow, each lost in their thoughts.

"Where exactly are we going?" Elaina asked, perching herself between Caitir and Ainsley on the rocky outcropping they had dusted off as they ate some of the provisions Mrs. Davies packed for them, washed down with copious amounts of whiskey to warm their cold feet.

The horses busied themselves beside a small stream, snorting through the snow in search of winter grass.

Ainsley sighed, "My home is near Ben Leu."

"I'm not sure why I asked. I'm not from Scotland, so it means nothing to me."

Ainsley gave a little smile, tension and grief written on his face. "No, I dinna suppose it would, my lady." His gaze rested on the half-eaten bannock in his hand.

She placed a hand upon his shoulder. She wanted to wrap him up in her arms and hold him, but he was a proud young man who was trying heroically to keep himself together. The transition from a young boy into a man was a challenge in and of itself, but to accomplish it by delivering your murdered brother's body to your parents was unimaginable.

There is a place called Balquidder that has a gaol. We need to avoid it and the soldiers and possibly some members of The Watch." Ainsley fiddled with the bread in his hand.

Puzzled, Elaina turned to Caitir. "Wouldn't we want to go through there? We might find the soldiers or maybe word of Robert Campbell."

"Nay, my lady," Caitir said. "Our mission is to get this lad to his home. We dinna want to be killin' British soldiers at the foot of their own gaol. I personally dinna want to hang."

Elaina realized she needed to snap out of these murderous thoughts, not as much for herself as for the people she cared about that her actions would affect. "Do you think the weather will hold?" she asked Caitir, trying to do just that as they mounted their horses to continue their journey.

Caitir studied the sky. "Aye. I hope." She frowned and gave the sky another furtive glance.

"A change is coming, is it not?" Elaina asked.

"Aye. I think so."

The three riders continued on their way in somber silence across the rolling, snow-covered hills. They received a definitive answer about the weather by the time night began to fall. The snow no longer remained an issue, the farther they traveled from Edinburgh, the less there was of it. The wind had steadily increased throughout the day, however, and howled towards nightfall. The trio finally came across a rocky outcropping that would offer some protection and allow them to light a fire.

Blustery gales turned out to be the least of their worries. As the sunlight began to disappear, they could hear the calling of wolves over the wind. The darker it grew, the closer they seemed to be. They decided to take turns guarding the body. Elaina volunteered to be the first watch. She wouldn't be able to sleep anyway. Whenever she closed her eyes, the fear that had filled Angus's face as he lay dying in her arms haunted her. How could they have taken his life over a few ducks? It was pure malice against the Scots. Hate-filled brutality. To threaten the boy's brother and beat them without reason. How had the soldiers expected them to react? She would gladly have done the same for William. Thinking of him, she wondered what his thoughts would be about the matter. He, being a British officer, might be able to bring a court-martial against the four soldiers— if she only knew who they were.

From the corner of her eye, she caught a movement in the dark, inching its way toward the end of the sled. She scrambled on hands and knees to the fire, using a foot to knock a half-burning log loose from the pile and yelling for Ainsley as she did so. Startled, the crouching wolf bolted. Not far enough, however. Elaina could see him rounding back on her.

"Ainsley! Wolf!" she yelled again over the violent wind while swinging her burning torch at the approaching beast.

Caitir appeared by her side with a burning log of her own. They were in a standoff with the snarling animal. He crouched low to the ground between the girls and the sled. Elaina slashed her torch through the air, accomplishing nothing except moving the animal closer to Angus's body. The animal lurched sideways, its cry carrying to Elaina on the wind. She stood uncomprehending at its unnatural movements as it fell to the ground.

Ainsley's wild mop of curls appeared over the top of his brother's body. As the women inched closer to the wolf, the light from their torches glinted off the hilt of the boy's sword protruding from the animal. Ainsley approached his prey, placing a foot on the dead creature, and wrenched his sword free.

"I-I didn't know you could throw like that." She watched him clean the blood from his blade.

"I didna either, but it's too bloody windy for an arrow. I believe we have scairt them off for the moment, mistress," Ainsley said, not taking his eyes from the dark void in front of them. "But they may return."

It was going to be a long ride to Ben Leu.

The following two days passed without any major incidents. Minor issues were another matter. The sled was a hindrance on the rocky terrain. She should have put Angus's body on a horse and delivered him that way, but horses tended to shy away from carrying dead things, and she thought the sled would be a suitable mode for transportation. She had been wrong. The sled harness broke the fourth morning of their travels, and Caitir and Ainsley headed to the nearest town in search of something to repair it with, leaving Elaina to guard Angus's body.

She sat alone next to a flowing stream, washing her face in the freezing water with hardly enough energy left to lift her hands. Sleep was an elusive concept none of them seemed able to grasp since the first night with the wolves.

Sadie snorted behind her as footsteps approached.

"Back already?" Elaina asked, splashing the icy water onto her face, the cold taking her breath away.

"I'm afraid I am not who you think, madam," a voice replied.

Elaina jumped to her feet, her hand on her knife.

"I didna mean to startle ye," the young man said, holding up his hands.

They eyed each other with wary apprehension. He couldn't have been more than eighteen or nineteen and was slight of stature. He looked oddly familiar, just something about him. His blonde hair hung loosely about his shoulders from under his blue slouch hat.

"Is this yer steed?" the lad asked, not moving.

Elaina climbed the embankment coming to stand close to Sadie. "It is."

"I am afraid I must confiscate her in the name of the king."

"You what?" Elaina knew she must have heard him wrong.

"As a member of The Black Watch, I may take your steed. Mine came up lame, necessitating he be put down a few days ago. By law, madam, I may take ownership of any horse in the name of the king."

"I am sorry, sir, but you may not have my horse. I am transporting a dead boy to his parents for burial." Elaina now saw the boy wore not only the trademark blue hat of The Watch but also the red coat and dark tartan.

The two stared at each other for a moment, then the man reached out and took hold of Sadie's reins.

Elaina immediately pulled her knife, grabbing Sadie's bridle. "I think not."

"Madam—"

"Lady," she corrected him. "Lady Elaina Spencer, sister to William Spencer, the 3rd Earl of Strafford and a Lieutenant in His Majesty's 8th Dragoons. You are not taking my horse." She stepped closer, pointing her knife at him.

"Alex Campbell, member of the 43rd Foot Patrol, and I am confiscating this steed." His hand was on his sword, but she could see in his eyes that he was unsure of whether to pull it on a lady or not, although she currently had her weapon pointed at him.

Elaina stepped forward, placing herself on the same side of her horse as the young man. "I thought The Watch were fighting in Flanders?"

"They are. We are a newly appointed band."

"Appointed by whom?" she asked, stalling for time while pondering her options and looking him up and down, gauging whether she thought she could take him.

"Appointed by the clans, Madam. Now, if you will…" he tugged at Sadie's reins.

"I do not mean to be difficult, Mr. Campbell, but I made a promise to someone and I intend to keep it no matter what."

"No matter what? My brother is the captain of our order of The Watch, my lady, and I assure you he will—"

"I don't care who your brother is. I am telling you that under no circumstances are you taking my horse and this conversation is—"

Sadie, startled by movement in the trees, swung herself around to face the sound and knocked the young man onto Elaina, sending them tumbling down the embankment and into the stream. Her breath taken by the cold, she fought to gain her footing, but her heavy skirts and the full weight of the man held her submerged. He looked as shocked as she felt, as she shoved and squirmed to free herself of his grasp. As black spots began to form in her eyes and her lungs seized with the need for air, the two of them were drug from under the water. She collapsed face down on the bank, coughing and choking.

A pair of black boots stood in front of her. "Are you quite recovered?"

"Getting there," she gasped, looking up into the face of another man dressed in a similar style to Mr. Campbell.

"Get her up," he barked.

Two pairs of hands grabbed her, one under each arm, and dragged her to her feet.

"What is your name?" The man stood with his arms behind his back, dressed in the same Black Watch uniform as the young man. His near-black eyes looked her up and down with distaste.

She repeated what she had told Campbell.

"Spencer, did you say? Elaina Spencer?"

He now stared at her with interest, and Elaina felt a chill creep down her spine. "Yes?"

"Lady Elaina Spencer, you are under arrest for the murder of Alex Campbell, member of The Watch, and," he added with a sneer, "for high treason."

"Murder? Treason? What the hell are you talking about?"

The man stepped to the side, and her eyes fell upon the lifeless body of Alex Campbell. The young man had the same startled expression he'd held under the water frozen upon his face and her knife protruding from his neck.

"I-I didn't kill him! It was an accident. My horse—"

"Your horse pulled a knife on a member of The Watch? I find that hard to believe."

Elaina glared at the man.

"Arrest her."

"You can't. I didn't do anything!" Elaina struggled with her captors, managing to wrench an arm free from one while cracking him with an elbow to his face.

Shoving herself loose of the other, she turned to run. She hadn't gotten more than two steps before there was a blinding pain on the back of her skull and her world went dark.

Chapter Twenty-five

S HE AWOKE FREEZING AND CONFUSED and laid still without moving for several moments. Had she fallen in the creek while washing? That didn't seem right. It had been mid-morning when she washed her face, and now it was dark. She grasped for pieces of memories about the day—breaking camp with Ainsley and Caitir, traveling several miles before the harness broke. The harness…the water…something about the water…she had fallen in the stream. She killed someone.

Her heart felt as if it slammed into the wall of her chest. Dear God, she had taken someone's life and The Watch had arrested her. Where had they taken her?

She lay on a stone floor, the coldness of it hard against her cheek and seeping through her clothing, but her eyes couldn't pierce the inky darkness. Pushing herself up to sitting, she listened for any identifying sounds. She was not alone. To the left, in the far corner, someone or something was breathing.

Closing her eyes, she rubbed the sore spot on the back of her head while trying to quell the fear and the resulting bile lodging itself in her throat. She took in what she could of her surroundings. The room was small and square, with the only light coming from transom windows so high up you could not see out. It must have been a moonless night for there to be no more light than there was. Elaina smelled snow on the air. The same scent had been in the air that morning as they broke camp, so she assumed it was the same day.

There was no furniture in the room. There was, however, a dark mound in the far corner that moved slightly, giving evidence of where the breathing came from.

"Who are you?" Elaina whispered into the night.

No answer.

She rose gingerly to her feet, pausing as a wave of dizziness washed over her. Christ, her head hurt. Following the rough stones of the wall with one hand, she made her way to a large wooden door. No surprise, it was locked.

Leaning her forehead against the door, she sighed heavily. *Now what?* Surely Ainsley and Caitir had missed her by now and were searching for her. Although, what if the pair had also been captured? She slammed her fist against the door in frustration.

"Ye'll get nowhere like that, lass," a voice came out of the dark.

Elaina squeaked, whirling around. "Who are you?"

"'Tis no matter," the voice sighed. "I will not be here much longer."

"Where are you going? Can I send a message with you? For my brother?" Elaina asked hopefully. Her eyes began to adjust to the dark, and she could just make out a small mound in the direction of the man's voice.

"Only if it is to God almighty or Satan himself, for I will hang—soon I hope, for I am tired of laying in this miserable, freezing place."

"Hang? For what?"

"Treason."

"Treason," she repeated in a whisper as the words of The Watch came back to her. *"...for murder and high treason..."* To the figure in the dark, she said, "Where are we?"

"The gaol in Balquhidder."

Balquhidder. At least some ten miles from where they had camped the night before, if she remembered correctly. They'd tried to skirt the area to avoid any interaction with Redcoats or The Watch. They had not skirted far enough.

"Ye may as well rest, lass. The night will pass whether ye stand or ye lie."

Elaina hugged her woolen cloak tightly around her, uncertain of what to do with herself. She tried to determine where the warmest spot on the floor would be.

"Ye can lay over here." The form moved slightly, making room for Elaina on his small mound. "I willnae bite," he said as she hesitated. "I cannae speak for the rats."

With the mention of rats, she chose the mound with the voice. The mound turned out to be a small pile of hay. Elaina was grateful to have even a slight barrier between her and the cold floor.

"When did they put me in here?" she asked as she settled in, trying not to breathe in the stench coming from her companion. Apparently, bathing was not a luxury granted to the condemned.

"A while ago. 'Twas still daylight."

"Mmmm," Elaina mused. "Must have been some knock to the head." She burrowed herself down in the small nest.

"Ye said ye needed to get word to yer brother?"

"Yes. Lord Spencer. Lieutenant William Edward Talbot Spencer, The Earl of Strafford. Have you heard of him?" she asked without much hope.

"Nay. I am sorry. I have been here for a time."

They lay in silence for a moment.

"Ye are a lady then? I mean, if yer brother is an Earl. Yer speech doesna sound as so, if ye beg my pardon, madam?" the man asked. "It's a wee bit odd."

Elaina laughed. "I had an English father and a Scottish mother. They raised me in the colonies."

"That explains it then," the man chuckled back.

"It's an eclectic mix to be sure."

"And what is your name, my lady?"

"Elaina," she replied. "And yours?"

"Lachlan, madam."

"Lachlan, I would say it's a pleasure, but under the circumstances…"

"The same, my lady," the voice said with a smile to it. After a moment he asked, "How does the sister of an Earl and a member of the British army find herself in a gaol in the middle of the Highlands, if I may be so bold?"

"You may, but it is a rather long story. It ends with an accident and the death of a member of The Watch."

"Did you kill him?"

"Yes and no. He is dead by my knife but not by my intent."

"They usually hang ye on the spot for such acts. Ye come here for interrogations."

Elaina mulled over his words in silence because her throat had seized and she could not speak.

"I'm sorry, lass. I didna mean to bring ye worries. Rest now. Ye will need yer stamina. Trust me."

The last statement did nothing to ease her distress.

Gray light filtered through the transoms as the lock in the door clicked and it slid open enough for an unseen person to throw a half loaf of bread through.

"Wait!" Elaina called as the door closed with a thud.

The click of the lock seemed to echo through her head. Something flew out from the hay like a shot, knocking her backward. Lachlan reached the bread one step ahead of a giant rat.

"Ye've got to be quick if ye want to eat," he said, tearing the bread in half and handing a piece to Elaina.

"Thank you," she said, trying not to swallow the thing whole. It had been at least twenty-four hours since she had eaten anything and then it was a breakfast of cold bannocks. She nibbled at the hunk of bread, not caring if it was stale or moldy.

Lachlan in the gray light of morning was much like Lachlan in the shadows of the night. A dark hunched shape. He sat with his back to Elaina, his long hair matted and wild with hay stuck here and there as if it grew from the depths of a great nest.

"How long have you been here?" she asked in between bites.

"I dinna ken. I quit counting."

That did little for Elaina's countenance. "Do you have family on the outside? Have you been able to correspond with them? I guess I am asking if they know you are here?"

"Aye, I've some. Some may ken, and others may not. 'Tis no matter. I have made my peace."

Elaina hoped she would be as calm if or when her time came, though his calmness may be more for the hope of leaving this world and ending this miserable punishment being inflicted upon him. She hoped it did not take losing all faith in man for her to come to peace with her own death.

The lock clicked in the door.

Elaina jumped to her feet as two officers entered the room. "Sir, I must speak to your superior at once. There has been a grave mistake."

The soldier shoved her backward onto the hay. "There is no mistake, my lady," he sneered her title at her. "We will deal with you later. It's this one we came for." They snatched Lachlan up by his frail arms.

"God go with ye, my lady," Lachlan called out as the door slammed shut.

"And with you," she whispered to the empty room.

She lay on the bed of hay, pondering her options. She didn't see she had any. Beg for word to be sent to William and plead for her life? She must convince them the Campbell man's death had been the accident it was. Not satisfied with that thought, she clambered to her feet and strode to the door. She put her ear to it, listening.

"Caitir!" she yelled, then listened.

She called for Ainsley as well.

Standing at each of the four walls, she held out hope for any sound as she called out until she was hoarse. Nothing—not even a soldier telling her to shut up. Sliding down the wall under the windows, she wrapped her cloak about her knees. Laying her head on them, she began to pray. She couldn't bring herself to pray for her soul. That would admit defeat. Instead, she prayed for Lachlan and that God grant him eternal rest.

"Madam." Someone kicked her leg.

She started suddenly at the young British soldier staring down at her. She had fallen asleep and not heard him enter. "If you will?" He motioned for the door.

Rising to her feet, she brushed the hay off her skirts and smoothed her hair the best she could. A pair of soldiers awaited them on the other side of the door, their muskets resting on their shoulders.

"This way," one of them said, turning sharply and leading the way down a dark hallway.

There were no windows to let in light, and although there were lanterns hung at regular intervals, they didn't have much luck dispelling the shadows. Elaina tried not to panic, making comparisons to coffins and hallways in her head. She thought she could smell Lachlan's odor remaining in the tunnel, or was it the rancid stink of fear seeping from herself? The quartet came to another large wooden door, and one of the guards opened it with a key he extracted from the many hanging on his belt.

Shielding her eyes from the sudden onslaught of glaring daylight, she stepped out into a courtyard of sorts. A dusting of snow crunched under their feet as they marched toward their destination. The ground had been trodden smooth by innumerable boot heels. She wondered, much to her chagrin, where the gallows was located.

They had locked her and Lachlan in a wing of their own, for theirs' was the only door on that side of the building. The only way out of the gaol appeared to be through a set of large wooden doors to the south that were barred against the outside, or through a part of the building itself.

The soldier with the keys unlocked a door in the middle of the east side of the building.

Elaina closed her eyes as they stepped across the threshold, to help her eyes adjust faster to the dimness of the room. She didn't know what she had expected, but her heart sank a little when she opened her eyes to a bare room with two chairs, a table, and a few candles.

Without speaking, the guards backed out into the courtyard and locked the door.

She stood alone in the room, trying to think of a way out of the mess she was in. Stalking the perimeter of the room, she listened at each of the walls, searching for any proof of human life but finding none. Dejected, she leaned against the locked door and surveyed the room. Her eyes came to rest on the candlestick in its pewter holder. Striding to the table, she lifted it and weighed it carefully in her hand. One never knew when one might need a weapon.

Chapter Twenty Six

"I'M AFRAID THE FURNISHINGS MAY not be up to your standards."

Startled, Elaina spilled melted wax on her hand and the tabletop.

"I am sorry, Madam. Here, let me." The officer took out his handkerchief. "I didn't mean to interrupt your contemplations." The officer wiped the wax from her fingers in long, slow strokes. "Please, do sit." He held the back of the chair for her.

She sat, taking in the gentleman's appearance. His handkerchief and tricorn hat rested upon the table beside his drumming fingers as he watched her. He was pristine from his powdered wig to his shining gorget, to the tip of his long, black boots.

They stared at each other without speaking long enough for Elaina to feel uncomfortable. She tried not to squirm in her seat. Instead, she sat up straighter and raised her chin, meeting the officer's eye.

He smacked the tabletop with the palm of his hand, making her jump. "And there it is."

Elaina raised an eyebrow in question.

"All I could see was a most handsome young woman, if I may, with eyes that would melt a man to his soul. Not an arrogant, impudent, traitorous Jacobite supporter and a killer of men."

"Officer…?"

"Captain. Captain Anthony Bernard Cummings of His Majesty's 2nd Dragoons at your service," he tipped his head as if remembering his manners.

"Captain Cummings, a mistake has been made. I did *accidentally* kill a member of The Watch. My horse shied and knocked us into the creek, and he fell upon my knife. But I am not a Jacobite. My brother is Lord William Edw—"

"I know who your brother is, madam. I also know who your father was and more importantly"—he leaned forward—"I know exactly what your mother was."

Elaina stared at him, shock rendering her speechless.

"Yes. I thought that might shut you up. Now. I want from you what your mother would not give me, my dear. I want to know who helped your mother on this side of the ocean. I want names."

"I have no idea what you are talking about," Elaina whispered. *They know about Mother. They know who she was. What in God's name is going on?*

"You are a terrible liar, my sweet." Captain Cummings leaned in closer.

Undaunted, Elaina did the same. "I know nothing of what you speak. If you knew my parents, then you would know they are dead. Murdered."

He ignored her words. "Your eyes, when you are angry, are even more magnificent—like the churning waters in a stream, almost black with bits of gold. A man could drown in them." The officer's eyes trailed down her neck, to the tops of her breasts that rose above the bodice of her dress. "They could make a man want to bed you in an instant, even if you are a traitorous whore."

She slapped him.

He moved quickly for a man of what seemed middle age. He wrenched her from her seat and pinned her arm behind her back, forcing her face-down onto the table and holding her there with his forearm. "Madam. You will only strike me once. You will tell me who your connections are if I have to beat it out of you."

"I know nothing of which you speak," Elaina said and sucked in a sharp breath as Captain Cummings wrenched her arm farther behind her back. She felt the weight of his descent upon her crushing her lungs against the table. The forearm that held her head to the table moved and his calloused hand grazed the side of her cheek, pushing loose tendrils of hair away from her face. She tried to struggle against him but felt her arm might snap in two.

"Now," he whispered, his mouth on her ear. "Tell me the names and where the money is."

"I will have you court-martialed—"

The captain licked the side of her face from her chin to her temple.

Elaina made a futile attempt to head-butt him. Impossible in her position.

"Nothing?" He grabbed her by a fistful of hair, wrenching her head backward to look her in the eye.

"My brother—"

"Your brother will do nothing. Your brother is a puppet safely performing his duties to his king, tucked away at Fort William. This is about you, my dear, and the knowledge you hold."

"I do not know," she hissed between her clenched teeth.

"Well, we will see about that." The captain reached down and started to ruck her skirts up.

"Get off me!" She kicked backward, grazing the captain's shin as she squirmed and fought with all she had.

"Captain?" An apprehensive voice came from the direction of the doorway. A young soldier stood looking in horror from the captain to Elaina and back.

"Yes?" Captain Cummings replied, not easing his grip in the least. Elaina's skirts were bundled in his hand, his crotch pushed firmly against her bare backside.

"General Shipley needs a word?" The statement came out more like a question from the young soldier, his face crimson as he looked everywhere except at Elaina.

"General Shipley? What the hell does he want?"

"I dinna ken," the young man replied. "He only said it was urgent."

With a sigh, Cummings released Elaina's arm. He pushed himself off her and patted her on the head. "Until next time, my lady." He turned and addressed the junior officer. "Escort the lady back to her accommodations, boy, but be careful. She's a live one." He bowed to Elaina and left.

She hurriedly pushed down her skirt and righted herself to a standing position. With shaking knees, she stepped away from the table and noticed the young soldier balked slightly. "I won't hurt you," she said and cocked her head.

"This way." A blush rose in his cheeks as she turned toward the door leading out into the courtyard.

They stepped out into the sunlight. The snow had melted, and the two trudged through the mud toward Elaina's door.

"Captain Cummings is quite the gentleman." She glanced sideways at the young man, contemplating his presence in the gaol. His red hair fell in waves from under his hat and his face still held the look of a boy not yet a man.

"I am sorry for his rough handlin', ma'am...my lady. He is a surly bastard." The boy blushed again as he said the words, looking behind him. "Pardon my speech."

"I think I would have to agree with you," Elaina replied. "Is he always the interrogator?"

"Not always, ma'am. There is another, but he is not at the gaol much. He is a member of The Black Watch. He is worse than Cummings."

"I can't imagine what could be worse, and I don't want to either. Let's hope he stays gone, shall we?" Elaina shuddered.

"Yes, let's."

"How old are you, lad?"

"My lady, I dinna think…" His voice trailing off betrayed his uneasiness.

"I don't think it would matter a great deal for me to know how old you are."

"Sixteen, my lady."

"You're so young, and obviously Scottish by your speech."

"They pressed me into service, my lady," the boy answered quietly, looking around, but they were the only two in the courtyard.

"Pressed? At sixteen? Is the British army hurting so bad they have to force young Scottish boys to fight?"

"Madam. I-I…" the boy stuttered.

"Don't fret." She laid a soft hand upon his sleeve. "You are doing your duty to your king and country. Bravely, I might add. I will do and say nothing to jeopardize you. It is a wicked world we live in." She sighed, looking up to the sky. "The clear weather won't last long. Hopefully, the clouds return before nightfall or it will be brutally cold."

Through the darkened hallway, they walked in silence.

As she stepped into her cell, she turned and gave him her warmest smile. "Thank you for your kindness, soldier." She lowered a small curtsy before the boy.

"My lady, I have done no kind deed. I am only lockin' ye away in this." He looked grimly around her cell.

"You saved me from the captain. That is enough."

Elaina spent the remainder of the day mulling over the captain's words. He knew what her mother had been, and he wanted from Elaina what her mother would not give him? Names? She would have paced the floor if she thought her legs would support her, but her encounter with Captain Cummings had left her more than a little weak-kneed. The odds of seeing the young Scottish soldier again were slim, but if she did—would he be able to get a message to William?

Did she wish to put the boy's life in danger? After only a moment of thought, the answer was a definite no.

The cold started to seep into her bones as what sunlight there was dissipated into night. Curling herself into a tight ball, she wormed her way down into the small mound of hay, thanking God for her woolen cloak that could easily have been taken from her. She cradled what remained of her supper tight to her chest. A different soldier had brought her a new bucket of water, not any cleaner; two bannocks; and a hunk of cheese. She devoured one of the bannocks and half of the cheese, deciding to try to save the rest. The bastards could at least give her one candle, if not to keep her hands warm then to try to keep the rats at bay.

The thought of another meeting with Captain Cummings left her tossing in her makeshift bed, trying to escape the feeling of him pressed against her. She would be more on her guard the next time. God help her. Her thoughts turned to Caitir and Ainsley. Right now, they were her only hope, and that hope was slim.

The light had begun its subtle shift from the charcoal hue of the night into the silvery light of dawn when the cell door opened. Expecting stale bread to be thrown in at her, she sat horrified when instead it was the stark-naked form of a man, battered and bloody, his malnourished skin blue from the cold.

"Lachlan?" She scrambled to the lifeless form lying sprawled across the stones. "Lachlan? Speak to me!"

She ripped her cloak off, wrapping it around his body and rolling him onto it. Grabbing the edges, she pulled him across the floor, losing her footing once and sitting down with a bone-jarring thud. There was not much substance to the putrid pile of hay in the cell, but anything would be better than leaving him on the freezing stone floor. Laying her head on his emaciated chest, she detected a shallow breath and the rapid fluttering of his heart. He was alive, but for how long?

His silver beard, matted and gnarled, did little to hide the sunken cheeks of starvation. Praying a quick prayer to St. Christopher, she took in the worst of his facial features. It looked to be an old wound, one not inflicted in the last day, but it was unnerving, nonetheless. It was recent enough that the scarred skin surrounding the socket of the man's left eye was still freshly pink and had sunk in, covering the gaping hole left by his missing eye. A jagged scar made its way from the socket across to his temple and disappeared into his wild mane, showing the violent nature of his injury. It dawned on her he may have hidden the trauma from her during their time together, possibly to keep from frightening her or out of humiliation—or both. His body was stippled with bruises, some of them fresh and just turning from pink into purple, others already taking on the faded green hue of healing. Gashes also decorated his frail frame. They could have been from a knife or a whip, either one. His skin was paper-thin and it would not take much to tear it. She lay the corner of her cloak across his manhood, trying to give the poor soul some dignity, and rolled him to his side, staring at the lashes across his back—the unmistakable markings of a whip.

The frigid temperatures worked to staunch the flow of blood, but unfortunately, the cold might cost him his life. Wrenching herself to her feet, she ran around the room feeling like a fool but trying to conduct as much body heat as possible. She lay beside the length of the poor Scottish Highlander, enveloping as much of him as she could into her petite frame. Elaina performed the same ritual many times over. As her body cooled and she began to shiver, she would rise and do it again.

It was after about the fifth such time that a quiet moan emerged from her patient.

"Lachlan? Can you hear me?" she whispered, smoothing the hair away from the man's face, her voice hitching in her throat.

A tear fell from the man's remaining eye and slowly made its way through the web of wrinkles until it disappeared into his mass of hair.

"Lachlan?"

"Why?" he whispered through his cracked lips.

Elaina scrambled for the water bucket, breaking the thin sheet of ice resting on top of the water. She ripped a piece of her petticoat loose. Dunking the rag into the water, she wet Lachlan's lips and dribbled a small amount on his tongue.

"Why?" he whispered again, turning his head away from her.

"I don't know," she whispered back. "Because they are evil bastards, is my only guess."

"Why do you help me? Please let me die," he begged her in a ragged whisper.

Guilt seized her heart. The words echoed in her ears, and she sat frozen. He wanted so desperately to die, and here she sat prolonging his misery. He did not question the actions of their captors but her own. Should she step back and let him go peacefully? How long might he last? Until nightfall? Until the next day? Until they found some other barbarous way of tormenting him?

The cell door opened before a decision could be made, and Captain Cummings himself stepped inside.

Elaina positioned herself between Lachlan and the officer. "Come no farther, Captain," she said. Crouched in front of her patient, her voice did not sound like her own.

The slightest hint of surprise registered in the back of Cummings's eyes. Without removing his gaze from hers, he snapped his fingers towards the open cell door.

Two guards entered carrying a small pot of steaming broth, a woolen blanket, and a flask one of the men placed into the captain's open and waiting hand.

"I only came to offer nourishment to the inmate," the captain said. "I heard about the unfortunate miscommunication that left the poor gentleman unclothed and left in the cold overnight."

"Horse shite," Elaina hissed at him.

The captain clicked his tongue. "Such language for a lady."

He took a step toward her, and she rose slightly, one hand closing over the rope handle of the water bucket. Two steps closer and she would swing at his head with all her might. The captain must have read her mind, for he remained stationary.

"The erroneous officer has been dealt with accordingly," he said as if he spoke the gospel.

"Leave." Elaina stood fully, bucket still in hand.

"I would only like to extend my help," Captain Cummings said, looking from Elaina's eyes to the bucket and back.

"If you only wanted to help, we would not be in this bloody rat hole to begin with. If you only wanted to help, you would have hanged this miserable man when you took him from this bloody cell yesterday instead of beating him and leaving him naked to freeze to death. Please remove yourself from my sight, *officer*," she spat the last word like it was filth from her mouth.

"Have it your way, madam." The captain motioned the soldier to leave the broth, and he tossed the flask beside Elaina on the hay.

Elaina glanced at the soldier as he placed the broth by the captain's feet. He met her eyes when he straightened, and Elaina's hands broke into a sweat when the pock-marked man who had killed Angus stared back at her.

"Oh, and we will continue our conversation that was so rudely interrupted yesterday," Captain Cummings added as Elaina and the soldier eyed one another.

"I look forward to it," she said as he turned to leave the room. "Damned bastard," she grumbled under her breath, taking up the broth and the flask and returning to her patient. "Here," she told Lachlan, cradling his head in her lap and holding the whiskey to his lips.

He tried to turn his head away, but she held it firm.

"We cannot let that monster win. You must live, friend."

"You don't even know me," he whispered before taking a sip of the whiskey, which caused coughs to wrack his frail body.

"I know all I need to know. You are a man who has been beaten and tortured, your lands invaded by butchers and murderers. We will not let them win. We can't." She adjusted the cloak around him, adding the woolen blanket to it, and took up the spoon from the broth. "Here, let's get this in you before it is too cold to do any good."

She fed the broth to him a spoon at a time, interspersed with whiskey, and held him when the shivering consumed his body. Hugging him close to her bosom and wrapping her small legs around him, she clutched him tight, willing his body to stop convulsing. After a time, when he needed to piss but was too weak to stand, Elaina dragged the chamber pot to him.

When the soldiers came to fetch her, they found Lachlan still wrapped in her embrace.

She unfolded herself and knelt over him with her back towards the door. "Take this," she whispered, extracting the bannock and the cheese from her pocket and wrapping his chilled fingers around them. "I will return soon. Don't feed the rats while I'm away," she teased, kissing his forehead while tucking the cloak around his body.

Chapter Twenty Seven

THE SOLDIERS DEPOSITED ELAINA IN a different room than last time. It was larger, with a small fire in a hearth. She wanted nothing more than to stand beside it and warm herself, but she thought of Lachlan lying back in their frigid cell, so, instead, she remained by the doorway they had pushed her through.

"Good afternoon, madam." Captain Cummings entered the room, brisk and official. He plopped two glasses onto the desktop and filled them with amber liquid from a decanter before setting it firmly on the tabletop. "Please, join me?"

Elaina stared at him from her place by the door.

With an amused look, the captain took one of the chairs himself, crossing his legs, and sipped from his glass, watching her.

Straightening her skirts, Elaina took a deep breath and a seat in the chair opposite, her heart pounding in her chest.

"What happened the day you killed Alex Campbell?"

His question caught her off guard. She'd expected him to say something about her mother. Elaina felt her skin begin to crawl, and she picked up her glass, draining the whiskey without a breath, and didn't argue when Cummings offered to refill it. "There was an accident." She looked at her hands, remembering the feeling of drowning and the boy's eyes staring at her while they struggled underneath the green waters of the stream.

"What kind of accident?"

"He wanted my horse, but I couldn't let him have it. I needed to return Angus's body to his family. I drew my knife, and there was a confrontation."

"What kind of confrontation?"

"The kind where he wanted my horse, and I didn't want to give it to him."

Elaina began to gain control of her nerves, but unfortunately that loosened the hold on her tongue.

"So, you pulled your knife on him and killed him?"

"No. I told him he couldn't have her."

"And then you killed him?"

"No. I tried to pull the reins from his hands when something startled Sadie and she shied sideways, knocking the young man and myself into the burn. He fell onto my knife. I didn't kill him. It was an accident."

"Convenient story."

"It was not a murder. It was an accident. That is the truth."

"You did not know Mr. Campbell before that day?"

"No. I had never seen him before."

The captain drummed his fingertips on the table. Casting a glance at her, he reached into a drawer on the desk and pulled out several sheets of paper. "Tell me about these."

"What would I know about…" Elaina's words trailed off as her eyes lighted on the papers and the words written in Gaelic in her mother's hand. "What is that?" she said after a moment's hesitation. They'd burned her mother's papers. All of them. Where had these come from?

"You do not recognize your mother's writing?"

"I would recognize her hand if that was it. But it is not, and my mother was a Lowlander. She does not…*did* not…speak Gaelic. How do you come by these papers and assume they belong to her?"

"It is an interesting story. One you will love to hear, but first, what do you know about them?"

"Nothing." Elaina drained her second glass of whiskey.

"That seems to be your signature answer, my dear. I thought you an intelligent woman, but you seem to know…nothing. These"—he tapped a finger on the papers—"map out a plan between your mother, Diana Spencer, a member of a Highland clan, and a member of Britain's elite. I want to know who the players are in this little game."

"I don't read or speak Gaelic, sir. I cannot help you. I am sure there are any number of men in these parts to help you with your task. I know nothing about a game."

"I find that hard to believe, being as these were found in your home."

"Where and by whom? I knew nothing of them."

"Enter," the captain called out, still holding Elaina's gaze.

She gaped at the man walking through the door. His dress was that of The Watch. The blue hat pulled over one ear, his dark tartan and red coat set his blonde hair and intense green eyes off perfectly. Her lips moved, but she could force no words past her throat.

Rabbie strode to the captain's side and looked coldly at Elaina.

"The lady claims innocence in the matter." Captain Cummings waved a hand over the pages on the table.

"Indeed?" Rabbie answered, staring at Elaina.

"What are you doing?" she hissed at him. "Why are you dressed like that?"

"I am a member of the Watch," he answered.

"You are not. The Watch is in Flanders. Do not let them pressure you, Rabbie," she pleaded, desperate to turn his mind from whatever bribery or blackmail they'd deceived him with.

"Pressure me? Madam, I regret to inform you that I have been a member of The Watch for some years now. Not all of us are fighting on the front."

"You are a coachman. *My* coachman. My *protector*." Her mind was numb, unable to form a coherent thought.

"I was gathering intelligence."

"Intelligence?"

Rabbie raised his brow at her. "Intelligence, as in gathering information for military purposes—"

"I know what the hell intelligence means," Elaina interrupted angrily. "Why me? William hired you to protect me. You had references."

"Aye, I did." Rabbie smiled down at Captain Cummings. "Good ones."

Elaina rose to her feet, backing away from the two gentlemen and nearly upending the table in her effort to get as far away as possible. "I-I don't understand," she whispered, shaking her head slowly. The whiskey she had drunk sat heavy in her belly and sweat ran between her breasts. It was as if all the air in the tiny room had been sucked out. The man standing before her did not resemble the aloof coachman who had been her employee for most of the past year.

"I am a member of The Watch. My brother and I both."

"Your brother is a farmer."

"Maybe you should explain things to the lady, Captain." Cummings's mouth slowly turned up into a wicked grin.

"Captain?" Elaina asked.

"He is most modest. He is captain of The Black Watch." Cummings leaned back in his seat once more, crossing his legs.

Elaina's eyes traveled to the papers and back to Rabbie's face.

"Oh yes. About those. I found them in a chest in yer room." Rabbie tapped the papers on the table.

"You didn't."

"I wondered why ye secretly hauled Mr. MacKinnon up to yer boudoir with yer maid. I kent it surely could not have been to bed the both of them, unless… it was?" His eyes traveled over her body.

"Go to hell," she hissed at him.

Rabbie advanced on her, and she flattened herself against the wall. He spoke the next sentence in rapid Latin. "Before things get out of hand, I can save you from this. Marry me."

Elaina stared at him gape-mouthed. Of all the things she thought might come out of his mouth, a proposal had not been one of them.

Cummings jumped to his feet. "What did you say?"

Rabbie spoke in Latin again. "He has no Latin. I beg ye, Elaina, let me spare yer life for ye will surely hang for treason."

Elaina replied in Latin, "Spare my life? I have committed no treason. You lied to me. You went through my things. You lied to William."

The captain stepped between the two. "Speak the king's English or shut your bloody mouths."

"Please." Rabbie held out his hand to her.

"Please what, Captain Campbell?" Cummings looked suspiciously between them.

Elaina stared at Rabbie's hand, contemplating. Swallowing hard, her gaze traveled from his hand to his eyes. They were intense and pleading. With a deep breath, she said, "Your name is not MacLeod."

Rabbie's jaw tightened.

"I knew the lass was smarter than she let on," Cummings laughed.

"Shut up," Rabbie hissed at him. "Marry me, dammit. I can save you." He had not switched back to Latin.

"Marry you? Are you out of your bloody mind, you fool?" Cummings said. When Rabbie did not respond, Cummings continued. "Well, I believe a marriage should start on the right foot. If you two are to wed, there are things you should know about one another."

Rabbie turned on the captain. "Shut your mouth before I knock every one of your teeth out of your head."

"Now, now. 'Tis not only your secrets I speak of. The lady has a few of her own."

"What do you not want me to know, Rabbie?" Elaina took a step toward him. "Where did you find the key to the chest?"

"That is interesting indeed," Cummings said. "We had it and never knew."

Rabbie closed his eyes.

"Who had it? What is your name, Rabbie? Your real name? Captain Campbell?" She took another step.

"My lady, you cannot tell me you do not know that Rabbie is a nickname for Robert here in Scotland."

"You son of a whore." Elaina's hand closed on a glass and smashed it against the side of Rabbie's head. "You damn bloody bastard! It was you—" Her voice caught in her throat and she doubled over, gasping for air. "All this time searching"—she choked on her tears—"and it was you…"

Cummings caught her hand mid-swing with the other glass and flung her into a chair, swiftly tying her arms behind it. "That'll be enough of that." He sat in the chair opposite her. "Clean yourself up, Campbell. You are bleeding on the evidence."

Drops of blood spattered the papers from a large cut on Rabbie's cheek. If she only had her knife, she would slit his throat from ear to ear.

"Now, let's return to business, shall we?" Leaning forward on his elbows, he studied her. "I want the names." He dragged the words out, emphasizing every syllable. "And I want the money."

"I told you—"

Her head flew sideways as the back of his hand connected with her face.

The iron taste of blood floated on her tongue. If Cummings thought he was getting anything out of her, he was dead wrong. She had her suspicions of who the 'British elite' might be, but she would be damned if she gave up a secret her mother had given her life for. Instead, she spit at his feet. A nice fat splat of blood and saliva landed on the captain's pristine black boot.

He stared at her with no expression on his face, then bent over and wiped his boot clean with his handkerchief. He then reached into the desk and pulled out the ledger to her mother's glass company, slamming it on the desktop and causing her to jump. "When your mother left this world in a most tragic fashion, this company reverted to you. The money kept coming through even after your mother's death until a couple of months ago. Now. I want to know the names and where the money is. I have spent the last five years in this miserable rat hole, and this, my dear, will buy my freedom. You cannot tell me your mother would leave you her company without telling you what transpired within it. You will tell me what I want to know."

"You can beat me all you want, but I cannot tell you what I don't know."

"If you think I will give up, let me set you straight on that matter. Let me tell you a little story." He leaned back in his chair, pouring himself a glass of whiskey that he held with his index finger pointed in the air. "There once was a woman named Diana Spencer," he said as if telling a fairy tale to a child.

Elaina's eyes rested on Rabbie, who perched himself on the corner of the desk, his arms folded, eyes trained on the far wall.

"We intercepted letters from her to an unnamed person in the Highlands. The only problem was that the woman lived across the ocean. Oh, how to get her to Scotland?" He tapped his chin as if thinking. "Ah, yes. We killed her brother-in-law."

She gawked at the captain, unbelieving. Their scheme was so elaborate that they killed her uncle, knowing her father would have to return home and claim the title of Earl.

"Sure enough, a year later and the Spencer family disembark from the *Victoria* onto Britain's lovely shores. However, I needed them in Scotland, so we sent Captain Lord Spencer's orders, knowing where he went, his dutiful wife would follow. Now to the good part."

Elaina closed her eyes, wishing to be anywhere else in the world.

"One foggy morning, a carriage traveled alone on the road between Newcastle and Edinburgh when it was suddenly set upon by thieves." His voice took on a dramatic tone of an actor on a stage.

Elaina wanted nothing more than to kick in his teeth.

"That's not actually how it happened, though, was it, Captain Campbell?"

Rabbie cut his eyes at Cummings.

"The lovely Lady Spencer was captured and interrogated. Her husband, an upstanding British officer, was shocked at the accusations, and even though we believed his innocence, he was a complication. So we did the only thing we could do. We killed him, and we let his loving wife watch," the captain said matter of factly.

Elaina choked back a sob.

"We thought that might persuade the lady to give us the names we wanted. Unfortunately, it did not, did it, Campbell? He did try so diligently to beat it out of your mother, but I have to admire her for her strength and loyalty to her cause."

"You beat my mother to death, and you killed my father, and you thought I would marry you?" Elaina spit out between her sobs, drawing Rabbie's eyes to her. "You thought I would never find out? Are you truly that stupid?"

"Nay, I kent ye would find out, but it would be too late. Ye would be mine." He smiled down at her, and she lunged at him, but Cummings caught her and seated her firmly back in her chair. "I didna ken ye then, Elaina. I didna love ye."

"Love? You think you *love* me? You are a damned fool, Robert Campbell. Go to hell."

"Your bickering is interrupting my story. Now, where was I? Oh yes. Your mother died before I could get a name, so we staged the robbery. I mean, if you never found your parents' bodies that would be a problem. The killing of your coachman…" Cummings barked out a laugh., "That was pure genius, planned out by this man right here." He slapped Rabbie on the knee. "And voila, you have a new coachman, and after your first little present arrived, a bodyguard. Ah, then the third present. Who knew the key was in the necklace the whole time? The key to the chest that you moved from all of your parent's things into your room and placed discreetly in a corner."

"You placed the necklace in my room? Did you go through our entire house? When?"

"While ye were sleepin'. I found the key when ye were horsin' around with the boys one day." Rabbie raised his brow at her.

"Who knew those two would be your ultimate downfall? It was so convenient one was murdered. Rabbie was right when he said you would be so loyal as to escort his body to his poor, dear mother."

"You-you killed Angus?" She couldn't breathe.

"I didna kill him. You were there. You ken that."

"No, my dear, I set that one up. Rabbie was only an adviser on the matter."

"You killed my boy," she whispered, her mind numb. He was responsible for everything. This man who she thought was protecting her.

"Now we get to the juicy part." The captain grinned at her and laid a knife upon the table. Her knife. The knife Rabbie had given her the day of their run-in with the Griers. "Look familiar?" Cummings asked Rabbie.

"Aye. I gave it to the lady for protection."

"Well, it did come in handy. That is why I sent for you."

"What has it to do with me?"

"She killed a member of the Watch."

"Well, surely to God ye could handle it without me here. Ye seem to be so adept at handling matters." Rabbie's voice dripped with sarcasm. "We could have avoided all of this."

"Well, it held a special interest for you, Captain, seeing as it was your brother she killed."

Elaina's eyes flew to Rabbie. She could see it now—the blonde hair and green eyes. Not as bright as Rabbie's, but yes. They did resemble each other.

"Alex?" Rabbie said to the captain. "Alex is dead?"

"Yes. Done in by none other than our illustrious Lady Elaina Spencer." The captain clapped his hands with glee at the cleverness of his storytelling.

Rabbie rose to his feet, turning on Elaina, and roared, "You killed my brother?"

"Isn't this grand? You kill her parents. She kills your brother. You live forever in wedded bliss. Oh, wait. That last part hasn't happened yet."

The captain was a sick bastard and given the opportunity, Elaina would do him in, but for now, she turned her wrath on Rabbie. "It was an accident, Robert, but given the knowledge I have now, I would have gladly slit him from neck to ballocks and spit upon his dead body."

"You bloody whore."

His blow threw her from the chair, nearly into the fire. Rabbie jerked her to her feet as she tried to shake away the blinding spots. Her eyes focused on his only an inch away from hers, his breath hot on her mouth.

His voice broke as he hissed, "You killed the only thing that was ever good in my life. God damn you!"

She head-butted him in the face.

He staggered backward, releasing his hold on her, and she nearly lost her footing. Blood oozed between his fingers as he pulled his hand away to spit out a piece of tooth. Elaina launched herself at him, knocking him to the floor. She didn't know what she hoped to accomplish with her arms still tied behind her, but she got two good kicks in before he managed to pin her face down, snatching her head back by her hair.

"You bloody bitch," he hissed, his blood dripping warm onto her face.

"But you want to wed me, remember?" Elaina grunted as his knee added pressure to the middle of her back.

"It was all part of the plan to get the money, my dear. I wadna stick my cock in you if ye paid me to."

"Liar." It came out in less than a whisper, for no air remained in her lungs.

He threw her head to the floor and pushed himself off of her just as she was on the verge of losing consciousness.

Chapter Twenty-Eight

THE POCK-MARKED SOLDIER AND ONE other had the honor of escorting Elaina to her cell. Her mind swirled in circles, unable to grab a single thought and isolate it in her brain. The man her brother had trusted to protect her, and the man she had spent numerous hours alone with on horseback was the man who murdered her parents. He'd "protected" her from the MacGregors, but he'd beat her mother to death. He was a twisted man and an incredible liar. Sickness at the truth burned in her belly.

She stumbled, her hands still tied behind her back. The soldier caught her by the arm, but she jerked away. The bloody British and the damn Watch—she hated them all at this point. Her trek to the frigid cell was too short. She didn't have enough time to plot her next move. Three people absolutely must die, Rabbie MacLeod, Captain Cummings, and this scarred up bastard walking behind her.

Unlocking the heavy door, the soldier swung it open and allowed her to step inside. Lachlan looked up at her, still wrapped in her cloak and the blanket. She gave him a subtle nod as his eyes took in her face, which she was sure looked a bit unsettling.

"Gentlemen," she said as the soldiers moved to step back into the hallway. "Could I ask you to untie me and would it be possible to get some fresh water." She feigned politeness as best she could.

The two soldiers glanced at each other.

"Are you afraid of me? Or are you afraid of this poor sick man who can barely raise his head? All I would like is some water that does not have rat shite in it. I don't think it is too much to ask, and he is too weak to untie me."

"Stirling, fetch the water." The pock-marked soldier nodded to his younger counterpart.

"Aye, Officer Taylor." The young man saluted and scrambled to fetch the bucket.

Taylor set about untying Elaina's hands, lingering on her buttocks in the process.

Elaina kept her eyes on Lachlan's. Her thoughts must have been easily readable for Lachlan gave her the slightest shake of his head. She tried to will her heartbeat to remain slow and not give her intentions away. Breathing deep through her nose, she closed her eyes, letting calmness flow through her. The smell of the rotten chamber pot, the fresh air flowing through the transoms, and the meaty scent of her captor behind her helped to ground her. She focused all her attention on his fingers and his knife fumbling with the knot around her wrists. Why he didn't just cut the rope was beyond her, but the longer he took, the more time she had to plan and to calm her mind. The knot finally broke loose, and the rough hemp slid from her wrists.

She stood for a moment, rubbing at them before offering him an offhanded "thank you." The sound of him sliding his knife back in his sheath reached her as his partner returned with a bucket of water. She turned to where Stirling bent over the bucket on the floor and took a deep breath. In a single move, she placed her foot on Stirling's back, kicking him to the floor and unsheathing his knife, then turned on her heel and the blade of the knife sliced through the air slightly above eye level. The point caught Taylor in the spot she'd wanted. His eyes bulged with fright as a frantic hand sought his throat. He turned scrambling for the door, but collapsed after only two steps, hat tumbling across the floor as he lay writhing on the stones with his life's blood pooling around him. His companion retched behind her. Squatting beside Langley's body, she looked him in the eye—eyes that looked just as scared as Angus's had.

As his spirit began to leave his body, she smiled at him. "Rest in hell," she whispered and patted his cheek.

She turned to the junior officer with the bloody knife still in her hand, causing him to stumble backward. His eyes darted around the room, searching for a way to escape as he wiped his mouth with the sleeve of his jacket. Elaina cleaned the bloody knife on her skirt and held it out to the boy, hilt first. He stared wide-eyed with fear. Elaina laid it at his feet and backed away, then knelt on the floor beside Lachlan.

"I have no grievance with you," she said to the boy as he stared at Langley's body. "That man killed a boy who was like a son to me. I have made good on a promise. I will not harm you."

The young soldier turned his wide blue eyes upon her and Lachlan. He never took his gaze from them as he squatted to pick up his knife and eased his way slowly out of the room, closing the door with a soft click rather than the echoing boom as everyone before him had done. She heard his footsteps retreating as he ran up the hallway.

"Do ye ken what ye've done, lass?" Lachlan asked, laying a bony hand upon her knee. "Ye will hang for certain."

"I am to hang anyway," Elaina said softly, staring at the blood on her hands. "It just so happens I am responsible for killing the brother of Robert Campbell, captain of The Watch. I am destined to hang at the gallows as it is. I had to avenge young Angus while I had the chance. Lie down, friend. You are trembling."

Elaina wrapped the blanket and her cloak tighter around him before she rose and dipped water over her hands, washing the blood from them. She took a small handful of hay and scrubbed the man's life from her hands.

"Well, well, well," Cummings's voice came from behind her.

She didn't bother turning around.

"It seems like you just cannot stop killing."

"You are a fine one to talk." Elaina's gaze rose to the transom windows above her head, taking in the gray skies and the clouds swirling across them. Would this be her last day to see the sky?

"Get him out of here," Cummings said to his unseen companions.

Elaina heard the shuffling of feet and the sound of dragging boots. Smiling to herself, she rose and turned to face the man whose presence she had just left. Rabbie stood by his side, his eyes traveling over her. When he'd looked at her like that before, she could imagine him undressing her with his eyes. Now she felt him considering all the different ways he would torture her. She shuddered, feeling as though the cold finger of death traced itself down her spine.

"Whatever are we to do with you?" Cummings studied her for a moment before a sickening smile spread across his face and he turned his gaze to Lachlan.

Elaina followed his eyes and stepped between her cellmate and Cummings.

"Ever the nursemaid, ever the mother hen," Rabbie sneered.

She stood her ground in front of Lachlan, arms loose at her sides, waiting. She could hear footsteps coming up the hallway through the open door. A towering soldier stepped into the room behind Rabbie.

Cummings's voice was flat. "Seize her."

The soldier advanced on Elaina. She waited until he was within arm's reach and then launched herself at him, the crown of her head colliding with the man's nose and causing a grotesque crunching sound. The two of them landed with a thud, rolling over and over with the soldier, unfortunately, landing on top of her.

"Aargh…thupid bith broke by nothe," he bellowed, shaking his head like a bear. He held her pinned to the cold stones of the floor, crushing the breath out of her.

Rabbie reached Lachlan in two strides and inflicted a sickening kick to the invalid's ribs.

Elaina heard the cracking of his bones and cringed at the man's strangled scream. She struggled to free herself from her captor. "Leave him be," she screamed at Rabbie. "He has nothing to do with you and me. If you want to torture someone, torture me."

"Oh, yer time is coming, lassie. Dinna fash yerself."

Lachlan lay immobile, face down on the hay.

"Take him out," Rabbie said to a second soldier who had entered the cell. "He doesna weigh enough to break his own neck if we were to try to hang him. Feed him to the wolves."

"I hate you!" Elaina screamed at Rabbie as the soldier grabbed Lachlan by his feet and drug him, blanket, cloak, and all, through the door of the cell. "I'm going to kill you. I swear it."

Rabbie curled his lip at her. "Not if I kill you first." He turned his attention to the man still pinning her down. "I would tell ye to have yer way with her, but ye may come out of it without a cock. Dinna turn yer back on her."

The man stared at Elaina through eyes that had already begun to swell. He glanced around and seemed startled to find the two of them alone in the cell. She could see the wheels turning in his mind. He raised himself from the floor and backed his way out of the room.

Elaina lay motionless, tears sliding down her temples into her hair. She winced as the cell door slammed shut. Now, she was truly alone. Rolling over and crawling her way across the stone floor, she lay down on the small pile of hay where the heat from Lachlan's body lingered. She inhaled the stench of him and lost herself to the guilt consuming her at having caused him such misery the last days of his life.

After a time, she dried her tears and rolled onto her back, staring at the ceiling. What would William think, his sister hung for treason and murder? Another thought struck her. Would Rabbie return to Duart Manor and resume his charade? How much did William know of his mother's actions, and would his life be in danger? They might meet each other on the other side if there was one. She had her doubts. What kind of God would let these horrible things happen and continue to happen? She hadn't meant to kill Alex Campbell, but if it came down to it and Sadie hadn't stepped in, would she have killed him over a horse? She honestly didn't know. Her drive to return Angus to his parents had been strong. She hoped Ainsley and Caitir had finished the journey without her instead of wasting time searching for her, that is if The Watch hadn't grabbed them as well. She didn't think it to be the case but wouldn't put it past Cummings to torture the duo to force a confession she didn't have to give.

Laying on her bed of rotting hay, she tried to make her peace with God as best she could. Guilt over the pock-marked soldier was non-existent, however. She found herself wondering if they would bring a priest in for her last rites. They hadn't afforded Lachlan the courtesy, so why would they extend it to her? She only prayed the man was dead before the wolves got to him. The thought made her shudder, and she lifted a special prayer for his soul to the heavens.

She awoke with a start in the morning, her heart tight in her chest, bile thick in her throat. It was only a nightmare. She rose on rubbery legs from her fetid bed of hay, her dress stiff with the dried and frozen blood of her captors. Breaking the thin sheet of ice that covered the surface of the bucket of water, she splashed the frigid water onto her face to wash away the dream that wouldn't quit replaying in her mind. Calum had gazed down at her in the gardens. His large, warm hands cupped her face as he smiled his infectious smile, the dimple in his left cheek showing. As he leaned in to kiss her, she closed her eyes in anticipation of the soft touch of his lips against hers. A warmth spread over her face, like the moment the sun comes from behind a cloud and its rays caress your skin. She opened her eyes to find Calum's head removed and his blood raining down on her. She scrambled to get out of his grasp, but he held tight. Rabbie's face could be seen over the headless form of her friend, laughing so that tears filled his bright green eyes—laughing as Elaina screamed.

Pacing the floor, she kept moving to stay warm and to ignore the hunger gnawing her belly. The first part of the day she spent in anticipation of her impending death. The longer the day progressed, however, the more her thoughts turned to food. She dug through the hay looking for any scraps Lachlan may have inadvertently left her. If there were any, the rats had found it before she could. She wondered if Cummings planned on starving her to death but decided it would be too easy for the lying bastard. By nightfall of the following day, she changed her mind. The evening before, she decided to try conserving her water, knowing you could live longer without food than you could without water. If she wasn't getting anything to eat, she assumed they wouldn't give her water either.

Darkness fell, and she sat rocking herself, her arms wrapped around her legs. She might freeze to death before she starved to death. Dancing the line between sleep and wakefulness, she emitted a scream when something scurried across her feet. Damned rats! They were hungry too. It might be a contest between them and her to see who could hold out from eating whom the longest. The thought made her ill on both accounts.

How had everything gone so wrong? She would give anything to go back in time, to return to the colonies and her old life with her parents and her brother. Her problems with almost-husband Richard seemed laughable now. She had never felt more hopeless or alone. Reaching into her pocket, she pulled out her amulet and squeezed it to her heart. She would see her parents again…soon, she hoped. She laid her head upon her knees, too tired to cry.

During the night, a soft scraping sound brought her slowly to consciousness. Footsteps. She lay still, trying to keep her breathing the same until the shadowy figure was close enough for her to grab it by the legs.

"Madam!" it hissed as it hit the floor. "I mean ye nay harm!"

"Who are you?" she whispered.

"The Scottish soldier. I escorted ye back the first day."

"What are you doing here? Are you getting me out?"

"Nay. I am sorry, my lady."

He'd sounded ashamed, so she reached over and patted him, trying to comfort him. "No worry. I am making my peace with it, but why are you here?"

"I brought ye some bread and cheese. They mean to starve ye. I thought it was the least I could do to sneak ye some of my supper."

"God bless you, son!" Tears welled up in Elaina's eyes as she held herself back from attacking the young man to gain his food. She groped in the darkness for his hand, and he placed the gift in her outstretched palm. "I thought I would have to eat a rat."

"Yuck."

"My thoughts exactly," she whispered around a mouthful of bread. "What do they mean to do with me? Will I hang soon?" The eagerness in her voice surprised her. She didn't know how much more starvation and freezing cold she could take.

"Maybe in two days, my lady. Cap'n Campbell will return by then." The boy cleared his throat. "He said he wanted the honor of doing it himself when he returned."

"I'm sure he would. Thank you, son. You have been a blessing to a dead woman."

"Ye are not dead yet. Do not give up until the end. From what I hear, ye are a braw lassie if there ever was one. The guards are all scairt of ye."

"You are not scared of me?"

"Me? No. I have seen yer heart. You seem to be a good woman caught in a bad situation."

"It doesn't bother you that I have murdered two men?"

"Not in the least. Cap'n Campbell is a horse's arse, pardon my speech, madam. His brother was near as bad. Good riddance is all I say. As for the guard, I heard yer reason. I think it was a fair one. I must go before I am missed. If I can, I will bring ye more tomorrow."

Alone again, Elaina tried not to think about the possibility of more food the next day. Instead, she pulled the few remaining pins from her hair and tried to pick the lock on the large door. They were too weak and the lock too heavy. With her plan shattered, she sat plaiting her hair. When she reached the ends, she would undo them and start over. It was a rhythmical act that brought a calmness to her spirit. She said her rosary as her hands did the work, commending her soul to God, and said her mental goodbyes to those she loved, hoping they would feel her in their spirit after she was gone and forgive her misdeeds.

The soldier did not return that night, and she saw no one the following day. By nightfall of the second night, she had taken to trying to find decent pieces of hay to chew on, trying not to think about what had laid or pissed on them. Sleep was nonexistent, as was water. It had run out midday. She would have hung herself and saved them the trouble if there was anything to hang herself from or she wasn't sure she would go straight to hell. She probably would anyway.

She ignored the sound of the door being slid open after having hallucinated it several times during the night.

"Elaina," someone hissed in the dark, shaking her.

A startled scream came from her throat before a hand clamped over her mouth.

"Shh. Ye'll get us both killed."

"What the hell are you doing?" she stammered when Rabbie released her.

"Keep yer voice down. I'm getting ye out of here."

"Why in the hell would you do that? I killed your brother, remember? I am not going anywhere with you."

"Come on. We dinna have much time. I have water and food hidden out-side the gates."

Thirst conquered her suspicions, and she let him help her to her feet, nearly toppling over.

Throwing his arm around her, he helped her down the dark hallway and out into the courtyard.

"Stay close to the wall," he whispered.

They passed through the shadows and another door. Rabbie placed a warm finger against her lips. They rounded a corner to find two soldiers at the end of the corridor, standing sentry outside a door. Their voices rattled down the hallway toward the two escapees.

Rabbie dragged her back around the corner with his hand on her mouth. "Dammit." He looked around wildly. "This way."

"I can't," she gasped, shaking her head. "I cannot go farther."

"Just a little farther." He wrapped his arm around her waist, dragging her through a door and down yet another hallway before bursting out into the frigid night where Elaina slid out of his arm to the ground.

Rabbie gathered her into his arms and carried her into the woods surround-ing the gaol, then set her gently on the ground against a large tree. "Sit here. I will fetch the food and water."

"Why are you doing this?" She laid her head back against the rough trunk of the tree, closing her eyes to the spinning world.

"Because I love you." He kissed her forehead and fled into the night, leaving her alone with his absurd words lingering on the air.

She was not sure how long she sat before he returned and shook her awake.

Snatching the canteen from his hand, she took several large gulps that immediately came back up.

"Slowly," he whispered, putting the canteen back to her lips.

She took two small sips that stayed down.

"Have my coat." He took it off and wrapped it around her shivering body.

"Food?"

"Yes. Here."

She crammed the bread into her mouth and tore at it like a madwoman, and she nearly choked on it.

"Slowly," Rabbie instructed as if she were a child.

"I'm starving," she mumbled around another bite. Her hands shook uncontrollably, and even though the bread was hard and stale, she had never tasted anything better.

"I ken it, and I am sorry. When I returned and found out Cummings was starvin' ye, I thought I was goin' to kill him. I had to get ye out. He is a sick bastard."

"I don't understand you, Rabbie. You killed my parents—beat my mother to death—but you save my life? Save me from starvation even after I killed your brother? It truly was an accident."

"I believe ye, and for what it's worth, I'm sorry. I was only doin' my duty as a member of The Watch when that…that happened with yer parents. They would have killed me if I refused. And then they sent me to watch ye and Lord Spencer. I didna ken I would love ye so."

Elaina jerked away from his hand as he tried to stroke her cheek.

"I truly am sorry," he whispered, staring off into the dark.

"What do we do now?" She tried to sort out his nonsensical words.

"We wait until mornin' is close and we can see to make our way through the woods. We will have to go farther into the Highlands to hide."

"And after that?"

"Well, it will be up to you, my lady."

They sat in silence for some time. Elaina dozed off and woke with a start, not knowing where she was. Her head rested on Rabbie's shoulder, his arm tightly around her. In a panic, she tried to struggle to her feet.

"It's okay, Elaina. I've got ye."

Fear and confusion overcame her, and she laid her head on her knees and wept while Rabbie softly stroked her back.

"Ye truly didna ken about yer ma, then?" he asked quietly.

Her voice came muffled by her skirts and her sobs. "No. I told you."

"But the papers in yer room? I cannae say I'm sorry enough. I wadna blame you if you took my dirk right now and slit my throat."

"I can't read Gaelic, Rabbie, and I have considered killing you several times in the last few hours."

"Ye've always been a brutally honest woman," he chuckled. "But MacKinnon read them, no? That is why you three were all bundled up in yer room."

"Why so many questions? I don't know how many times I have to repeat myself. If you read the papers, you would know they didn't name any names."

"Do ye think it could be the Duke of Newcastle?"

"I don't know, Rabbie! Dammit. I have no bloody idea," she lied.

"I'm sorry. Sleep now. Ye will need yer strength in the mornin'."

Elaina did sleep, but not well. The wind increased throughout the night, and it was a full-on winter storm by morning. Even though it was hidden behind clouds she couldn't see because of the pelting sleet, the sun eventually gave enough light that the pair could make their way along the tree line, the deeper part of the woods still too dark to see. They huddled together for warmth and support, Rabbie holding her up on quivering legs. She needed something besides stale bread to eat.

Her plait had come loose, and her hair whipped in the wind like writhing snakes, blinding her as much as the sleet. Between strands of flying hair, she could make out the ground and dodge rocks and fallen limbs. Then the forest floor cleared away and they were on a path.

She looked up. "Where are we?"

Before her at the edge of the wood stood redcoat soldiers waiting for them. They were not fifty yards from the gaol. Captain Cummings stepped from behind them, a sinister smile upon his face. She turned to run but slammed into the chest of another soldier.

Chapter Twenty-Nine

"WELCOME BACK," CAPTAIN CUMMINGS SAID as the red-coat shoved Elaina into the clearing. "Tie her hands."

She hadn't the strength to fight them.

"We can add escape to your list of charges. Not that it matters. Come." The captain took her arm. "I want you to see what you've done."

"I have done nothing," Elaina said jerking loose from his grasp. She looked around for Rabbie but could see little for her hair whipping wildly in the wind.

As they approached the gaol, Cummings grabbed her by her hair and wrenched her head back. "Open your eyes, my dear, and witness your work."

"What nonsense are you laying on me now?" It was then she noticed the black boots and red coat of a soldier. As the wind spun the body in a twisting arc upon the gallows, she spied the red hair and her breath left her body. She fell to her knees, her arms painfully yanked up behind her where the soldier still held her rope. "Why?" she choked on her sobs. "Why would you kill him?"

"He was declared a spy having been seen sneaking from your cell during the night. On the other hand, it could have been other matters besides Jacobite money he attended to." Cummings slid one cold finger down her taut throat.

"He was no spy." Elaina ignored his touch. "He brought me scraps of food. He was a good lad." Her head hung in shame. Guilt washed over her in waves. So many people had died because of her. It was time to escape the madness and the pain. Stumbling to her feet, she raised her head and turned to Cummings. "Kill me," she whispered. "I am ready to die."

Cummings looked appalled. "Oh, not here, my lady. We will make an example of you. This way."

Someone shoved Elaina into step behind Cummings, almost taking her feet out from under her. They made their way across the yard within inches of the hanging soldier's body. She would have vomited if she had anything on her stomach. A small entourage marched with them now, as the storm buffeted the parade of redcoats and the one lone woman.

The farther they walked, the angrier Elaina became, almost as if the rising wind stirred her wrath until it was at a rolling boil, her thoughts tumbling through her mind until they matched the pace of the rushing wind.

"What did she tell you?" Cummings asked.

Rabbie's voice answered, "MacKinnon read them. I truly think him to be the Highland connection."

Elaina turned with speed and strength she didn't know she possessed, ripping the rope from her guard's hands. She rounded on Rabbie, almost reaching him before she was knocked to the ground, cracking her head on the rocky earth. Someone unceremoniously yanked her to her feet and shoved her back into step.

"Now, now, my love," Rabbie said in her ear. "No need to be cross. We were only having a little fun."

Steam roiled from her mouth as if she breathed fire. Her bones rattled both from anger and the unbearable cold, blood dripping down her face. She stumbled on the uneven ground but was wrenched up, saved from falling by the rope binding her hands behind her back.

The guilt and sorrow drowning her moments ago had turned to rage at Rabbie's betrayal. She threw herself sideways at him as he held her arm, dragging her along. "You bloody bastard!" She collided with him, nearly taking them both to the ground.

"I may be a bastard, my dear," he hissed in her face as he yanked her head back by a fistful of hair. "But you are a traitor and a murderer, and today I shall have the honor of taking your life on my brother's behalf. Too bad you won't be around to see me take the life of your friend MacKinnon. I look forward to that one."

She spit in his face.

A sickening crack and blinding flash of light took her sight as he broke her nose with the hilt of his dirk. She hit her knees, gagging and choking. With nothing to break her fall, Elaina's face smashed onto the frozen earth. The cold ground was a relief from the searing fire burning through her head.

Captain Cummings's maniacal laugh sounded in her ear as he jerked her to her feet and shoved her forward. Blood ran from her nose and down her throat, threatening to close off her airway. She turned her head and spat at Rabbie.

"You've got a mighty big pair of ballocks, my dear," he growled, wiping the blood and mucus off his coat and smearing it on her face.

She jerked her head and caught his hand with her teeth.

He screamed in pain, trying to tear his hand free, but she held on, her teeth sinking deeper into his tender flesh. She felt his skin break, and the metallic taste of his blood mingled with hers. He struck her with his fist, still screaming and trying to break her hold. With each punch to her head, the muscles and tendons in his fingers tore a little more. Then, with one final incredible blow, it was over.

~•~

The world was weightless and dark. Empty. Death had taken her. But if she were dead, where were the streets of gold? Where were the burning fires of hell? The brimstone? The angels? Nothing lay before her but gray stones and bitterly cold wind whipping around her. She was neither in heaven nor in hell. It must be purgatory. Her head felt like a large boulder attached to her neck—eyes opened to nothing but slits. She squinted through the forest of her hair. There were bodies. Angels? No. Angels didn't say words like that, and they didn't throw stones. She tried to lunge at them as they pelted her with more rocks, but she could not reach them. Her arms were spread, tied tightly between two poles. She raised herself carefully to her feet, trying to take the pressure from her shoulders.

Icy water slammed into her face, bringing her fully alert and squinting into the sneering face of Robert Campbell, the lying, cheating, murdering rat of a man. He stepped back before she could spit on him again. His hand wrapped in an oddly shaped bloody cloth caught her attention, and she took pleasure in the fact that she had achieved some significant damage before he had beat her unconscious.

"Here stands before you a lying, murderous traitor," Cummings announced to the crowd gathered for the show. "She has betrayed our king, and she has killed three members of our guard, one just this morning. One of you. A poor Scottish lad but performing his duty for his country."

"Liar!" Elaina shouted, strangling on the dried blood in her throat. Her eyes nearly swollen shut from the beating, she turned her face toward the crowd. "I have not been a traitor to the crown. I did not kill that boy. He was—"

She heard the crowd gasp as the air exploded from her lungs.

"Still, she lies."

Her arms felt as though they would rip from her body as she hung all her weight from them, trying desperately to get air into her lungs. She would kill Cummings. He would die a slow, tortured, and terrible death at her hand.

Someone yanked her to her feet by her hair as she still gasped for air and tears streamed down her face. She felt a sawing and tugging at the back of her head, then it fell free and she dropped once again, her knees dragging the ground. Wafts of her chestnut mane floated away, carried off by the roaring wind. Visions of Rabbie floated with them through her mind. The day he entered the kitchen, catching her with her hair down around her face…his kiss in the stable…him staring at her as she tied her stocking to her thigh after the encounter with the MacGregors. Was this all because she'd shunned his advances?

She raised herself to her feet and held her head high. They would not break her. Ever. She stood stoic with her wet clothing clinging to her, chilling her to the bone as the wind whipped and roared about them. "If you are going to kill me," she chattered, teeth clanking together, "get on with it so these people may go home to their fires and their supper."

She could hear a rumble of agreement from the masses.

"They will have their fire, but we are just getting started," Cummings said motioning to Rabbie still holding his dirk. He slit the back of her dress to her waist, exposing her bare skin to the frigid air.

She knew what was coming as she heard the crowd gasp and braced herself as best she could, but the first lash nearly buckled her knees. She straightened herself, clenching her teeth, determined not to cry out. She kept her feet, even as each lash tore her skin and her blood ran through her skirts, down her buttocks and legs. She didn't know if it was Cummings or Rabbie behind the whip. Did it matter? They both would lose their lives.

They struck her once more, and she lost her footing from the force of the blow. Hatred flowed through the cat o' nine tails with every strike across her back.

She struggled to regain her footing but lost it in the blood soaking the ground around her. She felt the weight of the amulet strike her leg, still hidden in her skirts. Her mother's face drifted through the fog of her mind. Diana Spencer had withstood these same men without breaking. The strength gained through that vision drew her to her feet. He struck her again, knocking her to her knees.

There were murmurings all around. The crowd was turning. She could hear the cries for mercy.

"Are you done?" Cummings whispered in her ear. "Are you ready to end this? Give me the names."

She raised her head, and through narrow slits, could see the dirty face of a young boy in front of her and the horror and fear in his eyes. He shook his head at her, urging her to stay down. She offered him a weak smile and, turning her near-blind face toward Cummings, she stumbled her way to her feet, concentrating on the strength of the amulet and the images of her parents. "Go to hell." It was only a whisper, but it was enough.

Cummings nodded to someone behind her. "Campbell, continue."

Rabbie inflicted her punishment, and the realization nearly broke her. She never knew such evil could exist in the world. The blow came so hard it pitched her forward, and she wanted to cry out for mercy. She wanted to stay on her knees, but a force she could not control raised her to her feet.

Something changed, however, as she gained her footing. Her heart pounded in her chest. Thump, thump, thump. Faster…harder.

Screams echoed off the hills.

Were they coming from her own throat? No. It was farther away…somewhere behind them…it surrounded them. The realization came over her. Pipes. It was the pipes screaming.

An unearthly roar rose to the heavens, "*Ard-Choille!*"

Her heart leaped at the sound, and she caught a glimpse of black and red tartan and bare skin in the distance. Her head fell to her chest, and she took joy in the screams of her tormentors as they rose on the frigid air before a white-hot pain erupted in her side and she heard no more.

Chapter Thirty

MOMENTS OF LIGHT WERE TATTOOED by searing agony, followed by the blissful peace of nothingness until the next flash of misery.

Cold. She was freezing, and then it was as if she burned in the fiery pits of hell. Why couldn't she die? She just wanted to die.

"Shh, lass. Ye must be still." A comforting hand rested on her head.

"More laudanum," another voice ordered. "Ye must keep her still. Bind her to the bed."

The bitter liquid gagged her. Someone wiped her mouth and face with a cold, wet cloth.

Please no! The words would not pass her thick tongue. She could not fight as someone wrapped the bindings around her hands and her feet. *Please!* Troubled darkness overtook her.

Swirling images floated in and out of her consciousness. Hunting with her father and his deep boisterous laugh. Calum's face buried in her hair, his tears warm on her frozen cheek...the smell of parritch with honey...the burn of whiskey... *Oh God, the burning!* Fire ravaged her skin. Rabbie's face sneered inches in front of hers—his handsome features transforming into fangs—snarling and snapping at her throat like a wolf. She could feel the screams welling up inside her...something weighed her down. *No! No laudanum!* She spit it out. Rough hands held her face tight, forcing her mouth open and filling it with the demon liquid. The hands violently disappeared from her face.

"No more. You will kill her." A man's voice...familiar, but she could not open her eyes.

"She must—"

"Get out!" the man roared.

Darkness came again with rancid visions of Angus, bloody and stiff, snakes slithering from the empty sockets of his eyes and making their way down in a swirling-circular dance until they wrapped themselves around her wrists, binding her to the dead boy. A white-faced, red-headed soldier, his freckles showing dark upon his skin as he swung in a never-ending arc. Red hair, then his eyes bulging and sightless, his tongue large and blue protruding from his screaming mouth.

When the light did return, it was with the foul taste of vomit.

"Here. Drink," a male voice said.

Elaina tried to pull away.

"It's only water." His voice was soft as he held her head steady.

She turned eagerly to the cup, gulping desperately.

"Easy," he said. "Not too fast. Ye dinna want to be sick again."

"Where am I," she whispered, unable to open her eyes.

"The castle at Balquidder," he replied. "This is going to hurt. I am sorry."

She was splayed out, lying face down with arms and legs bound.

"Take my hand," a soft female voice said and gripped her hand as liquid flames seared across her back and side.

She cried out, squeezing the given hand tightly before leaving the conscious world.

❦

"Open yer eyes, love," Caitir's soft voice whispered. A hand rested on Elaina's head, gently stroking her forehead with its thumb.

The objects in question seemed glued shut, and she hadn't the strength to force them open. "I can't," Elaina croaked.

"Try."

"I don't want to."

"I see our patient is more like herself this morning," a male voice said wryly.

Elaina struggled to open one eye to a small slit and raised her head just enough to catch Calum staring down at her.

"Welcome back. We thought ye might be leaving us for good," he said, the corner of his mouth turned up.

"I wish I had." She dropped her head. "Water?" Her throat felt like she had swallowed shards of broken glass.

Caitir obliged, holding the cup to her lips.

Elaina struggled to drink, but after a few tortured sips, it became easier.

"Can ye stand some broth?" Calum asked.

"Yes, I think. How long? How long have I been here?" she whispered to Caitir as Calum left the room.

"Nigh on a week," Caitir answered, wiping her friend's face and dry, cracked, and bleeding lips with a damp rag.

"How bad?"

"Bad enough."

"My hair?"

"A mess."

"Angus? Ainsley? Did you make it home with his body?" A tear escaped down her cheek.

"I sent Ainsley on with him when we found ye missing," Caitir replied. "He did make it home. I wish we would have buried him on the spot so Ainsley could have helped me look for ye. Maybe we would have found ye sooner."

"I would never have forgiven you. Besides, there was no way to break me out of the gaol. Why am I bound? I need to turn over."

"Let Calum get back. Rabbie tried to extract your gizzard with his dirk before he fled. You are mighty lucky to be alive."

"Yes. Lucky," Elaina said with sarcasm.

"Why do ye have such a death wish?" her friend snapped angrily.

"I don't have a death wish."

"Could've fooled me the way ye were spoutin' yer mouth and spittin' and fightin' that damned Rabbie Campbell."

"And you would have me do differently?"

"I would have ye quit being so damned bullheaded! Why must ye anger him more? He is a vile, wicked bastard without any help from you."

"He is a wicked bastard," Elaina agreed, more tears escaping and rolling across the bridge of her swollen nose. Fear seized her heart as a realization hit her. "He lives? Rabbie is alive?"

"Aye. He escaped. I am sorry."

"I am too."

Caitir planted a soft kiss on Elaina's cheek.

Sleep overtook her. She woke long enough for the broth Calum brought back. She convinced her two nurses to untie her, groaning as they released her wrists from their hold. Caitir massaged a horrid smelling grease around the chaffing on her wrists and ankles. They were raw from her apparent thrashing.

The next time she woke, it was dark. She was shivering and curled up in a knot.

She groaned, reaching to find the blanket on the floor. Her hand skimmed something furry, and she shrieked as it jumped, first from fright, then from pain.

"Elaina! 'Tis only me!"

"Damn you, Calum! Christ, are you trying to kill me?" she demanded, her heart trying to pound out of her chest. She held her side where Rabbie had stabbed her as her rescuers had poured down the mountainside. "Oh God," she moaned, rocking back and forth.

"Are ye all right?" he asked, sounding concerned.

"No. I'm f-freezing," she hissed.

"The fever must've broken. Ye were a ball of fire earlier." He threw a blanket of fur over her shivering form.

"Wh-wh-whiskey?" she croaked through her chattering teeth. She downed several swallows and eventually got her shivering under control. "How long have you been laying there?" she whispered into the dark.

"Near a week."

"Ever the witty one," she whispered. "Why?"

"Someone had to stay with ye through the night. I drew the short stick." He chuckled.

"How did I come to be here?"

"That is a long story."

"You shouldn't have come. We have put everyone in danger."

"What? Ye want I should leave ye to be hung or worse yet, burnt alive?"

"No. It's just...I don't deserve to live." Elaina couldn't stop the tears from coming.

"Ye've nothing to be ashamed about, lassie. Ye've done no wrong that I can tell."

"You don't know," she wept as she drifted toward the sweet relief of sleep. "You just don't know."

She clung to his large, warm hand as she faded into sleep, replaying her sins in her mind. She should have died.

Elaina refused to be treated as an invalid for long, although recovery tarried at a slow pace. Her hair was just long enough to be tied back in a tiny bundle at her nape, which helped her feelings somewhat. What would help them better was if she could get off the bed by herself or even take a piss in private. The worst part of all was treating the healing yet still open wounds, which involved pouring whiskey on them. In the beginning, she would pass out. As the tears in her skin from Rabbie's whip started closing more, she stayed conscious but nauseated. Finally, she refused to let them do it at all, saying she would rather die from disease than endure that hell any longer.

Caitir bound her ribs and the stab wound tight, so Elaina could stand movement better, although, she was weak as a kitten. Holding on to Caitir, she could meander somewhat more easily around their wing of the castle where they had brought her while trying to save her life.

The first time she ventured from what she called her cell, she made it as far as the blue velvet settee immediately outside the door. Trembling from the act of walking a few feet, she sat panting, with her eyes closed and her head spinning. Groaning, she eased herself back against the wall behind her.

Calum planted himself beside her.

Elaina could not bring herself to look at him. She was beyond grateful that he'd helped rescue her, but shame overwhelmed her every time she thought about it. Shame that a group of people she didn't know had laid their lives on the line to save a murderess from a deserved death.

Suppressed giggles trickled down the hallway, and Elaina opened one eye, catching a glimpse of a shaggy brown head as it darted back around the corner, joined by more high-pitched titters. She smiled despite herself

"That is a welcome sight." Calum's voice was quiet and almost melancholy.

"What?"

"A smile upon yer lips."

Elaina sighed, holding the tears in that threatened to rise to the surface.

"Mistress?" a small voice squeaked in front of her.

"She's a lady—a real one. You have to say 'my lady,'" another higher-pitched voice corrected.

She opened her eyes to find three pairs of brown eyes staring intently at her.

"You may call me whatever you wish. We are far away from anywhere they ever considered me a lady." She offered the child a smile, easing herself up off the wall and waving away Calum's proffered hand of help.

"Miss…my lady," the little boy, started again, sheepishly looking back at what had to be his sisters. He turned his intent gaze back to Calum and Elaina. "My lady. A gift." He bowed his shaggy brown head before Elaina and lay in her hands a rustic offering. A sprig of mistletoe adorned with shiny emerald holly leaves and its red berries and what appeared to be dried berries from a Rowan tree, threaded onto a red string. They were bundled haphazardly together and presented to her in a most solemn fashion.

"It's beautiful. You are so kind, sir." Elaina offered the giggling girls a nod. "Ladies."

"The Rowan twig and berries and the red string will bring ye strength and healing, my lady."

"And protection!" the girls twittered from behind their younger brother.

"Come." She waved the young lad closer.

He could be no more than five or six years—all legs and arms. She thought of Angus, and her chest squeezed tight. God, she had loved that child. She lifted the boy's chin and planted a soft kiss upon his cheek.

He turned as crimson as the berries in her bouquet but scampered off with a broad smile, holding the site of her kiss and flanked on either side by his giggling sisters.

"How sweet," she sighed leaning back and closing her eyes. She tenderly fingered the pointed holly leaves. "Are there any more?"

"Gifts? You vain woman."

"Children," Elaina grumbled swatting Calum on the leg.

Calum chuckled. "Aye. A lass of about fourteen or so."

"Who is being so hospitable? I have yet to see an adult, besides you and Caitir, of course."

"Hugh Graham and his wife, Letitia. They are friends of ours."

"It is kind of them to allow us to stay here. I should like to thank them."

"You will have a chance. They are away but will return in about two weeks. 'Twill be close to Christmas when they return, and there will be a small to do."

"Christmas?" She had lost all track of time. "Have you heard anything of William?" Was he safe at Fort William or had Captain Cummings been lying to her about that as well?

"No, my lady. We have not. I'm sorry." He squeezed her hand.

She fought the urge to pull her hand away. She did not want to hurt Calum, nor could she accept his affections.

The two weeks passed with Elaina venturing farther and farther away from her room. Down to the end of the long hallway, eventually to the sitting room that graced their small wing, then back to her room where she would collapse from exhaustion.

The children were a constant source of entertainment. Their nursemaid, Hilda, was a plump harried-looking woman who spent her time trying to keep them from bothering her, but Elaina loved their sweet attention. Wee Simon often held her hand, steadying her as she walked. He would tell her stories of all the animals they had, and when she was well, he would take her to see the giant one-horned ram, but it was a vicious beast and they mustn't get too close! He often presented her with gifts—pretty rocks, random buttons, and other odds and ends he would come across. Elaina kept them all in a small, black velvet drawstring pouch the girls had brought her.

The girls, Finolia and Garia, brought her food and cups of whiskey every time she sat down to rest, "to keep up her strength," they said. They also took turns brushing her hair and tying it back, clucking like mother hens over the state of it. Elaina was tempted to cut it all off, but the girls absolutely would not have it. They relentlessly fought her short hair back into the leather thong, smoothing and grooming it.

"See, it's no so bad!"

"If you say so," Elaina retorted, thinking she was addressing Garia, but it was hard to remember because they looked so much alike.

She tried to pretend she didn't notice Calum watching her. Either he or Caitir was always by her side. Since the night she woke to find him on the floor next to her bed, Calum no longer slept in the same room. Caitir took to sleeping in the bed with Elaina and helped her to perform all her personal duties. She learned Calum had refused to leave her side from the moment he'd cut the ties binding her to the posts outside the gaol and carried her in his arms on the back of his horse to the safety of the Castle at Balquidder. He'd stayed with her, sleeping on the floor beside her bed until she regained part of her senses. She knew her distance and coldness to him confused and frustrated him. He had seen her at her most vulnerable. He'd doctored her wounds and saved her from the inept physician who thought laudanum was the answer to it all. God help her, he may have seen her naked form. She hadn't the nerve to question Caitir. He'd saved her life, and she had no idea how to repay nor face him.

Elaina tried never to be alone with him to avoid it all. She wasn't brave enough to face her demons.

Chapter Thirty-One

EARLY ONE MORNING, THERE WAS a light knock on her door. A slight comely girl of about thirteen or fourteen entered the room at Elaina's bidding.

"My lady." She bobbed a curtsy. "My mam and da request all to dine in the small hall early this evening to make acquaintance before the feast tomorrow eve. Also, Mam sent this for ye, for Christmas dinner. She kent yer dress, it... Well, it was a bit mankit."

"To say the least," said Caitir who had sewn up the back of the dress and tried to get as much blood out of it as possible.

"How kind." It touched Elaina that people she had never met cared enough to house her in their home and supply her with clothing. She rose gingerly from her seat and accepted the lilac gown.

"'Twas my auntie's gown. She died before I was born," the girl offered. "Ma said she was a braw lass, like you." She ducked her head, bashfully. "Strong and brave. Ma said the gown might as well be given to you. That ye seemed to be as hard-headed as my auntie was. It's time it was worn again."

"I don't feel strong or brave at the moment," Elaina whispered.

"But she is hard-headed," Calum offered with all seriousness.

Elaina shot him a look.

The girl snickered, then said, "But, my lady, ye are so brave. I heard ye gave ole Rabbie Campbell and that terrible captain pure hell as they were draggin' ye to the stake. I mean you near bit off Rabbie's finger. Ye are the talk of the land."

"What is your name, lass?" Elaina asked.

"Mairi, my lady."

"Mairi, I thank you for this gift. I do not deserve your kindness. I am thick-headed, reckless, irresponsible, and rash. You and your family have already done me the greatest of services by saving my pig-headed life. I am most humbled." Elaina bowed her head and dipped a deep, long curtsy before the astonished lass.

"M-my lady," she stammered, flushing.

"Thank you. Truly," Elaina said as she rose from her curtsy.

The stunned girl gave her a curtsy in return, a quick one, and fled from the room.

"Now ye have taken to scaring the weans," Calum said. "Have ye no manners at all?"

"Can ye breathe?" Caitir asked, securing the laces on the back of Elaina's frock. The lilac gown donated by the Grahams was tucked safely in the wardrobe, waiting for Christmas Eve.

"Yes, actually, it feels good. Supportive." Elaina touched the stays of her dress. Her body moved with more ease, although her wounds remained tender to sudden actions. "But am I presentable?" She self-consciously touched her hair and ran her hand down her cheek.

"You look lovely." Caitir adjusted the green ribbon that tied back Elaina's hair.

"My bruises match my ribbon wonderfully." The swelling had gone down in her face, and the dark purple bruises had faded to a lovely shade of green.

"They do, don't they?" Caitir giggled. "You look much improved over the last time they laid eyes on you."

The Grahams had visited Elaina several times in the first days of her arrival, bringing in the physician and then the priest when they were not confident she would survive her ordeal. They were called away when word came that Letitia's brother needed them.

A knock at the door announced Calum's arrival to escort the women to the small dining hall, which in all actuality sat about forty people around a long rectangular table. A large, gray stone fireplace encompassed an entire wall and kept the room toasty. The Grahams were all present when their guests entered the hall.

"My lady!" Wee Simon came running, wrapping his skinny arms about Elaina's waist.

She gave him a big hug in return.

"Look, my lady! I pulled it all by myself!" He held his missing tooth in his small hand and bared his teeth to show her the gap.

"You are so brave!" she exclaimed. "I knew you could do it." She ruffled his soft brown hair.

Calum, in the meantime, scooped Garia onto one hip and Finolia onto the other. They each wrapped their tiny arms around his neck.

"Children, you should let our guests enter the room before you start assailing them." A bear of a man approached the new arrivals. "Run along and take your seats." He scooped Garia from Calum's arms and swatted her playfully on the rump as he set her loose.

"Yes, Papa," she giggled. She grabbed Finolia's hand, and they scrambled for the table.

"Lady Elaina, you are looking spry." His sizeable hairy hand engulfed hers. His eyes glittered like little black beads beneath dark woolly eyebrows. The whiskers of his beard and mustache tickled her hand as he kissed it.

"I was in capable hands." She smiled at Caitir and Calum. "Mr. Graham, I presume?"

"Please, call me Hugh. My wife, Letitia." The great man ushered to his side a petite woman whose soft brown eyes looked Elaina over.

"Lady Elaina." Letitia gave her a warm smile, her gaze lingering, studying Elaina. Turning her attention to Calum and Caitir, she said, "My dears." She placed a hand on either cheek, peering up at the two of them.

"How is he then?" Calum asked with concern.

"I think he may be taking a turn for the better," Letitia answered. She looked worried and tired. "They have sent for another healer, from Strathyre. We will see, but come, let us sit and eat. Lady Elaina." Letitia motioned for her to sit across from her at the large table.

Hugh took his place at the head of the table immediately to Elaina's right, and little Simon scrunched up close to her on the other side before anyone could get his spot. She wrapped an arm around him and pulled him close. His mother shot him a stern look but smiled at Elaina with a wink.

The conversation centered on Elaina and how she had come to Scotland.

"How did ye ken Robert Campbell?" Hugh asked, eying Elaina with interest.

Elaina swallowed her bite of bread. "My brother hired him on to be a coachman and a bodyguard of sorts when we first moved to Edinburgh. Although, at the time, we knew him as Rabbie MacLeod. He came highly recommended. As we now know, that was a farce."

"And this"—Hugh waved a hand at Elaina—"came to be how?"

"Not to be of any offense, but I would have thought you, Calum, and Caitir would have cleared all of this up already?" She looked from Hugh to Calum with a raised brow.

"We have discussed it, yes, my lady. I only wanted to hear it from your point of view to make sure we get the full story," Hugh answered without apology. "How did you happen to get separated from your companions?"

"A member of the Watch came upon me while Ainsley and Caitir were gone to have the sled harness repaired. There was an accident, and we fell into the burn. He did not survive it." She glanced sideways at Simon, who sat glued to her every word. She didn't want to frighten the children.

"What happened in the gaol?"

"Need the children be here for this?" Elaina asked with some incredulity.

"Yes," Hugh said. "They need to know how dangerous the world can be."

"I think they have already been witness to it," Elaina argued.

She looked around for assistance, but the adults stared at their plates.

Damned cowards. Oh well, if he wants the gory details, that's what he will get. She left out nothing.

The room was silent except for the sniffles of the girls. Wee Simon sat stoic, keeping his chin lifted and eyes on his father for reassurance. Mairi's eyes rested on her hands.

Elaina could not look at Calum or Caitir. She had not told them everything that happened. Now they knew. They all knew what a fool Rabbie had made of her and the part she'd played in the death of the red-headed lad.

"Do ye ken where the money is goin'?" Hugh asked.

She turned a burning gaze on him that would have withered any other man.

He merely stared at her, studying her face with interest.

"No."

"You may not, but I may—at least part of it," Hugh said bluntly.

"How...what..." she tried.

He pushed himself away from the table and looked at his wife.

Letitia gave him a small nod and patted his arm.

He rose and crossed the room to the fireplace where he stood staring into the flames, his hands clenched behind his back. He was silent for a long while, and Elaina began to wonder if he was going to speak at all.

"One and twenty years ago, my brother and his wife were murdered in cold blood, in their own home," he finally began, not at all how Elaina imagined he would. "They were killed by the Campbells. It was a revenge killing for a cattle raid my uncle and my brother had orchestrated, which netted all of five head. My uncle was stealing back his own cattle. The Duke of Manchester had seized his land and everything he owned because he'd refused to renounce the MacGregor name. The Duke awarded the rights to my uncle's house, his land, and all his belongings to Stewart Campbell—Robert Campbell's father."

Elaina stared at the back of Hugh Graham, unblinking.

"My brother, Thamas, and his wife Mairi had a bairn, only six months old. The bairn was never found." Hugh's voice wavered, and he cleared his throat.

Elaina thought her heart stopped for a moment at the mention of Thamas's name, but then it jumped hard in her chest, nearly taking her breath from her. She found herself twisting the fabric of her skirt into a tight knot. Forcing her fingers to stop, she smoothed out the wrinkles and placed her hands flat on her lap.

"The bairn's nursemaid disappeared as well. Her family assumed the worst, that the Campbells had either killed her or taken her captive. One spring day, she appeared on her family's doorstep. She had been in hiding, she'd said, fearing for her safety and the safety of her family. The bairn, she sadly reported, had been taken by the Campbell men and thrown into the Loch. She barely escaped with her life and hid in the woods for several months while making her way to Edinburgh. She was afraid to lead the Campbells to her own home, fearing for the lives of her husband and daughter, then but two years old. She said she finally deemed it safe and returned to her daughter, Caitir, near a year later."

Elaina turned her eyes to Caitir whose gaze was fixed on her, but her emotions unreadable. She looked at Calum and Letitia, and her skin began to crawl.

"Money began appearing, sent by messenger to the remaining family of Thamas MacGregor, from an anonymous source. It didn't make sense. We wondered for a while if the Duke of Manchester had grown a conscience after the murders of Thamas and his family. The money continued to arrive at regular intervals for the next twenty years or so."

"Why are you telling me this?" Elaina whispered. Was he insinuating the money her mother sent to Scotland all these years had gone to his family, the family of Thamas MacGregor, a Highlander?

"Thamas loved another before Mairi. He carried a profound love for a fair-haired, blue-eyed lass—the daughter of a nobleman from the Lowlands. Her parents had put a stop to it immediately when they caught wind. They sent her away, to family in London."

"Why would my mother send money to Thamas's family…to you?" Elaina could not stay seated any longer. She rose on shaking legs that she prayed would hold her up.

"We didn't even consider Diana Leicester Spencer as being the benefactor until several weeks ago." Hugh turned from the fire to face her.

Elaina backed away until she was flat against the wall, having an all too familiar sense of hearing news she did not want to hear.

"A family heirloom came up missing after Thamas and Mairi's murders. Everyone assumed it stolen by Laird Campbell. It had been passed down for generations upon generations to the heir of the Laird of the Clan MacGregor. Thamas was Laird."

Elaina's hand went to the cairngorm pendant hidden in her secret pocket. "Wh-what did it look like."

"'Twas a cairngorm crystal topped with a silver bell of two pinecones with Scotch pine needles etched upon the stone. The tree of the clan MacGregor. The pendant was believed to offer protection to its owner."

Elaina reached into her pocket, her hands trembling, and pulled the pendant from its hiding place, nearly dropping it in the process. "Why would I have it?"

"Thamas's bairn had a unique and remarkable marking upon her tiny body."

Bile threatened to choke Elaina.

"'Twas a scarlet marking on the back of her right thigh," Caitir whispered.

"No." Elaina shook her head. "No."

"When ye arrived from the gaol near dead and we saw the marking upon yer leg as we doctored yer wounds, we didna think much of it, but when we saw your hidden pendant… Well, we paid a visit to Caitir's father."

Elaina was still shaking her head, searching her friend's face.

Caitir looked down at her hands.

"One and twenty years ago, while men battled for their lives in front of a castle, Mairi MacGregor wrapped her infant daughter in her arisaid with a family heirloom and sent the bairn to where she knew the child would be loved and cared for. Her parents sent her in the arms of someone who held their utmost trust. Mistress Murray delivered the babe to a blonde-haired blue-eyed lass who had once been in love with a rogue Highlander." Here, Hugh paused, swallowing hard. "'Twas a grave matter."

Elaina could feel her knees trying to buckle. Calum appeared at her side, his hand under her arm, supporting her.

"Don't touch me," she hissed. "Do not touch me." She choked on her tears. "It's not true." She looked from face to face, but she could see it in their eyes. The pity and the secrecy. "I am the daughter of Diana and Edward Spencer."

"You are the daughter of the Laird of Clan MacGregor." Hugh took a step toward her.

"You knew?" Elaina turned from Calum to Caitir and back. "You both knew, and you brought me here and ambushed me with...with..." Her voice rose into an unnatural squeak, unable to find any more words.

Caitir whispered, "I am sorry, my lady."

"Do not call me that. I am no lady." Elaina edged away from Calum, who reached out a tentative hand toward her. She jerked away from his touch, leaning over and laying the pendant on the edge of the table next to wee Simon. She could not bring herself to look at the children. "I'm sorry. I can't..."

"They loved ye so much." Letitia stood with tears streaming down her cheeks. "We loved ye. We love ye still."

Elaina turned and fled from the room, tripping on her skirts and bouncing off the doorway.

Chapter Thirty-Two

CAITIR HAD COME LOOKING FOR her and found her in the stables. They walked together to the short stone wall meandering its way behind the crop of buildings housing the animals. She tried to get Elaina to talk to her, but Elaina had few words.

"Do you believe in fate?" Caitir finally asked.

"I don't know what I believe anymore. Everything I've ever known is a lie." Elaina couldn't wrap her head around it. Her soul was lost; it had no home. Looking back, she analyzed the small moments of her life when she had felt out of place.

She didn't look like her mother, fair hair, eyes that would change from blue to green depending on the color of her frock or the color of the sky. Her father with his black hair and brilliant blue eyes. William's eyes…his hair…his build. William's everything. She suddenly hated him—her brother. She hated him for who he was and for his roots that were planted deep and would never change. She felt like a tree that grew in a rocky crag, roots too shallow to take hold of anything, the storms pounding her until they ripped her from her precarious perch and tossed her into the heaving sea.

"I've got to go," she whispered to Caitir, standing up from the low rock wall they shared. She wiped her hands on her skirt.

"Go where?" Her friend reached out, placing a hand on her arm.

"I have to get out of here. I can't think. I can't breathe. I-I need to be alone." Elaina bolted for the woods.

Hibernating gorse bushes drug at her skirts and leafless branches tugged at her hair, ripping the ribbon from it. Loose stones rolled underneath her, and her feet slipped on the thick carpet of wet, rotting leaves. She paid no mind to the freezing rain starting to fall, her tears mixing with the sleet stinging her face. The stabbing pain in her side did nothing to deter her, and even when she thought her heart and lungs would burst, she found she couldn't outrun the feeling of nothingness encompassing her. Stumbling and falling against a tree, she stood bent over with one hand on a frozen trunk as she gasped for air, the cold shredding her lungs like knives. Dropping to her knees, she knelt there gasping and weeping. Burying her face in the earth, she screamed until her throat was raw. It was dangerous. The Watch would have extra patrols searching for her. Why hadn't Rabbie finished what he started? She wished, not for the first time, that she was dead.

The damp from the decaying leaves and the thin layer of sleet seeped through her skirts. The scent of the wet earth and its decomposing blanket invaded her lungs, her nose only a few inches from the ground, and she tried to inhale its strength. God, she had none left. Easing herself from the wet forest floor, she found a dry seat on a fallen log and laid her head upon her knees. The emptiness of her life hit her with a pounding force. She had lost her parents, Angus, the Carolinas, now her home in Scotland—her brother. She was truly alone in this foreign world.

The awful truth sunk in as the shivering began.

Lifting her head, Elaina peered at the darkening forest around her. Nothing looked familiar. She would never be able to find her way back tonight, and she'd fled without even a cloak. Now she had to figure out how she was going to make it through the night. Although she felt as if she wanted to die, her stubbornness wouldn't let her freeze to death in the woods just as it had not let her freeze to death in the gaol.

Kicking at the pile of dead leaves and rubbish, she unearthed a decent-sized stick. Looking down at the large log, she knew it would be her answer for the night. On her hands and knees, she started rooting the dirt from under the fallen tree. The rhythmic motion of her digging took over her thoughts as she focused only on the job at hand. The shivering slowed and finally stopped as she neared the end of her task. She sat back, inspecting her work.

With a last glance around the darkening woods, she burrowed down into the narrow space as her father had taught her—*her pretend father*—and pulled the leaves and branches to cover her body. The body heat she generated with her digging became trapped by the leaves, engulfing her in a warm nest. After a time, exhaustion overtook her and she fell into a troubled sleep.

The smell of smoke woke her. Fuzzy at first, her brain started to panic at not knowing where she was. The next thought sent her scrambling from her hole, slipping on the wet leaves. She whirled around expecting to find flames licking up the black outline of trees but instead found a dark figure seated on the log under which she had slept. A fire blazed, and the smell of sizzling meat hit her senses, making her mouth water.

"A hoard of wild boars could have torn through here, and I dinna think ye'd have stirred." Calum turned the rabbit he was cooking without looking at her.

"What are you doing here?" She stared at his back, puzzled. "How did you find me?"

"Well, first off, the screamin' could've drawn half the country. Second, if ye're trying to hide, ye need to learn to cover yer tracks better."

Elaina felt the color rising in her cheeks.

"Here." He handed a bottle back to her without turning around. "Warm yer bones."

She sat next to him with her back to the fire, staring out into the inky blackness that had descended while she slept. Taking a long swig from the bottle, she hoped to warm some parts and numb others.

Calum took the bottle from her grasp. "Slow down. Ye might want some by mornin'."

They sat without speaking for several minutes, the crackling of the fire and creaking of frozen branches the only sounds disturbing their thoughts.

Calum turned to her, "Are ye quite finished feeling sorry for yerself?" He caught her arm before she could hit him.

"How dare you," she hissed.

He turned to her, straddling the log and taking her by both arms "How dare *you*," he returned, his voice thick with anger.

"Me?" Elaina struggled against his grasp. *My entire life is gone. I have no home…no family this arrogant bastard has the nerve to tell me I'm feeling sorry for myself?*

"You. Are ye so dense ye cannae see?"

Elaina sat with her mouth gaping open, speechless.

"I ken it is a shock to ye. Hell, it's a damn shock to everyone. We thought ye was a crabbit wee Sassenach, but it turns out ye're just a Scot. Dammit, lass. I ken ye've no folks. I ken ye are damn lonely and scairt. But do ye no see? Ye've just become a cousin to loads of MacGregors, which explains yer temper, by the way," he added, the corner of his mouth turning up.

Elaina glared at him.

"Do ye no understand the ways of a clan, then? Do ye no understand they will stand and die by ye whether ye were raised here or no? The blood Rabbie Campbell spilled on the ground at the gaol, your blood, runs through the veins of every one of those people back at that castle. The weans ye find so dear? Yer blood. Yer kin. Do ye no see how much they admire ye? How much they idolized ye even before they kent ye were blood? These people, this clan, put themselves in harm's way hiding ye from The Watch and nursing ye back to health because of who Caitir and I are and who Rabbie Campbell is. Now they will lay down their lives to avenge yer honor."

"But I don't want them to," Elaina said adamantly as she sniffled, her nose cold and running and tears welling in her eyes.

Calum held her arms tight. "It doesna matter whether ye want them to or no. Ye're clan. Ye're blood. That's all that matters." He stared into her eyes, waiting for a reaction.

She had none.

"If I let go, will ye no try to wallop me?"

"I haven't decided."

He cautiously released one of her arms and drew out a handkerchief, all the while watching her with wariness.

She tried to snatch the handkerchief from his hand, but he jerked it away.

"Give it to me."

"No." He grabbed her hand as she reached to snatch the handkerchief again. He wrapped both of her small hands in one of his and held them tight to his chest. He leaned forward and wiped her nose with the handkerchief.

"Stop it! What are you doing?" She tried to dodge him and wrench her hands loose, but he held her tight. "I am not a child!"

"Then stop acting like one."

"Did you follow me here to insult me all night?"

He tried again with the handkerchief, and she jerked away, glaring at him.

"You have lost your mind, Calum MacKinnon!"

Calum scooted closer to Elaina and too quickly for her to even know how he did it, he had his legs wrapped around hers, pinning them to the log and her arms behind her back. He pulled her tightly into his chest and proceeded to wipe at her face.

"You are crazy," she exclaimed dumbfounded, and quickly turned her face into his chest and wiped her leaking nose on his plaid. "There." She sneered up at him. "We both win."

"Why, ye wee besom," he grinned down at her.

She flung all her weight forward, knocking them tumbling into the black of night. They scrambled furiously for several seconds, ending with Calum pinning her to the ground.

"Ye are quite the wee scrapper," he said.

"Uh-huh," she quipped with renewed vigor.

He blocked a strategically aimed knee.

"Let me go!" Elaina struggled against him.

"No."

"Why are you doing this, you…you…brute!" She tried to butt him with her head, but he held himself out of reach.

The night was black as pitch with the log blocking the light from the fire. Her eyes struggled to adapt to the change in light.

"Let us help ye, Elaina."

"What?" she asked with exasperation. "Help me *what*?" She was too tired to struggle anymore, but Calum didn't ease his hold.

"Let us in. Open yer heart, lass. Can ye no see how much we care for ye?"

"I can't." Elaina turned her face toward the night, avoiding his burning stare that she couldn't see but could certainly feel.

"You can," he said softer.

"I can't. Everyone I let in has either died or betrayed me." Her voice caught in her throat. "I don't want to hurt anymore, Calum. I can't."

"I ken Rabbie hurt ye, Elaina, physically and emotionally, and I swear to ye that ye will have yer vengeance. Ye trusted him. Can ye no bring yourself to trust me to do ye nay harm?" he whispered. "Have I not proven myself to ye?"

She couldn't speak for the emotions welling up inside her. She closed her eyes, wanting to burrow back into the frozen ground to get away from him, from these feelings she had locked away deep inside her. They swirled up from the pit of her stomach and were going to drown her.

"I'm scared, Calum," she whispered, opening her eyes. Her vision had adjusted somewhat to the night, and she could make out the line of his jaw, tense and unwavering. Fringes of his hair hung loose, and the glow over the log from the fire danced through the curls. "In the stables with the horses…with Rabbie…I could keep my walls in place but open a window and let a small shred of sunlight in. I didn't have to worry…I thought I didn't have to," the last part she whispered.

"Ye needn't worry now. I will protect ye. I will never harm ye," Calum whispered, his voice thick.

"I can't."

"Why? Is my comin' to save ye no proof enough of my love for you? Nursing yer wounds? Laying on the floor beside yer bed every night. Weeping over ye when I thought ye were dying?"

"I am cursed, Calum! Don't you see? Everything around me is cursed. Everyone around me is cursed. I am not worried about you hurting me. I am scared to death that something will happen to you or Caitir." Elaina choked on her tears. The dream she'd had when she was under the laudanum was no dream. With vivid detail, she recalled the feel of his face buried in her hair and the warm tears on her cold cheek.

"Nonsense. Bad things happen. They happen to everyone all the time. They happened in the past, and they will happen in the future. Ye cannae let that keep ye from lovin'. What kind of life are ye livin' if ye can no have feelin's for anyone or anythin'—if ye keep yer heart closed off from the world? It's a dark place ye bide in, Elaina. Ye cannae live there. Your heart will turn as black as Rabbie's. Let me in, lass," he pleaded with her.

She could feel his breath on her face, cooling her tears as they flowed down her temples, wetting her hair. She hiccupped, trying to slow her sobs. "Calum, my actions have caused the deaths of innocent people. You deserve better than that. You do not deserve a life of hiding and running from the British. We cannot be, Calum. We can never be."

Calum was silent for a long moment. When he spoke again, his voice choked with emotion. "Dinna tell me what I need, Elaina. Ye did nothin' wrong."

"I killed two men. I am responsible for the deaths of two more."

"Whose deaths are ye responsible for?" His voice rose angrily in the night. "Lachlan? The young soldier? I heard ye tell Graham your tale, remember? I dinna see how you could ever believe their deaths lay on your shoulders. Their deaths are the result of Robert Campbell's and Captain Cummings's insanity. Do ye no think I have killed also? I am a Highlander. Do I like killin'? No. I hate it, but one must do what one has to do to survive. Do ye no think I killed that day on the hill in Balquidder? The rage that came over me when I saw ye, hen—" Calum's voice broke. "I cannae tell ye how many redcoats we slaughtered. And I would do it a thousand times over for ye, lass."

Elaina buried her face in the crook of his arm as she lost control of her tears.

"Let it go, Elaina. Ye needn't be brave all the time. I will be strong for ye," he whispered and rolled his weight to the side. Drawing her close to his body, he embraced her, wrapping his plaid around her in a warm cocoon that melted the icy places remaining in her soul.

She wept into his chest, her body wracked with grief—grief for her parents; those that had raised her and those that had given her up to save her life. She wept for William, and Angus, and the red-headed soldier. She cried over Rabbie's sick and demented betrayal. But most of all, she mourned her actions that had cost innocent people their lives. She was no longer the same person she was before. The innocence of her youth was gone.

As her sobs slowed, Calum took the edge of his plaid and gently wiped her face. This time she let him. Softly he traced the line of her tears with his thumb. "Let us help ye through this. Ye dinna have to handle everything on yer own. Ye are a braw lass, but it is not a sign of weakness to seek help."

She said nothing, turning her face towards his.

His thumb tenderly traced the outline of her mouth. "This time I will ask ye," he whispered. "May I kiss ye, Elaina Spencer MacGregor?"

Her breath hitched in her throat as he spoke her name. "No," she answered after a moment.

"No?"

She felt him tense at her words and heard the doubt and sadness in his voice. She nearly began to weep again. Instead, she grasped his face, the stubble of his unshaven skin rough against her hands. Her eyes strained to find his in the dark. She wanted to look at him. Instead, she traced the outline of his face with her fingers, her mind's eye recalling the curve of his jaw, the slope of his brow, his hazel eyes that seemed to read her every thought. She traced his lips with her frozen fingertips and felt him shudder against her. Slowly, as if afraid she might press the door he had opened closed, Elaina moved closer into his embrace. Steeling herself in his strength, she drew his face to hers and found his mouth with a whisper of a kiss.

His lips were as soft and warm as they had been in the garden in Edinburgh a lifetime ago, his nose once again cold upon her cheek.

"I have thought about your kiss a thousand times over," she breathed into him, her lips skimming his. "You need not ask for permission, nor apologize."

"Well, then." He drew her close into his body, one hand on the small of her back and the other buried in her short hair.

Their mouths met with a passion that took her breath away. His tongue found hers in a tantalizing dance of sweetness and the threat of temptation before his lips left hers to trace the curve of her face, following the path of her tears. "God, I love ye, Elaina," he whispered into her hair. "Yer fiery temper, yer hard-headed ways, yer foul mouth when yer temper is riled—"

"If you are trying to woo me, Mr. MacKinnon, you might try a little harder," Elaina interrupted.

Calum chuckled, his breath hot on her throat as he made his way across her collarbone and up to the soft spot just behind her ear.

She melted into him—against the hard, firm lines of him.

"I love the excitement in your eyes when ye are with the weans," he whispered into her ear, causing her to giggle and shiver at the same time. "I love how strong ye are even when ye think ye are weak. I love yer short hair."

Elaina snorted, but his words and his mouth were igniting a fire on the verge of burning out of control.

"I love the way yer brown eyes light up when they see me and how they turn dark as night when I annoy ye. I swear to ye I will keep ye safe," Calum whispered against her lips. "But..."

"But?" Elaina sighed breathlessly.

His teeth nipped her bottom lip, and she shivered against him.

"But, as much as I am enjoying the current state of things, if I dinna stop now, I may not be able to protect yer virtue."

Elaina was not certain she wanted him to protect her virtue, even though she'd never dreamed she would lose her innocence on a frozen forest floor.

"And..."

"And?" she whispered.

"I am also starving, and I think the rabbit may be on fire."

Chapter Thirty-Three

HUNDREDS OF CANDLES AND TORCHES lit the large dining hall. The small group numbered over seventy-five. A much larger party would be held on Hogmanay in a week. The thought of that evening made Elaina weak in the knees. Many members of the MacGregor clan and their friends would be in attendance. For now, Christmas Eve consisted of the Grahams, Caitir, Calum, several of the neighboring families living near the castle at Balquidder, and the best surprise of all, Auld Ruadh who had arrived that morning.

Elaina stood in the corner of the room beside one of the four massive fireplaces, sipping on her third glass of cider. She would have drained it, but Calum had an eagle eye on her. He stood conversing with a young couple who worked land for Hugh Graham. She raised her glass in salute to his reassuring smile before her eyes traveled the length of him, remembering their moment in the woods the night before. She flushed at the memory of his body pressed tight against hers, the corner of his mouth turned up as her gaze found its way back to his face. His dark eyes burned with an undeniable hunger, and she turned into the fire, hiding her smile from the room.

"Ye look lovely in Mairi's dress—yer mother's dress," Letitia said, gliding up beside her.

Elaina nearly dropped her glass onto the stone hearth.

"I didn't mean to startle ye, lass."

"My mind was elsewhere." Elaina smiled and smoothed a hand over the lilac fabric wrapped tightly around her waist. "Thank you for the dress," she added. She didn't know what to say to this woman—her aunt.

"Come. I have something to show ye while the men are jawing." Letitia jerked her chin in the direction of Hugh entertaining Calum and a small cluster of men with one of the many dramatic tales tucked away in his arsenal.

Letitia led the way through a side door, out of the dining hall. The corridor was dark and felt somewhat damp, much like the hallway at the gaol. Elaina gulped the last of her cider, trying to tamp down the bile and panic she felt rising in her throat. *You are safe. You are safe.* She repeated the mantra to herself over and over until Letitia led her through another doorway, into a large, well-lit sitting room.

"Here, I wanted you to see."

Elaina followed her aunt's gaze to a line of portraits hanging on the far wall of the room. Stepping closer, she viewed what must have been Hugh in his younger years, his beady eyes and massive beard being his give away. There had been markedly less gray in his beard then. Letitia's portrait hung beside his. Her looks had not changed much since it was rendered. Her dark hair cascading around her shoulders in ringlets held no silver, yet even in her youth, Letitia's eyes held wisdom beyond her years. The slight scar cutting through her left eyebrow was already present. Her gaze traveled to the next portrait, and she felt her knees buckle.

Letitia grabbed Elaina's arm and helped her to a sitting chair. "I should have warned ye," she said, taking the chair next to Elaina but not letting go of her hand. She squeezed it reassuringly.

"An occasional warning would be nice." Elaina held tight to Letitia's hand, her own eyes staring down at her from what she presumed to be her father's face. She didn't have to ask who the woman was because Elaina looked so much like her that it could be her portrait hanging there, except for the eyes. She studied Thamas's rugged features. The strong jaw and broad forehead. He looked like a Laird, like a man who could command armies and lead men, but his eyes—if the portrait was accurate—were soft and wise. Her mother's eyes were a pale gray and her father's dark brown speckled with the gold of her own. The plaid draped over his shoulder was the same tartan pattern that was in the chest in Edinburgh.

"Ye look so much like yer mother. If ye'd not been in such a state when ye arrived, I would've seen it immediately, but…"

Elaina only nodded. Her face had been so swollen from Rabbie breaking her nose and punching her teeth loose from his hand that she hadn't been able to open her eyes. Her hand moved to the bridge of her nose that would forever be slightly crooked and would, more than likely, be sore for a while longer. She swallowed the lump in her throat. "I have the plaid," she whispered.

"The plaid?"

"The one I was wrapped in when Caitir's mother saved my life." Elaina wiped away the tear that escaped down her cheek. God, she was so tired of crying. Never in her life had she cried as much as she had in the past year. It was time to stop. She took a deep, settling breath and turned to her aunt. "I want to know about my family. Will you tell me about them?"

Letitia wrapped her arms around Elaina, holding her tight for a long moment. When she pulled away, it was with tears in her eyes. "I would love to."

"Where have ye been hiding?" Calum whispered, leaning over Elaina's shoulder and handing her a glass of cider.

"Plying me with drink, are you?"

"Aye, if that's what it takes."

"It may take more than that."

"How much more?" Calum trailed a finger down her back and wrapped his hand around her waist.

"Are you being forward, Mr. MacKinnon?"

Calum glanced over his shoulder at the dwindling group and pulled Elaina into a small alcove behind a heavy brocade tapestry.

"I'm being forward and backward and everything in between, Elaina." Calum pushed her roughly up against the stone wall and kissed her. He tasted of expensive whiskey.

"Are you drunk?" Elaina whispered, gasping for air as Calum's lips trailed down her neck. She braced one hand on the wall for support, the other still holding her drink.

"Maybe a little," he hissed into her ear.

Elaina burst into giggles at his honesty and the chills his breath sent down her spine.

"Marry me," he whispered.

She placed a hand on his chest, trying to push him away. She could feel his heart pounding wildly beneath her palm. "You are not drunk. You are completely blootered!"

Calum snickered. "Marry me," he repeated with more urgency.

"I will not."

"I want ye, Elaina. I need ye so. I loved ye the first time I laid eyes on you." Calum's arm snaked its way around her waist, drawing her closer.

"Now I know you are pissed out of your head because the first time you saw me, I was covered in shite." Elaina struggled to push him away.

"Aye, I'll give ye that. The second time then. Ye were lovely, your skin like ivory against the gold in yer gown with the little buds in yer hair matching the flowers on it. When ye dressed down Harry Everson without a moment's hesitation, ye made me weak in the knees, and I burned for ye when ye blushed after I caught ye eyeing me with lust."

"I most certainly did not—" Her protests were rudely interrupted by his tongue in her mouth. "I can't believe you remember what I was wearing," she panted when they came up for air. Squirming and trying to push him away only worked to make her more conscious of how deep his need was.

"Remember? I relive that night in my dreams. Watching ye laugh at the Duke's poor jokes, the way your eyes turned near black as ye argued with yer brother. How ye avoided my gaze as Lady Caroline retold yer wild tale. But mostly…" He leaned close, nuzzling her cheek, and whispered, "Mostly I remember standing on the veranda alone with ye and ye smelling like roses, the feel of your tiny hand in mine, the way ye quivered when I took it, and the silkiness of yer skin. His fingers glided soft as a feather up her arm, sending chills through her body. "And then there is my favorite part…"

"And what would that be?" Elaina wrapped her arms around his neck, his words and his actions having had a marked effect on her willpower.

"The hunger in yer eyes when ye threatened to throttle me when I suggested William give ye a thrashin' for bein' reckless. I kent then we would be mairiet."

"Oh Christ." Elaina shoved him, ducking under his arm and out of the alcove in a swish of skirts.

"He knew it too!" Calum called out after her.

Chapter Thirty-Four

LAOCH SNATCHED THE RIBBON FROM Elaina's hair as she bent over to scoop his warm mash. He was the offspring of her father's horse, Gairdh. Uncle Hugh brought her out earlier in the morning to introduce her to him, explaining that Laoch was the Gaelic name for a warrior. They should have named him the Gaelic word for Devil because he had the attitude of one.

"Damn you." Elaina grabbed at the ribbon, but the ornery stallion flung his head up out of her reach. "Oh, that's how it is, is it?" She narrowed her eyes at the massive beast while raking her hair out of her eyes. "Two can play at that game. No mash for you." She picked up the bucket and turned from his stall to find Calum reclining against a wall, watching her.

He chuckled. "Is this big fella giving ye problems, my lady?"

"Yes, and don't call me that."

"Gimme the ribbon." Calum stepped around Elaina, ignoring her annoyed comment.

Laoch jerked his head away from him.

Elaina snickered.

"Give it," Calum growled.

Laoch stamped his hoof.

"Give it." Calum grabbed the horse's mane.

Laoch dropped the ribbon.

"That's more like it." Calum bent over to pick it up, and Laoch nipped at his shoulder. "Merde! Ye rotten bastard!" He swatted the stallion with his hat. "Yer damn ribbon, my— Yer ribbon." Calum handed Elaina her ribbon while rubbing his shoulder.

Elaina tried to hide the laughter in her voice as she said, "How bad did he get you?"

"Och, nay so bad. Here let me help." Calum tried to take the ribbon back from Elaina's teeth where she held it as she struggled to pull her short hair back into a small nob.

Elaina jerked her head.

"Aye, just as stubborn as the beast." On a second go, Calum snatched the ribbon from her teeth.

She snapped playfully at him.

"And near as wicked too." He jerked his fingers out of danger. "Sit." He ordered her to a low stool.

"I am not a dog," she said over her shoulder while obliging him.

"Why do ye no wear it down?" Calum asked her, raking his fingers through her hair and causing gooseflesh to rise on her arms.

"Wear it down?" Elaina cut him a look over her shoulder. "I can't wear it down!"

"Aye, it's no so bad since wee Mairi trimmed off the scraggly pieces." Calum flicked the back of her hair.

Elaina thought he must still be drunk. When she wore it tied back, she could at least pretend she still had some hair. She tried to make out like it didn't bother her, but deep down it did. Did that make her a vain person because she had been proud of her hair and now missed it? Probably, but she couldn't change the fact that she did.

Calum said nothing of their encounter in the alcove the night before, and Elaina wondered if he remembered it at all. He had drunk a fair amount of alcohol. Having wrestled her hair successfully into the ribbon, he flopped down in the hay next to her stool.

"Feeling a little worse for the wear this morning?" Elaina grinned down at him.

"Aye." He closed his eyes, his face slightly pale in the early morning light. "Never mix expensive Scottish whiskey with cider and brandy." He grimaced and gave a small shudder.

Elaina burst out laughing. "Brandy too? You lush!"

"Well, Hugh had some fancy imported stuff he wanted us to try. Who was I to refuse?"

"I bet you wished you had."

"Aye." Calum reached up, his eyes still closed, and searched out her hand. Having found it, he dragged her down onto the hay beside him. "If ye think I was too drunk to remember what I asked ye last night, ye would be mistaken."

"Well, I am surprised you do remember."

"I've been thinking about it for months. That is part of the reason I came back to the Highlands. To prepare to bring my new bride to her new home."

"Well, aren't you arrogant? What if I say no?"

"I dinna think ye can."

"You don't think I *can*? Well, I have news for you—"

Calum pulled her down to his mouth, cutting her off. She struggled against him at first but then fell into him. He knew how to manipulate her.

"Let me rephrase. Ye can say no, but I dinna think ye will, if for no other reason than ye would get to wake up next to this handsome face every morning." He grinned his crooked grin at her groan. "And ye cannae return home. Not until Robert Campbell and Captain Cummings have been brought to justice."

"Brought to justice?" Elaina scoffed. "He is the captain of The Watch. I am the outlaw. They are the supposed law. There will be no justice."

"Highland justice." Calum opened his hazel eyes and stared at her.

Elaina sat startled for a moment. The warrior side of Calum was not something she thought about. He was witty and handsome, always with a smile upon his face.

A slow smile spread across her face. "You speak my language, Mr. MacKinnon."

"Good, then it is settled. We will marry on Hogmanay shortly after midnight."

"What?" Elaina sat straight up. "I didn't—"

Calum stood up out of the hay, dusting himself off. He kissed the top of her head and headed toward the doors of the stables. "One week. Be prepared!"

"I didn't say yes!" she called frantically after him.

"Aye, but ye didna say no."

Chapter Thirty-five

"WHY AFTER MIDNIGHT?" ELAINA MOANED.

"In a hurry, are ye?" Caitir asked her friend with a devilish grin.

"Don't be brash." Elaina rolled her eyes. "It has made for a long day."

"Aye. Ye should have taken a nap like I told ye. Ye are goin' to fall asleep before ye consummate the marriage."

Elaina swatted at her. She couldn't have napped if she wanted to. Letitia insisted on handling the arrangements, leaving little for Elaina to do except pace the hallways fretting. "I cannot imagine what a priest would have to do on Hogmanay that would tie him up until after midnight."

"Well, he didna give us a schedule of his day's activities," Caitir said. "Who are you to question a man of God, anyway?"

Elaina snorted. "I want to wear it down," she said as Caitir started to pin her hair up.

"Down? Are ye sure?"

"Positive."

"As ye wish."

"I don't know why you are still waiting on me hand and foot when I am no longer a lady. You are no longer my employee," Elaina said, gazing at Caitir in the looking glass.

"Who says I am doing this as yer servant and not yer friend? Every woman needs help on their wedding day." Caitir cut her eyes at Elaina. "Wedding night?" she said, laughing.

"Well, thank you. You are the best friend I could ever ask for. I still don't understand how he got a priest to consent to perform a wedding when the banns have not been read. This is completely against the book."

"How are we supposed to go by the book when ye are an outlaw? And don't ye worry 'bout it. It's covered."

A light tap sounded on the door, and Mairi slid through it. "Seems I am always bringing ye a dress when I come," she giggled, laying an ivory frock in Caitir's arms. "Ma sent it…of course."

"Stay with us," Elaina said to the young girl as she turned to leave. "I think we could all use a drink. What do you say?"

Mairi nodded, and Elaina poured the three of them a cup of wine.

"What do we drink to?" Caitir asked.

"To friendship, family, and midnight weddings," Elaina said, raising her glass.

The two women saluted the toast.

"Now," Elaina said after draining hers. "What do we have here?" She fingered the delicate fabric.

"'Twas yer mother's wedding dress," Mairi whispered.

Elaina's fingers froze. "My mother's?"

"Aye. Ma said ye needed a proper dress for yer wedding, and the other fit ye so well we made hardly any changes to it at all."

"You worked on this dress?" Elaina turned to Caitir, who nodded at her.

"You have become quite the secret keeper."

"Who said I only just became one," Caitir grinned. "Now let's get ye into it and do something with this"—she waved a finger at Elaina's hair—"or ye're going to be late to yer own wedding."

The two women curled Elaina's hair and darkened her eyelashes. Caitir decided against rouge because Elaina was already flushed from drink. Her nerves were getting the better of her.

"Now the dress," Caitir said.

Elaina stood naked, looking at herself in the mirror while the other two fumbled with the garment. After tonight, she would no longer be a virgin.

"Are ye cold?" Caitir asked. "Ye are shaking."

"I'm scared."

"Scairt? You? Of what?" Mairi asked.

Elaina blushed. "It's nothing."

"Raise yer arms then if it's nothing. Let's get on with it," Caitir said impatiently, holding the gown to slip over Elaina's head.

Obedient, she raised her arms, and Caitir slid the dress over her head. The feel of it against her bare skin caused her to shiver.

"What is the matter with ye? Ye are skittish as a cat."

"I am not." Elaina wiggled uncomfortably in the gown.

"Be still then, so I can do the laces proper like. I would hate to have to thump ye on the head and mess up yer hair."

"Will you get me some more wine?" Elaina whispered to Mairi, who stood watching Caitir fiddle with the back of the dress.

"More wine? Ye tryin' to get snockered before ye say I do? Is it that bad?" Caitir mumbled behind Elaina.

"Do you think...what I mean is...will it..." Elaina sighed. "I'm nervous about...after."

"After?" Caitir burst out laughing. "Ye who slit a British soldier's throat in front of his comrades in their own prison, ye who spit in Rabbie Campbell's face while being dragged to the stake and then was near beat to death—ye fear yer wedding night?"

"Thank you for being so understanding." Elaina cut her eyes over her shoulder at her friend.

"I just never," she giggled.

"You can stop any time now."

"I cannae." Caitir's laughter grew stronger until she doubled over with it and Mairi had joined in.

Elaina crossed her arms and glared at the two girls, causing them to fall into gales of laughter. They held each other up as tears ran down their faces.

"I'm s-sorry," Caitir hiccupped. "I just never in all of my d-days thought ye would be scairt to have relations with a man." She snorted, trying to quell her laughter.

"Are you not scared for your own wedding night?" Elaina asked with a huff as Caitir spun her around to finish dressing her.

"Aye, I might be," she sniffled. "When the time comes, but it's no me havin' to worry about it tonight."

"I would be scairt," Mairi offered up. "I've heard it hurts something terrible."

Elaina eyed the young girl. "That quite sets my mind at ease. Thank you."

Mairi giggled and shrugged.

"Do you think he has…you know?"

"Experience?" Mairi offered.

"Yes, that."

"I dinna ken," Caitir said. "Ye want I should ask him?"

"No!"

Caitir chuckled. "There, now one last thing." She reached around Elaina's neck and laid the cairngorm pendant at her throat. A red velvet ribbon held the delicate piece, and Caitir tied the ends of it underneath Elaina's bobbed off hair.

"Now take a look." She turned the bride-to-be toward the large looking glass.

Elaina stared at her reflection in the mirror. Her soft brown hair lay in waves that nearly grazed her bare shoulders. Small ringlets from both sides were swooped back and pinned with pieces of dried white heather. Her fingers grazed the crystal lying in the hollow of her throat, and she swallowed the lump that rose as she thought about her parents—all of them. The gown's flowing sleeves reached her fingertips. The bodice held her small waist snug, and her breasts swelled over the top. She tried to wriggle it up just a bit, and Caitir slapped at her hand. The gown was simple—a tight V-shaped bodice flowed into a full skirt with a bit of a train. No lace, no pearls. The only adornment fell to the delicate drape of the MacGregor plaid. It swooped just in front of her hips, then around to the back where it cascaded its way down into the train. Elaina never in her life would have thought a piece of fabric would bring her to tears, but she felt them coming on like a tidal wave and worked to keep them down.

"Ye are breathtaking," Mairi whispered.

"Do you think so?" Elaina wiped at a tear trying to escape. "Do you think Calum will be pleased?"

"I think Calum would be pleased if ye showed up in burlap rags as long as ye showed up," Caitir said. "Are ye ready?"

After a deep breath, the answer was, "Yes."

Chapter Thirty-Six

L ETITIA MET THE TRIO IN the corridor bridging the gap between what had become known as Elaina's wing and the rest of the castle. A smile flooded her face as Elaina turned the corner. "So beautiful. Ye look like yer mother did on her wedding day. Just as nervous too, I think," she said.

Caitir and Mairi snickered.

"Don't you two start again," Elaina snapped. "Is the priest here?"

Letitia shook her head.

The women made it into the substantial circular entryway that led into the great hall as the grandfather clock chimed the midnight hour. The large double doors were closed in preparation for the coming nuptials. A heavy pounding began from another large door, the one leading outside into the courtyard surrounding the castle. Servants usually greeted visitors and determined their business with the inhabitants, but there were none present.

Mairi giggled at Elaina's puzzled expression. "It's the qualtagh. Do ye ken nothin' of first footin'?"

"Her father was British, ye have to remember," Caitir said. "The first foot to step in the house after midnight on Hogmanay should be a dark man bearing gifts. Open the door, Elaina." Caitir nodded toward the door.

Elaina crossed over to the door and wrenched it open, expecting Calum to be on the other side. Instead, she found a tall, thin man, his long black coat whipping in the wind.

"Well, let him in before we all freeze to death," Caitir urged.

The man stepped into the castle with a nod to the women.

"Father," Mairi greeted him with a bob of her head and took the man's cloak from him and gave it to the servant who had appeared.

"Letitia." The man bowed his head to the lady of the house as he presented her a basket with several items poking out of it. He handed her two small pouches that Letitia also placed in the basket before she set it aside.

Caitir whispered to Elaina as the exchange was taking place. "The dark man brings gifts of what is hoped for in the new year. A gift of silver for prosperity, bread for food, coal for warmth, whiskey for good cheer, and evergreen to symbolize long life."

"How lovely," Elaina said, hating that at one and twenty it was the first time she was a witness to the tradition of her birthplace. "Father, thank you for coming at this late an hour on such a blustery night," she said.

He smoothed his silver hair as he turned toward her. "I wadna miss it for the world," he whispered, his voice thick with emotion.

Something about him struck a familiar chord, but Elaina couldn't put her finger on it. He grasped her hand, his skin cold from the winter weather. The patch over his eye might have been almost frightening if it weren't for the warmth of his smile and the love emanating from his good eye.

"Do ye not remember me, child?" he whispered, stepping closer to her.

She looked up, studying his face.

"She's fainting!" The words came garbled as if they were declared from under water.

Multiple pairs of hands caught Elaina as her knees buckled beneath her.

She awoke reclined on the large settee with someone patting her cheek. "Are ye all right, lass?" the priest said as her eyes fluttered open.

With a hand that would not stop shaking, Elaina reached out a tentative finger and stroked his cheek. "Lachlan?" she whispered.

"Aye."

"Am I dead?"

"No," the man chuckled. "I am not a ghost, and neither are you. Ye saved my life."

"No." Panic gripped her wame and tears rose in her throat. "They killed you. They fed you to the wolves. It was my fault."

"Ye can see I am alive and mostly well. I have not been eaten by wolves." He smiled as he stroked her hand. "I wasna dead either. Near, but not quite."

"It was Lachlan who led us to ye," Caitir whispered.

Elaina looked at her, confused.

"It was luck they did not run me through with their bayonets when they threw me out onto the pile of corpses," Lachlan started. "If it were not for your cloak they threw out with me, I would have surely frozen to death. I managed to crawl out of that pit of bodies after I had come to. I dinna ken how far I walked before I came upon a small group who was combing the area, looking for a missing lass." Lachlan turned his gaze to Caitir, who smiled in return.

"We thought he was a ghost as well," Caitir said with a laugh. "He was a damn frightful sight—sorry, Father—but when he told us he had escaped the gaol and there was a beautiful angel of God near her demise…well, we knew it couldna be you."

Elaina cut her eyes at her friend.

"But then he also described her as fearless, a tad bit reckless, and with a massive heart and we knew it had to be."

"I am so sorry that Robert Campbell—"

Lachlan put his finger to Elaina's lips.

"Ye do not control Robert Campbell. Nor Captain Cummings. Ye are not responsible for their actions. If it hadna been for you, I would have surely died in that prison. Ye brought me back to life, and I drew upon yer strength and courage to guide me to seek help on yer own behalf."

"Oh, Father." Elaina threw her arms around the man she thought she'd killed. "I cannot believe you are alive…and *here*." She pulled back, studying his face. "You do look and smell better, I must say," she said with a chuckle.

"I wadna miss this celebration for anything in the world. After all, 'tis only fitting that I wed ye and Calum since it was I who baptized ye at birth."

"Now do ye believe in fate?" Caitir whispered in her ear.

Chapter Thirty Seven

THE DOUBLE DOORS OPENED BY a force unseen.

Elaina willed her knees not to collapse as wee Simon stepped forward, meeting her as she emerged through the doorway. He bowed solemnly before her. Upon rising with an impish grin, he held out a horseshoe threaded with a red silk ribbon. Elaina beamed down at him as she gave him a curtsy and added the good luck charm to her bouquet of dried white heather, fresh holly leaves, and mistletoe. Large bunches of evergreens tied with red tartan hung throughout the great hall. The scent of them filled the vast room and added a calming scent that mingled with the smell of hundreds of candles burning. Elaina stood looking at the faces of hundreds of Highland men and women glowing in the warm light of more candles that she had ever seen. Not a sound whispered through the great hall even with the enormous amount of bodies filling it. Elaina closed her eyes, sucking in a deep breath.

"Scairt, are ye?" Auld Ruadh whispered, sliding his arm through hers to escort her down the aisle.

"It shows?"

"Verra much," he chuckled. "Just breathe, lassie. This is yer family, and welcome to it."

Elaina nodded to him and straightened her posture. She could do this...but could she do it without throwing up?

Finolia and Garia led the procession down the narrow alley formed by the Hogmanay guests. Elaina was distracted by the smiling faces of the strangers who seemed to be overwhelmed with joy at being present at their wedding. She could now hear the sniffles of a few. The attention shown to her for no more reason than the respect and affection these people held for the parents she'd never met humbled Elaina to her core.

Her gaze fell upon Lachlan standing at the end of the aisle of bodies, and she thanked God for the miracle of his presence. Closing her eyes, her steps hesitated. Holding her breath, she opened her eyes and searched for him.

He stood to the father's left, magnificent in full Highland regalia of the MacKinnon's shades of green tartan overlaid with fine lines of red and white. His dark hair was pulled back tight into a leather thong, his curls tamed for the moment, dirk and broadsword attached at his waist.

She realized with a start that a small part of her worried he would not be there, that she would be jilted once again. Staring at the fine figure before her with his dimple showing, she thanked God, not for the first time, that Richard had been a coward.

"Ravishing," Calum whispered to her when she reached him, his hazel eyes dancing as he took her hand. "I was afraid ye wadna show."

"And let you off the hook that easy? Never." She was surprised to hear him echo her own fears. The slight tremble in his hand was the only outward sign that the man might be the slightest bit nervous.

Lachlan performed the first part of the service in Gaelic, and Elaina was lost. The second half was in traditional Latin, and she found her nerves calming over the familiar words and rituals. Mairi and Simon stepped forward, each with a strip of tartan in their hands—Mairi's the MacGregor colors, and Simon's the MacKinnon. Father Lachlan spoke Gaelic over the two cloths, and Mairi and Simon presented the pieces of tartan to the couple.

"We must tie them together in a knot," Calum whispered at Elaina's puzzled look.

Mairi took Elaina's bouquet from her and Elaina fumbled with trembling hands to tie a knot between the two clans.

"Yer temper is rising," Calum whispered with a chuckle as she struggled with her task.

She raised a menacing eyebrow at him. Finally, they got them together and the service moved along at a quick clip.

"You may kiss your bride," Lachlan said with finality.

The couple stared at each other, neither one moving. A slow smile spread across Elaina's face, and she raised onto her tiptoes to kiss her husband. Calum gathered her up in his arms, lifting her off her feet.

A deafening whoop erupted from the hall followed by whistles and inappropriate suggestions from the rowdy clan member who had started drinking hours ago. The pipers broke into a rousing song, and Calum deposited Elaina on her feet and swung her around in a dizzying postnuptial reel. Uncle Hugh broke in and finished the dance, surprisingly light on his feet for such a large man. When it ended, she was panting and searching for Calum.

"Come along, lass. Ye need to meet yer people." Hugh led her to a place of prominence and pushed a glass of excellent whiskey into her hand. "Get that look off yer face. They willnae eat ye." With a stout pat on the back that caused her to stumble, Hugh began his introductions.

They were a blur. Elaina heard their names and tried to smile as Hugh introduced her to the clan. What an odd thought to wrap her brain around. She was a full-blooded Scot. Her hands trembled as she took a large gup of whiskey, causing her to have a coughing fit.

"Slow down, lass. Ye dinna want to be pished on yer wedding night," a voice at her elbow whispered. "Or maybe ye do?" Auld Ruadh gave Calum a wink and a slug in the arm as he joined the group.

"Och, on with ye, ye auld bugger." Calum swatted at Red. "Ye look scairt half out yer wits," Calum whispered. "Not having second thoughts, are ye?"

"I'm not sure I had first thoughts," Elaina retorted out of the side of her mouth as she smiled at yet another MacGregor. "Where did all these people come from, and is it safe for them to be wearing their colors? I mean, with them being MacGregors and all."

"Yer father was a well-loved man, and yer mother cherished by all. Every time the clans would gather when I was but a lad, there would be many a tale told of yer da and his bravery and his wise heart. When word got around that the legendary woman who was such a braw fighter on the hill was none other than the missing daughter of Laird Thamas MacGregor, well, let's just say the entire British army couldna have kept them from this castle on this night. As for their colors, well, the colors are not outlawed, only the name."

A man stepped forward wringing his hat in his hands, his face drawn and eyes downcast. "I feel I owe ye the deepest of apologies, and I beg for yer mercy." The man fell to his knees at Elaina's feet.

Startled, Elaina looked to Calum for help, but he merely shrugged.

"Get up," she urged the man, but he remained kneeling with his head down.

"I don't know what grievance I would have with you when I've never met you. Please get up." She reached down to help the gentleman, but he wouldn't budge.

"But we *have* met. We met, and I did ye a grave wrong in not realizin' who ye were, nor the deceit Robert Campbell had pulled over yer eyes. It is my fault ye were beaten." The man's voice hitched.

Elaina could see the darkening of the stones in front of her where his tears were falling. She dropped to her knees in front of the man. "I don't know what you are talking about." She drew the man into her arms, confused over his guilt and feeling terrible for it.

He lifted his head, turning his sorrow-filled eyes to her own. His gaze traveled across the contours of her face. "That day at the burn, when we were watering our horses. Ye looked so much like her. I thought my heart would stop."

What was his name? Grier? "Mackenzie?" Elaina whispered.

"Aye, and may God strike me dead with the shame of not warning ye about the man ye were with."

"You couldn't have known." Her heart broke for the man who was in apparent agony in front of her.

"'Twas like I had seen a ghost." He studied her face now. "Yer mother had a beauty like no other and a love for horses. The way ye handled yer steed and swung yerself up in the saddle, I thought I would fall over it was so much like Mairi. I should have known."

"There was no way to know," Elaina consoled the man. "Everyone thought I was dead." Elaina looked up to Calum for help, but he only shrugged yet again, and she rolled her eyes at him.

"I could have saved ye. The sight of ye tied to the posts and being whipped... yer beautiful face when we cut ye loose... We thought ye were dead by the time we got to ye. I could have saved ye such agony." The man lowered his eyes to the floor, his shoulders shaking with silent sobs.

"Y-you were there? You saved me?"

Mackenzie nodded silently.

"These men that are here?"

Mackenzie nodded again.

Elaina looked around the room with a fresh set of eyes. How could it not have dawned on her that these were the MacGregor men who had saved her life that blistering cold day? Shivers rolled down her back at the memory of their war cry rolling off the Braes around Balquhidder. They'd rescued her without even knowing she was one of them. The thought of it humbled her and overwhelmed her at the same time.

Elaina grabbed Mackenzie's head, kissing the top of it. "God bless you. Thank you," she whispered.

"If only I had told ye before."

"It would have done you no good. I wouldn't have listened. I am so pig-headed I would have just thought you a crazy old loon."

The man chuckled. "Aye, ye are like yer mother then."

"Get up. Dry your face, and let's toast to my new-found family and that the curtain has been lifted from my eyes. Let's toast to revenge. For one day, Robert Campbell and Captain Cummings will pay with their lives."

"Aye. Now that is a toast I can drink to."

And toast they did. Apparently the Scottish toasted to everything—revenge...the scar on Auld Ruadh's leg...new family...Seamus MacGregor's calf returning home...the arrival of wee bairns, that one making Elaina's gut twist in a knot.

Nearly half an hour later, Mackenzie Grier swirled her out into a sea of bodies, the pair escaping the continuing toasts and joining the other couples on the dance floor.

Her chest swelled with emotions she had no words for. The rowdy Scots, the endless toasting and hugs from faces that resembled her own, filled her heart to bursting. She spied her husband watching her from across the great hall. *Her husband.* Even when he catered to the young women and obliged them in a twirling dance, his gaze lay upon Elaina. Her heart warmed at the adoration she saw in his eyes, swelling with pride at the thought that he was now hers and hers alone.

She found herself blushing, which seemed to amuse him and infuriate herself. Someone pushed yet another glass of whiskey into her hand and another toasted to their wedding and her fertility. Hours passed in a swirl of drink and dancing, laughter and love.

Lost in conversation with some of the other young wives, Elaina hadn't noticed Calum come up behind her until he removed her glass from her hand and swept her to the dance floor.

"One last dance and then the party is over." The side of his mouth turned up.

"You may be mistaken. It doesn't look as if anyone is planning on going anywhere." Elaina looked around at the Highland crowd still going strong.

Whiskey flowed, and a never-ending parade of servants toted food in from the kitchen.

"*Our* partying will be over." Calum's broad smile held a wolfish quality to it that made Elaina's knees turn soft.

His strong arms wrapped tightly about her waist, and he held her so her feet skimmed the ground. He kept one of his legs firmly wedged between her own as they made their way around the hall. Their bodies could not have been any closer together if they were smelted in a blacksmith's forge.

The pipers ended on a high peal, and Calum stopped her in her tracks. Without a word, he swept her up into his arms and kissed her with such ferocity that she felt she might melt right through his arms. The crowd erupted in a roar, and Elaina buried her crimson face into his chest as he burst through the double doors. The hallway was much quieter and a hell of a lot cooler, thankfully. Between the whiskey, the dancing, and his kiss, Elaina was over-heated.

"I can walk," she said as Calum weaved slightly. "You can't carry me all the way to my room."

"Aye, I bet I could if that was where we were goin', but it's not."

"It's not?"

"No. They have prepared a room. The priest has blessed the bed." He grinned down at her.

"Blessed the bed?" she asked warily.

"Aye." Calum kicked open a door at the end of the small hallway and carried her into the room.

A few candles were lit here and there, giving it a soft glow. A small fire in the hearth gave just enough heat to take the chill out of the air. Elaina was still sweltering, however. A small table adorned with food and drink and flanked by two chairs stood in the corner. The bed held a place of honor in the center of the room, its tall wooden posts carved with intricate thistles and swirling ivy. Calum carried her across the room and deposited her on the ivory lace covering on the bed, of which she catapulted off of as if it were on fire.

Calum barked out a laugh. "Maybe the father needs to come back and bless it again. It seems no to have taken the first time."

"I just...I need a drink." Elaina grabbed a decanter from the table and filled her glass and Calum's.

His fingers lingered on hers as he took his glass of wine from her. "To my beautiful bride. A lovelier lass never existed." He raised his glass in salute, his eyes dark and seductive.

"To my most handsome and flattering husband," she returned in kind and then continued nervously, "It is stifling in here." She lifted her short hair off of her neck.

Calum crossed the room and stuck his head out the door, speaking to someone.

"What was that all about?" she asked him with wariness.

"I'm gettin' ye some relief. What is a husband for if not to see to his wife's needs?" He inched closer to her, and she took a step back. "Ye are so bonnie when ye're scairt."

"I am not scared."

"No?"

"No." To prove it, she stood her ground as he gathered her into his arms.

"Ye were just playing hard to get, then?" he whispered.

His eyes searched her face, and he lowered his mouth to hers, pausing at the moment before their lips touched. The greens and browns of his eyes held her mesmerized. She had never looked this closely at them and never wanted to gaze at another thing. The corners crinkled as a smile formed on his lips. Elaina could not help but return it. This man, with his teasing ways and infectious smile, made her whole. He filled the empty parts of her heart she thought would forever be void of happiness. She wanted to spend eternity staring into his eyes. Her hands slid up the ivory sleeves covering the solid curve of muscle attaching itself to a set of broad, square shoulders. Her fingers smoothed their way up his neck and untied the leather thong attempting to hold his curls in check. A knock at the door interrupted their moment as Elaina's fingers were releasing his silken locks.

"*Ifrinn*," Calum uttered against her lips before giving her a quick peck—the same oath he had said on the evening of their first meeting.

It had the same effect. Elaina giggled while he opened the door. A young servant girl deposited a large bowl of water into a washstand.

"What does *ifrinn* mean?" Elaina asked as the girl pulled the door closed behind her.

"It means hell." Calum gave her an amused look over his shoulder.

"I see." Elaina laughed.

"Drunk, are ye?" Calum grabbed her arm, pulling her close.

"No," Elaina answered without conviction.

"Aye, I think ye are and on yer own weddin' night, no less. Are ye still over-heated?" he whispered in her ear, sending shivers down her back.

He didn't wait for an answer as he ran the cloth that he had dipped in what was possibly a bowl of half-frozen water from a well down the back of her neck and to the top of her dress, causing her to squeal and arch her back, the frigid water taking her breath away.

"Ah, the bride is an eager one," Calum teased, clutching Elaina tighter.

"You are incorrigible, Mr. MacKinnon."

"And ye are a breathtaking bride, Mrs. MacKinnon."

Elaina wasn't sure if her heart fluttered at his words or because his mouth was making its way slowly down her neck.

"I see ye wore your hair down," he whispered in her ear. "I love it."

"Do you?" Elaina put a hand to her hair. "It doesn't bother you that it is so short?"

"I didna marry ye for yer hair."

"No?" she asked. "And why did you marry me, Calum?" She squirmed out of his arms and poured herself another drink, trying to vie for time and build her courage. She planted herself in one of the chairs by the table of food and popped a piece of dried fig into her mouth.

"Well," Calum leaned against the hearth, watching her with amusement as she tried to hide the shaking in her hands. "I love the way ye sound when ye speak my name."

"Oh?"

"Yes, and I love that ye are a braw lass with a stubborn mind." He walked around behind her with the cold rag and slowly ran it down her arm.

After nearly dropping her glass, she drained it and set it on the table.

"I love the way ye look strong and confident when ye are in the saddle." He ran the cloth across her shoulders and down her other arm.

She sighed and leaned back against his solid stomach, closing her eyes. Her head was spinning, and she didn't think it was from drink alone.

"Right now, at this moment," he whispered, running the rag across her chest. "I love the way ye look in yer weddin' dress, but I do believe, I would love how ye look out of it even more." He scooped her out of the chair and traded places with her, depositing her on his lap, laying his forehead against her own.

Her heart pounded in her chest, his words playing over in her mind while his hands encircled her waist. As they slid to the back of her dress and worked their way up, she wondered if he would do just that—remove her from her clothing—but his hands continued their journey until they reached her bare shoulders and drew the cold rag once again across her back.

She arched against him. "You are doing that on purpose," she whispered, their foreheads still reclining against each other's.

He chuckled, the motion of it vibrating against her chest. "Aye," he whispered back.

He smelled of smoke from the hearth with undercurrents of musk and whiskey. She entwined her fingers in his hair, pulling his mouth to hers with a sudden urge to taste him. Their kiss began soft and hesitant—lips whispering across each other's—but as Calum's tongue brushed across her lips, she melted against his chest and her fingers tightened in his curls as parts of her came alive that she'd never known existed. She ached for him. God, she needed him, this man—her husband.

Something in the fire popped, and Elaina jumped. She could feel the laughter in his chest, his lips curving against her own in amusement. He wrapped his arms around her, pulling her even closer, if that was possible. She heard the rag hit the floor and could feel his own need for her pressed against her leg. His hand, cold from the rag he had held, slid across her shoulder and over the other side, down inside the bodice of her dress, and caressed her delicate skin. His mouth worked its way to her ear where he took the lobe softly in his teeth.

"I like that sound," he whispered in it before his mouth found the tender spot where her neck met her shoulder. "Do it again," he growled.

"Oh bloody hell," she hissed. Everything moved so quickly from that one utterance.

Calum whirled her around to face him, his large hands cupping her buttocks, their mouths dancing in a frenzied ballet against each other. Instinct overtook their bodies, and the couple crumbled to the floor, not bothering with moving to the bed.

"I love ye, Elaina. God, how I love ye." Calum covered her face, her neck, the swell of her breasts with kisses while the palm of his hand slid up her bare thigh.

She couldn't breathe. She couldn't think.

"What do ye want me to do?"

"What?" Elaina could barely utter the one word.

Calum's hand rested on her bare hip under her dress. His thumb made lazy circles against her trembling skin. "Do ye—"

"Quick," Elaina whispered, cupping his face, her fingers skimming his lips as she shushed him. "Do it quickly."

His eyes held hers as he positioned himself between her thighs. He gave her the slightest of nods as if asking permission.

Elaina felt her heart would burst, or she would lose her confidence before anything happened. She pulled his mouth to her own in a crushing kiss and held him there while she raised her hips to meet his thrust. A small cry escaped her throat and she lay still for a moment, waiting for the small burning sensation to pass.

"Did I hurt ye? I'm sorry." Calum's forehead was creased with worry as his eyes searched her face.

"No. It was not as bad as I feared."

Calum chuckled, causing odd sensations to ripple through her body.

Closing her eyes, she dug her nails into the tender skin at the small of his back, pulling him into her. "Don't stop," she whispered against his lips.

"Dinna fash, love. I couldn't if I tried."

———— ❦ ————

They lay on the cold, hard floor, the room silent except for their ragged breaths. The world spun around Elaina, and she closed her eyes against it, trying not to smell the peat of the fire, her own sweat-soaked body, or the scent of their love-making. All the smells of the room seemed amplified as she desperately clung to the floor to keep from falling off the edge of the earth.

"Are ye okay?" Calum whispered, reaching out a finger to touch her hand.

Elaina wasn't sure she could answer, so she nodded slightly, the movement making things worse. Calum moved closer to her, and she could feel his breath on her face. She opened one eye to find him peering at her with concern.

"Ye dinna look so well. Ye look like ye did—merde!" Calum scrambled to drag the chamber pot over and held Elaina while her stomach turned inside out.

"That bad, lass?" He chuckled as he wet the rag again and dabbed it across the back of her neck.

"It was wonderf—" Elaina was rudely interrupted by her wame. "I'm sorry," she moaned. She was a wretched, horrible wife already.

"Well, dinna cry. Ye will make me feel terrible about it!"

"I have ruined our wedding night with all this damned whiskey." She wiped at the tears rolling down her cheeks. Her nerves had gotten the better of her, and here she lay pished on her wedding night, with her face in a chamber pot. She cringed at her behavior.

"Ye have ruined nothing for me, lass. I enjoy holding yer hair," Calum said with a laugh.

Elaina swatted at him as she fell backward onto his lap. He stroked her hair and dabbed at her face with the cool rag. She opened her eyes as he dampened her lips. His curls fell around his face, his dimple showing in his cheek. She reached, up grazing it with her fingertips. "You have the patience of a saint. I don't know how I am so lucky."

He leaned his cheek into the palm of her hand. "I enjoy carin' for piteous creatures."

Her head vibrated with his laughter after she swatted him again.

"Do ye think ye be finished?"

"Maybe." God, she hoped so.

"Here. Swish your mouth then." Calum gave her a swig of whiskey to rinse her mouth with.

Elaina gagged but managed to hold it in.

Calum scooped her up with little effort and carried her to the bed.

She didn't dive off this time—she clutched it for dear life.

"Ye truly have to quit the tears. Ye are killin' me." Calum wiped them away gently with his thumb, his concerned face hovering over hers.

"But I have ruined everything. I am so sorry."

"What have ye ruined? Besides maybe yer dress. We have joined as one. Now ye can never be rid of me," Calum whispered conspiratorially in her ear. "We have the rest of our lives to spend together, and I intend to make ye pay dearly." He lay beside her and wrapped her up in his arms.

"I have been warned," Elaina murmured as she drifted off to sleep.

Chapter Thirty-Eight

ELAINA GROANED, GRASPING HER HEAD in both hands. If she so much as smelled whiskey again, she might die. Gingerly rolling over and opening one eye, she found the bed empty. She raised onto her elbows to survey the room. It stood empty also.

Perfect time to relieve herself. She slid out of bed, only then realizing she was naked. Where the hell was her dress? Wrapping an arm around her exposed breasts, she took care of the business at hand and scrambled back in bed as the door to the room opened. She squeaked, drawing the covers up to her neck.

Calum threw his spirituous smile at her as he set down a platter loaded with what appeared to be a breakfast feast, which immediately made Elaina's stomach rise into her throat. "Good mornin'." Calum eyed her warily. "Are ye alive, then?"

"I'm not sure." Elaina closed her eyes, still gripping the blanket tight in her fists.

"This will help." Calum appeared by her side, handing her a small cup.

"Ech, I can't!" Elaina turned her head after catching a whiff of the stout whiskey.

"Ye'll feel better if ye do—the hair of the dog. Bottoms up." Calum tilted the cup toward Elaina's mouth.

She wrinkled her nose, eyeing him with suspicion, and downed the amber liquid. "Ugh," she groaned, covering her head with the blanket and laying back against the pillows. "Where are my clothes?"

"I couldna let ye sleep in that nonsense." Calum's voice was altered by a mouthful of something. "Are ye hungry? Can ye eat?"

No. Did you...well...did we..."

"Again? No. I want ye to remember it. Besides, ye smelled too bad."

Elaina lowered the blanket long enough to glare at him before pulling it over her head. "Did you…"

"Look?" Calum sounded amused.

Elaina felt her face go crimson under her shelter.

"I can hardly undress ye with my eyes closed what with all the laces and things. I tried not to ogle ye, but I must say the little mole on yer right breast is verra becomin'."

Lifting the blanket and peering down, she squeaked before covering her head again. She felt his weight on the bed next to her and tightened her grip.

"You're my wife, Elaina. I have carnal knowledge of ye, if I may be so bold." He reached out a finger and pulled the blanket away from her face. "I dinna ken why ye're so bashful. I dare say I am enjoying it, however."

She could hear the laughter in his voice.

"Our braw, fearless lass who will fight a man to the death is afraid to show her nakedness to her husband."

"Everyone has their weaknesses," Elaina mumbled.

"'Tis one we shall remedy soon—after ye have washed up a bit." Calum pulled the blanket back over her head, patting her on the leg. "I had them bring ye in a wash pot, if ye would like a bath."

Uncovering her head, she peered across the room. Beside the fire stood a large copper bathing pot.

"The water is warm, if ye would like to climb in." Calum took a smaller pot from the fire and poured its steaming contents into the large tub.

"How did I sleep through all of this?"

"I was afraid ye were dead for a time."

"Feels like I was."

"Well, do ye want a bath or no?"

"Turn around."

"Turn around she says to her own husband," Calum grumbled but obliged.

Elaina inched from the bed, taking the blanket with her and keeping her eyes on Calum's back. He stood in only his tunic. Her eyes followed the etched line of muscle as it made its way from under the hem. A smile touched her lips as she realized the view of his bare legs and feet had nearly been the same the first time they met, only then she had sat on the floor in front of them, oddly enough, feeling much the same way.

Testing the water with one foot, a small sigh escaped her as she slid into a warm cocoon. She pulled her knees to her chest before she told Calum it was safe to turn around, then closed her eyes and laid her head on her knees.

Calum knelt behind her, laying his cheek upon her head. "Ye have made me happy beyond measure, Elaina Spencer MacGregor MacKinnon."

"Have I now?"

"Aye." Calum reached into the tub and scooped the warm water into his cupped hand, pouring it over her shoulders.

"I must say I am quite content as well."

"I hope I can do ye justice as a husband."

"From what I remember of last night, you have things well under control."

"No what I meant, but thank God," Calum laughed. "I mean to protect ye from harm and to provide for ye in the manner in which ye are accustomed."

"If you are talking about the way I lived in Edinburgh, that is not the manner in which I am accustomed. We lived a much simpler life in the colonies, which is what I prefer. I am not a woman to be waited on hand and foot, although, I can say what you are doing right now...I could get accustomed to that."

Calum poured warm water over her hair as she spoke. With a hint of amusement in his voice. he asked, "But can ye cook?"

"Not particularly."

"No worries. My ma will teach ye everythin' ye need to ken."

Elaina stiffened at his words. "Your ma? Your mother is alive?"

"Aye, alive and well."

"I never thought to ask you about your family. I am a thoughtless, horrible person." She buried her face in her hands.

"Ye are not a horrible person. When have we had a chance to talk about such matters?"

"We had time to get married. We could have had time to talk about your family. Why were they not here?"

His hands made their way across her shoulder and down her back, and she relaxed under his gentle touch, the scent of roses rising in the steam from the tub. "I didna want to wait until they could arrive."

"Is it far? Your home?" There was so much she didn't know about her husband. "What will they think of you marrying an outlaw—a murderess? Your father? Is he alive as well?"

"So many questions," he chuckled. "Aye, my da is alive, and they will love ye as much as I. What will William think?"

Elaina sighed. The messenger they'd sent to Fort William had returned with word that William was sent into the Highlands with a small troop to root out Jacobite rebels. She hoped this was true and that he was not Rabbie and Captain Cumming's prisoner.

"Siblings?" she asked him, buying time to consider his question. How *would* William feel about her marrying without his permission?

"A brother, Aron, three years older. Also a sister, Isobel, younger by two years."

"What are your parents' names?" Elaina sighed as he massaged and kneaded the knots from her shoulders.

"My father's name is Micheil and my mother, Rhona. Lean back and let me wash yer hair."

"I can wash my hair." Elaina eyed him over her shoulder.

"Dinna be stubborn." Calum took her by the shoulder and pulled her back toward him.

Elaina reluctantly acquiesced but was soon grateful for his soft touch. "Mmmm, that is amazing," she whispered as his fingers worked her scalp and neck.

"That's funny," Calum said.

"What?"

"Those are the words ye used last night."

"It was not." Elaina looked up at him.

He grinned down at her. "No, I believe yer words were, 'Please don't stop.'"

She rolled her eyes.

Calum moved to the side of the washtub and took her face in his hands, his hazel eyes studying her.

"Do I smell better?" she asked, uncomfortable in his scrutiny.

"Aye," Calum whispered. He ran his thumb across her lips, sending chills to some parts of her and heat to others. "Do ye feel better?"

"Aye."

"Well, then. I'm coming in." Calum started to slip his tunic over his head. "Close yer eyes."

"What?"

"If I cannae look, ye cannae either."

Elaina laughed but obliged and scooted back, making room for him.

He sank into the tub with a groan.

The mere friction of his thick legs against her set her skin afire.

"Keep yer eyes closed," he whispered.

"Are your eyes open or closed?"

"Closed. Now, come here." He took her hands in his and pulled her until she lay upon his chest. "If ye willnae let me look with my eyes, I must look in other ways." His mouth skimmed her ear as he wrapped his arms around her.

His heart pounded swift against the wall of his chest, hers matching it beat for beat. One could tell through his tunic and the fit of his suit coat that the man was well muscled, but she could not have imagined how much so. With his arms around her now, muscles flexed firm against her bare skin, she felt safe for maybe the first time since her parents' deaths.

Their legs intertwined, making the deepest parts of her come alive. She shivered, burying her face in his hair as he ran his fingers light as a feather across the scars on her back.

"Does it embarrass ye, hen?" Calum sounded worried.

"Yes, a little." The fact that she was scarred shamed her and brought her sins back to the forefront of her mind. They also scared her. They stood as a reminder of how fragile life was and how quickly you could lose everything you ever had.

Calum's fingers traced the overlapping lines. "Dinna be ashamed. They are a sign of bravery. Wear them with pride. Whenever ye feel small or intimidated, remember them—remember what ye survived. Call upon the strength that kept ye risin' to yer feet. I have never seen a sight like it before." He hugged her closer to him and lay his head against hers. "My legs couldna carry me fast enough down the braes. My beautiful Elaina bloodied and battered. I thought my heart would split in two and I would fall over dead before I reached ye. Ye rose to yer feet, staring that bastard down and never cried out. I couldna believe ye were so strong, although I should have kent it as stubborn as ye are."

Elaina tugged his hair and tried not to sniffle so he wouldn't know she was crying.

"No, my sweet hen. Ye are stronger than ye ken. Ye are an amazin' woman."

"May I ask you something?"

"Yes, anythin'."

"Were you naked running down the braes?" Elaina snickered. "Caitir told me that sometimes…"

"Would ye think more of me if I was?"

"No. I would think you a knight in shining armor no matter what you wore."

"Good, because it was too damn cold to be naked runnin' down a blasted hill. Now Auld Ruadh, on the other hand…"

"Oh God."

Calum's laughter shook her, and she buried her face in his chest, stifling her own.

"Now then," Calum said, his hands moving lower. "Let's see what other interesting things we can find to explore."

Elaina yelped as his fingers curled around her toes.

"I see ye are ticklish."

She gave an irritated grunt before her breath caught as he raked his fingers up her calves, to the tender places on the inside of her thighs. He spread them wide, wrapping her legs around him. His hands disappeared only to reappear on her shoulders, leaving her aching with want.

Her hands slid down his ribs, causing him to squirm beneath her "Oh, ticklish as well, I see?"

"Dinna do it again," Calum growled. "I would hate to hurt ye."

Elaina's hands worked their way back up his firm abdomen, her fingers explored the fine hairs, pausing as they grazed over the long trail of a scar that started just above his navel and zig-zagged its way up until it stopped just above his right nipple which hardened as her thumb grazed over it.

Calum whispered, his mouth against her ear, "Impressive?"

"Aye, 'tis," she responded in her best imitation of a Scottish accent.

He huffed a chuckle in her ear, and she squirmed against him, giggling and breaking out in goose flesh. "I wish it came with a braw story of heroism." Calum moved his mouth to her neck, "but alas I nearly gutted my own self fallin' from a tree when I was of about ten. Now this one," He slid her hand down his stomach and around to his hip.

Elaina tried to remember to breathe as he kissed her neck and guided her hand down his body. Her fingers found the object in question that traveled from his hip across a ridge of well-muscled thigh to the inside of his knee. She had to move her leg to follow the progress.

"That gift was presented to me in a wee stramash with a few MacLaren men."

"A wee stramash?"

Calum shivered as her fingers trailed their way back up the scar, to his hip.

"The Highlands are full of wee stramashes," he whispered into her other ear. "Now, if we are finished explorin' our scars, *mo chridhe*, let's explore other things."

"What is…*mo chridhe*?" She found it difficult to get the question out with his mouth moving lower and his arms lifting her higher. "Oh Jesus," she whispered as his mouth skimmed the swell of flesh before it. The rose-scented water mixed with the peat burning in the hearth invaded her senses, making what his mouth was doing even more decadent. She twisted her fingers in his hair.

"Mmmm," he hummed against her flesh. "*Mo chridhe* means my heart, and you, Elaina MacKinnon, are my heart. Ye are my soul. Ye are what I have longed for my entire life."

Elaina couldn't speak over the boulder lodged in her throat. She chanced a glance at her husband and the breathtaking acts he was performing. His eyes were open, studying all the places his mouth explored. "Cheater," she whispered without reproof.

He tilted his gaze to meet hers, and the desire in his eyes made every part of her tighten in response. "I couldna help myself. I am a weak man. Ye're so beautiful," he added in a whisper of adoration. "Ye are the most beautiful woman I have ever seen." His mouth moved across her, trailing a winding and intoxicating path to her shoulder where he softly planted his teeth.

"And just how many women have you seen, Mr. MacKinnon?" She wrapped her legs around him once again, and he crushed her to him.

His mouth met hers with an assault that tore through to the heart of her. "No many," he breathed against her lips.

His hand slid under the water, exploring the depths it found there. She struggled to draw breath, her fingernails digging into his shoulder.

"If ye are askin' me if I've ever bed another woman"—Calum position her just so, his mouth working its way to her ear—"the answer is no, and there will never be another." He claimed her as her husband, and she lost herself in the flood of his words and the crush of his mouth against hers. Her cries of surrender muffled against his unchecked hunger as they shattered together as one, joined forever by destiny, love, and an irrefutable and undeniable attraction that had been there from their first meeting.

Chapter Thirty-Nine

"AH, THE NEWLYWEDS SHOW THEIR faces," Hugh bellowed as Elaina and Calm strolled into the hall still filled with clansmen and their families.

Calum had warned Elaina that many of the guests slept in the great room while at the castle. She was prepared for the greeting she might receive but not for Calum to drag her into the foray of lude comments and teasing with an announcement that he'd had to beg her to come down for breakfast, but that she had been too ravenous in other ways to make an appearance. She smacked him on the arm and strode off in a huff, but not before he swatted her on the derriere. She shook her head at the clansmen's reactions and hunted for an ally.

Auld Ruadh looked content as he lounged at one of the long tables, leaned back and elbows propped on the tabletop. He patted the bench next to him. "How is it then, lassie? Welcome to the family." He waved an outstretched hand to the crowd milling about in various states of entertaining themselves—some with food, some with drink, and some with feats of prowess like arm wrestling or wrestling in general.

"Thank you, Auld Ruadh."

"Would ye like to go for a ride in a bit?" he asked.

"I most definitely would," she replied, excited at the prospect of sitting astride a horse once more.

"Good. We've a bit of an excursion planned for ye."

"We?"

"Calum mostly, but I'll come along for protection."

"Can I ride Laoch?" Elaina asked,

Auld Ruadh widened his eyes at her. "Are ye sure ye want to do that, lass? Ye ken his nature."

"I can handle him. I would love to take him out."

Auld Ruadh thought on it a moment before answering. "Aye. I'll let ye, but if he gets out of hand, ye will be ridin' with me."

Elaina grinned at him. "You have yourself a deal."

He patted her knee before rising to his feet. "I'll go see to the horses, then," he said and kissed her on top of the head before he left.

As soon as he had vacated his spot, Caitir slid in next to Elaina. "So?" Caitir asked.

"So what?"

"So, how was it?"

"Aren't you nosy? A lady should never kiss and tell." Elaina arched an eyebrow at her friend.

"Ye're no lady, remember?"

Elaina laughed at Caitir, throwing her own saying in her face. Too embarrassed to look at her, Elaina instead stared at a group of young men in a heated game of dice as she proceeded to confess her actions during the evening's festivities that had left her feeling less than spry.

After a moment of silence, a strangled noise came from Caitir's direction.

Elaina snuck a peek at her, finding her facing away from her on the bench, her shoulders hunched around her ears. Elaina elbowed her. "It's not funny."

Caitir buried her head into the crook of her arm, her face to the table.

"It's not funny," Elaina hissed in her ear, causing Caitir to snort, her tiny body shaking.

"What's so funny?" Mairi plopped down across the table from the two women.

Caitir slapped her palm on the table and doubled over. She clutched her chest, trying to regain her breath, tears streaming down her face. "Crivens, she was worried about"—snort—"it hurtin'." Snort. "Poor Calum should have been the one a worryin'. He's damn lucky the drink didna hit ye beforehand, or the two of ye would still be virgins."

Elaina cleared her throat and coughed, jabbing an elbow into her friend's back.

Mairi stared in confusion at the two women.

From across the room, Calum gave her a raised brow.

Elaina could feel her face burning and elbowed her friend again. "Calm down."

"I'm sorry. I'm tryin'," Caitir giggled, wiping her eyes with her sleeve.

"You asked him?" Elaina hissed when Caitir's words sunk in.

"Aye. I couldna help myself. Then I wondered how the two of ye would get on when neither one of ye kent what to do."

"How did ye get on?" Mairi whispered, causing Caitir to lose control once again.

"To change the subject," Elaina said before Caitir could reveal all of her secrets. "Do you know anything about this little trip Calum is taking me on?"

"Aye," Caitir gulped, trying to regain her composure.

"More secrets?"

"Ye should be used to it by now."

"Indeed, I should."

The women were joined by several other members of the clan, saving Elaina from any more embarrassing conversations. She visited with her new family, garnering knowledge about them and their way of life. Apparently, most Highlanders could spin a wild tale, and they kept Elaina doubled over with laughter for an hour or more until Calum came to gather her and Caitir for their excursion.

Three burly clansmen joined Elaina, Calum, Caitir, and Red, as they picked their way through the dense woods, all on high alert for any signs of The Watch or Redcoats. The five broadswords surrounding her did little to alleviate the feeling of being exposed. The small dirk tied about her waist was her only protection against possible assailants.

"Try to bite me again, you wicked beast, and I will throttle the bloody hell out of you!" Elaina flicked her reins at Laoch's bared teeth.

"Is that what ye told Calum last night?" one of the men called out, causing a rumble of laughter amongst the others.

Elaina ignored them as she tried to keep an eye on Laoch and his teeth. She insisted on riding him even though Auld Ruadh had warned her. Her arrogance had made her think she could control him. Her sanity was now in question. Thankfully, Calum told her their destination was but a few hours ride.

Midday, they arrived at a small house set in a clearing at the edge of the forest. A thread of pale gray smoke trailed from the chimney and disappeared on the winter air. The group slid from their horses as a pair of dogs announced their arrival.

The door opened and a frail-looking woman peered out with a pair of tiny faces peeking around each of her legs. "Girls, tell yer da they have arrived. Get down the good whiskey," the woman said, and the girls scurried away.

The woman waved Elaina, Calum, and Caitir inside. The other four travelers tended the horses. The house was cramped but neat. There were three rooms, and they were encouraged to sit around a small table in the main one. Sleeping quarters lay to the left, Elaina assumed, hidden behind a thin piece of muslin for privacy. A small pantry emptied off the main room from which the two girls scurried out of, followed by a short dark-haired man carrying a stone bottle. The excellent whiskey helped to warm Elaina's frozen fingers and toes.

"I cannae thank ye enough for what you did for us...for our son." The man addressed Elaina as he held the woman's hand.

"Your son? I—"

A blast of cold air swirled through the room as a tall lad flanked by two smaller boys burst through the doors, all three carrying a dead hare in each hand.

"Ainsley?" Elaina stumbled from her seat and hurled herself at the astonished young man. Wrapping her arms around him, she clung to the boy she'd thought she would never see again.

"My lady?" After a moment's hesitation, he returned her hug, dead hares and all.

Elaina grabbed his face. "Let me look at you. You've turned into a man since last I saw you..." Those words brought her back to the present. "Oh." She turned to the couple who had risen and stood behind her. "Oh. Oh God." She buried her face in her hands, her words muffled by a sudden onslaught of tears. "I am so very sorry."

A pair of firm arms encircled her. "Hush now, lass. No one blames ye for what happened."

Elaina looked into the eyes of the man holding her. His wife stood beside him, her hand rubbing Elaina's back. Younger than Elaina first took her for, the compassion in the woman's amber eyes staggered her. "You left him in my care, and I failed him," she whispered. "I failed you."

Ainsley's mother pulled Elaina into her embrace and patted her head as she wept, soothing her as if she were her child.

The man placed a firm hand on Elaina's back. "'Tis no yer fault, lass. Ainsley told us everythin'. And we have seen the broadsheet with yer name upon it. We ken ye have avenged our son's death, and for that, we will be forever grateful."

"We thought ye would like to meet Angus's family and visit his gravesite. It might help ye heal a bit on the inside," Calum whispered beside her.

"Yes." Elaina sniffled, accepting Calum's handkerchief. "Thank you."

She braced herself against the cold air and the emotions already threatening to drown her at the thought of seeing Angus's final resting place. She found herself holding her breath as his family led her around the house to a small cairn.

The group held back while Elaina sat beside the grave that held her young friend, adding her own stones to the cairn. Ainsley eased down beside her, taking her hand and squeezing it tight. They sat for several minutes without speaking.

Ainsley took a deep breath. "My lady, if ye would have me, I would like to come back to work for ye."

How was she to address this statement? She couldn't go home. She might never be able to go home. "Ainsley, I am certain Lord Spencer would love to have you back at the stables. I will not be there. I am an outlaw. Truth be told, I don't know where I will be." Where would they go? To Calum's family? How much danger would that put them in?

"I would like to be with ye, my lady. I can help protect ye. I am so sorry for what they did to ye at the gaol at Balquidder. I am sorry I was no there to protect ye from The Watch. I willnae let ye down again."

"First, you have to stop calling me my lady. I am no longer a lady. Second, you might have been right there alongside me but not near as lucky."

"Lucky? That bastard MacLeod…I mean Campbell…he broke yer nose and beat ye. He whipped ye." Ainsley's voice hitched in his throat, and Elaina lay a hand upon his knee. "I was there. I arrived before the MacGregors came and saved ye. I am so sorry I couldna help ye. There were so many lobster-backs everywhere… It tore my insides out seein' ye like that, my…I mean, mistress. Please forgive me."

"There is nothing to forgive, Ainsley. I brought part of that lot upon myself. I took a man's life in cold blood. I probably deserved every bit of it. But, God, I would do it over again for Angus." She smiled sideways at him, sniffling. "Let's talk to Calum about you joining us, but what about your parents? They may not approve."

"Aye, they will. Ye see they have their hands full."

The pair sat a while longer, hand in hand as they said their goodbyes to the fearless young ruffian lying in eternal slumber. Rising, they made their way back to the crowded house where they discussed Ainsley's request. To Elaina's surprise and Ainsley's delight, all parties agreed. After Ainsley situated his few belongings, the group rose to say their farewells.

Ainsley's father stepped forward. "Elaina, we would like for ye to have this." In his hands, he held Angus's small broadsword.

"I can't—"

But the man shoved the sword into her hand. "It will fit ye well. Angus would have wanted ye to have it."

"But don't you want to keep it in the family?" Elaina turned the sword over in her hand.

"I want to give it to the woman who gave my son justice and brought him home to us."

Elaina closed her eyes and took a deep, calming breath. "I-I don't know what to say."

"Ye needn't say anythin'," Ainsley's mother whispered through her tears.

Calum did the honors of fastening the sword around her waist. It hung from her left hip, and the weight of it felt like Angus's small head pressed there, where it used to be.

Chapter Forty

AS THE PATH WIDENED, CALUM appeared on her left and Caitir her right. Elaina knew the three of them together would find Rabbie and she would exact her revenge. She and Calum would make a home and God willing, a family. Even with the unknowns, contentment settled in Elaina's soul as she gazed out over her new homeland with pride.

A sharp crack split the air and Laoch reared, nearly throwing her. As she circled, trying to rein him in, she saw Calum fall from his horse, a crimson stain spreading across his chest.

She screamed his name as chaos erupted around her, sending Laoch bolting into the surrounding forest and away from the shouting and firing pistols with his unwilling rider.

"Damn you, Laoch! Stop!" She yanked at the reins, but the blasted demon horse wouldn't stop.

Her only choice was to dive off of him before she got too far from the road and her injured husband. The broadsword strapped to her waist made it impossible to tuck herself into a ball and roll. The healing yet tender parts of her screamed when she hit the ground. She lay for several moments, gasping for air. Wiping the tears from her eyes, she struggled to rise, finding she could not move her right arm without the world swirling in a sickening dance. The entire right side of her body screamed with pain.

Clutching her arm to her belly, she managed to fight her way to her feet. A sick sweat soaked through her bodice as she leaned her head against a tree. The muffled sounds came from...*where?* Her heart pounded too loud in her ears for her to hear. She managed to push herself off the tree and turned in a circle, holding her breath, listening.

She stumbled off in what she thought was the right direction, stopping every few steps to listen and keep from retching. The vision of her husband's bloody form falling from his horse played over and over in her mind, pushing her forward. A flash of red caught her attention through the brush—the bloody British. She pulled her dirk with her left hand. Crouching behind a bush to avoid contact with the soldier running in the opposite direction of the fighting, she pressed her knuckles to her forehead and tried to pull herself together. She took his retreating form as a sign that the Highlanders might be holding their own. Keeping low to the ground, she held the bottom of her skirts and her dirk with the same hand and pushed on.

The metallic clang of steel upon steel pierced the air, and the tortured scream of a man caused her to lose her footing, sending her tumbling down a small ravine where she landed face down. Calum's cries edged their way through the din in her ears.

Trembling, she fought to raise her face from the dead leaves. "Calum!" she screamed and got as far as her knees before she vomited. Ignoring the searing pain in her ribs, she clawed her way to the top of the ravine. Her dirk was gone. She struggled to unsheathe her broadsword with the wrong hand, her own body fighting against her.

"Ye'll never get it like that, lass," a voice whispered in her ear as a hand snaked its way around her waist and slammed her sword back into its sheath. "Let's go." Rabbie shoved her forward, making her breath hitch with pain. "Injured, are ye?"

She couldn't garner enough breath for a response but cried out when he grabbed her right arm and yanked her forward.

"Oh, now ye scream. Couldna make a sound or cry for mercy while ye were strapped between the posts."

"Go to hell."

"Oh, dinna fash yerself. I have nay doubt about my final destination. I'll just no be gettin' there as quick as MacKinnon."

Grabbing her chin, he pulled her head back, revealing her husband. Calum sat propped against a tree, his face bloodied and hands tied behind his back with a gleeful Captain Cummings standing over him. A large circle of blood stained his right shoulder, and his thigh held another.

"Found her," Rabbie called out as the two approached.

Without a word, Cummings slammed the butt of his rifle into the wound on Calum's shoulder.

He grunted as he clenched his teeth, his face gray and slick with blood and sweat.

Elaina screamed, lunging at Cummings, but Rabbie held her tight.

"Do you have something you want to offer me?" Cummings's eyes slid down her body with a seductive grin as he leaned nonchalantly upon his rifle on the wound on Calum's leg. "Something like names? I want the money."

"I don't have any bloody names to give you. I don't *know* anything."

Calum's head slumped as he lost consciousness.

Glancing down at him, Cummings slapped his cheeks. "Wake up, son, you'll want to see this."

Cold steel pressed against Elaina's temple.

Calum's head bobbed as he came back to life, his eyes rolling into focus. "Leave...her... Elaina," he whispered.

"Confess." Cummings yanked Calum's head sideways by his hair. "Confess that you are the Highland connection."

"He is not!"

Rabbie squeezed tighter, taking her breath and keeping her from collapsing to the ground.

"Now, this is a fun game." Cummings looked from Calum to Elaina. "Who will crack first, the lovely Lady Elaina or the Highland bastard? My money is on the lady. She will speak or MacKinnon will die. What say you, Captain Campbell?"

Rabbie nuzzled his mouth against Elaina's ear, his teeth ever so softly nipping the lobe. "I want you to remember..." His words trailed off as his lips skimmed down her neck.

She tried in vain to jerk away from his touch.

Calum struggled to rise to his feet only to have the butt of the rifle slammed down on his injured leg.

"Stop it. Please stop." Elaina's voice dropped to a choked sob. "I will tell you. Just please stop."

"Elaina...hen..." Calum's chest heaved with the effort of speaking. "Dinna..." Their eyes locked on each other's. "Dinna lie for me."

"Don't be rude, MacKinnon. Let the lass speak her piece." Cummings shoved Calum's head with the butt of the gun.

Elaina opened her mouth to lay down the lie that could cost an innocent soul their life only to save her husband's, but she could not do it.

Rabbie's mouth was once more at her ear, the barrel of the pistol pressed tight against her temple. "Hen. How endearing. I want ye to remember, lass, remember I loved ye."

The click of a hammer pulled back sounded in her ear, and she squeezed her eyes shut.

The cold metal against her temple moved and then the crack of the pistol muffled Calum's screams as the air filled with the scent of burning gunpowder.

Her breath came in hitched hiccups. Unsure of what had transpired, she was afraid to open her eyes. Rabbie's arm remained about her waist, that much she knew. She heard the thud of the pistol hit the ground, and his arm began to relax. Had he been shot? Opening her eyes, she made a move to shove him off her, but his hand grabbed her chin and he brought his lips to rest softly upon her own. It was quick, like a tender kiss between lovers before they parted for the day. His green eyes were inches from her own.

"I will see ye again soon, hen" he whispered before he shoved her face down onto the ground.

A blinding flash of pain took the air from her lungs. She writhed on the ground, white light dancing behind her eyes as she struggled for breath.

War carried on around her—grunting and Gaelic, the clanging of steel upon steel.

She found the strength to open her eyes and watched, helpless, as Rabbie rallied the few British soldiers still standing and retreated into the woods, two of the MacGregor men following in pursuit. She turned her head to search for Calum but froze, her gaze lighting upon Captain Cummings's sightless eyes staring at her and then the round hole in his forehead. Blood ran in a jagged stream across it and had begun to puddle on the dead leaves beneath his face.

"Elaina?" Calum's raspy voice drew her eyes away from the puzzling image in front of her.

Pushing herself to her knees, she waited for the nausea to pass before crawling her way to her husband where he had fallen over, unable to right himself. She tried to untie his hands, but she had no use of her injured arm. She abandoned the task and collapsed onto her back in front of him instead. She reached out a tentative hand and stroked his cheek. His curls were plastered to his forehead in a sick sweat and his coloring unnerved her.

"What happened?" she asked him. "To Cummings?"

"Rabbie shot him." Calum closed his eyes with a grimace.

She stared at his mouth, his words echoing in her head. *Why would Rabbie shoot him?*

"What did he say to ye, Elaina?" Calum asked. It seemed an immense struggle for the words to leave his mouth.

Her gaze moved to his eyes. The golds and the greens usually present had been swallowed by brown. Furrowed lines etched his brow. She wanted to smooth them out with her thumb and kiss the pain from his face, but she couldn't move. "He said he wanted me to remember he loved me and I would see him again soon," Elaina whispered, a cold chill sliding down her spine.

Shaking with fear and pain, she turned her face to the sky and tried to catch the breath that had escaped her. The shouting and shuffling of feet around them did not drown out Calum's ragged breathing, and for that she lay thankful. As long as he rasped, he lived.

She stared at the dimming skies. The sun was setting. The thought flitted through her brain as a pair of hands lifted her from beside her husband. She hadn't the strength to fight them.

Calum?" she whispered into the dwindling light.

"We've got 'im, lass. Dinna fash. Ye are safe."

A laugh began in her lower belly and worked its way to the surface. She laughed, and she cried into the chest of whoever held her. The motion of it shooting pain through her body, but she couldn't stop. It was the most absurd sentence ever uttered.

"Ye are safe."

TO BE CONTINUED...

Thank You

A great big THANK YOU for giving up the most precious asset you own... your time. I hope you thoroughly enjoyed *Whispers of Deception*, and if so, I would love for you to share your experience with your friends and the world through avenues such as Facebook, Instagram, Twitter, Google, and/or Pinterest. If you feel so inclined, a review on your favorite retailer's site would be greatly appreciated.

To learn more about the upcoming sequels (yes, that word ends in an 's') to *Whispers of Deception*, you can swing on over to **http://www.reneegallant.com** and sign up for my newsletter and see what exciting things we have planned for 2020. Emails are always welcome. I love hearing from my readers!

Acknowledgments

Thank you to my husband, my parents, my siblings, my four kiddos, and my friends for their constant encouragement. You are the reason I dared to try, and you are the reason I will succeed.

Many thanks to my ever-present, ever-helpful, ever-encouraging editor—Debra L Hartmann. Her knowledge, support, and kindness carry me through the rough times and help to make it all worthwhile.

Thank you to my first readers for their critiques and encouragement. I couldn't have completed the task without them.

Carol Jackson

Vicki Holt

Elaine Schroller

Juliette Townsend

And…

An enormous thank you to Mrs. Nancy Herndon, my fifth grade reading teacher, for planting the seed that has finally bloomed into a reality!

About The Author

Although her name sounds rather French, Renée Gallant is just a good ol' Texas gal through and through, residing in the great state with her husband of thirty years. Renée is a writer, business owner, avid reader, Lyme Warrior, and lover of all things historical. Learning is a never-ending process she thoroughly enjoys… unless it involves computers.

Mother of four and grandmother of six, she spends her free time hanging with dinosaurs, painting, coloring, or sitting with one or more little person on her lap and staring at weird YouTube videos.

Strap on your broadsword, grab up your targe, and prepare to do battle! You're invited to join Renée Gallant on the harrowing journey she refers to as her writing life. It's exciting, occasionally hilarious, and at times terrifying, but it is NEVER dull!

http://www.reneegallant.com/

CPSIA information can be obtained
at www.ICGtesting.com
Printed in the USA
LVHW041101130520
655432LV00005B/69